Westbound

D1745276

WESTBOUND

Paul Krebill

Copyright © 2006 by Paul Krebill.

ISBN :   Softcover   1-4257-1631-8

All rights reserved. No part of this book may be reproduced or transmitted in any form or by any means, electronic or mechanical, including photocopying, recording, or by any information storage and retrieval system, without permission in writing from the copyright owner.

This is a work of fiction. Names, characters, places and incidents either are the product of the author's imagination or are used fictitiously, and any resemblance to any actual persons, living or dead, events, or locales is entirely coincidental.

This book was printed in the United States of America.

To order additional copies of this book, contact:
Xlibris Corporation
1-888-795-4274
www.Xlibris.com
Orders@Xlibris.com
30180

CONTENTS

Prologue: "Go west, young man." 9

PART ONE

Chapter 1: The Westbound 13
Chapter 2: Lunch And A Tour 19
Chapter 3: On Display 28
Chapter 4: Coming Home 33
Chapter 5: Racing In The Night 37
Chapter 6: The Song Of The Meadowlark 41
Chapter 7: Point Of No Return 45
Chapter 8: "White Christmas" 51
Chapter 9: House On The Beach 56
Chapter 10: In The Family 63
Chapter 11: Godspeed 71
Chapter 12: The Committee 77
Chapter 13: Blue Skies 80
Chapter 14: Under Gray Skies 85
Chapter 15: Home 91
Chapter 16: The "Reverner" 97
Chapter 17: Re-play 103
Chapter 18: Off And Running 108

PART II

The 1960s and 1970s

Chapter 19: "Fairest Of Them All?" 119
Chapter 20: Sitka 129
Chapter 21: Witch Hunt 134
Chapter 22: Out Of Town 138
Chapter 23: Settling In 150
Chapter 24: W lazy N 155

Chapter 25: On The Inside Passage 162
Chapter 26: John Lindsay 171
Chapter 27: Best Man 178
Chapter 28: Family 184
Chapter 29: At Home In Southland... 191
Chapter 30: A Cold Wind Blowing.. 198
Chapter 31: Firestorm.. 204
Chapter 32: Looking West Again.. 209
Chapter 33: Becoming A Proper Kiwi 217
Chapter 34: Decently And In Order.. 224
Chapter 35: Eastbound 232
Chapter 36: Decisions.. 239
Chapter 37: Seasons of the Years 250

PART III

The 1980s

Chapter 38: Bed & Breakfast 261
Chapter 39: Home Is Where The Heart Is... 265
Chapter 40: Cabin In The Mountains 270
Chapter 41: Heathrow 279
Chapter 42: Tragedy.. 284

PART IV

The 1990s

Chapter 43: Bittersweet.. 297
Chapter 44: Honorably Retired 308
Chapter 45: Return 314
Chapter 46: In Touch 326

PART V

Into a New Century

Chapter 47: Starting Over 335
Chapter 48: On The Shore Again 341
Chapter 49: On The Rocks.. 345
Chapter 50: Neither Here Nor There... 353

Chapter 51: Home Alone 360
Chapter 52: Naomi 367
Chapter 53: The Pendant 375
Chapter 54: Turning Point..381
Chapter 55: Pacific 386

Author's Note 395

PROLOGUE

"Go west, young man."

"Out on the western prairie a young flaxen haired girl walked beside her brown curly headed brother. Her long homespun dress fluttered in the wind. Beside them their family's Conestoga wagon rumbled and creaked. It bore its heavy load of household furnishings carrying also an ample supply of provisions for a long journey. Ahead under the first rays of an August sun, oceans of tall grasses undulated in the early morning breeze. The sun warmed their backs as they began another grueling day of trudging westward. They were part of a throng of hundreds of westbound immigrants, all seeking new opportunity in the lush green valleys which lay many weeks ahead."

Thus the teacher read to the class. A large map of the United States filled the wall behind him. The teacher continued. "A few years later Horace Greeley, editor and publisher of *The Tribune* in New York City, would coin the phrase, *Go west, young man.* In those few words he captured the lure which lay behind the eager and arduous effort of thousands of westbound immigrants."

The high school students had been listening to a favorite teacher expound poetically on the delights of "American History." Seated among his classmates, Earl Norris was especially taken with this particular class lecture. His imagination was ignited by a prophetic spark.

His teacher developed his westward theme. "And in making that statement, Greeley named a dominant thread which has been woven into the history of this continent. From the earliest settlers who plied the Atlantic on a westward journey bound for a virgin continent—to the pioneers who pushed west from New England across the Alleghenies, from Lewis and Clark on their voyage of discovery searching for a waterway westward to the Pacific—to the thousands upon thousands who crossed the prairies seeking fertile farmland in the Willamette Valley of Oregon, the movement of America has always been westbound."

He turned to the map and swept his hand across the continent. "And I believe that this inevitable direction is an ingrained compass in the subconscious soul of many an American today."

Earl sat deeply enthralled, envisioning the westward stream of covered wagons, winding their way toward the Pacific.

"And I predict that when you come back to these hallowed halls for a class reunion some day, many of you will be coming from regions to the west—places to which you will have moved."

With that the bell signaling the end of the period sounded. Notebooks were closed and books gathered up. And Earl, along with the others, left for his next class. Preoccupied by thoughts which had been set in motion, he barely noticed anyone as he passed along the hall to his next class. An intriguing desire had been imprinted upon Earl Norris' subconscious. His life would be influenced by what he'd begun to imagine during that day in his high school American History class. An intrigue which would impel him on his own westbound journey barely a century after the last Conestoga plied the Great Plains of the American continent.

PART I

CHAPTER 1

The Westbound

Behind the bars of the Northern Pacific ticket window the station master could be observed seated at his worn wooden desk. In brown suspenders over a white shirt with a black bow tie he worked his telegraph key as he prepared for the arrival of the Westbound. In the stale smelling depot waiting room there was an aura of anticipation among a dozen or so people seated on the shiny benches. Most were eagerly awaiting the arrival of the daily passenger train from the east. Some who were dressed up for travel with small hand-held pieces of luggage were waiting to board, while others in bib overalls or plain house dresses were there to meet passengers who would soon be stepping down onto the platform. Two or three of the men who were waiting spent the time pacing between the seats inside and the outside platform next to the tracks. The air outside was calm and warm with an aroma of early spring, which itself added another layer of pleasant anticipation. The sun shown brightly in an almost cloudless sky. Those who paced the platform could look far to the east along the narrowing track, hoping to spot a tiny image of an approaching locomotive in the distance.

After what felt to the crowd like a very long wait, the station master got up from his telegraph counter and took up a black microphone mounted on a desk stand. The loud speakers inside and over the platform crackled as he switched it on.

"Westbound is due in five minutes."

This announcement brought a stir among the little group of people in the waiting room. Grandpa Benson turned to his grandson, Dwight. "She's a'comin'! If you was to put your ear to the track out there you'd hear it a comin'."

"Really? Even if you can't see it?"

"Yep. And if you see it, you better not try it. She's too close by then."

"Can I try?"

You can't entice a ten year old boy like that and not let him try it, his grandpa reasoned. "Let's go out and see."

The boy and his grandfather got up and went out the track-side door, walked down the length of the station house to where the ties were exposed and where the track was raised enough for the boy to get down to put his ear to the shiny steel.

"Do you hear her a comin'?"

"I sure do!"

"Better get up now and we'll watch for the train."

By this time most people had joined them on the platform. Some carrying luggage were accompanied by family members already beginning their departure rituals. Others were obviously waiting for someone to arrive, as were Dale Benson and Dwight. At the west end of the platform a baggage handler wheeled a green and red Railway Express cart onto the platform making ready to receive luggage soon to be handed out of the baggage car.

A low pitched roar of the whistle could be heard in the near distance. Then in a moment the the front of the huge diesel with its powerful headlight shining along the tracks could be seen approaching. The bell on the engine was ringing. The brick platform began to vibrate as the sound of the electromotive engine was heard slowing down to approach a stop at the little prairie town of Saline, Montana. The westbound North Coast Limited was arriving from the east. The day before it had begun its journey in Chicago.

Dale took Dwight's hand, beckoning him to step back from the edge a bit. All other sounds and sights were overpowered by the rumbling sound of the locomotive's massive hulk now slowly rolling past, one set of steel shiny wheels after another. Looking east, the boy and his grandfather could see the string of passenger cars slowly approaching and then passing by, each with its conductor or trainman leaning out of the half door at the end of his car. Four of the cars had domed observation windows on their roofs, called Vista Domes on the Northern Pacific Railroad, the line which snakes across southern Montana for some six hundred and fifty miles from the North Dakota state line to the Idaho line. Before sunrise this train had entered Montana and would continue until after sunset when it would pass into Idaho heading west to the Pacific.

Some of the trainmen waved at Dwight as their cars slowly rolled past. After four or five cars had glided by ever more slowly, the train came to a very gentle halt. The dining car was positioned in front of Dwight and his grandpa. They could see people inside seated before glistening white table cloths. In the center of each broad window was a silver vase with a single rose.

Outside trainmen were helping passengers to step off onto the platform. Up ahead Dwight could see the baggage car attendants lifting down suitcases and parcels which were being stacked onto the green cart with huge metal red wheels. His attention was diverted when his grandpa pulled him along saying. "We better look for him so that he knows we are here to meet him, don't you suppose?"

"How will we know him?"

"Well, he'll be tall, around twenty-five years old, and dressed like an Easterner. And he'll be looking for someone! That's us."

Earlier that morning Earl Norris had awakened in his narrow Pullman bed when the sun had begun to illumine his little cubicle. He slid up the heavy leather shade and looked out his window. He was struck by the absence of trees. Trees which had filled his view the evening before as the North Coast Limited had pulled out of St. Paul to begin its roll across Minnesota. Trees as he had always been accustomed to them. This morning there wasn't a tree in sight. All Earl could see was mile upon mile of sunlit grass lands. There were breaks in the flatness now and then as the view progressed, areas which had little vegetation except for scattered clumps of sage brush and some scrub cedar hugging the ground.

The gray cloud bespeckled sky of the day before had given way overnight to one which was azure blue and cloudless. He couldn't get over how far he could see. There seemed to be nothing to block his view. A surge of excitement washed over him as he continued to survey the vast open land under a seemingly endless sky. From the narrow corridor outside his cubicle he heard a man's voice announcing, "Second call for breakfast in the dining car—third car behind."

Earl Norris got up, pulled down the tiny sink to shave and wash up. He put on the clothes he had carefully selected for his arrival. Brown slacks and a light tan suit jacket over a yellow shirt with a brown tie. When he pulled in his shoes from the shelf next to his door, he discovered that they had been expertly polished. He remembered then that Pullman porters do this during the night—for a tip, of course. Dressed now, he emerged into the Pullman passageway and headed back through two cars to the dining car, steadying himself as the train gently swayed.

As he entered the diner he was greeted by the dining car steward. "Mornin', sir. Come this way." The steward showed Earl to a table, held his chair, and gave him a menu. When the waiter arrived, Earl gave his order. For a few minutes he intently looked out the dining car window. Soon the waiter returned with a pancake the size of his dinner plate, bacon on the side and a silver pot of coffee. Earl's excitement mounted as he ate and watched the scenery of the Great Plains slip by his spotlessly washed window. *What could be more luxurious—like an ocean liner bound for the Orient,* he thought as he finished. He paid the waiter and carefully placed his napkin on the table. He pushed his heavy chair back, got up and walked out of the dining car and into the next car to the rear in which he climbed the narrow stairway to the Vista Dome. Now the panorama of the plains surrounded him, to his ever-increasing delight. The unmitigated sun against the immense blue sky filled the Vista Dome's enclosure. *Big Sky Country,* he thought. *I see what they mean.* And then he remembered. "*Go west, young man.*"

His mind turned to thoughts of his anticipated arrival in Saline. He checked his train schedule and looked at his watch. He estimated forty-five minutes if they were on time. He gave himself another fifteen minutes in the Vista Dome before returning to his Pullman compartment to gather his things for getting off. He felt a nervous tingle in his hands as he did his final packing. He was experiencing butterflies like a first day of school. In just a very few minutes he would be seeing some of the people with whom he might be associated for the next—who knows how many—years. He heard the faint squeal of brakes and felt a slowing down. Next the low drone of the whistle and then, as the speed became markedly slower, he heard the bell from the locomotive ringing. He took his briefcase and small bag and went out into the corridor, along which he made his way forward to the platform of the Pullman car where the porter in his white starched jacket was leaning out of the upper half of the exit door. Earl caught glimpses of a few framed houses and streets with a few cars and trucks parked along their sides.

The speed of the train had diminished sharply and then it came to a full stop. The porter opened the bottom half and put down a moveable stair step. Earl was the only person coming out of this doorway, as the porter helped him down onto the station platform. As he moved away from the train which had paused, waiting to move on, Earl smelled the freshness of the air and felt the brightness of the sun, unhampered by any foliage or canopy. *Now—how am I to find Mr. Benson?* He walked back toward the tiny depot.

Only a few others had gotten off the train, so he was pretty obvious, especially since the others were much more casually dressed and seemed to know where they were going or whom they were meeting. He spotted a man in a denim shirt and faded blue jeans, wearing a straw cowboy hat slightly crumpled. Beside him holding the older man's hand was a young boy similarly dressed. Earl and the pair on the platform walked toward each other.

Earl was the first to speak. "Mr. Benson?"

"Reverner Norris," the man said without a smile. "I'm Dale Benson and this is my grandson, Dwight."

"Hello, Dwight," Earl said shaking the boy's hand. He turned to Dale Benson and they shook hands as Earl introduced himself. "I'm Earl Norris."

Earl had never heard the term *Reverner*, but he would soon discover that this was a frequent mispronunciation of *Reverend*. There followed an awkward silence as the three headed into the depot and to the baggage door. When Earl found his suitcase he dragged it into the depot and prepared to lift it along with his overnight case. Benson noticed this and said, "I can take that." They left by the door opposite the tracks. Benson led the way to his battered Ford pickup. Putting the bag in the back and opening the door he motioned to his grandson. "Dwight, you sit in the middle and let the Reverner sit next to you." With that he got in behind the wheel. Earl carefully put his brief case and bag in the cleanest spot he could find in the pickup box behind the cab. As he did, he heard the signal coming from the platform. "All aboard." Then the rev'ing up of the engine, and Earl looked toward the tracks and saw the Westbound begin to pull away from the Saline station. He watched for a moment as the train slowly rumbled on. *On to the west coast*, Earl thought wistfully. He turned to Benson's pickup.

Before he hoisted himself up next to the boy, he noticed two decals on the rear window of the cab. An American flag and a round seal which he did not recognize at the time, but learned later that such a seal identified the owner of the truck as a member of the National Rifle Association. And against the inside of the rear window, a rifle was suspended on two brackets. He'd never seen this before, but he would become accustomed to seeing rifles displayed inside most pickup rear windows. Earl climbed in and banged his door shut, producing a metallic clank. Benson started the engine, backed out of the parking place and headed down the main street of Saline. Earl counted four places of business: a gas station, a bar, a small grocery store and a lumber yard. That was all. Further back there were apparently residential streets with a couple blocks of houses on either side of the main street. Beyond one of the streets Earl spotted the church building, white clapboard with a stubby sort of entry, above which was a steeple. He'd have to wait until later to get a better look at it.

"The missus is waiting lunch for you, Reverner. So we'll head out to the house before I take you to your place."

"That'll be fine."

More silence as they left the little cluster of buildings that was Saline, Montana. The spot on this earth where Earl's new life might begin on this Saturday in May. They drove along a dusty gravel road out from town a few miles to the Benson place.

For some unknown reason during the silent ride, Earl found himself remembering where he had been just a week ago. He and two of his friends in the seminary had gone downtown on the subway after dinner in the Commons. They had tickets that evening for the Chicago Symphony Orchestra concert in Orchestra Hall on Chicago's busy Michigan Boulevard. Now he could hear in his mind the music and feel the presence of the large crowd surrounding them in the hall. He then heard the sounds of the throngs on the downtown streets at night as they came out of the concert hall to return to the seminary. He "saw" the rain drenched streets reflecting the red and green stop lights on every corner, "heard" the whistle of a traffic cop, and the honking of car horns, and the drone of the diesel buses passing by—stopping and starting again at each corner. The sounds and the sights of the city a "million miles" away were still reverberating in Earl Norris' mind as he was being driven on a dusty deserted and silent road out west in rural Montana. Hereford cows contentedly munched the grass close to the road, unaware of what a momentous day this was in the life of the young man in a suit and tie riding in a dusty pickup. On this Friday noon in May, Earl Norris would face the people who were to consider him as a candidate to become the pastor of their church.

Me? A pastor? Earl felt a sudden loss of confidence. *I'm too young to be a minister here, I'm still "wet behind the ears" as Grandma would say.* He almost wished he were still riding along on the Westbound—or on Michigan Boulevard.

CHAPTER 2

Lunch and a Tour

A narrow gravel road led to the Benson place five miles from town. An easy drive if the road grader had been by recently, and if it hadn't rained since. However, neither rain nor grading happened very often, so the ride out to Bensons was rough, dusty and "washboardy,"—a term for successive ribbing in the gravel surface which Earl would come to know. He noticed a few rural mail boxes along the way, but he failed to see any houses. The road followed a shallow creek flowing along a circuitous cut in the otherwise flat prairie. Growing in the gully were various low brambles of one kind or another. Occasionally the water of the creek was visible from the vehicle. Earl could see that the creek was a mere trickle over an almost dry bed. At the top of the cut the grassland stretched seemingly forever to Earl's right, dotted here and there with cattle grazing on the short dry gray/green grass. To his left as he looked over Dwight's head and past Benson, Earl observed a pattern of crop land unfamiliar to him—strips of green alternating with strips of unplanted beige colored soil.

In the fifteen minutes it took them to reach the Benson mail box, they saw only one vehicle, a shiny black pickup traveling faster than Dale, and raising a billowing cloud of dust making it almost impossible to see anything in the wake of the passing truck. Benson had waved as the other driver had greeted him in similar fashion. Earl saw no one in the fields working, nor anyone else on the road. So different from the rides in the country he and his parents had taken back in Illinois, where lots of farmers could be seen on tractors in the fields, or driving by in farm trucks of various descriptions. The roadside itself was another aspect of this new scene which struck him as very different. Country roads in Illinois were often lined with corn fields reaching almost to the paved road. In other places mowed grass strips bordered the fields along the road sides. Here on the road out to Bensons the fields or the grass lands were separated from the road by broad ditches, which he would come to know as barrow pits. These were covered with straggly grass and thistles, certainly not mowed. Earl's excitement rose as he found himself in this totally new environment. Even the sky was different—bluer, and on this particular day, cloudless—and big. There would be many more such days in what he would come to know as the Big Sky Country.

The mailbox simply announced "BENSON." Earl's attention was turned to the lane into the Benson place. The small single-story farm house became visible after they lurched over a slight rise in the lay of the land. A little way up the lane they passed by an unoccupied feed lot with its dirt floor black and muddy. Some of its aroma was still in the air. Beyond the house were some sheds, with machinery in them, and other wooden structures of a nondescript sort. But, Earl observed, no barn of any size. To the right of the house was a large vegetable garden neatly laid out. A little fenced lawn was in front of the house with a sprinkler on the end of a garden hose showering droplets of water on the young plants. The yard around the left and rear of the house was a patchwork of dirt, gravel and stunted grass and thistles, unlike the paved farm yards Earl remembered from some of the farms back home.

Dale brought the pickup around to the back door of the house, stopped and announced. "This is it." He and Dwight got out and headed for one of the sheds, leaving Earl to wonder what he was supposed to do next. He got out, and as soon as he closed the door behind him, a woman in her sixties dressed in a faded house dress and an apron came out of the house and greeted him. "Reverend Norris! I'm Mae Benson. I'm so glad you are here."

Whereas Dale Benson's welcome had been subdued, his wife's was anything but. She made Earl feel immediately welcome and wanted. *"Reverend!"* He thought, *I'm not even ordained yet. Still have to graduate from seminary, and already I'm called "Reverend."*

"Come on in. I've got lunch ready."

Earl climbed the steps and shook Mrs. Benson's hand, "Hello, Mrs. Benson!"

"It's Mae. We don't use the *mister* or *missus* around here much."

"Well, you better not use the *Reverend* then either. Call me Earl."

"I like that. Now come in and make yourself ta' home. You can wash up and then I'll have our lunch on the table." She showed him through the living room to a bathroom off the hall."

Earl assumed Dale and Dwight would be coming in for lunch, but when he emerged from the bathroom he found that Mae had set the table for only two.

Mae apparently misinterpreted the question on Earl's face. "The other committee members are coming for dessert. I thought I'd like to have this chance to get acquainted." She must have noticed that her guest still had a question. "Oh, you mean Dwight and his Grandpa? They thought they'd just go ahead and eat by themselves. Dale—he's a little on the shy side when it comes to city folks."

After a delicious meal of cold sliced roast beef, tossed salad and homemade rolls Mae cleared the table just in time for the first committee member's arrival. By that time Earl had been moved to the living room. He heard the exchange at the back door. "Hello Gertrude. Come in."

"It's good to see you." Gertrude said. Then in a soft voice. "Is he here yet?"

"Oh yes, come in and meet Reverend Norris."

Earl rose to greet Gertrude Gelenik, and then in the next few minutes he rose frequently to greet the other committee members as well. Sue Stark, Wyoma Baxter, Jane Moss, and finally a man—Homer Stein.

"This is our pulpit committee." Mae announced, and then added. "Wilbur Wallace and Tim Fraser, the other two, told me they couldn't make it—too much farm work."

"I'm sorry," Earl responded. After Earl had greeted each one, everyone seated themselves in the living room, each person staring as unobtrusively as possible at this new minister candidate for their church in Saline.

"Yes, now I can put faces on the names I've been seeing on paper. An impressive bunch," Earl said with an intentional twinkle in his voice, hoping to make a good beginning with this group assembled for the sole purpose of having a look at him.

Each member had read and re-read Earl's dossier and had copies of bulletins of services which Earl Norris had led, including manuscripts of sermons he had preached. On the basis of this scrutiny the committee had invited Earl to come and "candidate" before the entire congregation. Earl had been informed through correspondence with the committee that on Sunday, after a service led by Earl and a sermon preached to the congregation, a vote would be taken by those church members in attendance. If the vote was unanimous—or nearly unanimous—and Earl agreed, he would come to Saline as its new pastor.

Earl felt at ease with this committee since they had already given their approval. Standing before the congregation on Sunday morning would be another matter. This, Earl anticipated with fear and trepidation. He had learned at seminary that this step in the process was by no means automatic. One disappointed classmate had returned to the seminary after preaching a trial sermon at a small church in Indiana. When Earl had asked him how his candidating had gone for him his answer shocked Earl. "They didn't approve me."

"How so?"

"Not enough positive votes—too many negative!"

The afternoon together over dessert at Mae Benson's gave Earl a chance to ask questions about the church and the community, questions which had not been covered in the church information material he had been sent earlier in the process. This meeting also gave the committee opportunity to ask questions of him which might still be unanswered. One area of interest on the committee's part was Earl's family situation. It was Gertrude Gelenik who led off. "Reverend—" She changed her manner of addressing him when she saw Earl's expression. "I mean, Earl, tell us a bit about your family."

Earl got right to the point he knew they wanted to hear. "Well, I'm not married . . . ." He paused just long enough for the question of divorce to trouble some of the committee members. Earl saved the day when he continued. "I have never been married. Close—once, but she did not want to be a pastor's wife. I'm a bachelor." He relieved his hearers. "So far as family is concerned it consists of my parents, both of whom are living, and a younger sister still at home with our parents in northern Illinois." This information about family was not as crucial a subject as his reference to his own singleness. That part they liked—especially Gertrude Gelenik, for she had an unmarried daughter.

The mood around the living room was friendly and upbeat. Meeting the ministerial candidate only confirmed the positive feeling the committee had had about "Reverend" Norris. He also was favorably impressed. Not yet fully ready to commit himself, however. He needed to see the entire congregation and get a feel of the group. This would happen on Sunday. After the service a potluck was planned, so that church members could meet the candidate on an informal basis before the meeting in which the congregation was to vote on accepting Earl Norris as its new pastor.

One can often tell when a meeting like this had come to an end, and the committee folk could feel that. Small talk emerges, some of it pertinent, other bits of conversation about other matters. And so, one by one the committee members made their courteous exit, thanking Mae and telling Earl that they looked forward to hearing him on Sunday. Gertrude was the last of the women to prepare to leave. She quite proudly announced to Earl, "Reverend, you'll be staying in my home for the weekend, so I can take you there now, if you'd like."

Earl could only answer such an invitation with a "Yes, I'd like that."

Before Homer Stein left, he went up to Earl and offered. "Mr. Norris, I'd like to show you around the community tomorrow, if you have time. Or will you need the day to prepare for Sunday?"

"No, Homer, I'm all set. I'd very much appreciate a guided tour."

"Good." Then Homer turned to Gertrude. "Gert, will you let me have Earl for part of the day tomorrow?"

She feigned reluctance and said that would be ok, if he didn't monopolize the Reverend.

It was arranged that Homer would come by Gelenik's around ten the next morning and return Earl in time for dinner.

When Gertrude and Earl drove into the Gelenik ranch, some fifteen miles further out of town, Gelenik's daughter, Ella Jean, was just coming into the yard on her horse. "Oh, good, there's Ella Jean. I want you to meet my daughter, Reverend." Gertrude gushed.

Once out of the car Earl was fair game. "Ella! This is our new minister! Come and meet him."

The girl sauntered closer to the car and still on her horse, leaned over and said. "How do you do, Reverend."

"Hello, Ella. I'm Earl Norris. Glad to meet you."

The girl turned and rode toward the horse barn.

Gertrude felt the need to apologize. "Ella Jean's a shy girl." And then she quickly added. "But very talented." At her own invitation Gertrude listed a number of attributes including, "plays the piano—good at drawing—and can she ever cook!" Only as an after thought did she add. "and she loves horses." Gertrude spotted her husband in one of the machinery sheds and called to him. "Karl, I want you to meet Rev. Norris."

Karl emerged from the shed almost immediately and with a welcome smile held out his hand. "Howdy, Reverner."

"Hello, Mr. Gelenik. Thanks for taking me in while I'm here in Saline."

"Oh, that's fine. We are glad you are here to look us over!"

That evening at supper Ella was very quiet, despite Gertrude's many attempts to draw her into conversation with Earl. On the other hand, Earl found Karl Gelenik to be an affable sort of man, tall and wiry with a ready sense of humor. He kidded Earl about what he might be getting himself into "here in this hot bed of conservative Montana farmers and ranchers." Earl didn't quite know what he was referring to—yet.

The next morning when Earl came into the kitchen for breakfast he found that Karl had already eaten and was out working on the place. Ella Jean was at the table while Gertrude was fixing eggs and bacon. Before her mother had a chance to push her into talking, Earl thought he might help out. "Ella, what's today going to be like for you? What do you plan to do?"

She smiled faintly and replied. "I'm going to work my horse some this morning, and then this afternoon I'm going over to my girlfriend's house."

"Is she close by?"

"Yeah, over in the next valley. About twenty miles."

"Wow, twenty miles is far where I come from."

"Where do you live?"

"Chicago, right now. I grew up in a suburb just outside the city."

"Oh." The conversation seemed to stop until the girl added a comment. "I've never been east of Minot. So I don't know anything about Illinois."

All during this exchange Ella's mother was listening. She explained. "Ella Jean's lived here since she was little when we moved here from North Dakota. Ella Jean's had all her schooling here and just graduated from high school."

Thankfully the eggs and bacon arrived, and Earl could turn his attention to something more productive.

When Homer arrived at ten, Earl joined him in his pickup. Once in the cab with Homer and away from the Gelenik's, it seemed to Earl that a heavy blanket had been removed. He could breathe more freely in Homer's presence. There had been something oppressive about the Gelenik home. He couldn't put his finger on it. From Homer's welcome, Earl sensed that Homer was aware of this condition. He gave Earl a slightly knowing look and then asked, "Did you get much chance to visit with Karl?"

"Briefly last evening at dinner. He was outside working already when I got to breakfast.'

"Well, you'll like him, I think. He's the only other member of the Farmers Union, besides myself, here in Saline. All the rest, if they belong to any farm organization, are in the Farm Bureau."

"I don't know much about either. What's the difference?"

"Oh, the Bureau is quite a bit more politically conservative than the Farmers Union."

"I take it that the area is on the conservative side, then." Earl cautiously guessed out loud.

Homer nodded, but apparently didn't want to say much more on the subject. "First we'll have a look at town," Homer announced as the two began their tour.

Saline is laid out on a typical grid pattern with five streets running east and west parallel to the railroad tracks which marks the "city limits" on one side. Intersecting these five streets are seven north and south streets, one of these, Main Street, crosses the tracks and turns into the country road going north. Railroad Avenue follows the tracks and becomes a county road leading into the surrounding country on both ends of town.

"Saline, Montana. Population 231, according to the last census in 1950. Not much has changed since. I reckon the number of deaths has been offset by about the same number of births." Homer began as he drove up and down and back and forth east of Main where the houses seemed to be in relatively good repair. "When you come down to it, it's mostly widows living here—also a few Main Street shopkeepers and officials like the depot agent, Ted Newhouse and his family. And then there's Thelma Oldham, our librarian. That's her house there. Never married—unless you subscribe to the rumor that she'd been married during the war when she worked in Minneapolis. Now as we go west from Main, most of these are rentals."

Earl could see that west of Main the houses were smaller and seemed more dilapidated.

"The folks on this side of town are mostly farm hands or laborers of one kind and another, who work for the railroad, the grain elevator, or the county road department—that kind of thing. As rentals they of course change occupants quite often. Can't really keep up with who they are, except over there in that ramshackle place. I tell you there's a pair. Brothers they are, a couple of years apart. But the fact that they're both alcoholics lends credence to what some of them city research doctors say—that it's a disease which gets its start in the genes."

As Earl listened to Homer he was reminded of the Stage Manager in the play, *Our Town*, who begins the play with a description of Grover's Corner, New Hampshire. Earl was tempted to mention this association, but decided against it. By this time they were driving along the outer edge of town where there were two or three new houses on neatly groomed yards. Unlike the other houses, these reminded Earl slightly of what he knew from suburban Chicago. "Who lives in these?"

"Well, this one here is the house Orville Hudson built after selling his farm a couple of years ago. He and Myrna Lou are retired. The one next to it is a newcomer. Moved over from Minot, to get away from the crowds. Dahlquist is their name. I don't know much about them, They seem to stay pretty much to themselves."

"How about church members? Some of these in town belong?"

"Not so much on this end of town, but I'd say most everyone east of Main is either a member or at least comes Easter and Christmas."

After going up and down the few residential streets of Saline, Homer commented. "That about covers the town. Now we'll go out into the country." Outside of town, when they reached a gate of a rural member Homer had more to say, telling about each particular farm operation, and which ones might be better described as livestock ranches. Not much personal information—thankfully. Earl had an idea that if Gertrude had been conducting the tour it would have included a running commentary of local gossip. Perhaps the most helpful aspect of Homer's tour was his reference to which activities in the church people were involved with. This helped Earl to gauge the strength of the congregation. As Homer pointed out the farms and ranches of families in the church, he came to one particular gate and slowed down, because he wanted Earl to be aware of its owner. "This is Jake Munson's gate."

Earl couldn't see beyond the ranch gate because there was a sizeable cluster of trees and undergrowth obscuring the view toward the farm house. "Is he a church member?"

"No. Just as well."

"Why's that?"

"He's an odd one. Been renting the old Cochrane place for years. He's let it go to ruin too, except he seems to make a living off it. But the thing about Jake is that he's a member of the John Birch Society . . . . In fact the society meets there."

Earl looked puzzled. "What's that?"

"A very conservative political group. They see themselves as the watch dogs of America. They are always looking for Communists—under every rock, you might say. Homer thought about what he was saying. "And you'll be lucky to stay out of their sights, I tell you! The last thing a preacher around here needs is to get onto their list."

"You say 'their'—are there others?"

"Oh, I'd say two or three other families. I don't know. It's pretty secret."

As they resumed their tour, one ranch was especially striking. The gravel road they were traveling began to curve downhill toward the Yellowstone River flowing along tree lined banks. "You can tell where the rivers are, by the ribbon of trees." Homer pointed to cottonwoods ahead which lined the river. "The river is the southern boundary of the community. In fact you can't even get over to the other side. No bridges for miles. There used to be a hand cranked ferry, but that's long gone. The old geezer who ran it died and nobody else wanted to mess with it."

When they descended to the level of the river, the road turned to run parallel to the river. A broad fertile pastureland stretched between the narrow road and the line of cottonwoods. "There's a place along here I want to show you, but they're not church people." Homer added under his breath. "No way! Not any more."

After driving a mile or so they came to a ranch gate which impressed Earl because of its size. Hanging from the cross beam was a wrought iron brand. It was a "W" with an "N' lying on its side. "That's the "W Lazy N" ranch. The Norlands have had the ranch for years. I doubt if you'll get to know any of them. They haven't darkened the door of the church—not in recent memory. In fact they don't take part in community functions either."

"Oh—why is that?" Earl wanted to know.

Homer was a bit evasive. "Can't say. There's some who have no use for 'em."

Earl got the feeling that would be all he should know. But it had made him curious, especially as they drove further over a slight hillock to a point where the ranch buildings could be seen from the road—all log. The two story ranch house was quite broad with its porch and front door facing the road. A rather large barn was surrounded by a number of smaller sheds and outbuildings. Dotting the grassy plain between the buildings and the road were quite a number of cows.

"Them's black Angus cattle, possibly a couple hundred—Aberdeen Angus." Homer announced as he found a widened place in the road in which to turn around. "Only one other place beyond here, but you won't need to waste your time there."

"Oh, why is that?"

"Well, a couple of bachelor brothers lived there for years—twins, in fact. *The Perry Twins*, they were known as, until one of them was killed. And that left just old Martin whom the kids around here call *Martin, the Hermit*. Some say he must be some sort of a college teacher . . . Oh that will give you enough of an idea about him."

Homer finished turning the car around and headed back up into the farming area they had previously toured. "Well, now you've seen Saline!"

"Thank you very much, Homer. It gives me a notion of what it's like here."

"At least on the surface for a start."

Earl thought Homer's reply had a bit of a cryptic overtone. But he guessed that any such tour would leave a lot yet to be discovered. He'd know a little more after the service and potluck the next day . . . and if he became pastor, he would no doubt learn a great deal more in time!

CHAPTER 3

On Display

Sunday was "show and tell." The committee very proudly put Earl on display before the congregation, both in the worship service and at the potluck dinner which followed. Earl succumbed to this same mood and did his very best. He felt that he'd preached a great sermon after leading in what he considered a good service of worship. Lots of women came up to him gushing before the meal began. The men were more reserved.

The basement fellowship hall was bustling with the people who had come down after the worship. Most of the women were working in the kitchen or outside the serving window loading the buffet table with the dishes of food brought for the potluck. In one corner of the dining room the youth had congregated, while here and there were clusters of men. A number of old timers were seated on chairs around the room.

Earl steered himself to various groups of men to meet them. They were always quite cordial, stopping their conversation to talk with him briefly. But in most cases they were quick to return to whatever matters they'd been discussing—mostly farming. Earl made sure to drop by the group of teenagers to visit with them.

Gertrude Gelenik was in charge of the potluck, presiding over the serving table as each dish was added. When the table was laden with what Earl would learn were called "carry-in" dishes, she asked Earl to pray. She tapped on an empty water class to get the attention of the various clusters of parishioners. When the group became quiet she announced, "I've asked the Reverend to bring us our blessing."

Earl gave a brief prayer asking God's blessing upon the food and the hands which had prepared it.

"Now we're ready to partake. Reverend! You go first." Gertrude was in her glory.

Earl took a china dinner plate and went along the table loading his plate with the best meal he had ever seen. He came to the coffee urn and filled a cup with coffee and sat down alone at a place at one of the long tables set up for the diners. It was awkward being alone, until some of the others had gone through the line and joined him. Everyone seemed to have many things to talk with each other about, and in a strange way Earl was left to fend for himself, until, fortunately, Homer Stein took his place across the table from Earl, making conversation easier. Earl had come to like Homer from their first meeting two days before, and it was apparent that Homer felt very positive toward Earl.

Toward the end of the meal the door opened and a man dressed in a suit and tie hurried into the room. He was an unusual sight, for very few of the men in the congregation had dressed in suits. Mae Benson rose to greet him and offered him a plate. He refused. She then announced, "This is Reverend Hapner from the Presbytery. He's here to moderate the meeting." Mae then brought him over to meet Earl. A place at the table was opened for him and Ella Gelenik brought him a cup of coffee. The two ministers visited with one another until Gertrude again was on her feet with an announcement. "In ten minutes we'll have our congregational meeting upstairs." She then turned to Earl. "Of course we'll want you to stay down here during the meeting. I've asked Ella to stay here to keep you company. After the vote we'll come down to get you, Reverend, to bring you upstairs to the meeting."

The noise level in the room increased noticeably as everyone finished up. Soon people were getting up and taking their plates and cups to the dishwashing window. After scraping and depositing these they made their way upstairs. Eventually the basement quieted down, leaving only Earl and Ella in the basement. A low rumble of indistinguishable voices could be heard coming from upstairs in the sanctuary.

Earl would have much rather stayed downstairs by himself to await the vote. Now he was obligated to make small talk with Ella, who was on the shy side. But, being thus occupied kept Earl from worrying over whether the folks upstairs would vote him in as their next pastor. However, he was not yet sure he would accept if the vote was favorable. This process upstairs took a long time. It worried Earl. Between various inane remarks he and Ella exchanged, he wondered if the long period of time the meeting was taking meant that he was not acceptable. Finally the door at the foot of the stairs opened and Gertrude came into the basement with an overly sly smile, "Come upstairs, you two!"

Earl arrived upstairs where Gertrude ushered him up to a position in front of the congregation. The low din of conversations throughout the group stopped. Mr. Hapner then shook Earl's hand and said, "Congratulations, Mr. Norris. The congregation of the Saline Community Church has voted to invite you to be its next pastor. The vote was 37 in favor." He lowered his voice a bit and added, "2 not in favor."

Mr. Hapner had pressed for a unanimous vote on a second ballot after the two negative votes had been tallied. This was customary in such a meeting to call a pastor. The rationale is that when the negative voters realize the near unanimous vote of the group, they will change their vote in order to give the new minister a vote of total approval, a courteous action which congregations usually take in such cases. However, here in Saline apparently the negative voters remained stubborn and refused to change their vote. Chances were that Earl would understand this and take it into consideration as he made up his mind on whether or not to accept the call. He would have two weeks in which to respond one way or the other to Saline's call.

Hapner closed the meeting with prayer and everyone got up to prepare to go home. Three of the women, however returned to the kitchen to wash the dishes and straighten up. Many of the folk came up to Earl to offer their support for the vote and to tell him that they hoped he would accept. The overall mood was that of joy and excitement as church members picked up their dishes and went out to their vehicles.

On the way back to the Geleniks' farm, Gertrude tried to put a positive interpretation on the vote. "You have to expect that there will always be a few hold-outs. Who knows why. Sometimes someone will vote negative merely because they don't agree with the salary package which is being offered. They think it's too high." She thought about what she had just said and offered an alternative idea just to dress it up. "Or too low. Maybe they thought we should offer you more money. Don't you think, Ella, that they might have been thinking that way?"

"I guess so, Mother."

"I see." Earl responded without much conviction on the subject.

"We certainly look forward to having you as our new preacher," Gertrude gushed. She turned to Ella. "Won't we, Ella?"

"Yes, we will, Mother."

When they got to Geleniks,' Earl excused himself saying that he had to pack since he was leaving in the evening.

"We'll have an early supper, Reverend. I'll call you in time."

In the privacy of his room he relaxed in an easy chair by the bed to sort out his thoughts. It was too soon afterward to formulate any reasonable thoughts. He needed some perspective which time and distance would give him. So he put on some casual traveling clothes and packed. It would be good to get back to the comfortable familiarity of the seminary, and his friends there.

After a while Gertrude called and he came downstairs into the living room for a supper. Karl stood up to welcome Earl and the two men joined Gertrude and Ella in the large kitchen where the table was spread with a full supper. While Gertrude continued to speak as though Earl had already agreed to come to Saline, Ella was a bit more reserved, not only by nature, but she must have understood the peculiar position Earl was in. It was awkward for him because he had not had time to sort out his thoughts and at this point did not know whether he would return to take the pastorate in Saline. Karl was a congenial host without making any premature assumptions, unlike his wife.

When the meal was finished, Karl announced that Homer Stein was coming to take Earl to the train station in town. In a few moments, Homer arrived. Earl said his goodbyes and thank yous, and then picked up his bag and went out to Homer's car. Now in the privacy of the car Homer said, with a knowing twinkle in his eye. "Well, I take it that Gert has you already moved in to Saline!" and then he added, "I shouldn't say this, but I will—and married to Ella."

Earl didn't know quite how to respond to Homer's frank appraisal, but there was something so genuine about the man that Earl felt that he could agree. "Yes, Homer, I believe you're right on both of those assumptions."

Then Homer said something a bit ominous. "And you'll not be on the good side of Gertrude Gelenik until you make her right on both counts."

"I hear you."

"Don't get me wrong—I'm not advising both—only the first assumption!"

"Well, I've felt good about today, and I will have lots of good things to consider, Homer."

Homer continued the subject. "Well, Earl, is there anything else that you'd like to know about us before making your decision?"

"Nothing specific that I can think of now. But I'd like to ask you a general question."

"What's that?"

"How do you feel about the presentation of the Saline church which has been given to me?"

Homer had a puzzled expression.

"I mean, frankly, did I see the real you—so to speak? Or might there be some surprises if I were to come here?"

"That's a very good question, Earl. You are prudent and wise to ask that." Homer thought for a few moments. "I believe that what you saw here this weekend is what you get, to use a shop worn phrase."

Earl's only reply was to say, "That's helpful." He was uncomfortable with moving this conversation forward until he knew his own mind and heart on the question of coming to Saline. He redirected the conversation. "Homer, tell me about yourself."

"Well, as you probably guessed, I'm a native of this community. I farm the place on which Mae and I were born and grew up. Just down the road from where Norlands are now.

"Mae?"

"Oh, I guess you wouldn't have known. Mae Benson and I are cousins. Our fathers were partners on the Stein place. When this country opened up, my father, Jacob, and his brother, Josiah, filed on adjoining homesteads. After each had proved up, they put the two pieces together and formed a partnership. So Mae and I grew up about a mile apart, but on the same farm. We were like brother and sister, growing up so close to each other."

"I see. Was that partnership idea unusual?"

"Yes, it was. But the bigger size of the operation gave them more leverage."

"Are the two places still together?"

"Yes. The brothers, of course, are gone. By that time Father had bought out my uncle. And now I'm in partnership with my son, Tom." Homer's mind seemed to drift before resuming his account. "Tom and his wife, Jenny have been a godsend to me, especially after his mother died. That was fifteen years ago that Vivian passed away—too young—too young."

"I'm sorry, Homer. Was it an illness, or something sudden?"

"Cancer—fast acting. Nothing the doctors could do, except maybe to give her a few more months—difficult months." Another pause with a distant look in his eyes. "Left two boys. Tom was sixteen in his last year of school. Ray was only twelve."

"Does Ray live nearby?"

"In Billings. He teaches in the high school—biology."

"I don't think I met Tom at church, did I?"

"No, I'm afraid not." Homer chose not to say more.

By this time they had gotten into town and soon would be pulling up to the station. So the story had to end at that point. To be taken up later—perhaps.

CHAPTER 4

Coming Home

On the Sunday of her arrival, the Westbound was unusually late, so late that it would be pulling into the Saline station only a few minutes before the scheduled arrival of the Eastbound. It would tax Ted Newhouse's energy and efficiency to handle both arrivals at about the same time. The waiting room was bustling with exited sounds of people waiting. The platform already had twice the usual number of people waiting for passengers coming off of one train or the other.

Walter Norland and his wife, Beth, were seated on the end of one of the long shiny pew-like benches in the waiting room. Typical of a small town it was obvious from the noise level of the conversations throughout the room that most of the folk in the waiting area knew each other. However, a stranger would have concluded that the Norlands were not part of the community, because they didn't seem to carry on any conversations with the people seated around them. If asked, most of the others would have said something like, "*Oh yes, they live here. But . . . .*" A code of silence toward outsiders would have closed off any further comment regarding the Norlands.

Walter Norland, a tall man in his late fifties, was wearing a gray woolen western suit jacket above neatly ironed Levis. His silver belt buckle matched his bolo tie worn with his white western snap button shirt. A new-appearing powder gray Stetson hat and cowboy boots rounded out an image of a well-to-do Montana rancher. Beth, also in her fifties, liked to wear denim and so had on a mid calf length denim full-skirted dress decorated with a flower brocade. This was touched off with a red bandana neck scarf. The two made an impressive pair. The lively twinkle in Walt's eyes and the gentle softness about Beth would make them not only impressive but appealing to an outside observer.

Walter Norland commented wistfully to his wife. "Not quite two years ago and we were here to see Kaye and Buck off. And now . . . ."

"I know. I thought of that too. And now Kaye and the baby." She sighed. "I just hope we can be the help she needs."

"So do I. I think we can, Beth. We'll try our best."

"She's been through a lot. More than I ever had to endure. My life's been happy thanks to you, sweetheart."

Walt reached for Beth's hand and gave it a squeeze.

Just then the high pitched drone of the train whistle could be heard in the distance. The noise level in the waiting room suddenly dropped briefly. "It's the Westbound," someone said.

Walter Norland smiled knowingly at his wife. "A few more minutes and you'll be holding your grandbaby again, Beth!"

"I can't wait."

Over the loud speaker came the Agent Newhouse's much anticipated announcement. "Westbound arriving shortly on track No. 2." The station master made the arrival official.

Soon the building shook as the massive diesel engine reached the east edge of the platform and proceeded to rumble by the depot. The Westbound came to a precision stop when it reached the tree shaded lawn on the west end of the pavement just beyond the depot. By the time it arrived and several conductors had swung themselves down onto the cement platform, at least half the depot crowd had funneled outside next to the tracks furthest from the depot.

The Norlands didn't see her step down but soon they saw her walking toward them with the baby in a stroller. They waved at each other and soon they met. In the next moment Walter was hugging his daughter while Beth had already knelt down to greet the baby.

Kaye Norland had left Saline almost two years previous as a young girl, turned bride. Now she was returning, a young woman in her early twenties, turned single mother. Somewhat tall like her father, she had the softness of her mother. Motherhood had given her new maturity of appearance. She'd "filled out" as her aunt in Minnesota would say. She was attractive with light chestnut-colored hair cascading down to her shoulders, a classic Nordic face with twinkling eyes. The kind of person whom it always seemed a joy to be near, making anyone who knew her situation conclude that her ex-husband had been a fool to lose her.

While the Norland family was reuniting out on the platform, inside the depot were those waiting for the eastbound Northcoast Limited. Soon they heard the rumble of the second engine as it slowly approached the station. Again it appeared that everybody was with somebody—except for one young man dressed in a sport coat carrying an overnight case. He made his way onto the platform to prepare to board. The Eastbound arrived and soon passengers were stepping off onto the platform. Earl Norris mounted the steps into one of the coaches. He was assisted up by a porter in a white starched jacket and wearing a black railroad hat.

In a matter of minutes, the powerful engines of both trains began to rev up about the same time. Soon each train was rolling ever so slowly. They both could be heard picking up speed as they departed from the Saline Depot. In a few minutes time, the waiting room was empty and quiet, while the cars and pickups which had been temporarily parked outside the depot were driving off. In the distance the train whistles sounded as each crossed intersecting roads. Inside the Eastbound Earl, settled in to watch the Montana scenery pass in review.

Back in Saline the four Norlands began their journey to the ranch. Twenty minutes later, as the late model Chrysler Imperial turned off and passed through the Norland ranch gate, Kaye exclaimed. "Oh, Mom and Dad, it's so good to be home again."

"Yes, dear. And you don't have to go anywhere until you're ready."

"I know, Mom."

Walter Norland, a quiet man but strong in every way, drove up to the house and turned into the half circle drive pulling up to the front door of his substantial log home. He stopped the shiny dark blue sedan at the front steps. He had washed and polished the car for the occasion. He got out and opened the rear door for Kaye. He spoke in a formal regal tone. "Welcome home, Kaye . . . and to you—young David!" Walter Norland, proud father, grandfather, and "lord of the manor," escorted Kaye up the broad front steps and into the door. Beth followed lovingly carrying the sleeping baby.

The two women tucked little Davey into the crib in the nursery which Beth had made ready. Walt carried Kaye's bags up to her childhood bedroom. Kaye and her parents returned to the spacious living room. There was enough chill in the May air so that Norland lit a fire which he had set in the fireplace. All three settled down in front of it to begin rebuilding the life they had shared together before Kaye had left. There followed an outpouring of thoughts and feelings each to the other until Kaye and her parents were basking in the bittersweet joy of her return home from what had been a most unfortunate marriage and a sadly unhappy home life in Minnesota. The only bright spot of those years had been Davey.

Kaye had grown up the oldest of two children in the home. Her brother, Ken, had a year remaining at Dartmouth, Walter's alma mater. Kaye had followed her mother's college path and had earned her degree from the University of Minnesota a few months prior to her marriage. While Beth's degree had been in Home Economics, Kaye's field had been political science, as her father's had been. Ken intended to enter law school. Obviously higher education was of primary importance in the Norland family, a cultural preference which did not go unnoticed—or unresented—by others in the Saline community. Current events and social/political issues were regular topics around the Norland dinner table. Often after dinner, in front of the massive living room fireplace the discussion revolved around the novels and other reading in which family members happened to be engaged at the time. Also in the living room the music frequently heard from the stereo would be Beethoven or Mozart. These educational and cultural interests too, had they been known, would have caused sneering comments among neighbors. But the fact of the matter was that very little was known about the Norlands. They kept to themselves, not so much because they were private by nature, but as a result of attitudes in the community towards the Norlands which had developed over the years and now had become set in the hard pan clay of the region, so to speak.

Other ranchers and Norland would visit as necessary at the local lumber yard or at the grain elevator, but that's as far as it went. Norland sold his livestock at the Public Auction Yards in Billings without much association with other ranchers from Saline who sold in Miles City. Beth had long since quit going to the monthly Extension Club meetings, having felt a certain undercurrent of shunning. For other reasons, more profound, the Norlands had ceased to identify with the Community Church in Saline. Even in school, Kaye and Ken had kept somewhat to themselves, unusual for a town the size of Saline.

Now, once again buried in the womb of her own family, Kaye anticipated the chance to heal, free from agitation and constant tension. That was good, she felt, as she sat in the large soft leather chair facing the glowing embers of late evening. Her mother was in the kitchen fixing some hot chocolate and her father had a few late chores to do outside. Coming home was good.

CHAPTER 5

Racing in the night

He was too keyed up to sleep, so he climbed up into the darkened Vista Dome and gazed out into the night as the Northcoast Limited raced eastward across the moonlit plains of North Dakota. Tiny dots of yellowing light could be seen in the distance as yard lights on farms passed by. Occasionally tiny towns sped by, made evident by a few street lights and the red neon glow of the local bar. When such towns were big enough to have an intersecting road he could hear the sound of the pulsating crossing bell in a crescendo as the train approached and then diminishing as the train left the town in its wake. But most of the time it was dark beyond the curved windows of this glass and aluminum cocoon in which an energized "soon to be" pastor sat immersed in his own thoughts. Racing eastward in the night.

Earl Norris, alone in the Vista Dome, was lost in his thoughts, also racing in the night. Two weeks to make his decision. The same two weeks to complete his course work for seminary graduation. If he decided on Saline, they wanted him as soon as possible. They'd been without a regular minister for over two years. You couldn't blame them. But he needed some time to make the transition. A transition from living among millions in Chicagoland with all that a major city could provide to the meager resources and the few people to make up Saline on the plains of Montana in a county numbering scarcely a few thousand. Not even a decent library in the county. He contemplated an awesome leap from the warmth and familiarity of his peers with whom he had spent the last three years at seminary, into a new group of people, most of whom were older than he was, and none of whom did he know in any real sense. In some ways threatening. He would be very much alone. He had been taught the dangers of becoming too close to any in the congregation he would serve. These folk would not be peers in that sense. Alone, yes alone. So far as social life was concerned he could think of no prospects for dating. He thought about church. Over the past three years he had worshiped for the most part in a large and prestigious church of his denomination, which was located across the city from the seminary. But worth the trip just to hear the great organ, to say nothing of the incisive preaching. Saline didn't have an organ, just a tinkly old upright piano, played not too well by a high school girl. And the preaching? Well it would be Earl Norris, for what that was worth!

And yet . . . there was Saline. He'd never seen a sky so blue, nor distances as great as those he saw when he had looked onto the plains in almost all directions from town. The eager enthusiasm he had felt as church people had introduced themselves to him and visited with him at the potluck. He couldn't put his finger on it, but the people were different from those with whom he'd been associated in his life up to that time. The men in their Levis and western shirts with cowboy hats and boots, the women in their faded house dresses. More dusty pickups in the church parking lots than cars. Something about Saline that intrigued him, and he'd have to admit to himself—appealed to him.

Earl Norris did not have any experience in rural or small town communities. The only knowledge of the farm came from children's books he'd read as a youngster. He was a city boy. He grew up in a suburb on the west side of Chicago. And now he lived in the heart of a large city—Chicago. It is commonly understood that many rural people are intimidated by the big city. In a turn-about way Earl Norris had been intimidated by Saline. Perhaps it was a fear of the unknown. But on a deeper level his intimidation stemmed from the radically different way people related to one another in Saline. Sociologists would label the Saline society as a *primary group*. All his life had been spent in *secondary groups* except for his own family. Groups in which there was always a comfortable distance between people. In the primary group there is a scary closeness. Everyone knows everybody's business. But not in a negative way, but as family members who care about what each member is doing and feeling. This can be terrifying to someone like Earl who has known only secondary groups. The anonymity of the city life was familiar and comforting to Earl. He sensed the reluctance of the small primary group in Saline to include an outsider. And he would definitely be an outsider . . . for a considerable length of time.

As the train kept a steady pace racing in the night toward Earl's destination in the heart of downtown Chicago, he could not explain his fears, but he knew what he felt. And yet he felt drawn to the very people who intimidated him. He thought of Homer Stein. He had been so gracious in showing Earl around the area. He had such an easy friendly way about him. He hadn't seemed so impressed with Earl's profession as others had. It had embarrassed Earl the way so many had paid him obvious respect, if not a sort of homage. Homer had acted more like a long time friend. As Earl pondered this he concluded that unlike the others Homer had seemed willing to let Earl into his own "inner circle" so to speak. The others had not. Earl remembered something one of his pastoral theology professors had said in a lecture on ministering in rural communities. "It can take as long as twenty-five years before a newcomer is allowed to become part of the community."

While the closeness of a primary group may be intimidating to the outsider, it is also true that those in such a group are well aware of the outsider, and do not readily accept the stranger into the group. In rural communities, it is often the case that clergy and their spouses remain outsiders for as long as they stay in the community. This is especially true when they come from more urban environments. This dynamic may very well account for the short tenures of many ministers who come to serve rural churches, only to move on in a year or two.

Back and forth his mind went. But somehow, down deep Earl knew that he would become the pastor of the Community Church of Saline, Montana. It made him feel tingly all over, just to imagine himself in that new role. Admitting that fact seemed to put his mind at ease. He thought about the inevitability of his affirmative decision. *I guess that's how the call of God happens. You just sort of know that it is what God wants you to do. You can do all sorts of "this way and that way" figuring, but in the end what matters is what God calls me to do.*

Having run out of thoughts, he rose and returned to his assigned coach seat. His sleeping accommodations were limited to the pillow and blanket the porter had brought to him earlier in the evening. It wasn't long before he slept.

When he awakened he pulled up the heavy shade and saw that the train was skirting along the edge of the Mississippi between St. Paul and Savannah, Illinois. Sometime during the night the train had made a lengthy stop in St. Paul. Now in the morning, after freshening up in the men's lavatory at the end of the coach, Earl made his way forward through three coaches to the diner. After a plate sized pancake and a cup of coffee he paid his bill and returned to one of the coaches with a Vista Dome. He climbed the narrow stairway and found a seat from which he could take in the familiar scenery of the Midwest as the North Coast Limited came nearer and nearer to Chicago. He found himself relaxing as the congested streets and roadways of the city came into view. Soon he saw in the murky distance the buildings in the Loop partially enshrouded in light cloud cover. The train rapidly passed through the outer edges of the city where well kept brick homes with attractive yards passed in review, Then block after block of two story frame houses on tiny lots whizzed by. After these came the industrial areas with factories and warehouse lots filled with various kinds of building materials and machinery parts. Interspersed in these sections of the city were ancient three story tenements with their rickety stairways and porches, as well as brick strewn vacant lots where apartment buildings had once stood. Before he knew it, he felt the train slowing up to enter the station south of the Loop. The end of the line. He gathered up his carry-on things and went to the end of the coach to await the porter's signal to step down onto the cement platform. Soon he was walking with the stream of passengers making their way rapidly to the huge railroad station.

As he walked along, excited to be home in Chicago again, he thought of what would come next in his life. Now all he had to do was to finish his course work and graduate. Chicago Presbytery had already scheduled his ordination in his home church. But first, when he got to his apartment he needed to call the committee out in Saline and tell them *"Yes, I'd like very much to come. I accept your call to ministry in Saline."*

The next time he would go west to Montana he would be driving. He hoped his Ford Fairlane would make it. It would be packed full. The committee had promised to furnish the parsonage—or *manse* as it was called, so he wouldn't need to take any furniture, only his personal belongings. Books were another problem. He had heard that the way to get your books out to the field was to send them by freight. This would take a few weeks, but he could coast on what was in his head for that long, he thought. Lots to do between now and then. His mind was still racing.

CHAPTER 6

The Song of the Meadowlark

The song of a meadowlark wafted into her bedroom window, passing through the lace curtains swaying in the morning breeze. The cheerful music of the bird bathed the sleeping young woman in a pool of sound which was both shocking to her and pleasantly familiar. Shocking because she hadn't heard it since the last time she had slept in her childhood bed, and familiar precisely because as a child she had often been awakened with that sweet sound. In the old days, that is. Before her unfortunate marriage to Buck.

She stirred, opened her eyes and stretched her legs down the length of the bed between the cool sheets. She laid back the bed covers enough to uncover the top portion of her sheer nightgown. The coolness of the morning breeze spread over her, stimulating her to awaken further. She sat up in bed, swung her feet onto the floor and sat for a moment to think about where she was. *Home.* The nostalgic rattle of pots and dishes came up from the kitchen where her mother was already preparing breakfast—a special breakfast for Kaye on her first morning home. Along with cozy memories of childhood flooding her mind, the aroma of bacon began to come through the hall from the kitchen below.

Next she heard the slight crying of her baby, apparently in the kitchen area of the house. Immediately there followed the soothing voice of Kaye's mother who had obviously gone to comfort the child. How long it had been since there had been someone else to help her with her child. Now, with her mother caring for him, Kaye could remain in bed a bit longer. She puffed up the pillow, swung her legs back onto the bed and lay back on top of the blankets. She discreetly pulled down her shorty night gown on the outside chance that someone might come in to greet her.

She had been alone with her baby for so long, since her mother had left the apartment after he was born. She'd been able to stay only a week. Buck had left while she was still in the hospital. He'd come to see her and the newborn once, and then *he was gone. Gone!* When she got out of the hospital she found *not a trace of his things. GONE!* She still filled with anger as she said it to herself. She had hoped that the baby would help their marriage. It had done the opposite. *Do I still love him?* She'd thought so, but now that she was home, she wasn't so sure. He'd refused to go to counseling. Now, after the fact, she felt she had a handle on some of what had gone wrong. Not that it made any difference anymore—except to help her avoid the same thing the next time. *Next time? No way!* But then, the baby. Davey would need a father. But she surely didn't need a husband again. *Certainly not yet.*

She and Buck had known each other as children. Played in the barn, in the woods down at the creek—all over the ranch it seemed. Buck's father had been a hired hand on the Norland ranch and lived in a small house just east of the lane leading to the Norland house. They were friends in high school and finally in their senior year they were going together. They became engaged the night before Kaye left for college in the fall after their senior year. It would be a long engagement until Kaye would get her degree. Four years later, when she returned to Saline, they were married. By that time she'd landed a job in a suburban courthouse outside the Twin Cities. They found an apartment, and Buck took what jobs he could, usually in service stations in the area. He was working in a tire shop at the time he disappeared.

Trouble in their marriage revolved around his resentment of Kaye's college degree and the relatively good job she had obtained. Buck's anger peaked every time Kaye had tried to persuade Buck to enter a community college, a trade school or anything to "better himself" as she had said. She now realized that had been an unfortunate choice of words. So far as he was concerned he didn't need any further education, or to "better himself." And so the tension mounted. Then the baby. Then Buck was *outta there,* as he declared to himself. He was gone. And Kaye became a single mom.

Fortunately Buck's parents no longer worked for her father. They had moved to western Montana, somewhere up around Kalispell. So there'd be no embarrassing meetings now that she was home. They'd shown no interest in the baby, so that was good now that Buck was out of the picture. The job in the courthouse folded when county funding was severely cut. At that point Kaye came home.

Here she was—home! And she smelled the bacon. She got out of bed, slipped off her gown, dressed herself in jeans and a sweat shirt, stopped by her bathroom, did a quick face wash, and came to the kitchen in her bare feet.

"Hi, Mom!"

"Morning, Babes. I've got Davey here with me."

"Thank you for that. I could stay in bed a little longer, Mom." Kaye reached down to pick the baby up from a little swinging seat he'd been put in. The baby cooed and it felt good to Kaye to cuddle him against her sweat shirt. He was warm and smelled "of baby."

While they ate, Kaye could hear the song of the meadowlark. It heralded a new life for her and for little Davey. But at the time she didn't know much of what that new life would be. She was still trying to repair her old life.

Repair had been the name of the game since Buck had left. A few months after his rude departure, divorce papers were served on Kaye. Another hit. Like a blow to the stomach which knocks one's air out. She was angry and hurt, but she decided not to contest it. Her first thought had been not to allow him his freedom. But then she discovered from a mutual friend that his disappearance had been a flight into the arms of another woman whom he had seduced during Kaye's pregnancy. When the divorce was finalized she felt a surprising relief. It was then that the repair of her life began.

Now it was a Saturday morning in Saline, Montana—her first day home, and Kaye was luxuriating. By the time Kaye had eaten her bacon and eggs, Davey had become sleepy and she put him to sleep in his crib, in a room near the dining room. This gave her a chance to take another cup of coffee. "Mom, come sit down with me. Bring a cup for yourself."

When the two were seated together Kaye shared what was on her mind. "Mom, I don't think I ever told you, but after the divorce I started going to church."

Her mother looked surprised. This had not been a pattern of activity in Kaye's background, although before her own marriage her mother had been active in the community church in Saline. But that had ended suddenly on a sour note.

Kaye sensed her mother's chagrin. "What happened is that when I was served the divorce papers, I was so devastated that I couldn't manage to keep it to myself. One of my co-workers told me of a certain pastor who had been a great help to her in similar circumstances a few years earlier. She suggested. "If you want me to, I'll give him a call and tell him that I've recommended that you see him. OK?"

I said, "Yeah, I guess so."

"Well, I went to see that particular pastor a couple of times, and he really helped me. So much so that I started going to his church—Peace Lutheran. It began to mean a lot to me to be in church during that hour every week. I felt a certain stability, which had been lacking since Buck left. They had a nice nursery for Davey, and so it was really a special time for me."

"I'm glad, dear, that you found such help. I wish I could have been there to help you."

"Oh, Mom, this was something I had to work out myself. Anyway, I've been worried that once I got home I'd have to quit going to church. Because I know you guys just don't like the church here in Saline."

"No, your father has been alienated from them for a long time. And they don't have anything to do with us either."

"I know. But you know what I'd like to do, Mom?"

"What?"

"If it's ok with you to keep Davey next Sunday morning, I'd like to go into Miles City to church."

"Sure, dear, we can do that, if that's what you want. What church, do you know any there?"

"I thought I'd try the big one on Main Street, Presbyterian, I think."

"Oh?"

"A girl friend of mine in high school—she and her family used to go there and she was always talking about it."

So when Sunday came Kaye attended worship at First Presbyterian Church of Miles City. It was a decision she would not regret.

CHAPTER 7

Point of No Return

Merle Johnson's petroleum business consisted of a bulk plant from which he provided fuel to farms and ranches in the Saline area as well as a service station for retail business on the west edge of town. It was affectionately referred to as "The Conoco." More than a gas station and auto repair shop, it served as the social center for its own *reg'lars*. It was a men's club, not as richly appointed as the Union League Club in Chicago—by a long shot! But it had its membership and its "ritual." The amenities, however were sparse, consisting of a battered aluminum coffee percolator and mugs, not too often washed. And a few antiquated steel folding chairs—quite cold in the winter. The "meeting room" itself left a lot to be desired. It doubled as the gas station counter area.

Tuesday morning the sky was a brilliant blue. Bright sunlight shone through the plate glass front window of the Conoco station, highlighting quite a number of smudges and spots. A good day for farming if there ever was one. However the beat-up metal folding chairs at "The Conoco" were occupied by members of "the club." In former times this ritual had been carried out at the lumber yard, until it closed a couple of years ago. After that the "regulars" began using the Conoco for their morning palavers. If you wanted to know what some folks thought about what was going on, this grimy service station was the place to go. That is if you were male, and had been accepted into "membership."

It was a couple of days after the Sunday Earl Norris had been voted upon. The subject was the "new preacher."

"Well what'd ya think of the new preacher, Hank?" Darrel Reisner asked, not having been there himself. He was aware that Hank Hurlbutt and his wife were active members of the Saline Community Church.

45

"Well, if ya really wanna to know, I didn't vote for him."

"How come? Can't he preach?"

"Well . . . yeah, he can preach . . . but . . . ."

"But what?"

"Well, if ya really wanna know . . . he's single, and that's not good."

This got Dale Benson into the discussion. "You may be right, Hurlbutt."

Merle came in from the oil changing bay. "What's the topic, boys?"

Reisner told him. "The new preacher. Hank voted against him because he's single."

Claude Miller had been listening and now asked. "What's that got do with it?"

Hank took a cigar out of his breast pocket, chewed off the tip, licked the end before taking it in his mouth. He lit it. After his first draw he seemed to settle back for one of his long stories. The guys were used to hearing long harangues presented by Hank Hurlbutt.

"Well, ya know . . ." he puffed out a cloud of cigar smoke. "There was this preacher over to Sage Creek. Young fella—full of . . . know what I mean?"

The listeners nodded.

"Well he got to fooling around . . . not with any of them that was in his church. Too smart for that. Well, he used to go into Miles City all the time. People over there to Sage Creek didn't like it. Thought he ought be there tending his flock, so to speak. And I agree. That's what a preacher's for. Well, anyway it seems like he got to going to this one store a lot—sorta like a dime store. Remember it?"

There seemed to be nods of familiarity with the place he was talking about.

"There was this young lady at the counter—married to a sheep farmer down by the river. Well anyway, the story was that this young single preacher got sweet on this clerk. She was a 'looker' so you can see why he might-a. Now, I'm not sayin' anything happened. Know what I mean?"

More nods.

"But next thing ya knew, that gal got a divorce and left the country." Hank looked around to see how this story was "playing," with his audience, before continuing. "Well anyway, the church people up to Sage Creek must 'uv put two and two together. Wasn't long before they asked that young preacher to pack." Hank paused for the full effect of the implication to sink in. "And so, I say a single preacher ain't a good idea. Right?"

One or two nods. Instead of agreeing, Darrel asked. "You the only one who voted 'No'?"

"There was one other 'no' vote. But I dunno who."

"When's he comin'?" Merle wanted to know.

"Not sure. He might not accept." Hank introduced this element of doubt.

Dale Benson added. "He seemed all right to me. Dwight and I picked him up from the train."

"Don't tell me you went to church?" Darrel chided.

"No, can't say I did. But the ol' lady did and really liked him."

"I don't mean anything by it. But . . . ." Darrel chimed in. "But did ya ever notice how it's them young single preachers the church ladies like the best?"

More nods of agreement.

Jake Munson had been quiet but now leaned forward and in a conspiratorial way asked Hank Hurlbutt, "So you heard the new preacher's sermon?"

"Yeah. Can't say I remember much of it, why?."

"Well, did he say anything about the UN, or our country?"

"No, not exactly. He talked about how there are hungry people in the world and here in the US. And how we ought to feed them."

"Oh, he did?"

"Yeah. But that's preacher talk."

Jake gave a knowing look and nodded his head. "But that may be more than just preacher talk."

Hank was bewildered. "Whad'ya mean?"

Jake became reluctant to say more. "Oh, I dunno . . . . know what I mean?"

The implication seemed to dawn on Hank.

"You keep me informed, Hank." More of a command than a suggestion.

The "club" went on to other matters—the weather and cattle prices.

About an hour later Hank announced, "Bout time for lunch. Gotta go. But, I'm gonna watch him like a hawk."

"Who?" Claude asked.

"The new preacher."

Not every man in the community chose to be a member of "the Club.' Harley Jensen was not a member. He had his reasons. So long as Gelenik was in "the Club," Harley stayed away. Harley and his wife, Charlotte, were members of the Community Church and old timers in the community. Some years back he'd had a falling out with his neighbor, Karl Gelenik. Something about a fence line between their farms, and some stray cattle. Whatever it was it mushroomed out of proportion and from that time on the two men had not spoken. Charlotte and Gertrude Gelenik were in the Ladies Aid and as such were involved in projects which kept them on minimal speaking terms. The Jensens were church members, but not too active, probably because of the Geleniks, it was thought.

A few days after the congregational meeting, Harley and Charlotte were discussing the "new preacher" over supper.

"I thought he was good." Charlotte admitted.

"That may be, but I voted against him." The anger in Harley's voice was not unusual, however.

"For heaven's sake, why?"

"Because that Gelenik woman was so enthused about him, that's why."

"Harley, that's no reason."

"It is for me, after what them Geleniks did to us."

"You know that was years ago and you're still mad. You ought to be ashamed."

Harley grumbled to himself. He'd heard this from his wife many times.

In a crowded city restaurant eleven hundred miles to the east, the town of Saline, Montana was the topic of conversation between two young students.

"Where in the world is Saline?"

"In eastern Montana, not too far from Miles City, Montana."

Phil was quick to counter with, "That helps a lot, Earl. Where's Miles City?" He thought further. "As a matter of fact I don't know a thing about Montana."

The Seminary Bar and Restaurant was uniquely located on the near north side of Chicago, across the street from a theological seminary. In fact it was an infamous spot because of an incident which occurred near it in the '30s. At the northeast corner of the seminary grounds, three Chicago streets intersect with Lincoln Avenue coming into the corner on an angle so that the building at the corner facing Lincoln on one side and Fullerton on the other is pie-shaped. The restaurant occupied the very point of the property. About a half a block west of the establishment, an alley cuts across to Lincoln where the Biograph movie theater is located. It was in this alley that the notorious outlaw, John Dillinger, was shot and killed by F.B.I. agents on July 22, 1934, as he came out of the Biograph. Now, a few decades later the neighborhood was a quiet ethnic area.

Earl Norris and Phil Otis, a friend, were having coffee at the counter of the Seminary Bar and Restaurant. The two young men were both seniors at the seminary, about ready to graduate. Phil had accepted a call to become an assistant pastor at First Presbyterian Church of Spokane, Washington. The two friends had been telling each other about the previous weekend when each had been out interviewing for positions after graduation.

Phil wasn't very encouraging to Earl. "You can have the little town and the solo pastorate. I'm glad I'm going as an assistant. Isn't it a little scary when you think about being out there all alone?"

"I guess it is a little scary. But that's outweighed in my mind by the excitement I feel when I think about going out to Saline to start my ministry."

"More power to you, buddy," Phil concluded the discussion. "I better get going. I have a preaching class in fifteen minutes."

"See you later. Think I'll stay here and read my book."

After Phil left for class, Earl opened a book he'd been loaned by Homer when he had been out in Montana. Homer had said, "You might find this helpful in understanding our area. Kraenzel is a rural sociology professor at Montana State College in Bozeman. His understanding and observations about the plains will describe us for you, Earl."

The book was *The Great Plains in Transition* by Karl Kraenzel. The book would be the first of a number which Earl would read to try and get a handle on what would become his newly adopted home. It was ironic that he should begin his study of rural Montana while sitting at the counter of a busy restaurant in the heart of one of America's most typical cities—Chicago—in some ways the most American city in the sense of being in the heartland and having such a melting pot diversity of ethnic and racial groups. You couldn't conceive of a sharper contrast than between Chicago and Saline. It was across this wide and deep chasm that Earl Norris was about to jump. His phone call the night before to the committee out in Saline to tell them that he would accept their call was the point of no return for Earl Norris.

Finally, after having drained his third cup of coffee, Earl paid his bill and walked out of the Seminary Bar and Restaurant onto Fullerton Avenue. He didn't have any more classes that day, so he turned east and walked out to the lake shore. In the spring warmth he found a place to sit on the edge of the retaining wall, from which he could look at the white/gray breakers coming in, wave after wave off of Lake Michigan. His eyes traveled out to the horizon beyond which was the Michigan side of the lake. His mind turned back to the little tourist town of Saugatuck where he and Lynette had spent many an afternoon riding a tandem bicycle around the little town.

He thought of Lynette Ellerton. An empty feeling.

In his farm home in Saline, Homer Stein had made himself a ham sandwich, and had heated up a can of beef barley soup. He put these on the kitchen table, poured himself a cup of tea and sat down to his usual solitary lunch. Some years back he had enlarged the kitchen window, so that Vivian could get a full view of the wheat fields, while they took their meals together. Now, Homer could enjoy the view, though alone. When the wheat was up enough to wave in the wind, he liked to think that he was looking out over a vast lake, or perhaps onto the ocean. The land was flat, and nothing in the distance obstructed the horizon, as if it were out at the far reaches of the sea. He'd never seen the ocean, nor much in the way of lakes, either. His whole life, it seemed, had been spent right here in Saline, and on the Stein place. He smiled to himself. *If it wasn't for my reading, I'd really be bound to this place.* As he pondered "his ocean" of wheat, he thought, *Maybe next fall after harvest I could take a trip out to the coast.*

The phone rang. It was Mae. "Homer, I've got good news."

"What's that?"

"He's coming,"

"Who?"

"Reverend Norris! I just got his letter of acceptance. He'd phoned a few days ago, but we decided that he would send a formal acceptance."

"Oh, that is good news. I really wasn't sure he would accept. But that's very good news, Mae."

"We'll be getting the committee together to plan for his arrival and all."

"Good. Let me know when."

After hanging up the phone, Homer finished his lunch and cleared away the dishes. He would wash them afterwards with his supper dishes. He relished his few minutes in his living room before going back into the fields. This was a special time for him to read. His easy chair near the fireplace was surrounded by his favorite fare, on the side table and in the bookcases on each side of the hearth. *National Geographics,* current and from years back, were there. He "traveled" that way. There were history books, especially of the American West. And interestingly he had quite a number of books on theology and church affairs—current and past. A life of John Calvin. Some of the Barclay *Daily Study Bible* commentaries, Bright's, *A History of Israel,* as well as some Friendship Press books on various mission fields. It was obvious that these were not window dressing. Homer had read or was currently reading the books and periodicals in his living room. On this particular noon hour he was poring over a *Geographic* on New Zealand.

CHAPTER 8

"White Christmas"

His first date with Lynette had been at Christmas time during his high school years. The way Earl felt about it at the time, this relationship seemed to have the potential of something very wonderful in his life, and hers too. Both were members of the youth group at their church, but it wasn't until a caroling party during their senior year that they "discovered" each other.

Theirs was one of the older established suburbs on the west side of Chicago. They belonged to a large and prestigious church. The building itself spoke of the position First Presbyterian held in the community. Located on the main business street, it was not far from Marshall Fields, the upscale department store in the area. Close to other retail stores, it occupied the better part of a block. Its facility accommodated a large, broad "Akron style" sanctuary and included a newer Christian education wing forming an "L" shaped complex wrapped around a landscaped parking lot. The illuminated sign in front of the building listed two ministers and a director of Christian education. The worship services were greatly enhanced with a very good four manual pipe organ and a superb organist known for his position as organist for the venerable Chicago Sunday Evening Club in Orchestra Hall on Michigan Boulevard.

For the most part, members of this suburban congregation were well-to-do. While many had businesses in downtown Chicago, their residences were in a community far enough from the city to be quiet and safe. These features were ones which residents often recited to one another. Most of the homes north of the of the main business street had been built on lots twice the size of lots found in Chicago's residential neighborhoods. The streets were lined with large American Elms and most of the spacious front yards were enhanced by mature trees of varying kinds. Most of the houses along these shady streets were two storied, imparting the accurate impression of long standing wealth. Roughly two-thirds of the church's youth group members lived on such comfortable streets. The palatial homes of these members were often the location for social activities not only of their parents but of the young people as well. The youth group frequently scheduled gettogethers in some of these homes on Saturdays.

The architecture of many buildings in the business district mimicked the style of an English village. The Chicago Northwestern commuter line ran through the business district, and in many ways its tracks separated the fine single family residential streets north of the commuter line from a concentration of apartment buildings south of the tracks within walking distance from the downtown shops. South beyond the apartment buildings, one would find that the houses were smaller and closer together than on the north side of the rail line. Earl's parents rented one of the three bedroom apartments south of the tracks close to downtown. This had always been home to Earl and his sister, Anne.

On a Sunday evening, four days before Christmas, a light snow was coming down upon an already snow-covered landscape. As Earl walked to church in the crisp night air, snowflakes fell gently on him, melting as they touched his face. Already dark, the streets were illuminated by cheerful lantern shaped streetlights against which the snow came down in sparkling silver streaks. In the city park across the street from First Presbyterian, a huge Christmas tree had been brought in and decorated with colored lights. Soft snow had also decorated each bow of the tree, adding to Earl's joyous anticipation as he walked by. When he reached the church door he was met by the youth leader.

"Hi, Earl! Leave your coat on. We'll be going out to carol in a couple of minutes. First, we are gathering in the fellowship hall to get organized."

Earl joined the others already assembled, and found a place next to a couple of his buddies. The group was forming itself into a lopsided circle to await instructions. Earl knew everyone. Yet on this magical night he was struck by one particular person. She stood opposite him. She was Lynette Ellerton. They'd known each other since first grade Sunday school class. Bundled up in a royal blue winter coat, a yellow woolen cap and white furry ear muffs, she was a sight which caught Earl's eye as never before. Earl couldn't keep his eyes off of her. As the youth group waited for latecomers, they sang Christmas songs. The lights in the room gave her brown eyes a captivating sparkle. Her hazel hair beneath her yellow wool hat cascaded around her perfect face. It was during the singing of "White Christmas" that Earl was especially smitten. So much so, that in the years to come Earl would see a dream-like image of Lynette whenever "White Christmas" was sung."

He barely heard the instructions, and so when the group went out into the snow covered street to the waiting cars, he followed his friends. The parking lot was covered with a bright white coating of new snow. An itinerary had been arranged so that the cars drove to a succession of church shut-ins, stopping at each place where everyone poured out of the cars and gathered in front of the door. At the signal from the leader, they would begin the first of two carols they were to sing at each home.

On that destined, night Earl managed to stand next to Lynette "by accident" at the first house at which the group visited. Though riding in different cars it became obvious by the third house that each looked for the other as they walked up to the house. After the final carol-sing Earl took her mittened hand and walked her back to her car. When the group returned to the church for hot chocolate Lynn and Earl sat together in the circle which the group formed for the traditional ending of their meeting. As they always did, they sang a verse of "To the Knights in the Days of Old." For this particular closing song the leader chose the second stanza:

> And we who would serve the King,
> And loyally Him obey,
> In consecrated silence know
> That the challenge still holds today.
> Follow, follow, follow the gleam;
> Standards of worth o'er all the earth;
> Follow, follow, follow the gleam
> Of the light that shall bring the dawn.

Earl had often sung these words, for it was a favorite of the group. But this time the words seemed to stand out—"follow the gleam"—while the meaning seemed to attach to his attraction to Lynette, he knew the meaning was more spiritual. Years later he, as well as Lynn, would each come to experience these words in a life-changing way.

After this favorite hymn was sung the meeting adjourned with the Mizpah benediction spoken in unison: *The Lord watch between me and thee, when we are absent one from another.* The high schoolers once again put on their coats and hats and mittens, this time to disperse to their own homes

Earl turned to Lynn as she was slipping on her royal blue coat. "May I walk you home?" He knew that Lynette's home was within walking distance of the church, one of the large houses north of the church.

She didn't hesitate. "Sure."

On the short walk to her house Earl held her mitten-encased hand. The Ellertons lived only three blocks from the church on tree lined Forest Avenue. Away from the lights of the downtown, the street lights sparkled in the darkness of the winter night, casting illuminated circular patches on the snow. Colored Christmas lights shown on many of the houses. The air was calm as snowflakes gently fell on Lynette's knit hat, and Earl's bare head. They talked of the evening's activities, about some of the others in the group and finally about what was ahead in the remaining days of school before Christmas. When they arrived at Lynn's house they walked up the long curving sidewalk to the house. They stepped up onto her glazed-in porch. Before she left him he took her in his arms and they gave each other a good night kiss. The attraction felt for each other had been mutual and instant. This good night kiss surprised them both.

Later in their lives each would come to realize what a fortunate experience they had been given through their church youth group. And specifically they would each remember this night as very special and magical. The youth group was called *TUXIS*, which was an acronym for the sentence, *Together United In the Service of Christ*. Instead of using the *C* for Christ, the Greek *X* was used as the central letter. *TUXIS* met formally each Sunday evening at the church, but the members of the group had become such good friends that often during the week, especially on Saturdays, the group came together for informal social times in the homes of members. During the summer months these extra gatherings often included picnics in nearby parks or Forest Preserves and occasionally involved a trip down to the lakeshore to attend the outdoor evening concerts of the Grant Park Symphony Orchestra.

Christmastime had been a beginning for them. During the remaining months of their senior year, Earl and Lynn were inseparable as they participated in the *TUXIS* meetings and the group's social events. Other members of the youth group took great pleasure in acknowledging Earl Norris and Lynn Ellerton as a couple who were "going steady." If they hadn't been regular church attenders before, they certainly were now, always sitting together in the balcony. In addition they dated regularly, and of course were together at the Senior Prom and other commencement celebrations.

The joy and excitement of graduation was diminished for Earl because he and Lynn would be separated for the summer, and who could tell what would happen after that when they would be apart from each other in different colleges. A week after commencement, Lynn was scheduled to go up to the family cottage in Michigan for the summer. Earl needed to find a summer job near home so that most of what he earned could be saved for college expenses. Lynn's family resources made it possible for Lynn to spend the summer at the lake without having to work. Her father would be paying her way at college. Unlike Earl, whose family was not in such a bracket.

The night before Lynn was to leave, they went to the movies together and then, after ice cream cones, they went to the local park to sit quietly, savoring their last moments for a while. They found a bench in the trees away from the main walk through the park. Neither spoke after sitting down. Earl put his arm around Lynn and held her close. She lay her head on his shoulder. He responded by putting his face against her hair.

Dreading their impending separation and feeling the warmth of each other's bodies brought them closer to letting down the bars of intimacy than ever before. Each sensed this but said nothing. They leaned in more closely to each other and remained silent, hearing only each other's breathing.

Earl broke the emotion laden silence. "Lynn, what's to become of us?" In the silence which followed, each was aware of how much they wanted each other.

"I don't know." Lynn thought some more about this. "We are going different directions with our lives. We'll only have holidays—not even summers. Daddy would be upset if I didn't spend my entire summers at the beach house."

"And I won't make college if I don't spend my entire summers trying to earn some money."

"If I wanted to get a job here in town, he would be angered and wouldn't hear of it. So, I guess we'll just have to wait and see. Maybe something will work out." Lynn spoke with little conviction.

"Right, but we need to get you home now."

They rose and held each other in a prolonged embrace with a tear-filled kiss. And then they walked home to the Ellerton house. They kissed "good night" on the porch and parted. Earl walked back to his apartment deep in thought.

In late June, after Lynn had been at her family summer home for a couple of weeks, Earl got a phone call from Lynn inviting him up to her family's place at Saugatuck for the July fourth weekend.

"My brother will be back from Purdue, and there'll be some of my cousins visiting. There's always a bunch of friends from nearby beach houses too. We always do this on the Fourth. And this time I'll have you with me, Earl. You'll love it, I know."

By June he had fallen hopelessly in love with Lynn, and whatever she suggested he'd love to do. Of course he agreed.

"Yes, I'll be there—with bells on!"

CHAPTER 9

House on the Beach

She had given him simple directions. "Just go down to Gary and take the road along the lake shore through Benton Harbor and north 'till you get to Saugatuck. Drive down to the dunes and you'll see a sign saying *SHORE CREST—The Ellertons—Gerald and Eleanor.* And you'll be there."

It hadn't been easy for Earl to arrange to have the week end of the Fourth off. His boss had required him to arrange for substitutes who could stand in for him. While his parents had been more or less supportive of his relationship with Lynette, they were painfully aware of the economic gap between their family and the Ellertons. Earl's invitation to the Ellerton's beach house served to rub in that difference, which made them a bit reluctant to have Earl gone for the Fourth of July weekend. In the past this had been a time of holiday fun for Earl's family. They traditionally had a family picnic in the local park, and then a trip to the community fireworks display in the evening. This year would be different for them with Earl at the lake.

Earl's eager excitement over the prospects of the weekend with the Ellertons was dampened as the time for him to leave home for the drive to Saugatuck came nearer. Nothing was said, but Earl felt like a deserter nevertheless as he put his suitcase in his car and said goodbye to his parents and sister. But soon he was fighting traffic on the South Shore Drive. Thoughts of home had dissolved and were replaced with an imagined scene of the beach house and the fun he'd have once he was with Lynn—and her friends and family.

He felt all tingly as he left Benton Harbor and soon was driving through South Haven. Saugutuck was next on the map. He couldn't wait to see her, but he was apprehensive about meeting all those others. Her brother, Jack, he had met once. He'd seemed sort of distant. He knew nothing about her cousins, but he would soon meet them. When Lynn had mentioned the family summer home, he thought of the little rustic cabin his parents had rented a time or two at a lake in Indiana. The sort of cabin in which the living room, dining area, and kitchen are one room with a couple of small bedrooms off to the side. Across the road there had been a wooden walk through the trees down to a public beach. What he was soon to find would be quite a contrast.

By now he was driving along a narrow road parallel to the shoreline along which were a number of mail boxes and lanes leading to lakefront properties. His heart jumped into his shoes when he spotted the mail box with the sign, *SHORE CREST—The Ellertons.* He turned his little pre-war Chevy onto the asphalt lane leading to the shore. The lake was fully visible beyond the knoll he was passing over. There weren't many trees, mostly native grasses. Not far ahead of him were the sandy dunes along the shore line beyond which pounded the successive waves of Lake Michigan with their breakers sending glistening sheets of water onto the wet sand.

He didn't see the house at first, but when the lane veered to the left the Ellerton summer home came into view. It was large. Intimidating. It must have contained seven or eight rooms, he thought. Twelve, he'd later be told. Bright yellow with white trim. Two stories with a wrap around porch facing the shoreline as well with a lane approaching the building. The porch on the far side was glassed in, he would discover later. At first he saw no one around. He pulled his car into a parking area on the side of the house away from the lake, and began to make his way to the house, feeling eager and apprehensive all at the same time.

Tentative—until Lynette came bounding around the side of the house coming toward him. She was wearing a one piece white swimming suit which contrasted stunningly to her now tanned body.

"She threw her arms around Earl. "You're here!"

"Yeah—finally—long trip!"

They kissed.

"Come, le'me show you the house."

She dragged him up the steps onto the porch and into the house. She showed him the entire first floor and as much of the second as she could. The living room was large. It covered most of the lake side of the house just inside the long porch. On one end stood a huge stone fireplace with overstuffed chairs facing it. Over the mantel a painting of an impressive boat was displayed. When Lynn saw Earl staring at it she said,

"Oh, that was daddy's yacht. His pride and joy. He lost it in a storm a few years ago. It was tied to our pier, but the winds were almost gale level and the boat capsized and broke up. It sank."

"Too bad."

"He has another now."

She continued to walk Earl through the room. Couches and side tables seemed to be everywhere. Covering the hard wood floor was a large woven rug with an American Indian pattern in reds and browns. A series of oak beams seeming to support the white ceiling spanned the width of the room. French doors on the long wall of the room opened to a formal dining room furnished with a long polished maple table with twelve chairs. On one wall was a buffet and china closet with silver pieces and fancy china visible through its glass doors. Next to the dining room, the kitchen was furnished with a large island counter with a meat block over which hung a square utensil rack, in addition to the usual appliances and two separate sinks. On the other side of the kitchen, a breakfast room extended onto the glazed-in porch with four separate tables for four. On the opposite end of the living room toward the fireplace, another French door led into a library with all of its walls lined with dark walnut shelves filled with books. Lynette's father's desk occupied the center of the room. A large globe sat on a study table to the right of the desk. This room also had a fireplace. The room was permeated with the rich odor of cigar. Her father's, no doubt.

As Earl climbed the stairway to the second floor, his attention was diverted from the Ellerton summer house to the white bathing suit ahead of him, displaying Lynn's golden tan legs and arms. Earl was very glad to be here, even if a bit apprehensive about meeting the others. He wondered, "Where is everyone?"

"Oh, on our beach. We spend most of our time there. As soon as you change we can go down there."

Lynn showed Earl her room and then brought him down the hall to the guest room he would be occupying.

"Why don't you run down and get your stuff? I'll wait for you."

Earl brought in his things and changed into his swimming trunks, while Lynn puttered in her room. They went down to the beach together and she introduced him to her four cousins, three girls and a guy, all about Lynn's age. They lived in a house a few hundred yards down the beach. Their father was Mr. Ellerton's brother. There was an assortment of neighbor kids whom Lynn introduced as "members of our bunch."

"They live in some of the other houses along the shore line," she informed Earl.

Earl had worried about being on display. But, if anything, he was more or less ignored as the others seemed to let Lynn and Earl to themselves while they took turns water skiing behind Lynn's brother's boat. Otherwise, sun bathing and frequent short dips in the water was the order of the day. The overall impression Earl gained of his new found "friends" was one of continual fun and excitement. Lots of talk and shouting. Someone had a portable radio playing the latest hits. The air was filled not only with the steady drone of Jack's boat, but by the sounds of other motorboats going by, up and down the shore line. Lynn, herself, seemed more animated than he had known her to be as she took him around to meet her cousins and neighboring friends.

It was obvious that the beach at Ellertons' was the place to be for the younger set. Earl had never been immersed in this much youthful summer fun and games. A contrast to the more quiet fishing holidays he and his family had been accustomed to. But this new atmosphere was seductively appealing to Earl. His first thought was that he wanted to become one of this gang, and by the end of the weekend that's more or less how he felt about his relationship to the others.

Dinner was served at 6:30 in the dining room after everyone had come in and changed into casual clothes. Lynn's mother had hired one of the local women in town to do her cooking for the summer as well as to do other household chores, while her main activity seemed to be reading, on the beach during the day—her bronzed wrinkled skin proved it—and on the porch in the evenings.

"Daddy is still in the city. He'll be here for the Fourth." Lynn announced as she and Earl came down the stairs to dinner.

Everyone was in high spirits and ate heartily, seeming to talk constantly.

Toward the end of the meal Jack asked, "Who's for a movie tonight?" There was general agreement and soon after dinner almost everyone drove into Saugatuck for a movie, except Lynn and Earl, and her mother. Her mother disappeared to her chair at the far end of the porch. Lynn took Earl by the hand and they went down onto the beach to walk as they watched the golden orange of the sun sink into the water.

"Well, how do you like it here?"

"Great! I've never been to place like this, or with a bunch of live wires like your cousins and friends."

"Aren't they a 'hoot'?" She added, "It's this way all summer."

"Don't any of them have to work during the summer?"

"No." Her answer fell about as flat as his question.

Over the next three days Earl entered into the acceptable routine: sunbathing, water skiing, volleyball on the beach and whatever else Jack suggested. He seemed to be the activity director. Lynn and Earl had time alone together mostly in the evenings on the porch. They found that they could be perfectly natural in each other's company. No pretense. So different from the way Earl had been forced to feel in the company of her cousins and friends. With Lynn there was no trying to build up his own image. Earl couldn't think of anyone else with whom he could be himself. One evening when he told this to Lynn she impulsively brought her lips to his for a joyous kiss before she replied, "Oh Earl, that's exactly how I feel when I'm with you. With my cousins and friends I'm always a little on edge wanting to make the right impression. With you—who cares!"

They were alone and it was dark. They both were wearing shorts, Earl a tee shirt, Lynn a halter. In the warmth of their embrace they experienced as never before the passion which the entwining of their young bodies pressing against each other induced. Not wanting this feeling to go away, and yet afraid that their restraint would not hold, they remained locked in the silent mystery of desire.

When Earl woke up on the morning of the Fourth he felt a surge of new-found excitement. One more day with Lynn and her family and friends amid the excitement of the holiday festivities. Lynn had explained. "We always do a cook-out on the beach for both meals. Hot dogs at noon and steaks at night. Then Jack does a really big fireworks display on the beach when it gets dark. All the neighbors always come. Daddy is in his glory presiding over the crowd." Then Lynn became pensive. "And Mother—if she's not under the weather—comes out of her shell and visits with the other wives—usually."

Earl went over to the window, brightly lit with the morning sun. He looked down onto the parking area and saw his little Chevy and Jack's convertible. Next to these, a new white Lincoln Continental sedan had arrived since the night before. *Lynn's father's, no doubt,* Earl concluded. While dressing he thought about his new experience at the beach house. The time went by far too quickly for Earl who had gotten into the swing of things. He told himself that he felt pretty much a part of the Ellerton beach crowd. But before returning to the city he would be summoned to an obligatory visit with Lynn's father.

After a final morning on the beach, Earl and Lynn walked over to where Mrs. Ellerton's cook was roasting hot dogs. "We're famished!" Lynn exclaimed.

"Well, this here is the right place, Miss Lynn. You and your friend just take one right now and put on your favorite fixin's."

"Thank you, Josie."

On the afternoon of July fourth, Lynn's father cornered Earl before he had time to change for the beach. "Say, Earl, come into the library. I'd like to talk to you." This was a command, not a suggestion.

When Earl followed him into the library, Mr. Ellerton motioned for him to sit in a chair across the desk from him. Lynn's father was a strikingly good-looking man in his early fifties. Most of the time at the beach house he wore white duck trousers with a neatly tucked in white, polo shirt and a soft yellow cardigan. Now, as he sat in his executive chair behind his desk in the library, Ellerton lit up a cigar and took a draw, blew out a cloud of blue smoke and began what might be termed an interrogation. "Now, Son, what do you plan after graduation?"

"College, sir."

"Good. Have you been accepted somewhere? And what do you plan to major in?"

"Rock River Community College. Liberal Arts."

"Oh? Where's that?"

"Out in Rockford, Sir."

"I see." It was evident that this decision did not meet with the man's approval.

Earl thought he should explain further. 'It's just a two year course. Then I'll probably go somewhere like the University of Illinois."

"Good. Get yourself a good business degree. Companies like mine always need sharp young business majors." As if to himself he said under his breath, "Jack will have a mechanical engineering background. We need that too." He then launched into a long account of his own college experience and his accomplishments in the manufacturing business since college. He finally concluded with what appeared to be the crowning glory of it all. "And now I own Ellerton Manufacturing—precision parts and equipment for major heavy industry in the area. That's how it is that all of you can play on the beach here all day."

"Yes sir, and I have really enjoyed being here. Thank you very much."

"Good."

Earl realized that the implication of the personal account was to encourage him to do the same. Earl would later realize that underneath this conversation was the old man's warning to the effect of: "Anyone who wants to marry my daughter had better do as I have done."

When Earl had a chance to tell Lynn about the fatherly talk in the library, she went a step further to add, "And I think he would take you into the company if you get the right kind of education to where you could do a job in it."

On the evening of the fourth when it became dark enough Jack put on an extensive fireworks display on the beach. The older folks from the other beach houses came over for his display, dipping in to Ellertons' ample supply of beer cans. Earl had never seen a home fireworks display as extensive as Jack's. He had things on the ground and in the air, which went on for an hour and a half. There was frequent applause and lots of "oohs and ahs" from the crowd of twenty or thirty folks of all ages.

Afterwards Earl and Lynn walked on the beach beside the dark lapping water for the last time. Their mood was bittersweet. In the darkness before going up to the house they sat on a log nestled among some tall grasses beneath a dune. They held each other, kissing passionately. Lynn pressed against Earl's chest. They remained in this embrace for a very long time held by a wall of moral restraint, like children pressing their noses to the window of a closed candy store.

As Earl drove back to the city on the fifth after a whirlwind weekend, he thought about what Ellerton had said and about Lynn's apparent agreement. This troubled him. It made him feel swallowed up in the family and the family business. In fact, as he reflected on the weekend, he had felt a bit like that, especially when Jack so readily called the shots and Lynn and all the others had followed along so easily. And yet he'd found this exotic life style exceedingly appealing. He admitted to himself that he could live like this without a backward glance.

He had fallen even more deeply in love with Lynette. But her family? Her brother? Her father? Ellerton Manufacturing? He didn't know. He wondered about her mother. She seemed so mousey, without much personality. She had been cordial to him, but that was all. She hadn't really asked him any questions, like most adults do. He would later discover that she had an alcohol problem which she assumed she was managing to keep secret. Each time he thought of that magnificent beach house, he felt a little threatened—but also intrigued.

However, the closer Earl got to Chicago the more his mind held onto a glossy picture of the house on the beach. What a house, he thought. And to think that it is their second home. And they owned their portion of the beach! Always before, Earl's beach experiences had been at public beaches. The Ellerton house on North Forest Avenue in the "city" was also impressive with probably eight or nine rooms. A solid two story brick house amid tall American Elms which grew in the lush lawn around the house. The house occupied what was apparently three or four lots which comprised a large yard. Quite a contrast to the apartment his family had been renting for the past fifteen years. Coincidently it also was on the same street, but south of the main part of town. If Lynn was right about her father and what she predicted were her father's plans for Earl and Lynn's future, then the life style and the Ellerton beach house he'd experienced over the past three days could be in his own future. He and Lynn had already discussed marriage. If he were to get a business degree, chances are he could go to work for the Ellerton Manufacturing Company, and in time, who knows, as one of the family he could be part owner. After the old man retires, why not Jack Ellerton and Earl Norris as the owners of Ellerton Manufacturing? Like the seductive glitter of gold nuggets in the mind of the miner, Earl felt a strange new sensation a little like he felt each time he and Lynn embraced passionately. Earl had never thought himself capable of attaining the sort of life he now pictured. But thanks to Lynn and her family, this scene had slipped into range. His sights had never been set that high. He assumed he'd have a comfortable life like his parents and drive a Chevy like his dad. But a Lincoln Continental like Gerald Ellerton . . . maybe.

His imagination was going a mile a minute as he entered onto the rain-slick South Shore Drive. This would be the night he decided on a degree in business. He could get his start at Rock River, and then really go for it down in Urbana. After Rock River he and Lynn could get married and go down to the U. of I. together! After two or three years in Champaign-Urbana they would move back to Chicago, he'd go to work in the office at Ellerton's, they'd find a nice starter house in their neighborhood, and soon be raising children. And think of the summers when they would pack up the kids in a new Buick station wagon and drive to the beach.

Earl Norris' imagination was going a mile a minute, and Earl Norris was on the way to glory.

CHAPTER 10

In the Family

College for Earl Norris was a means to an end. And the end was to be the dream which had been conceived at Shore Crest. It became his dream to become a full fledged member of the Ellerton family, and of Ellerton Manufacturing Company. One day he too would have a house on the beach where he and Lynn would take their family each summer. His children would have their own beach crowd. Perhaps one of his boys would take over Jack Ellerton's highly respected role among his peers. The key to unlock this treasured future would be a degree in business and with it his marriage to Ellerton's daughter.

Earl had become convinced that this dream was right for him and that one day it would be realized. Except, there were times when he was home with his family during college breaks when in the silence of his boyhood room in the Norris apartment, that Earl would experience a niggling question. *Is it Ellerton Manufacturing and all that goes with that . . . or is it Lynn, that I really want?* At times like this he would often recall Lynn's response to his dreaming. *She never seems to share my excitement about becoming an Ellerton in every sense of the word. I wonder why she doesn't dream like I do?* He usually concluded with an excuse. *Maybe it's because she's already "an Ellerton."* But when Earl was quite honest with himself he didn't think that was the reason for her reluctance about his dream. But his was a seductively powerful dream. It impelled him through his college courses.

During the summer vacation between his freshman and sophomore year of college, Earl spent as many weekends as he could with Lynn and her family at the beach house. Not only were Lynn and Earl inseparable but he had grown to enjoy her cousins and friends as much as she did. Already he'd been allowed in the family so to speak. He'd come to love the beach house as if it were his own—or Lynn's and his. He often found himself talking with Lynn of the day when they could have such a beach house, perhaps on the same dunes. Often as they walked up and down the beach looking up at each place they passed, he would play a game of "Which house will be ours some day?" Occasionally they drove into town and rented tandem bikes on which to ride around town. He liked to pretend that they were important residents of the larger community of Saugatuck, as were the Ellertons. Earl believed they were on a path which would bring them into full fledged membership in the society in which Lynn's parents enjoyed status, both here in Michigan and at home in Chicago. No longer would Earl have to live in a rented apartment as he and his parents did.

An important step in accomplishing this dream was Earl's college work in the business department. Mr. Ellerton had made that clear. And so Earl applied himself to the task at hand. He was indeed motivated and did very well at college, taking as many business courses as he could fit in. He saw himself on a fast track which pointed to the University of Illinois at Urbana and then on to a successful business career in the family company. While at college he didn't get involved in any social activities. That aspect of his life he left to his summers at the beach house with Lynn and his new crowd.

The summer after his sophomore year, Earl moved up to Michigan and found a job, so that he could stay in the beach house full time. He had found work as a desk clerk in one of the motels in town. Mr. Ellerton had warmed up to Earl after Lynette told her father that Earl was getting his degree in business.

This was especially true after Earl switched to the U. of I. for his third and fourth years. "You make good contacts at a school like that." Mr. Ellerton told Earl. "And you never know when those connections will pay off handsomely." Life was running smoothly for the young couple, who were beginning to make tentative plans for marriage. Their only point of disagreement was the location of their marriage ceremony. Lynn had always assumed it would be in her home church in the suburbs. "It's your church too, Earl. And all our youth group friends will be there."

"I think it would be just right to have it here at Shore Crest." He pondered this and added with a gleam in his eye. "I can see the invitation now! . . . inviting people to *Shore Crest*. Wouldn't that be impressive! And all our beach friends and family here would come. It would be a blast!"

"Oh, Earl, I want it at home." The designation of Shore Crest didn't hold the same aura of wealth and prestige for her as it did for Earl.

They discussed a probable date for their wedding. It would be after Earl's graduation and after he was settled into a position at Ellerton Manufacturing.

"That'll work." Lynn declared. "I will have graduated as well."

"How about the Fourth of July weekend, a year after graduation?"

"I know why you want it then. It's when we will all be here." She gave him a knowing glance.

"Well, I guess that's right," he said with a smirk

"I'll think about it—and talk to father. We could still have it at home on the Fourth."

However something happened to Earl which was destined to change the course of events in his life and in Lynette's as well, effectively settling the question of wedding date and location with a resounding "nowhere." It occurred in July of his final summer at the beach house. In June of that year he had received his bachelor's degree in business from the University of Illinois. He was ready, he thought, for an invitation to join Ellerton Manufacturing. However, Lynn's father had been silent about the matter. This disappointed him, but he rationalized. *He's probably got a lot on his mind regarding the business, and besides, it's summer. Maybe in the fall . . . .*

On July fourth of that summer, a Sunday, the promising young couple became formally engaged. This was the occasion for an important celebration at Shore Crest. Friends from up and down the beach were invited to a barbeque and fireworks to celebrate not only Independence Day but Earl's intended loss of independence, as the cousins had quipped. Lynn and Earl were higher than a kite. It turned out to be a picture perfect day. Cousins and friends all joined in the gala event. The only downer had been the fact that Earl's parents had declined to attend. None of the Ellertons, including Lynn, could understand this. But down deep in Earl's consciousness, he knew the reason, and it made him feel badly for his parents and for himself.

Earl knew how much out of place his mother and father would have felt, had they come to the party. Worse yet . . . he also felt that they would indeed have been out of place. In this regard Earl had to admit to himself that he had been relieved that his family would not be at Shore Crest. But he felt ashamed of feeling relieved. He remembered the Sunday afternoon in his senior year when he had brought Lynn home to his house to meet his parents. Even though the Norris family and the Ellertons were in the same church, there had been no social contact between the two families. Later in his life, Earl would come to admit to himself that there had been a hidden caste system operating within the congregation. He had sensed the awkwardness which he knew his parents must have felt. Now he sensed that feeling in connection to the invitation to the beach house. They'd been very cordial, not at all critical or disapproving of Lynn. But his intuition told him that they, especially his mother, were slightly afraid of Lynette Ellerton. And Earl had picked up on a sadness in his father after telling him about Mr. Ellerton and Ellerton Manufacturing. Afterward

Earl chastised himself. *I wish I hadn't spoken in such glowing terms about Lynn's family and about the Ellerton company.* Later he realized that Lynn had recognized none of this and had only good to say about Earl's parents. She also had not seemed to understand the way in which Main Street in their town made a difference between those who lived south and those who lived north of it. It was the dividing line for more than merely the street numbering system.

Earl's parents sent Lynn and Earl a lovely congratulations card in which they promised to host a simple dinner for them and a few of their friends sometime later to celebrate their engagement. Earl was touched by the card in a way he did not understand. Lynn took the message in stride and said that she looked forward to meeting some of his family friends.

On the morning of the Fourth, Mr. Ellerton and Jack, as well as Lynn and Earl attended worship in Saugatuck, in a church which they called their own during the summers. After the service Earl asked a question of Lynn which she did not want to face.

"I missed your mother. How come she didn't join us?"

Lynn was evasive. "I guess she is under the weather this morning. She doesn't always attend."

"I see." Earl, however, did not understand. "I hope she'll be all right for the party later."

"I hope so too."

Earl felt that this had been an especially significant way to start the day of their formal engagement. Unlike so many students, Earl's college years seemed to be having the effect of making him more religious. Later he would believe that *Someone* had been trying to tell him something!

At the university he'd gotten to know the campus ministers at McKinley Memorial Church in Champaign and had found them stimulating in the way they had talked about the faith. Unfortunately Lynn had not found such a deepening experience in her college experience at Lawrence University in Wisconsin. Perhaps this accounted for their differing responses to a vesper service they would attended by accident in August of that year, a month after their engagement party.

After church, the barbeque at Shore Crest began. Friends and neighbors arrived. Cousins and aunts and uncles as well. A canvas canopy had been erected by the caterers, who had been hired to provide the outdoor banquet. Beer and wine were in abundance. Earl noticed that Lynn's mother seemed to be consuming more than most of the other women. At the close of the meal champagne was passed around and Mr. Ellerton rose to make the formal announcement.

"It gives me great pleasure to announce to you this afternoon Ellerton Manufacturing's latest acquisition." He paused for effect. "Yes, we are acquiring a bright and promising young man, Earl Norris." He stopped at this point and the group didn't exactly know how to respond. Most gave a joyous laugh, knowing that this was not supposed to be an Ellerton Co. meeting, but an engagement party. It certainly took Earl by surprise . . . a happy one, though. Ellerton then completed his announcement. I have given my permission to this young man here . . ." He turned to Earl. ". . . to marry into the Ellerton family . . . that is to marry our daughter, Lynette!"

Everyone applauded. Earl took Lynn's hand. Someone in the audience shouted, "Kiss the bride to be!" Earl and Lynn kissed, but were somewhat embarrassed. Something about the announcement troubled Earl, but he couldn't quite put his finger on it.

"Now, let the party go on!" Ellerton thus ended the formalities. In no time at all most of the younger set had changed into their swimming suits and headed for the beach. The older folks sat around in various clusters on the broad lawn between the house and the beach. Ellerton excused himself. "I have a bit of phoning to do—for the company." Mrs. Ellerton disappeared.

Strangely, Earl and Lynn found themselves alone after the celebration had ended. Alone and wistfully saddened by the brash manner of Lynn's father.

"Daddy could have said a bit more about you, Earl."

"And about us." Earl added. "But he didn't, and that's OK. Instead he talked about my coming into the company!"

The matter was dropped and only later would Lynn have cause to think about this again.

The two took a walk along the beach, hand in hand as they did regularly each evening. Now as an engaged couple they found themselves often talking about their future together and as future residents of Shore Crest. Earl spoke often about his anticipation of working for Lynn's father.

"I'm glad that you want to work for Daddy. I can just see it now. You and Daddy coming home after work to Forest Avenue. He turning off at his house, and your going a block or so further and turning in to our house. I'd kiss you as you come in, and you'd take off your tie and sit down on the floor to play with the children . . . and I would say *Forget about the company now, dear.*"

"Yes, and then in the summer you and I would sit on porch of our beach house watching our kids swimming with their friends."

Lynn now joined the reverie. "What shall we call our beach house?"

Earl thought for a few moments. "Why not *Earlynn House?*"

"I like that!"

On one particular evening a few days later, while Lynn and Earl were walking hand in hand along the beach they heard singing. They stopped to listen before discovering its source.

"That sounds like church! Out here on the beach?" Earl remarked.

"It does. I wonder. I've never heard that before."

About a mile north of the Ellerton Beach House there was a church conference grounds located on the lake. Frequently in the evenings, conferences held on the grounds conducted vesper services on the beach. Lynn had not remembered coming this far along the shore line.

Lynn and Earl kept walking during the gradually darkening dusk as the sun sank into the evening calm of the lake. They came to the crest of a dune and looked down on one of the conference vesper services. Earl and Lynn moved closer to the group assembled on the beach in order to catch the words of the hymn. The waning sun casting its golden beams across the water added a mystical spell, making the words of the song touch Earl deeply:

> Day is dying in the west;
> Heaven is touching earth with rest:
> Wait and worship while the night
> Sets her evening lamps alight
> Through all the sky.
> Holy, holy, holy Lord God of Hosts!
> Heaven and eath are full of Thee!
> Heaven and earth are praising Thee,
> O Lord Most High!

As unobtrusively as they could Earl took Lynn's hand and they dropped down from their position above the little congregation and walked to the back of the group. They identified it as a group of young people seated on the sand. In the fading light of dusk they faced a leader at whose back was the glistening water of Lake Michigan. Above his head they could see the first stars of the evening sky. Earl led Lynn to a place on the sand behind the group where they sat down unobserved. They hummed along as the group sang another verse.

> Lord of life, beneath the dome
> Of the universe, Thy home,
> Gather us who seek Thy face
> To the fold of Thy embrace,
> For thou art nigh.
> Holy, holy, holy Lord God of Hosts!
> Heaven and earth are full of Thee!
> Heaven and earth are praising Thee,
> O Lord Most High! Amen

The leader was a young man not much older than Earl. Dressed in light seersucker slacks and a white cotton shirt he spoke with a pleasant and sparkling voice. At the conclusion of the song he gave a brief prayer and then began a short meditation. The earnest intensity of the speaker and the quiet attentiveness of the young people made Earl listen with expectation. Years later Earl would not be able to remember what the leader had said, but he would always know the feeling which that brief sermon had brought to Earl on a very special night in August. Something about the stars in the darkening sky and the fading sunlight reflecting on the blackening water stirred Earl's consciousness to the point that he felt he was hearing the "voice" of God speaking within his inner being. Not in words so much as in an overwhelming impression. But if he could put words to the message he was receiving it would be ***There is more, Earl.*** As the young worship leader spoke Earl felt impelled to look as far across the water as his eyes could take him. What Earl was experiencing in that moment was like a trance. His attention became fixed entirely in a westbound direction. He felt as though he was trying to keep up with the sun as it left the dome of his immediate sky and moved inexorably westward. It was as if the sun was the source of his life and in order to live he must travel westward with the sun. He "saw" across the lake the city of Chicago in the distance, and beyond it the western suburbs, the farm lands of the Midwest. In this trance-like state, Earl "saw" still further west. He envisioned the mountains which he had never seen in real life. And behind the mountains he "saw" that the sun was still shining at that very moment on regions of the country he'd never seen. He felt as if there were some specific place illumined by the sun beckoning him to visit. This exotic feeling reminded him of having felt something similar in the high school class when the teacher had used the phrase *go west, young man.* He blinked his eyes, and looked around him. He saw Lynn sitting next to him and the group of worshipers getting up at the close of their service. At the time he had no knowledge of what this might mean. Only gradually would Earl begin to understand the pull which "a voice" in the western sky would have upon his soul.

Earl was unusually quiet as the two walked back to the beach house. Lynn seemed to be lost in her own thoughts as well. When they reached the house they embraced and gave each other a warm good night kiss after which each went to bed.

The next day Earl went to work at the motel in town. Throughout the day whenever he was not engaged in the usual activity of the motel, his mind would drift back to the lake shore and to the young man who had led the vespers. He had never felt such an intense pull upon him. On the way back without anyone knowing, he stopped by the conference center to inquire about the vesper leader. The young woman in the office gave him the young man's name. "His name is Clemens McNulty. We call him Clem."

"Is he available, do you know? I'd like to meet him."

"I think he's on the grounds today. Here's a map of the grounds. Clem is this cabin right here—just down that walkway." She handed him the map.

Earl found him in his cabin and introduced himself. The two arranged to meet for lunch at the conference grounds the next day. It would be the first of a number of occasions when Earl would visit with Clem to talk about Clem's experience in seminary and his anticipation of entering the pastoral ministry of the church.

The more the two young men talked the more sure Earl became of his desire to pursue a course which would lead him into the ministry of the church. McNulty put Earl in contact with his seminary in Chicago. By the end of August he had applied for admission and was accepted, Much to the surprise of his parents and to the bewilderment of Lynn, Earl began his three year seminary studies in September.

In succeeding years Earl would often look back upon these conversations with Clem and say to himself: *That's when it all started, when my life began to be re-directed . . . when I was given a new map, another dream.*

CHAPTER 11

Godspeed

Almost four years after Earl's first conversation with the vesper leader at Saugatuck, a procession of young men in caps and gowns walked solemnly down the aisle of Chicago's Fourth Presbyterian Church on Michigan Boulevard in preparation for a service of worship and commencement. For most of the men this night marked the end of a three year course in theological education, and on this night the degree of Bachelor of Divinity would be conferred upon each one.

The candidates for the B.D. degree sat in the first five pews in the stately gothic cathedral-like church. Tall stone arches flanked the pews on both walls. The seminary president and dean as well as the preacher of the evening sat behind the center pulpit on the high front platform. Above and behind them sat the robed choir. After the sermon the large pipe organ led the congregation in the singing of the hymn, "God of the Prophets."

The words of the final stanza hung in Earl's ears as he sat among those waiting the commencement ceremony.

> Make them apostles! Heralds of Thy cross;
> Forth may they go to tell all realms Thy grace;
> Inspired by Thee, may they count all but loss,
> And stand at last with joy before Thy Face."

The president and the dean stood. The dean began to read the names of the candidates. One by one they walked up the steps to the level of the pulpit and received their diplomas and were given a handshake by the president. Soon the names beginning with "N" were read and then Earl heard his name.

"Earl Whitman Norris."

When his name was read by the dean, Earl left his pew and walked across the front of the sanctuary to the point where he was handed his diploma and given a hearty hand shake by the president of the seminary.

After the commencement exercises, there were many *goodbyes* to his friends and teachers. His parents and his sister, Anne, had joined him. His mother and sister both gave him warm hugs. His father shook his hand heartily.

"Your mother and I are so very proud of you, Earl. As you know, your decision has pleased us deeply."

"Thank you, Dad. I hope I can live up to your expectations."

Anne took her brother's hand and looked at him and said, "You've done the right thing, Earl. That other life wouldn't have been right for you."

Just then a man came up to Earl. Dressed in a dark suit with a white shirt and a tie, Earl had not expected to see Clem McNulty and almost didn't recognize him. "Clem. I'm so glad you came to my commencement. Thank you for coming. I owe much of this occasion to you!" McNulty demurred and offered his congratulations.

"What are you doing these days, Clem?"

"I'm on the staff up at camp. Year around. Where are you headed?"

"I have a call to a small church in Montana."

"Wow. That sounds like the mission field!"

"Well, I guess it is—sort of."

"Anyhow, I wish you the best, Earl."

With that the two separated and Earl turned to his family.

Later on that evening, Earl and his mother and father and sister were sitting at a table in a favorite restaurant on Chicago Avenue near the old Water Tower. This would be Earl's family's special time to celebrate this significant milestone in his life and preparation for Christian ministry. Also this evening would be a poignant time to bid him farewell and Godspeed. He would be taking off for the west in the morning. A celebration he would cherish for many years to come.

Before their dinners were served, a discussion about Earl's forthcoming assignment began on a note of reluctance.

"You're going so far away." There was anguish in his mother's voice.

Earl didn't know quite how to respond. His father rescued him.

"Now, Esther. Earl's a big boy. Remember, we promised we wouldn't say anything about losing our child!"

"He's not a child, Dad," Anne insisted.

"Yes, Annie. You are right."

His mother responded to her husband's admonition. "I know, but it seems so far. Montana—none of us have ever been there."

"I have, Mother, and once you're there it doesn't seem so far." Earl was going to say "or different" but thought better of it since that really wasn't true. *It was different—very different*, he thought to himself.

His sister, Anne, wanted the facts. She was a young mathematician as everyone liked to remind themselves about her. "Just how far is it, Earl?"

"Twenty-two hours by train—three days by car."

This didn't relieve his mother one bit. "What'd I say? A long way! And you'll be all alone."

"Oh, Mother, once I get there I won't be alone. All the folks are so friendly."

Then she said a surprising thing. "I sometimes wish you still had Lynette." Earl's mother had been less tentative about Lynette Ellerton than her husband had been. He had been threatened by the social difference between the two families. Earl's mother had seen the love the two young people had held for each other.

There was silence around the table. This had not been a subject for discussion in the family since the two had broken their engagement after Earl's first year in seminary.

"Mom, you're forgetting. Going to a little po-dunk place like Saline was the very reason Lynn couldn't stick with me any longer. She could barely leave Chicago and the beach house to go to school in Wisconsin. What would she have done in Montana. For her it certainly would have been far away—too far—off her map."

"Beyond which 'there be dragons,'" Ann added.

And then Earl shared the most telling reflection on the break-up. "And besides, her father would never have tolerated it."

Earl's father gave a knowing nod.

His mother tried to conclude the matter. "Anyway, I'm sorry that it has to be so far from home."

This time it was Anne who bailed Earl out of an awkward conversation. "I know I shouldn't say it. But I think Lynn was not the girl for Earl. I thought that even before he decided on the ministry."

Earl's dad had always been hesitant about Lynette. "Why do you say that, Anne?"

"If you'd seen that beach house and been with the beach crowd there, you'd know what I mean."

This struck Earl between the eyes. "Is that what you always thought, Anne?"

"Yes, I know it hurts you, but it's true."

Earl thought for a while and then admitted. "You may be right. But it's old news now. I'm off to conquer new worlds—right?"

"Where there *be dragons*?" Anne asked with a grin.

"No way. They're all Americans. He had a flickering light in his eye. "I'm WESTBOUND!" He paused to hear the words reverberate in his mind. "Doesn't that have a ring to it?:"

"Yes, I suppose it does." Earl's father commented, and then revealed that he had been thinking about what Anne had said. "I sensed what you mean, Anne, but when it was just Lynette, it seemed to me that all that class difference could be handled."

"I'm not so sure." Anne wasn't convinced, perhaps because she herself had always felt intimidated by Lynn's crowd.

At this point the waiter brought their meal

"Come on—let's lighten up and celebrate!" Earl's dad proposed a toast. "Raise your glasses." (water glasses in the Norris family) "To the soon-to-be Reverend Earl Norris, pastor of the Community Church of Saline, Montana. May your sermons 'wow' the congregation, your friendly wit and humor make them all glad you are their new pastor and may you find a delightful young woman out there to become your *Mrs. Norris!*"

They all gasped.

He then took on a more serious tone. "And may God grant you an ever deepening sense of His presence enabling you to minister effectively for Him!" This sounded more like a prayer than a toast. If not audibly, at least in thought everyone in the family uttered an "Amen."

The four settled down to enjoy a favorite menu of broiled Atlantic salmon. After the meal the waiter cleared the table and then returned with a decorated cake which he set before Earl. Amid a floral motif the words: *Congratulations, Earl and Godspeed* had been placed on the top. This marked the end of the celebration and the final day of Earl's life in the Midwest. The next morning he would be westbound on US 12—westbound to the rest of his life!

Bob Norris stayed home the next morning long enough to see his son off. Esther and Anne also were home for the occasion. Earl had packed up his Chevy the night before, and now was ready. His mother had fixed him sandwiches and fruit for his lunch. "Here, Earl, you can stop at a city park along the way and have this for lunch."

"Thank you, Mom."

He hugged his mother. She was teary-eyed.

There was excitement in Anne's face as she hugged her brother.

His father shook his hand, patted him on his back, and when Earl was in the car, Robert Norris bid his westbound son, "Godspeed." And off he drove.

The night before, on Sunday evening at Shore Crest in early June, Lynn's parents had been invited to a party next door. Her brother was in town with his friends. The house was empty, and depressing. Lynette went up to her room, slipped off her white bathing suit and put on a pair of shorts, a plain white blouse and grabbed a pull over sweater in case it got cool during her walk. Lynn knew where she wanted to go. She went down to the beach and began a lonely walk up toward the conference grounds. She located the spot and sat down. This had been where they had been seated during that fateful vesper service nearly four years before, the service which had touched Earl so deeply. This is where they had first heard the song, "Day Is Dying in the West." She looked at the place on the sand where the young leader had stood. The young ministerial student who had so captured Earl's imagination that it caused Earl to decide on the ministry and to go to seminary. Here she was on the very spot. At first she had resented deeply the influence that ministerial student had exerted upon Earl. Resentment bordering on jealousy. She used to say to herself, *"He stole my Earl."* She had returned for a private celebration of sorts. But strangely, she no longer held it against the young man who had conducted that fateful service. Jealousy had turned to envy. This surprised her. She had become envious of both this young man and of Earl. *They've got a mission in life. They know where they're going.* She thought about her life. Working at Ellerton Manufacturing had become drudgery. *It's getting me nowhere.*

Earlier in the afternoon she had been aware of the commencement going on in the city and now she knew that he would be with his family at their favorite restaurant. She also knew that the next the morning he would be headed west—alone. Judy Waymann, a friend of Lynn's, was also acquainted with Anne Norris. She had been keeping Lynette posted on Earl ever since the break up. Such knowledge had been bittersweet. And now she most likely would no longer hear much, for Earl was sailing off her map—westbound.

She had no way of knowing what Montana was like, much less Saline. But she found herself wondering now. Would it be exciting? How will he do as a minister there? And then she surprised herself by wondering, *How would I like it?* Surprised because the prospect of Saline or someplace like it, and of being a pastor's wife had been the reason—she thought—for breaking off the engagement. The strangest thing was that she felt this wistful envy. At a time like this when she was alone and feeling introspective, she had to admit that *it was really Daddy who didn't want Earl's chosen life for me.* Her father was a church member, but when it came to ministers and their wives, that was for somebody else. People who wouldn't be very good at business. No, he and his family had bigger things to do.

As a member of the family, it had been expected of Lynn that after her college graduation she would go to work for Ellerton Manufacturing. From time to time during her college years she had entertained other ideas. But in the end, following college, on the day after Labor Day Lynn went to work for her father—a decision of his with which she had been satisfied—more or less—at first.

The golden sun was turning to orange sending deep yellow ribbons of glimmering reflection across the water skittering up to the very shore before her eyes. She fixed her eyes upon the western sky as it was becoming more and more streaked with pinks and reds. While she looked, the colors were becoming less vivid and growing darker until the life giving ball of fire disappeared into the lake beyond the horizon. Lynn had long been fascinated with thoughts of the way the sun progressed—always westward illuminating one continent after another as it made its rounds only to return again in the morning. Oh, she knew it was the movement of the earth, bur she like to think of the sun making the rounds.

With the setting of the sun a cool breeze stirred, prompting Lynn to get up and begin walking up to the house. As she made her way along the beach to the Ellerton property, she said to herself *the next time I see the sun it will be shining on him as he loads his car and takes off westbound.* She thought about her own life as it would be in the morning. *Another day on the beach with the gang. I'm already tired of them and its only a week of my vacation. And worst of all Daddy wants me to marry one of them. Which one? They're all the same. Full of fun and games now, but soon they'll be all business, working to make the bucks—like Daddy. With no time for their wives.* Then her thought took a further plunge. *I don't want to wind up like Mother.*

She remembered that after their fateful walk to the conference Vespers they had gone back to their youth group and encouraged them to sing "Day Is Dying in the West" often in their meetings. She had come to know the words by heart. Now alone on the beach after the slowly setting sun had disappeared in the west, Lynn quietly sang the third verse to herself.

> When forever from our sight
> Pass the stars, the day, the night,
> Lord of angels, on our eyes
> Let eternal morning rise,
> And shadows end.

She took one last look toward the darkened horizon. Tears came to her eyes as she said out loud over the lapping of the water on the wet sand of the beach—*Godspeed!*

CHAPTER 12

The Committee

In matters concerning the Community Church of Saline six family names are crucial to any progress. No one ever said it, but anyone who had been a member for any length of time knew it to be true. When it game time to elect a Pastor Nominating Committee the hidden wisdom of the voting members had dictated the make-up of the committee. It was as if the roof of the church was supported by six pillars, each with an important name: Benson, Gelenik, Stark, Baxter, Moss and Stein. In the past—at some cost—the congregation had learned that if you wanted to get anything done you needed to have representatives of these six families involved. None of those so named would ever have admitted it, but each enjoyed the responsibility thus silently conferred. Over the years, pastors who came to serve the Saline church needed to learn this at their peril. If not, their time in Saline would be limited.

The unanimous approval which Earl Norris had received from the Pastor Nominating committee was a very good sign. A year or so earlier the congregation had seen to it that the six names appeared among the members on the committee to elect a pastor. Thus when members of the congregation became convinced that the committee vote had been unanimous—with no silent hold-outs—then they felt confident in voting Earl Norris to be their new pastor—the two negative votes not withstanding since neither was one of the six pillar families. Presbytery's approval was assured, and Earl Norris' acceptance was given.

Now on a bright and sunny June afternoon the committee was gathering to prepare for Earl Norris' welcome. He would be on hand the following Sunday. Mae Benson, the committee chairwoman, had regularly hosted the committee meetings, and this final meeting would be a celebration of sorts.

The Bensons were old timers in the community. Dale's father had homesteaded the place where Dale and Mae farmed. It was a bone of contention in their family that Dale's father still owned the farm even though he had long since retired and moved to Miles City. Mae had been a Stein. Her father and Homer Stein's father had been brothers, making Mae and Homer cousins. Homer was a widower. His wife had died young, at age forty-five. Homer had lived alone for the past fifteen years. Gertrude Gelenik and her husband, Karl were considered newcomers. They had bought their place thirty years ago. It had taken a while for the Geleniks to "fit in." The fact that they had moved to Saline from a similar area in North Dakota had helped to remove the "outsider" stigma. However, the fact that the place they'd bought had long been a rented farm tended to downgrade its new occupants at first. Baxter was a descendant of one of the earliest families in the area. Sue Stark's first husband had been raised in the area on the Hubbard place. But he was killed in a farm accident a few years back. Sue had remarried Buck Stark from Miles City. Jane Moss had also come from Miles City to Saline to teach school. She had retired early but remained in the community, living in a small house in town. Her father, Norbert Moss, had been one of the founders of Saline.

Of course, it would be important for a new pastor to become acquainted with these items of family histories. It would fall to Homer to help Earl in this regard. Homer was a sort of unofficial historian not only for the church but for the community of Saline. He reveled in the knowledge that his family roots "go way back" as he often said. "Almost before the fences."

This group, and to a great extent, the entire congregation, had learned how to relate to each other in ways that honored past history, and took into account the idiosyncrasies of each person. They knew how to get along with each other, an essential facility in a small community. This dynamic had frequently been hard to understand and learn by new young ministers coming from city backgrounds. Earl Norris would be the next to try.

By common unspoken consent, Homer Stein was a necessary arbiter of church affairs. When a controversy arose, it would be Homer who would mediate. It was commonly held that there wasn't a hateful bone in his body. Over the years, pastors of the Community Church who failed to allow Homer Stein's wisdom to influence them did so at their peril. Not so much that Homer would be offended, but often times his wisdom was crucial to moving ahead. Fortunately Earl Norris would be one to take heed of what Homer had to say. Not only would Earl find Homer's wisdom helpful, but his friendship very supportive to him. Perhaps at first this was because both men, though widely different in age, were single. Earl's marital status, however, would not always be helpful to him.

The remaining job for the committee was to plan the welcoming potluck for the following Sunday when the new minister would have his first service. Custom pretty well dictated who would do what at such an occasion, and so there wasn't a lot to plan. If the truth be known, the underlying reason for the meeting was to get together. They had always enjoyed their meetings. This was no doubt in Mae Benson's mind when she had invited the committee to her home. After the plans were made, Gertrude Gelenik added one more idea for which she volunteered. "I'd be glad to take care of the place cards and of putting them around the tables."

There was a look of question on the faces of other committee members. Sue Stark responded, "Gert, we don't usually have name cards. Everybody just sits where they want to."

Others seemed to feel the same way. But Homer saw the point. "Well, this is a special time. Rev. Norris won't know people. It might not be a bad idea."

Gertrude agreed, of course. "Yes, he'll need to be helped to know people's names."

"Instead—why not have name cards for people to wear?" Wyoma suggested.

"Well, that too . . ." Gertrude did not want to let her idea drop. Her hidden agenda would be discovered on Sunday when she placed her daughter's card across from Earl Norris. Another little nudge was putting Homer next to Jane Moss.

Soon it became apparent that things were pretty well planned for Sunday. Everyone left the committee meeting with their assignments for Sunday and offered their thanks to Mae for the "delicious lunch."

Meanwhile the trustees had been over to the parsonage—or *manse* as it was calld—to make sure it was ready for the new minister. Since he was single, the nervousness attached to this job was cut considerably. Homer Stein was a trustee and had volunteered to bring the new preacher to the manse the morning after his arrival. Rev. Norris would be staying at Benson's the first night—Friday.

This preparatory work happened with some frequency in Saline since ministers tended not to stay very long. Three years, maybe, rarely as many as five. Church members were aware of this as they anticipated Sunday's welcoming. Some thought that because he was a bachelor, he might not last long. But they would give him their best welcome, nevertheless. What they did not know was that Earl Norris would be their pastor for some years to come.

In many ways Sunday would be the beginning of a possible success story! There would be many of the normal ups and downs, but the overall trend would be up. Hank Hurlbutt, one of the dissenting voices, had it partly right when he felt that hiring a bachelor would present a problem. Not because of inappropriate action on Rev. Norris' part but because of congregational disagreement over whom their pastor should marry. Of course, Ella Gelenik had been put forward as an eligible candidate from the start. Her mother had seen to that suggestion and now served as Ella's campaign manager. But at least one other contestant would emerge, and therein would lie the problem. Otherwise it looked as though things would work out beautifully between Earl and his congregation. That is, if the two nay sayers would forget the reasons for voting "no."

CHAPTER 13

Blue Skies

Earl drove into Coon Rapids, Minnesota, where he found a motel along the highway. Still energized by the anticipation he had been feeling, he was nevertheless ready to stop for the night at the end of his first day of driving, westbound on US 10. Earlier in the day the heavily overcast skies lying low above the Chicago area had turned into pelting rain as he entered the rich farm lands of Wisconsin. After crossing the Mississippi at St. Paul, the rain had continued, but with less intensity. By the time he reached Coon Rapids for his first overnight the rain had abated, though the partially overcast sky ushered in an early dusk. The land of 10,000 lakes had been getting replenishment for its lakes from life-giving rain all day long. Coming from Chicago, Earl had taken the rain from granted and as an unwelcome intrusion. That's not the way the people in Saline feel about rain. For them it is critically needed and rare.

Now at the end of day he was ready to relax. Fortunately he could walk from the motel to a small café, also on US 10, where he ordered a chicken fried steak, which he finished off with gusto—and with apple pie. Good to have his right leg free of eight hours of pressing the resistant accelerator.

When Earl returned to his motel room he stripped for bed, crawled under the covers, turned on the bedside lamp and took out some intriguing reading material which he had been given. The presbytery office in Montana had sent him a packet of materials in preparation for his coming to Saline. In the packet he had found a paper written by his new friend, Homer Stein. He had skimmed it quickly while still in Chicago, but now he wanted to read it carefully. He could see that it pertained very specifically to the new life and ministry he was about to take up.

WHERE THE SKIES ARE BLUER AND THE PEOPLE ARE FEWER
An Introduction to Ministry in Montana by Homer Stein

Ministry in Montana territory for Presbyterians began in the 1880's under the Board of Foreign Missions, "to convert the heathen natives."

Foreign missions! Wow—that's where I'm going! he thought to himself, and then continued.

A little later, under the Board of Home Missions, the focus of mission was upon American frontiersmen. The Board folk feared that "professing Christians could not be trusted to keep their faith as they moved into the west!"

To get at our ministry in Montana it is necessary to look at the way our history, geography, climate, and sociology have interacted to make us what we are. It is helpful to describe the history of Montana as a series of successive frontiers, each of which has left its marks upon present day life in this area.

First the fur trapping and trading frontier. In the early 1800's these hearty mountain men came up the Missouri River to trap the beaver and to sell the pelts for the stylish beaver hats so prized in the East. But when the styles changed and the beaver was no longer a prize, the trappers floated back down the Missouri to return to civilization.

In the summer of 1862 the first sizeable discovery of gold in Grasshopper Creek in the Beaverhead Valley of Montana touched off the *second frontier*—hard rock mining. However, when the price of gold and silver dropped or the mines petered out, the miners left. Somewhat later, copper was being taken from the "richest hill on earth" at Butte to be refined in Anaconda. This lasted until it was determined that copper could be produced more cheaply elsewhere in the U.S. and the world. The mines and the smelters closed and workers were forced to leave what is still called "The Treasure State."

The *third frontier* was the open range livestock frontier, the era of the cowboy, and the colorful days of roundups and cattle drives and *the fourth* was homesteading which caused the end of the open range. While ranching and farming have continued, the number of farms and ranches has decreased as agricultural operations have become larger, with new machinery making for fewer farm and ranch laborers. As a result, population in farming areas has decreased since the opening of these two frontiers.

In the 1900s the *fifth frontier* broke open—the Energy Frontier with its coal and oil bringing people up from other energy producing areas of the nation. But the energy surge ended, reducing the number of workers in energy-related jobs.

The *sixth frontier* was timber. Wood products for in-state activities like mining, railroading and construction and for exportation to world markets. Due to environmental considerations and changes in the market, many mills are now shut down while raw timber is being shipped out of state for milling elsewhere.

Tourism and recreation are the *seventh frontier*. By its very nature tourism brings people into the state on a very temporary basis, whose participation in the life of Montana is minimal.

Earl's eyes had begun to droop. This was as much of Homer's paper as he could read for now. He'd get to the rest of it the next night. His total trip of about eleven hundred miles would take two more days of driving.

The next morning he returned to the highway café for a country style breakfast of bacon and eggs. He imagined that both had come from local farms. They were better tasting than any he had ever eaten.

On the road again, he sped west toward his lunch stop at Wadena. The sky had been partly cloudy all morning, but at noon there remained only a few clouds. After a hamburger Earl was back on the highway heading toward Fargo, and then on to Bismarck, North Dakota, before dark. He crossed the Missouri River on the west edge of Bismarck and entered Mandan, where he checked into a motel for his second night. And another chance to read more of Homer's paper in his motel room before sleep would overcome him.

He resumed reading the portion of the paper following its description of the frontiers which made up the history of the settlement of Montana.

The legacy of the temporary nature of these frontiers is symbolized by some of the typical catch phrases of the frontier: *Here today, gone tomorrow. Boom and Bust. Get rich quick and return to civilization.*

Earl stopped reading to ponder this remark. He had felt the the westbound urge to take a church on the coast some day. He had to admit that he viewed his call to Saline as temporary—for the time being—until he would have the opportunity to move further west. But now, he felt a guilt pang for feeling this way. After reading Homer's thoughts on the subject, he realized that it was unfair to Saline to hold to the idea of wanting to go further west eventually. His call was to Saline—PERIOD. Earl returned to his reading.

Of all the frontiers which formed our history, the only one which seems to have had some measure of lasting stability is agriculture. However, as technology has expanded and farms have increased in size, fewer people are required to farm these larger tracts, causing a significant number of farm families to leave the land. Periodic droughts have also forced many to leave the state. As a result hundreds of small farming towns throughout the state have dried up because of the exodus of their populations. And mid-sized towns have stagnated as major purchases of goods as well as the marketing of produce has moved to distant cities.

But yet, it is agriculture which has held up. It is agriculture more than any other phase of our development which has brought the church into Montana. Many Presbyterian Churches across the state were organized in the early part of this century when agriculture was on the rise.

Ministry in Montana necessarily means involvement in some very special problems related to the conditions of climate and geography on the Great Plains. The most significant and influential climatic factor is low moisture, and along with sparse rainfall, hot summers. We are in a place where the skies are bluer!

However! This area has some of the most beautiful scenery in the world: majestic mountains, verdant river valleys, rolling plains, magnificent sunrises and gorgeous sunsets, bright sunshine and wonderfully blue skies! The air is clear and the streams remain unpolluted. It is a joy to live where the skies are bluer!

But the weather will always be unpredictable. In many ways this is a hostile land, once called, not inaccurately, "the great American desert," and considered in an earlier time to be unfit for human habitation by the earliest European visitors to the area.

The climate, together with the resulting soil and growth cycle, has produced the conditions of the particular agriculture and sociology of this area. *Because* the skies are bluer, the people are fewer! Because the land cannot support the rich and more intensive agriculture found in the more humid areas of the country, a low density of population is inevitable here. Sparse population with its resulting isolation is a most significant underlying factor of our agricultural life here.

Earl was about ready to call it quits for the night when he came to the declaration in the paper that the sparsity of population on the plains is caused by the weather. Low rainfall results in low population! And so that's where Homer got the title for his paper: *Where the Skies are Bluer and the People are Fewer.*

Time to let that sink in as he sank into a second night's sleep on the road. *Tomorrow I'll be in Saline—at home in Saline,* he thought as he drifted off to sleep.

CHAPTER 14

Under Gray Skies

She'd already put on her rain coat and was lifting her umbrella off the hook when the phone rang one more time.

"Ellerton Manufacturing. Lynn speaking . . . . No, he's not in the office . . . . not until next Tuesday. May I take a message for Mr. Ellerton? . . . Thank you for calling."

Lynn hung up and quickly shut off the office lights and made for the door. She stepped into the hall, locked the door, and as she turned toward the elevator she heard the phone again. *Not another call. It's after five. They can call Monday.* All day long she had taken calls for her father, who was out of town on business. As she entered the elevator which would take her down to the street she thought about her day. It seemed like she had barely accomplished anything else, besides covering for her father. *Oh well, another week is over. I'm glad.*

When she left the building to begin her walk to the elevated train station, a sharp wet wind almost pushed her over. She opened her umbrella, wrapped her coat around her and walked as fast as she could to the El station a block from the Ellerton Building. The sizzling of tires on the wet pavement of a street full of cars filled her ears. All had their lights on reflecting against the shiny street. An already gray day was even darker now that it had begun to rain.

Lynn brushed past a swarm of pedestrians as she hurried into the dingy El station. She climbed up the steps and onto the platform, a routine she followed every day after work. The difference on this particular Friday was that she had stepped up onto the other side of the platform, where she waited for a train bound for the loop, instead of the usual outbound train to take her home. Earlier in the week she had phoned Gail Abernathy to ask if they could meet for dinner on Friday evening.

"Gail, this is Lynn . . . I know, not since last September when we closed up the beach house. . . . . what I'm calling about is to ask you if you'd like to go to dinner with me sometime. I'd like to catch up. . . . Oh, I wondered about Friday . . . . Good. How about downtown at the Heidelberg? . . . Good. I suggest we meet around quarter to six. Gail, I'm glad we can get together. See you then, OK? . . . . Bye."

For the most part Lynn did not have any contact with her Michigan beach friends during the year. But it was different with Gail. The Abernathys had a beach house just north of Shore Crest. In the last two summers Lynn and Gail had become good friends. The Abernathys lived up in Evanston so it was usually more convenient to meet downtown. Gail was the one person in Lynn's life with whom she felt she could share whatever was on her mind. In fact this seemed to be mutual. Each listened to the other seriously.

Things had been building up for Lynn and she needed to talk. All day she'd looked forward to their getting together. As the El bumped and swayed noisily along the ancient elevated tracks Lynn peered out the dirty window into the rain streaked gray. She turned over in her mind what she wanted to tell Gail. Soon she heard the squeaking of the brakes and the conductor swung into view and shouted over the crowd of passengers, "State and Dearborn." Lynn's stop. She got up, pulled her coat around her and started inching toward the folding doors in the center of the car. The train came to an abrupt stop and a stream of passengers walked out onto the rain-soaked wooden platform past an equal number waiting to board. Down the steps and onto the street. With her umbrella up she made her way quickly to the chosen restaurant and went in through the revolving door. Out of breath, she folded her umbrella, took off her coat and shook out the rain drops which had collected. Lynn looked around and soon spotted Gail coming in.

"Gail, I'm so glad you could come."

"So am I. Let's find a table. I'm hungry."

A hostess led them to the back of the bustling dining room to a table for two which had just been vacated and cleared A waiter came, gave them their menus and poured ice water into the glistening goblets on the white linen covered table. He was soon back to take their orders, and in no time a meal was set before each of the young women. By the time they were on their desserts, fortunately the crowd had begun to thin, so that they could keep their seats to talk over coffee. They had exchanged pleasantries while they ate. Now Lynn was ready for some heavy duty talk.

"The reason I wanted to see you is that I've got a problem."

"What's that?"

"Well, I met this guy, and I really like him. We hit it off from the start. Now he's getting serious. You know what I mean?"

"Yeah, do I!" Gail had had her share of false starts.

"But the thing is, I'd like to get serious but just can't."

"Why not?"

"You remember Earl?"

"Sure."

"I don't know if you ever heard why he and I had to split," Lynn questioned.

Gail hesitated, not wanting to appear to have known more than Lynn had expected. "You didn't want to become a minister's wife?"

"That was part of it, but not all. The worst was Daddy."

"Your father?"

"Yes, my father. He wouldn't let me marry a loser, as he called him." Lynn paused as if to take stock of her predicament before going further. "Now I've got Don who in Daddy's eyes is a worse loser."

"How so?"

"He's an artist. He lives and paints in an attic, sells a few, but mostly lives off his widowed mother, who's loaded."

"Oh, Lynn," Gail pleaded. "Pardon me, but how'd you ever get stuck on him?"

"It was last spring. I met him in a park by our house. He was sketching. I was jogging, and I tripped on a tree root right near where he was. He helped me up and onto his bench. I'd twisted my ankle and couldn't walk on it. He was so sweet to me."

"Lady in distress and all that?" Gail looked skeptical.

"No it was real. I was in pain and he was genuinely concerned. He was so sensitive and caring."

"You sure it wasn't your cute skimpy outfit?" Gail gave a leer.

"No, it wasn't that, Gail."

"All right, go on."

"After I caught my breath and decided that I'd better get home so that I could get to a doctor, he folded up his art things, put them under his arm and held me up with his other arm and hobbled me home."

"What's his name?"

"Don—short for Eldon. Eldon Drury."

"All this sounds interesting."

"Well, anyway, when we got to my house, just before he rang the doorbell, he asked if he could have my phone number so that he could find out how I was mending. We exchanged numbers—and we've been talking with one another ever since."

Gail, who had been listening intently, wanted to know more.

"And when I could get around again, he would meet me in the park and we'd talk. And then we began going on dates. And—you know—it just went on from there."

"And now he wants to get serious?"

"Yes."

"You mean marriage, Lynn? Or just . . . you know . . . ."

"No, Gail. Marriage!" Lynn was emphatic.

Gail pondered this a while. "Wow. And that's what you want?"

"I know it sounds stupid. But I do." Lynn then added, "Don is leaving Chicago to to go down to New Mexico, to some art colony where he says artists do quite well. He wants me to come down with him."

Both friends were quiet for a prolonged moment.

"I dumped Earl because of Daddy, and now am I supposed to dump Don too?"

"No, not really . . ."

"I'll be an old maid for sure."

Gail launched into the matter with her best effort at wisdom for the situation her friend was in. "Lynn, it seems to me that you have to be the one to decide. You know how you felt after you lost Earl. And now you've told me that it was really your father's decision. Do you want to be in that position again?"

"No, but the other side of it is that I'm all Daddy has." Lynn stopped herself, knowing that she was about to divulge some family secrets.

However, Gail picked up on this. "He has your mother."

"No, that's just it. Mom's a drunk, and I'm sure she's worthless as a wife." She paused to think about what she had said. "I can't add insult to injury."

"Your brother still at home, isn't he?" Gail asked further.

"He's moved into an apartment on his own. He rarely visits. I think his is more of a business relationship with his father than as a son."

"Oh, I guess there's more to the situation than I thought."

"Yes, and it boils down to who I hurt: Daddy or me."

Casting about for something to say, Gail asked. "How long do you have before you have to decide?"

"Don's pushing me. And Daddy told me before he left on this business trip. This is what he said word for word, Gail. 'When I get back on Tuesday, I want you to be able to tell me that this artist-creep is out of your life.'"

"Oh, wow."

"So I've got until Tuesday. Three more days. That's why I wanted to see you tonight." Lynn thought some more. "I know you can't tell me what to do. But it has helped to talk about it. I don't know what I'm going to do. But I'll let you know."

"Will you be OK?"

"Yeah, I'll make it. Ellerton Manufacturing or the art world, I guess." Lynn tried to end on a light note.

Gail wasn't completely satisfied she had helped. "Wait, Lynn, let me ask another question—another way of looking at it."

"What question?"

"Lynn, suppose you make a clean decision and tell Don you'll go with him. Imagine that situation. How do you really feel about it?"

"OK . . . I think I would . . . ."

Gail looked deeply into Lynn's expression "You're not sure?"

"Well, as a matter of fact, when I thought about going off with Don, I thought of Earl."

"Lynn!" Gail took on a stern mood. "Whichever way you decide, you have to get rid of your lingering feeling for Earl."

"Yeah, I know." Lynn had had enough. "Well, I'll let you know. Thanks. You've been helpful."

The two got up and left the restaurant together. The gray sky was now almost black.

They mounted the Loop El platform where they separated so that Gail could wait for a northbound train to Evanston.

The El train bound for the western suburbs was almost empty as Lynn boarded. By this evening hour the trains coming into the city were crowded with those seeking its night life. Inbound trains passed on their way into the Loop. Lynn's window reflected black except for dots of city lights whizzing by as she was hurried toward her home. Pondering her talk with Gail, Lynn leaned toward quitting Ellerton's and joining Don in New Mexico. *I need a new life.* she told herself. *This one isn't going anywhere . . . NOWHERE AT ALL.* She felt an anger welling up, directed toward her father. But it made her ashamed. Nevertheless a resolve was taking shape in her mind. *Daddy'll find someone to take my place, a mousey little thing! He'll get along without me. Ellerton will continue its success story. Even though I'll be financially strapped until I can get something in Santa Fe, or Don makes it big! I'll get a job. We'll find a little apartment, get married and then as things get better we'll move into one of those neat adobe style houses Santa Fe is famous for. And Earl? He's old news.* Thinking of herself far away and bound to Don in New Mexico gave Lynn a hollow nervous feeling in the pit of her stomach, like standing on the edge of a pool before jumping.

Lynn's reverie continued until she reached her stop and got off the train to walk home. She thought about her mother and hoped she'd be in and in shape to talk. Lynn thought she'd try to sound out her mother, to see if she might possibly get some support for her plans to move and marry. She would skirt the issue in a round-about sort of way, just to see what kind of response she might get out of her mother. She'd had a conversation like this back in the days of Earl and her mother had been supportive.

When Lynn walked up the tree shaded lane to her house she noticed that the front door was open, which seemed strange, especially since there were no lights on in the house even though it was dark outside. She opened the screen door and started to step inside and to reach for a light switch, when her foot came against something in the doorway. A shiver went up Lynn's spine realizing that it was the body of a person. She stretched around it to put on the lights and discovered that it was her mother lying in the door way. The sickening smell of booze mingled with the putrid odor of vomit left no doubt in Lynn's mind. She leaned over to feel a slow pulse, and knew immediately that she must get help. The woman next door was a nurse and fortunately Lynn found her home.

"It's mother . . . Yeah, again, only this time I think its pretty bad. Could you come over?"

She hurried over to Lynn's house. The neighbor quickly assessed the situation.

"Lynn, you must call an ambulance. I'll call Emergency. Your mother needs to be hospitalized right now!"

From the emergency room Lynn phoned her father at his hotel. "Daddy, this is Lynette. Mother is really out of it this time. I found her on the floor. She'd barely gotten in the door. Marge, next door, advised immediate hospitalization . . . Yes, it's that bad. She's in E.R. right now. . . . No, I haven't heard from a doctor yet. But I think you better come, if you can, Daddy."

"I don't think I can. I've got an important presentation to a client tomorrow morning. A lot depends on this. You understand. And with you there, Lynn, I feel I can delay a day or two. You understand. I don't know what I'd do without you, Lynn. Phone me tomorrow morning before nine. That's when I leave here for the meeting. You understand. Good bye."

"Good bye . . . ." *Yeah, I understand. So much for Santa Fe—at least for now.*

CHAPTER 15

Home

The blazing sun reflecting on the prairie greeted Earl as he drove west out of Mandan. Like Lewis and Clark after their wintering in Mandan, Earl was setting out on his own "journey of discovery" on this spring morning. He was bound for Montana. And, yes, the skies were indeed bluer on this morning than he'd seen them on the other two mornings of his journey. In fact, bluer than Earl had ever seen the sky. Traffic was noticeably thinner now. Occasionally a pickup passed him. Oncoming vehicles were miles apart. Towns had become scarce and further apart now, and what towns there were appeared to Earl to be tiny and seemingly insignificant. Not so, however, Earl would later come to realize. Each town was indeed very important to the few who lived in it and to those on farms on the surrounding plains.

A little before noon he passed through Beach, North Dakota, and very soon after that he came to the "WELCOME TO MONTANA" sign. *In Montana! On the home stretch!* His hands on the steering wheel felt a tingle of nervous excitement as each mile brought him closer to Saline. Forty-five minutes later he came to Glendive. The Route 10 took him down the main street which followed the Northern Pacific tracks on his left. In the heart of town he came to the Jordan Hotel. He found a parking place near the hotel let himself out to stretch as he walked to the door of the Jordan where he stopped in for lunch in the hotel café.

Passing the reception desk, he entered the café and took a stool at the counter. In a matter of fact way, a middle-aged waitress in a plain white blouse brought him a glass of iced water. She greeted him and gave him a menu. When she returned, Earl ordered a hamburger and a cup of coffee. On his interview trip his meals had been in homes. Now, for the first time he was on his own in a Montana café away from the over-zealous attention of the committee. Not much to remind him of the Seminary Bar and Restaurant on Halsted! The other men who sat on stools up and down the counter for the most part were dressed in Levis and western work shirts. He was struck with the fact that they kept their hats on while eating—many wore cowboy hats, others had on baseball caps. Unlike the café on Halsted everyone seemed to know each other here in Glendive, making for a jovial atmosphere. Earl felt out-of-place, an impression which would only gradually recede in the coming weeks. But this new area was to be home—for better or worse! The other patrons watched him as he got up and paid his bill at the cashier by the door.

After lunch he stopped at a gas station for his last fill up. He found a pay phone from which he called Mae Benson to tell her where he was so that she could gauge when to be at the church in Saline to meet him. He was soon on highway 10 again following the Yellowstone River on his right. Another fifty minutes or so and he was passing through Terry. The next town of any size would be Miles City. Saline was east of Miles City a few miles before the junction of US highways 10 and 12.

As is so often the case, the final miles of a long journey seemed to go by very slowly. This gave Earl plenty of time to try an imagine what would be in store for him. He looked forward to seeing the folks who had been on the search committee, especially Homer. For three days he'd not seen a soul whom he knew. He felt a certain loneliness and so it would be good to see some familiar faces. The closer he got to Saline the more he could start to imagine that he was looking at his new home. Not many farms were visible from the road, but occasionally in the distance he could see clusters of trees, indicating a farmyard. He wondered if these would be places at which he would be making pastoral visits. A green Ford pickup overtook him. As it passed he could look into the cab to see that it was driven by a young woman with blond hair tied back into a pony tail. Dressed in farm work clothes she appeared so different from the young women he'd been associated with in Chicago.

Earl had thought about Lynn less and less frequently in recent months, as he had been slipping into his new "parish pastor mode." But something about the image of the local farm girl in the pickup brought thoughts of Lynn to the surface. *I wonder what Lynette would think of this area. If she had stuck with me, she'd be here beside me. Would she be as excited as I am? I doubt it. In fact, I think that she would be turned off.* And then he thought about what had actually happened. *That's exactly what she did—she turned off the track I'm following, choosing to remain in her own familiar way of life—or in her father's!* And yet he missed Lynn. *I wonder if we'll ever meet again. I wonder if I'll ever have the chance to share any of this new experience with her.* His thoughts circled back to his anticipation of his new home. And the new relationships he could expect. The miles kept slowly grinding by.

Finally he spotted the grain elevator in the distance and then a few buildings came into view. He slowed down as he passed a *Reduce Speed* sign and then he came to a small sign announcing *Saline*. He had arrived in Saline. He drove very slowly, savoring the view in every direction. *This will be my town,* he thought as he left the paved highway and rolled over the gravel streets. He found his way to the church building. There were three or four cars parked beside it. He pulled in next to them and turned off the engine. For a moment he sat in the now quiet car. Then he got out and began walking to the main door of the church. As he did the door opened and members of the committee rushed out and down the stairs to greet him. Mae had phoned around and Gertrude Gelenik had come to the church. Homer Stein was there. Sue Stark and Jane Moss had driven over to the church together.

Earl was overwhelmed by the obvious joy in the warm greetings he received as each one shook his hand in turn. Mae was quick to announce. "We have coffee and goodies downstairs, Reverend. We know you must be ready for something like that."

"Sounds great," Earl said as everyone filed back into the church and down to the fellowship hall.

"You sit right down, Reverend, and we'll bring some refreshments," Mae directed.

Homer intervened. "Or perhaps you'd like to use the facilities."

"Thank you, I think I will." This also gave Earl a chance to comb his hair in place and ready himself for the impending "viewing." He came out and found the seat set for him.

The women seemed to trip over each other bringing Earl his coffee and specially baked cookies. Homer sat down next to Earl and also became the recipient of the hospitality offered by the women members of the committee. Thus began the first of many such social occasions Earl would enjoy in Saline, Montana. No longer alone as he had been during his three days on the road, he was now surrounded by his new friends. He was home! He turned to Homer. "I've been reading your paper."

Homer looked at Earl with a question. "What paper is that?"

"The one about blue skies and fewer people."

"Oh that. I'd forgotten that new ministers coming into Montana have been getting that. I hope it is helpful. I wrote that up a few years ago when we had a streak of extremely short pastorates. Two years at the most. One was less than a year. The presbytery decided the new pastors had not been properly oriented—or better yet—*warned!*"

"I can see where this could help. Or at least I'm finding it most interesting."

"Good."

Gertrude came to sit across from Earl and Homer. "Pastor, Ella is sorry she couldn't be here to help welcome you."

"That's quite alright, Mrs. Gelenik. I'm feeling quite welcome."

"She'll be here Sunday."

"So will everyone else!" Homer quipped. He explained, "Like spectators coming to see a new species at the zoo."

After this informal reception, everyone accompanied Earl to the manse next door to welcome him to his house. They had redecorated and furnished the parsonage throughout. Earl was thrilled with what they had done for him. There was a vase with freshly cut flowers on the dining room table. And in the refrigerator were milk, eggs, cheese, cold cuts and a head of lettuce. The pantry cupboard was stocked with canned goods, mostly home canned, coffee and cereal, and fresh fruit was on the counter.

"This is marvelous!" Earl exclaimed as he surveyed all that the committee had provided. This was met with a glow of pride on the faces of the committee members. After a discussion of what else was planned for the next few days, the committee took their leave. And Earl was at home.

That night Earl re-read the last few lines of Homer's paper which he'd been reading on the way to Montana.

> Related to the drought cycles and the mechanization of agriculture, population of small towns has declined and some have shriveled up and died, while larger towns are experiencing economic hardships.
>
> Low population density as well as population transience means that there is a lower tax base available for the provision of basic necessary public services throughout the state. We have limited services because we have fewer people to pay the tax bill.
>
> In many cases the "extras" taken for granted elsewhere are unavailable here. Thus, there are fewer cultural and artistic opportunities across the state. It simply takes more people to support those kinds of "luxury" services.
>
> What does all of this mean to us who are leaders in the name of Christ in Montana? I believe it means "right out of the chute" that we must love Montana and want to be here; and that we must love the people, and enjoy being one of them. I mean really love, in a way that is uncalculating and equalitarian. This must be the emotional footing for all that we say and do in ministry.
>
> Let us feel about this place into which Christ has called us, as Arapooish, a Chief of the Crow tribe felt:

The Crow country is a good country. The Great Spirit has put it exactly in the right place: while you are in it you fare well; whenever you go out of it, whichever way you travel you fare worse . . . The Crow country is exactly the right place. It has snowy mountains and sunny plains, all kinds of climates and good things for every season.

When our love for Christ is joined by such love for the state in which we serve, we will be more able to minister in this area of sparse population, isolation, and transience; and we will be able to approach our task with enthusiasm and vigor in Montana: WHERE THE SKIES ARE BLUER . . . . AND THE PEOPLE ARE FEWER!

A lot in this to think about, Earl said to himself as he put the paper down and prepared for bed.

And so ended Earl Norris's first evening at home in "Crow country" among the people he would come to love.

Earl was so taken with this introduction to his new home that he hadn't let himself get sleepy until he'd finished the paper. Then when he did go to bed, sleep overcame him almost immediately. But he was restless. Perhaps it was the fact that the next day he would begin his new life in Saline—his permanent home! Or was it his mind which had been filled with ideas and images in Homer's paper? . . . . *The Crow country is exactly the right place . . . . where the skies are bluer and the people are fewer . . .*

Earl's introduction to his new life would not be complete until he and the congregation had a chance to see each other on a Sunday. He spent his intervening time getting ready for his formal debut. Sunday came and the sanctuary of the little church quickly filled up as more and more pickups and cars arrived at the church before the scheduled time of worship. The five children in the Sunday school had been well rehearsed for an opening song in the service. They sang "Tell Me the Old, Old Story." At the conclusion of Earl's scripture reading the adult choir sang "Blessed Assurance." Earl felt that his sermon went very well. In fact, he felt on "cloud nine" about the entire service, which he thought had proceeded without a hitch.

The Sunday service was followed by an informal potluck. The basement fellowship hall was filled with excitement as members of the congregation filled their plates from an over stocked banquet table. Of course Earl was the honored guest and invited to fill his plate first. Somehow Gertrude Gelenik managed to steer Ella and herself to seats at the same table as Earl. Fortunately the conversation around the table included others who were seated near the "new reverend." As Earl came to the end of his ample plateful, and an enticing dessert dish, he remembered a tidbit he'd heard in his practical theology class. Acting on the hint, he stood up to say a few words. The crowd suddenly quieted down to hear what their new pastor would say.

"I am overwhelmed by your welcome and most eager to get to know each and every one of you in the coming weeks. Until then I'd like for us to thank the ladies who have put together the best meal I've ever had! Might all of you come out of the kitchen so that we can thank you."

The women feigned reluctance but came out anyway. The group applauded, the four women who had come out smiled proudly. Earl topped it off with, "Thank you, ladies, so very much for the best meal I've ever eaten—in my whole life!"

And so, Earl began his ministry in Saline with confidence and with almost total congregational approval. The committee had done well.

A few weeks later at the congregational meeting called for the purpose of issuing a formal call—or contract—to Earl, an action of the congregation would be to disband the search committee, commending it for having done a good job.

CHAPTER 16

The "Reverner"

Earl's ordination and installation as pastor of the Community Presbyterian Church of Saline was scheduled to take place a month after Earl's arrival in Saline. A commission of ministers and elders had been appointed and guests had been invited. This would be an occasion for both a potluck and a reception in addition to the service itself. The members of the presbytery commission and out of town guests would need a supper before the evening service of ordination and installation. And of course, everyone would want to greet the new pastor at a fancy reception afterward. The women of the church had their work cut out for them. But they were used to it. This had happened frequently at Saline over the years. Ministers hadn't stayed very long in the experience of most of the current members, oftentimes to their disappointment, sometimes to their relief.

Earl's parents would be arriving on the Westbound the day before his ordination service. His sister, Anne, would arrive a week earlier to give Earl a hand in sprucing up his "bachelor quarters" and to prepare some meals for the family during the time they would be all together. Anne had a couple of weeks between her college graduation and a summer job before starting. her career as a math teacher out in Oak Park in the high school.

Earl met her at the train station. Anne was an attractive young woman resembling her mother in complexion and build. Earl, on the other hand, favored his father in appearance. When she stepped off the train onto the platform Earl was there to greet her with a hug and a kiss. They began immediately to jabber, like old friends, which they were. The two had always been close. Earl was eager to show her around his new surroundings. After picking up her bag they left the depot and got in Earl's car to take her to the manse where the two renewed their brother-sister relationship with zest. Her arrival did not go unnoticed.

Ten o'clock the next morning and "The Club" was in session at the Conoco. "Hey Hank—who's that good looker stayin' over to the preacher's house?" Darrel Reisner liked to goad Hank Hurlbutt.

"Whad'ya mean? I don't know about any woman over there. Tell me about her."

"Well, I just happened to be driving by the depot while the Westbound was in. I saw the preacher meet this babe. Good lookin' blonde. Really stacked." Darrel waited for the full effect of this revelation before continuing his lurid saga. "They was a kissin' and a huggin' when she got off the train." Now he knew he had Hank's attention. "I thought I'd just swing around and see where he was a'goin on with her. Next thing I knew he'd driven up to the parsonage, and was helpin' her in—right into his house—and she had a suitcase."

"Is that a fact?" Merle had come in from the garage to listen in on Darrel's story.

"It's true. I swear."

Hank was taking this all in. "I know'd it would be trouble—him bein' a bachelor." He took time to picture what he'd heard—and what he was imagining. "And right here in town—in the parsonage."

"Yeah, Hank. Not even over to Miles City," Merle goaded.

"Some Reverner you folks have got yourselves," Darrel added with a sly look on his face as he gave Merle a wink.

The ordination-installation was scheduled for Sunday evening. By Thursday evening Anne and Earl had done all the household preparations needed. Their parents would arrive on Saturday. As they were clearing the breakfast dishes, Earl suggested, "Why don't I give you a tour of the parish this morning. I'd like to show you the farms where some of the folks live and the other 'sights' such as they are."

"Sure, I'd like that. Let me put on something decent."

"Great! I'll go and get gas in the car and be back for you."

"No, let me come along and then we can go from there."

"OK, I'll wait for you then."

In a few minutes Anne appeared, ready for the tour. She was dressed in a snug white sweater and a plaid skirt, rather short. They drove over to the Conoco.

"Somebody get that?" Merle called from the garage when a car pulled up to the pump. He was at a critical point in replacing a part on a pickup he was servicing.

"Yeah, I'll get it." Hank Hurlbutt volunteered. He'd been having coffee with Darrel Reisner at "the Club."

He walked out to the apron of the gas station and up to the driver's window of the waiting customer. "Oh, it's you, Reverner! What'll it be?"

"Yes, it's me, and I'd like to fill'er up."

After putting the nozzle in and starting to pump the gas, Hank began cleaning the windshield. When he got to the passenger side he slowed down to make sure to get a good look at Earl's passenger, whom he assumed was the girlfriend who'd come in on the Westbound a week or so ago. Anne's skirt had ridden up enough to give him a good view of her legs, which made him slow down his window polishing considerably. He reluctantly moved to the side windows and then topped off the tank, hung up the hose and returned to Earl's window to take Earl's money—and to get another look. Earl and Anne drove off to begin their tour.

Hank returned to his metal chair and his coffee mug. "She's a looker!"

"Who?"

"That girlfriend of the Reverner's."

"Oh, she was in the car with the Revener?"

"Yeah, nice legs—and her sweater was a knock-out."

Away from the Conoco on a gravel road not far from town, Earl and Anne passed a pasture on which a herd of antelope were grazing.

"Look there!" Anne pointed. "What are those?"

"Deer, I think."

This false identification would eventually stand corrected as Earl became more and more acquainted with his new surroundings. He would learn that one of the qualifications for a pastor in Saline was the ability to make positive identification of local wild life. He would have to be correct in such matters, for in this field of knowledge, unlike the Bible, his parishioners would know when he was wrong. He would learn that these were antelope.

They drove up and down the roads close to town, looking at the farms, which Earl said probably were occupied by parishioners. Earl then turned onto a road which took them near the Yellowstone River and they passed by the Walter Norland ranch with its massive gate carrying the W lazy N brand.

"Wow, that's quite a ranch!" Anne was obviously impressed.

"Yeah, that belongs to the Norlands." For some reason Earl remembered this place from his tour with Homer. "But they aren't members."

"Too bad."

Further down the road they saw that their way was blocked by a herd of cattle, all of them black. The cows were ambling down the road the same direction as Earl was going. Behind the herd there were two men in cowboy hats on horseback guiding the bunch. When they saw that Earl wanted to pass they began to split the herd to make way. But Earl drove up next to one of the men and yelled. "We don't need to go through. We'll turn around."

"You sure?" The drover talking was a man in his fifties, tall and straight, giving Earl the correct impression that he was the boss, probably Norland himself.

"Right! You go ahead, we'll make a U turn as soon as we can."

Earl slowed down, and when he saw a slight widening in the road he managed a turn around. As he drove away from the herd he watched Norland on horseback in his rear view mirror. Earl was unaware that the time would come when he'd be much more closely associated with Norland and his family.

Sunday, the day of Earl's ordination and installation, arrived. After the morning service, Earl's mother and sister prepared a chicken dinner for the family. It was good to spend part of the day with only his family, before the ceremonies of the evening would take place. In fact his ordination would in some sense set him apart from his family. In the days to come Earl would often think of this Sunday dinner and afternoon of conversation with his family.

At six o'clock, Earl and his family joined the members of the presbytery commission in the church fellowship hall for a meal together before things got started. The church women were most attentive to the guests including Earl's family. In a curious way they treated Earl as their own, unlike the guests. The social stage was set for what some had called the marriage of a pastor and his congregation.

Years later, Earl would look back wistfully on this night, seeing it as the official start of his Montana odyssey, an all-consuming experience which would extend well into the years ahead. Different as they were from one another, the people who came to Saline that night would become Earl's closest friends. Friends with whom Earl Norris would share his frustrations and his accomplishments as pastor of the Community Presbyterian Church of Saline, Montana from June of 1959 onward.

The first commission member to arrive was Dr. Cecil Graham, a gray haired man probably in his mid-seventies, Earl guessed. Medium height and build with a bushy white mustache. He came down the stairs into the basement fellowship hall carrying his black pulpit gown over his left arm. He looked immediately into the kitchen where some of the Saline women were getting ready to serve the meal.

"Howdy, ladies."

The woman nearest the serving door greeted him. "Oh, Cecil, I'm so glad you'll be part of the service tonight."

"It's an honor. Saline's been a favorite of mine for a long time."

One of the other women added, "And that's how we feel about you. How many times you have helped us out when we didn't have a pastor!"

Mae Benson turned from the oven where she had been occupied. "Yes, Cecil, you have been a God-send to us more than once."

Gertrude Gelenik came around from a storage pantry in the back of the kitchen. "Dr. Graham, I want you to meet our new pastor." She took him by the arm and directed him out into the dining room to the place where Earl was visiting with some of the session members who had come for the occasion.

"Reverner Norris. This is Dr. Graham . . . And this is Earl Norris."

At that the two men shook hands and fell into a get acquainted sort of conversation, while Gertrude returned to the kitchen where the Saline women were going about their preparations.

"I wasn't at any of the meetings when you were being considered. I'm retired and don't get to all the presbytery functions anymore."

"I see. Were you a pastor in one of the churches nearby?"

"More than once over the years, Earl." The older man was obviously pleased to share some of his history with this very young man. "More than one. I've been in the presbytery forty-three years. I came in 1916 as a Sunday School Missionary for the Board of National Missions."

"I guess I don't know what that position was."

"We were sent out to sparsely settled areas of the West to bring church services to isolated farm and ranch families."

"You mean you started new churches?"

"No, we didn't do that so much as we held services out in the ranch and farm houses. And we tried to teach Sunday School to whatever children there were on those places."

"That sounds like real frontier ministry."

"It was that all right. Some day I'll tell you some of the stories. Then later I served the church in Terry and up at Poplar. Finally I was pastor in Miles City. Then I retired."

"You live there now?"

"Oh no. In my day we didn't believe in that—staying on in the town you had been pastoring. The wife and I bought a little place along the river east of Forsyth, near Rosebud. We go to church at Forsyth."

By this time the other members of the commission had arrived. Merleen Oldham, an elder from Forsyth, had gone immediately into the kitchen to visit with the Saline women, while Homer Stein and Reverend Hapner from Miles City were upstairs in the sanctuary arranging chairs in the chancel for commission members. The two men were well acquainted, having both served on the Ministerial Relations committee of presbytery, the committee in charge of the ordination and installation. Bob Taggert was the last to arrive. A young man only a few years older than Earl, he was the minister in Terry, his first call after seminary in San Francisco. Or rather, he breezed in wearing a yellow corduroy sport coat over an open collar. Khaki pants and argyle socks completed his attire. He would give in to a tie later when he put on his pulpit robe. Earl had met him in the presbytery meeting in which he had been examined and approved. The two had hit it off at first sight, in part because both were still single, and now as Bob bounded down the steps he went over to greet Earl immediately.

"Hi, buddy! This'll be a great night, pal. After that it's work, work, work!:"

"Thanks a bunch."

Homer and Ray Hapner came down from the sanctuary. The last of the guests to arrive were Earl's parents and his sister Anne. They had waited 'til it was time for supper, and slipped over from the manse. Earl joined his family and then motioned for a pause in the conversation so that he could introduce them.

The kitchen committee came out to meet the three Norrises and then announced that the supper was ready. Mae asked Hapner to give the blessing. After the prayer she invited everyone to fill their plates at the serving table. Earl's ministry at Saline was beginning! By the end of the evening he could properly be called *The Reverend Mr. Norris.*

CHAPTER 17

Re-play

Saline folks don't like being up too late "of an evening." Chores require early rising. So, by 9 o'clock Earl and his family were in the living room of the manse with shoes kicked off and ties loosened. Bob Taggert was included along with Earl's mother and dad, and Anne. All were elated as each contributed to a re-play of the evening.

Bob found a place on the couch next to Anne. Robert Norris kicked off the recounting of the day with, "I'm proud of you, Son."

"Thank you, Dad."

Earl's mother admonished her husband, "Robert, I don't think you can talk that way after this evening."

"What do you mean, Esther?"

With a grin she replied. "Well, if we were Catholic you would be saying, 'I'm proud of you, Father!'"

This caused an outburst of laughter.

Bob Taggert chimed in, "Or Episcopal. That reminds me of a woman in seminary who was Episcopal. Mary O'Riley was her name, and she used to talk about how someday her church would allow women to be ordained. So at that point some of the wise guys would chirp. 'Then we'd have to call you 'Father Mary' Then she'd add, "And when I marry and have kids I'm going to make them call me Father!'"

This was followed by more laughter, especially by Anne.

Not to be side-tracked, Earl's father reiterated his feeling. "Whatever we call you now, I think this is a red letter day for you, Earl, and for us as a family."

All agreed and Bob reflected on his own ordination which had taken place three years previously.

"Seriously, it is a significant step in your life, Earl. It was for me. I remember that one of my immediate reactions was that I decided that from that time on I ought to be much more serious, and not so 'flip' about everything."

Anne had a quizzical look when she responded. "That's interesting? Didn't last long, though. Did it?"

"Ah! Touche! I guess I had that coming." Again everyone laughed.

It was Earl's turn to comment. "I think I know what you mean, Bob. It must be what I think a wedding service would be like. You go in single and in twenty minuets you leave the church married. And your life will never be the same again."

Bob agreed and became strangely quiet. It was Esther who picked up on this. "Bob, is it difficult being single as a parish pastor?"

"Yes, it is."

Anne was uncomfortable with such a brief answer. "Why, I wonder. Priests aren't married. They have a lot more time to devote to their work that way."

"With us it's different." Bob continued. "People expect you to be married and so they are always on the look-out for prospects. I sometimes think getting me married off must be an unwritten goal of the Terry church women's association."

No one seemed to know quite what to say. Earl was taking all this in.

"And then when you do look around, if there is anyone in the congregation, you get in a big tangle if you select a girl from one of the church families. Ministers ought not to become close friends with people in their own congregations, let alone a member of one of the families. It becomes a political mess, I hear."

Anne stirred and was about to say something when Bob turned to her. "So, Anne, it's nice to sit next to someone who is not politically allied."

Anne blushed.

Esther could see her embarrassment and said, "Back to the service this evening."

"Yes," Anne was quick to agree.

"I was interested in what Dr. Graham had to say in his *Charge to the Pastor* about service in Montana." Earl's mother went on. "I had to shudder when he read that poem."

"Right." Earl said. "I asked him for a copy of that, and he gave it to me."

"Let's hear it again," Anne asked. "He was describing what life on the plains is like, wasn't he?"

"Yes, and here it is:

HOPE CRUCIFIED

Spring! And Hope is smiling again.
First tinge of green across the rolling plain;
A blanket of soft, wet snow, and then
The gentle patter of rain.

Fragrance of early flowers and freshly upturned earth;
Bleating of baby lambs, it is Nature's time of birth.
Bird songs fill the air, thrilling the hearts of men,
And Hope is smiling again.

Then comes the Wind!
Like a devil casting a spell;
Suddenly, blazing hot—its fetid breath
Like a blast from the mouth of Hell!

Hillsides sear and brown, clouds of scorching dust
Shriveling up the plain—covering it with rust;
Taking the lilt from the meadowlark's song.
And I can only cry out, "Oh, God! How long?"
—Annie Knipfer

"Who did he say wrote that?" Esther asked.

"A young woman who came out to the area around Baker, Montana, from Massachusetts in the early days—in 1919. She came out to teach school and she wound up marrying a local farmer."

"How true are her words, Bob?"

"Anne, believe me they are pretty much on the mark. I've seen some years like that."

"Oh, wow! Are you sure this is the place for you, brother?"

"It is. Such writing only makes me more convinced—not less. I guess it's the challenge. The sense of mission to join in the pioneering life style, if but a few years late."

"Atta boy!" Bob said, only half in jest.

With a mirthful glint in her eye, Anne teased, "Watched it. We established that he's Reverend Earl now!"

"Oh, I'm so sorry. I forgot why we're here tonight. Thought it was to get acquainted with the new pastor's family—especially his sister!"

Anne blushed again.

To make amends Bob steered the discussion back to the installation. "I thought what Ray Hapner said to the congregation was especially good."

"What part are you referring to?" Earl's father wondered.

"The way he talked about the need to love their pastor, to take him into their homes—in some sense to care for him as much as he is called to care for the congregation's needs. 'It can be a lonely life,' he said."

"Is it?" Anne asked bluntly.

"Yes, especially for someone who does not have a family with him."

The little group was quiet for a few moments.

In an effort to conclude the conversation, Robert Norris asked his son. "Earl, tell us how you felt about the evening."

"Dad, it was everything I'd hoped. I feel as if it verified God's call to me to the ministry and to this particular place at this time. What more can I say?" And then Earl thought further. "I'd like to thank you, Bob, for your sermon. That advice you drew out of John 1:8 I found most provocative—that, like John the Baptist, we are not the light ourselves, but our job is to point people to the light."

"I'm glad that hit you, Earl. There are a lot of clergy who think—or act like they themselves are the light. When it is our role to bear witness to the light—to Christ."

This got Anne to thinking. "You know, it strikes me that a lot of young people get turned off exactly at that point."

"What point?" Esther asked.

"When they have a minister who acts like he's the light. If more ministers were like John, as you pointed out, Bob, such people might stick with the church."

"I think so, Anne . . . . Well, it all begins tomorrow morning, Pal. I hope you can hang on to what you have felt tonight, Earl." Bob was offering a serious challenge and he added. "I sort of think you will."

There was general agreement and well-wishing in the group as the evening's re-play concluded.

"I've got to drive home to Terry, so I better say good bye. It's been really good meeting you all. I hope we'll meet again." As he said this his gaze settled on Anne. Then he thought of one more comment. "If you all stick around 'til next Sunday, come over to Terry. I'm preaching!"

"Just may do that!" Anne quipped.

Earl gave her a brotherly push for uttering something so disloyal.

Bob made his exit, leaving the Norris family to prepare for bed.

"Nice young man," Mr. Norris said.

"Yeah," Anne said as she made her way to the guest room she'd been using.

The next day found the Norris family in the Northern Pacific waiting room. Earl was now ordained and fully installed as pastor of the Saline Church. His parents and sister needed now to return to their lives. Still thinking about the previous evening, Anne brought up something strange she had heard.

"Last night at the reception Mrs. Oldham from Forsyth came over to where I was sitting and asked if she could sit down. I asked her about her town and church and she told me that they were looking for a minister. Their former pastor and his family had left in a hurry and no one had come to replace him."

"What was the hurry for?" Earl asked.

"That's the strange part of the story. They left because they thought the manse was haunted!"

"Haunted! Really?

"Yes, haunted, Mother. They kept hearing this strange sound of footsteps seeming to come from the attic. Always at night. When they checked the attic the next morning it was always empty. So they put a lock on the door leading to the attic stairs—a dead bolt which could only be opened from second floor side of the attic stairway. And the minister himself kept the only key around his neck at night."

"Yeah—go on." Mr. Norris was impatient.

"When they discovered the door unlocked they decided it was time to leave the house, and Forsyth!"

"Must have been a prank." Robert Norris concluded.

"No," Anne proclaimed. "Merleen Oldham said it was not, and furthermore, there had been stories like this abut the old manse going around for years."

Earl thought about what Anne had reported. "I'll have to ask Bob Taggert what he knows about this. In fact, Anne! When I talk to him, I'm going to give him your phone number so he can check out the story with you! You'd like that, wouldn't you?" Apparently Earl had picked up some of the vibrations from the night before.

"Oh Earl. You wouldn't." Anne blushed.

"Yes, I would."

Just then the station master announced over the public address system, "Northcoast Limited, eastbound, arriving on track number two. Scheduled to depart immediately. All aboard." Outside the rumbling sound of the heavy locomotive moved past the depot and the screeching of the coach wheels stopping became louder as the depot door opened for people to prepare to board.

With that, Esther and Anne stood up and hugged Earl while Earl's father shook his son's hand. They walked out to the platform and in minutes the three Norrises stepped up into the coach, and Earl stood alone next to the track at the station in Saline, Montana—his home for the foreseeable future. *Unless the Saline manse has ghosts! What a story!"* he thought.

CHAPTER 18

Off and Running

A brief gust of warm wind stirred Earl's bedroom curtain awakening him the next morning. Earl tossed back the sheet and swung his feet to the floor to begin the first new day as an ordained minister in Saline, Montana. He shaved and dressed and by half past seven he was having the first of many solitary breakfasts—simple, just orange juice, cereal, toast and coffee. By eight-thirty he walked across the church yard to his study which was located in a little room behind the chancel. It was a bit chilly, though the sky was clear blue on this June morning. It would be warm by mid-morning, but for now Earl plugged in the small electric heater on the floor of his office, before sitting down at his desk. He was off and running, so to speak.

Raw pine boards on cinder blocks along the wall to the left of the door held his books, mostly seminary text books and a few he'd bought since. These almost filled the middle shelf. The bottom shelf remained more or less empty, but would soon hold an assortment of magazines and papers. Along the top shelf were a few items like a clock and photos of his family. In time more memorabilia would occupy the top shelf, and a couple more shelves would eventually be needed. For now, one group picture in a cedar wood frame was his first item of memorabilia. It was taken at Shore Crest, showing Lynette Ellerton with her brother, cousins and friends, including Earl. A happy-go-lucky bunch in bathing suits with their arms around each other against a background of the beach house and a bit of the Lake Michigan shore line. He looked at this photo and thought, *A million miles away and worlds apart.*

Opposite the door stood the small wooden desk at which Earl sat. It had been used by a succession of Saline pastors. Not much on it—yet. Behind the desk chair was an even smaller typewriter stand on which Earl had installed his battered manual Smith-Corona. He'd soon replace it with an electric Smith-Corona. There weren't many pictures on the walls. A few left over from Sunday School rooms like the familiar painting, showing Jesus and the children. His own selections would come in time. One photo he kept in a desk drawer—a studio photograph of Lynn Ellerton in a bare shouldered evening gown.

The tall windows behind his desk, and the higher one on the wall opposite the bookcases would need some drapes to hang on the empty rods above the windows. Whatever had been on them previously either belonged to the former pastor or they had been discarded due to sun rot. Two other pieces of furniture were the two un-matching side chairs in the area in front of the desk. The room was quite Spartan, but before too many years Earl would be wishing for a larger room to accommodate the inevitable accumulation of things. During daytime use the two tube fluorescent light on the high ceiling was adequate, but for study in the evenings another lamp would be needed. The most awkward arrangement was the wall phone behind the desk. Earl would need to ask the local telephone co-op to replace it with a cradle phone for his desk.

Otherwise Earl felt a mellow thrill as he took his seat and placed a blank piece of lined paper on his desk to begin planning his day—or days ahead—his life, really! Four years of college, three years in seminary and now he was ordained, installed and ready to be off and running. *Am I ready for this?* This thought made him open up the Bible on his desk to spend his first moments in personal devotions—reading some Scripture and uttering a silent prayer—the first of many in the days to come. The first phrase in the Bible reading of Psalm 133, suggested for the day caught his eye.

How very good and pleasant it is when kindred live together in unity! (Psalm 133:1)

It appeared to Earl that this summed up the experience of the congregation in Saline. He'd observed already how much people enjoyed each other's company at church functions. In listening to conversations informally and in the meetings he'd had with the selection committee he had been impressed with a prevailing unity of thought and opinion. Later in his life he would look back on these early Saline days and realize that in the 1950s unity and agreement prevailed in the church nationally. It was a condition which would begin to erode in the 60s.

In the midst of his thoughtful devotion he heard someone come into the building and walk down the bare wood aisle toward his office with echoing footsteps. It was Gertrude Gelenik.

"Good morning, Gertrude."

"Hello, Reverend."

"What can I do for you?"

"I came about Vacation Bible School."

"Yes."

"It's June 23 to 27."

"What are the plans?"

"That's what we've been waiting for . . . for you to come. We thought maybe you should call a meeting to let us know what we should be doing."

Earl was floored. He had never even attended a Vacation Bible School, let alone planned one. "Did you have one last summer?"

"Oh yes, we do this every year."

Earl thought about this for a few moments wondering how to begin. "Well, Gertrude, I suggest you call the people who usually help with this, and set up a meeting in the next day or two, and start to plan for this year."

"That sounds good, Reverend. That way we can all hear your plans. I'll get us together at my house tomorrow afternoon. You'll be there."

This was more a command than a question.

"Yes, I can be there."

"Good. Rev. Jones used to always plan this and assign us our various jobs."

"Well, I think we should all work that out together. I'll be there to help with the plans and arrangements. But you folks know how to do this, I'm sure."

Gertrude seemed hesitant at this statement but, having accomplished her mission, she excused herself. "I must do some things in the kitchen. Ella and I will see you tomorrow, Reverend."

Earl would discover that his predecessor had planned just about everything except the Women's Association meetings. Things would be different under Earl Norris's leadership. They would begin to discover this at the meeting the next afternoon.

The phone rang as Gertrude was going out the door. Earl got up and took the receiver off the hook on the wall. "Hello, this is Earl Norris."

"Hi, ol' buddy!"

The solemnity of the pastor's study in the church was shattered. Earl recognized Bob Taggert's voice and breezy approach. "Checking up already, are you?"

"Yeah, wanted to be sure you're up and at 'em."

"I am. Already had a caller—wanted me to plan Vacation Bible School . . . . no way, that's their job . . . . I told her to set up a meeting and I'd come to it, but that's all."

"Good start, pal. And good luck." He switched subjects to get at the real purpose for calling. "Seriously, Earl—your sister—I can't stop thinking about her! What I want to know is—is she 'spoken for' as they say?"

"No, my friend. Fair game, you might say."

"Is she still at the house?"

At this Earl felt sorry. "No, Bob, she left on the eastbound train yesterday."

"That's too bad. I was going to suggest I come by tonight and show her a big time in Miles City."

"The best I can do is to give you her address and phone number."

"She lives in the Chicago area? Is that the number I was given when we were at your place?"

"I assume so. Right now she's still at my folks'. In a week or two she'll be in Oak Park where she will begin her teaching career."

"I guess I'll have to start looking for a continuing education conference in Chicago."

Earl gave Anne's address and number. He hesitated, but then added, "If it's any help to you, friend, I think she was sort of taken with you."

"Thanks for that! Gives me some hope. Well I gotta run, but let's you and I get together one of these days."

"I'd like that."

"I'll phone."

Earl thought about the Forsyth ghost story. "Say, wait a minute. . . ."

"Yeah, what?"

"Have you heard that story about a ghost in the Forsyth manse?'

"Sure have. Why?"

"Well somebody was telling Anne about how it drove a minister and his family out not long ago. Is that true?"

"Sort of, but there were other reasons and the ghost gave him an excuse, is what I heard." Then Bob added, "But you know, I've got a book on ghosts in buildings in Montana. It's a serious book, but I don't believe most of it . . . but then . . . ."

"Well, thanks, Bob. I need to get to the land of the living in Saline."

"O.K. buddy. See you around."

Hank Hurlbutt was the last to arrive at the Conoco for the morning "club" meeting. When he did, Claude Miller wasted no time getting to the most current subject. "Well, did you folks get your new preacher put in?"

"Yep. Now he can handle all the old women."

"I suppose you got a good look at his girlfriend."

Hank turned to Darrel Reisner, but didn't say anything for a moment.

"Well—good looker—huh?" Reisner hoped this would get Hank going.

"Turns out she's his sister, not girlfriend. I guess she was here to help him fix up the manse before the big doin's." Hank looked a bit sheepish. "But I'm gonna keep track of him. Don't want any of this messin' around." Hank took a cigar out of the pocket in his bib overalls and chewed off the end before lighting it. After his first puff of smoke he continued. "Messin' around like that young buck over to Sage Creek. Don't want none of this Miles City stuff. And I found out there's another one of 'em around."

"Whad'ya mean?" Merle cut in after joining the group.

"Another single minister. Over to Terry. Taggert's his name. He was there at the meeting. Looked the type to me."

"What type's that?" Claude asked.

"The ladies' man type." Hank was quick to judge.

Reisner pushed him. "You better check things over ta Terry, Don't you think?"

"Well, I don't know. They better do that themselves."

"So what else's new?" Claude was tiring of the banter.

The best part of the Vacation Bible School meeting, as far as Earl was concerned, had been the caramel rolls fresh out of Gertrude's oven which she served with coffee as people gathered to plan the VBS. He had spent most of the time transferring responsibility. Gertrude had begun the meeting by reminding everyone. "Rev. Jones always used to be the VBS director. And so I suggest that Rev. Norris do that, and . . . ." She looked at Ella with a knowing glance. "You'd like to be the assistant, wouldn't you, Ella?"

It had taken some further new interpretation of the minister's job, to get things re-arranged. But before the meeting was over, Jane Ross had been persuaded to direct the school and with two assistants would plan the event. Earl would gladly advise. "But you folks have the experience and know-how. I'll learn from you!"

That was a revolutionary thought which those who had gathered at Geleniks carried away with them. An approach in which Earl had believed as he drove home from his first vacation Bible school meeting in Saline. When he got home he entered the empty manse. The silence struck him. The loneliness of the manse begged a new thought. *I ought to get a dog or a cat—something to greet me when I get home.*

He opened a can of spaghetti, heated it up for his supper and finished with a can of peaches. Such a supper was quickly over and the dishes were done quite easily. This gave Earl a chance to settle down in his living room with his current book—fun reading as he called it, a Thomas Hardy novel, *Return of the Native*. The phone rang. He made his way to the kitchen where the phone hung on the wall.

"Hello, Earl Norris here."

"Earl, this is Anne."

"Anne! What brings you to my ears?"

"I got a call from Bob Taggert last night."

"Yes?"

"Well, he was really friendly, and he wants to know if I plan to come out again to see you. And if I do, he sure wants to see me. When I told him I had no idea when I'd be out again he said that he was working on an idea for a study conference at Chicago Theological Seminary down on the south side, and if he came to that event maybe we could get together."

"How did all that sit with you, Anne?"

"I'm thrilled. I thought he was neat. But just my luck for him to be eleven hundred miles away. What do you think of him, Earl?"

"I really like the guy. I think we are going to become good friends."

"But he's so different from you, big brother!"

"I know. That's just it. He's a welcome change from thinking my way all the time."

"I guess you're right. Maybe that's part of the attraction I feel."

Earl thought abut the eleven hundred mile distance.

"There's the phone, you know."

"Expensive."

"You can write."

"He suggested that."

"OK, see where that gets you two."

After they concluded their conversation Earl returned to his book, but he kept thinking about his sister and his new friend. The idea intrigued him.

Earl's official board, the session, would be meeting in a week. The monthly session meetings would consider and direct the life of the church in Saline. From his study of church government in seminary, Earl was aware of a symbiotic relationship he and the session would share. He would conduct its meetings as its moderator and would lead the session to a deepening understanding of its responsibilities. He would be the "idea person" introducing the session to his vision for the church in Saline and the session's roll in developing new church program. But at the same time the session would be in some sense a supervisor over Earl's ministry and performance, although according to church law Earl was under the jurisdiction of the presbytery. In fact the session itself was under presbytery's governance charged with the task of providing Presbyterian worship, education, fellowship and pastoral care in Saline, Montana. The congregation and the presbytery had called Earl Norris to help in this mission.

Armed with this philosophy of service, Earl met with Homer Stein, the clerk of session, a few days before the session meeting. Over succeeding months the two would meet in this way each month to prepare for the forthcoming meeting. In his first consultation with Homer, Earl discovered that his predecessor had not been as symbiotic as Earl intended to be.

Homer began by asking. "Rev. Norris, what do you want us to do at the meeting next Thursday?"

"First off, Homer, I'm Earl, just like you are Homer!"

"I like that, Earl. We always used to call our minister *Reverend Jones*. Never *Burton*."

"Well let's go for *Earl!*" Homer's statement didn't surprise Earl judging from what he had discovered about his predecessor's style. "As to what you should do, I think we should begin with the question, 'What is your customary agenda for meetings?' And what items seem to surface as needing attention next week?"

"That's what Rev. Jones used to outline for us."

"Besides the usual minutes and treasurer's reports, I assume there will be reports from committees."

"Well, yes, but Rev. Jones usually spoke for the committees." Homer seemed to hesitate, wondering if he should add to that. "If you really want to know, Earl, the minister usually told the committees what they should decide and do."

"Didn't people on committees have their own opinions? What if they didn't like what the minister was suggesting?"

Homer pondered these questions for a moment. "I think the thing that made this approach work is the fact that most everyone was of one mind on things and usually their ideas were pretty much what the minister was suggesting." Homer thought about this some more. "A lot of what we did was by consensus—following Rev. Jones' suggestions."

"If that was the case, what in the world did the committees do after he left?"

"That's just it. They didn't do much of anything—just maintaining absolutely necessary things. During the interim, so often, matters up for discussion were shelved in committee meetings and in session with the comment, 'We better wait to see what the new minister wants.'"

Earl leaned back in his chair, closed his eyes as he looked up toward the high ceiling—a prayer passed through his mind. He looked at Homer. "Homer, things are going to be different. The way I look at my role and relationship to the session and its committees is going to be very different from what apparently you have been used to."

Homer smiled and admitted,. "I sort of thought so."

At that Earl launched into a description of his philosophy of leadership and how he thought that should play out in the life of the church in Saline.

"Like a breath of fresh air!" Homer was enthusiastic. "I think you need to share this with the folks at our meeting next week. Let's give them a chance to discuss this fully. I think most of the elders will take to this idea as I do. There may be one or two who will see it as involving more work."

"It will be more work for the elders, but that should be more satisfying than just being rubber stamps."

Homer agreed and together the two men put together the docket for the upcoming meeting.

The following week both Earl and Homer were delighted to find that the session liked the new approach. In the coming months and years, this style of leadership on Earl's part would enhance the life and effectiveness of the Saline church beyond measure.

This approach allowed Earl to devote his time and energy to his role as worship leader and preacher and his ministry as a pastor to members of his congregation.

Months went by and Mae Benson got the idea of inviting the former pulpit committee members to her home for a social evening. But her hidden agenda would be Earl Norris and how he was doing. Proper church procedure would never permit such a behind-the-scenes meeting, but a social evening would slip through unnoticed.

She phoned Jane Moss. "Jane, I'm inviting the committee members and spouses for dessert next Sunday evening . . . . No, I know, the committee doesn't function anymore, but I thought it would be fun to do a "quality check on our work" so to speak now that Earl has been with us for a time . . . . Good. I'm glad you can come . . . . While you are at it, could you come early and give me a hand with the party? Thanks, Jane. . . . Come at sevenish."

Jane arrived at seven and the others around seven-thirty. They obviously enjoyed getting back together and the conversation quickly turned to Earl. "Well, what do you think, Homer?"

"I am pleased. He is making the rounds of the congregation, visiting in as many homes as he can. After he gets around, he plans to call on others in the community who don't have a church home."

"And Wyoma and I think he's a good preacher, don't we, Wyo?"

"We sure do. He's got the young people listening."

Mae had been listening and seemed troubled. Jane picked up on this. "What do you think of his sermons, Mae?"

"Oh, they're fine . . . but . . . ."

"But what?" Jane pressed her.

"Oh, I've heard some criticism of his always mentioning the hungry and how we ought to be feeding them."

"Well, we should." Jane declared.

Mae was still troubled. ". . . . But I guess it's when he gets into trying to explain why there are poor and how we ought to change things so that there wouldn't be so much poverty."

Jane accepted this and let the matter drop. But she would remember this and there would come a time when she would be compelled to defend Earl.

"He's doing a good job with the youth group. Our Ella's too old for it, but I've been sending her over to the church with cookies and refreshments for the meetings," Gertrude crowed.

"That time last month when our hired man, Wayne, got hurt working with the hay bailer, Pastor Norris was at the hospital to see him that very night. And Wayne isn't even a member."

Buck more or less drew the assessment to a close when he said. "Now all we have to worry about is that he stays here."

"And finding him a nice wife!" Gertrude added.

Everyone knew whom she had in mind.

"Talk about him staying, Homer, has he gotten your *Blue Skies* paper?"

"As soon as the presbytery office heard of his acceptance they sent it to him, along with other information about the presbytery. They do that for each new pastor."

"Well, I hope he has it and has read it. That usually helps—if they read it and take it to heart."

Homer assured the others. "I know he has it and has read it. He told me."

As the group continued to discuss Earl, it became apparent that Earl had made a good start. He was off and running smoothly—for the most part. And a few times when things were not going so smoothly Earl found in Cecil Graham an experienced mature wisdom which would help him more than once.

In his later years Earl would remember his early days in ministry at the end of the late 1950's. *That was a good time to start, a time when the church and faith were firmly held in people's view of things. What God wanted, most everyone wanted. And so what the church taught and what preachers preached was pretty generally accepted. Unanimous or near unanimous votes were the common experience of session and committee meetings. Eisenhower was in the White House, there was a new and widespread interest in church. Things were going well for Christian efforts nationally—and in Saline, Montana.*

Earl was off and running.

PART II

The 1960s and 1970s

CHAPTER 19

"Fairest of Them All?"

The first year of a new minister's life in a community like Saline is often referred to as the "honeymoon," during which both the pastor and congregation enjoy each other and are willing to overlook any flaws which might be emerging. After the honeymoon, trouble can sometimes begin to appear. However, for Earl Norris and the Community Church of Saline, Montana, there didn't appear to be any trouble on the horizon. In fact, things were going quite well as he began his second year. He was doing all the expected tasks: preaching on Sundays, of course, teaching a Sunday school class, and leading a youth group each Sunday evening. By and large his style of leadership had been accepted, and by most, it was appreciated. From that first session meeting, Earl had encouraged initiative and follow-through on the part of elders and committee members. Earl adopted the time-honored minister's schedule—in his study in the mornings and out and about in the afternoons, calling on people in their homes and in the hospital. And there were funerals, but not many weddings. A mark of the age profile of the congregation.

Earl was busy, but not too busy to avoid periods of loneliness. He often thought about how his life would be different if Lynn had stuck with him. Somebody to come home to after an afternoon of calling, or to curl up with in the evening after church meetings were over. They could have enjoyed days off exploring the area around Saline, so different from anything either of them had known in the Midwest. But this life which Earl had chosen wasn't for her, apparently. She hadn't caught the spirit of adventure, or the sense of call to ministry, both of which had motivated him. When he was honest with himself, he knew very well that the life he and Lynn had planned was that of the Ellertons and Shore Crest. It would have been too great a jump to bring Lynn to Saline. But, nevertheless, he yearned for her to be near him again.

In contrast, Earl, observed what was going on in Bob Taggert's life. Soon after meeting Earl's sister, Anne, Bob had begun correspondence with her. Phone calls added to their growing long distance relationship. In the fall he had taken a study leave in Chicago. This gave them a chance to make up for lost time. During Anne's spring break she had come to Montana—to visit her brother—but more important to be with Bob as much as possible.

Earl's own loneliness peaked after Anne returned to the manse from her last evening with Bob. Earl was up late reading.

"Earl! I've got some news!"

It was obvious to Earl that his sister was deeply excited. "What's that, Sis?"

"Bob asked me to marry him!"

"What! I had no idea things had progressed to that point."

"They have."

"Well, did you say 'yes'?"

"Oh Earl—can't you tell? I did! We haven't set a date yet. I need to finish out this school year. And I don't know whether to sign a contract for next year. It depends on how Bob feels about Terry, and whether or not he'll look for another church."

"I see." Earl was quiet for a moment. "Anne, have you honestly looked at what being a minister's wife will involve?"

"Sort of. What are you getting at?"

"Well, obviously I don't know the whole answer, but I've seen some unhappy minister's wives."

"Oh, Earl, you're a worry wort. With Bob it's going to be all right—in fact it'll be great!"

Earl could sense Anne's happiness and he had a change of heart. "I'm really happy for you both. I can't wait to talk to Bob."

She looked a bit sheepish. "That will be sooner than you think. I've invited him here for breakfast tomorrow morning before I have to leave on the train. Is that OK?"

"Sure, if he's satisfied with Puffed Wheat!" Earl grinned.

"I told him I'd fix him bacon and eggs."

"I bet he'd come if it was just an old piece of dry toast!"

The next day after Anne had left for Chicago and Bob had gone back to Terry, Earl felt an aching emptiness.

Church people in a town like Saline, Montana hold on to what has become an outmoded evaluation. The members of the Community Church of Saline still regarded the minister, or "preacher" as he was most often referred to, as a person with a higher status than others in the community enjoyed. Without a physician in town the preacher would be at the top of the list, even surpassing the local school principal. While some ministers seemed to enjoy this adulation, Earl found it embarrassing, especially during his first year in Saline. This caused him the most difficulty when it came to how the people responded to his bachelorhood. In plain terms he was considered a "good catch." This caused a good bit of speculation from time to time on the part of the people. What he didn't know was that it had often been a subject for conversation at the Women's Association meetings. Earl felt himself to be in an awkward situation. There seemed to be only one eligible candidate in the congregation and everyone knew it. The older widows didn't qualify. No other prospects in Saline. Where else was he to find prospects?

From the very start Gertrude Gelenik had been most solicitous. She had arranged on many occasions for the Rev. Mr. Norris and her daughter, Ella, to be in close proximity. Gertrude had Ella's cap set on Earl, though it seemed less likely that Ella had any such ambitions. Gertrude considered her Ella to be "the fairest of them all," no matter that there weren't any others nearby to compete for the new minister's attentions. As a single man, Earl found himself often invited to meals in the homes of his parishioners, but nowhere as often as at the Gelenik home.

Finally after a year of having experienced such campaigning, Earl thought he should at least invite Ella on a date. No harm in that. It was only right, considering all the delicious fried chicken he'd consumed at her mother's table. The day he'd phoned to speak to Ella became a red letter day for Gertrude, if not for Ella. After she hung up her mother asked in anticipation. "What did he want, dear?"

Ella replied without enthusiasm. "He's asked me to go to the movies with him in Miles City next Friday evening."

"You said 'yes,' I hope."

"I told him that I would go with him."

"I hope you showed a little more interest than that."

"Oh, Mother."

Friday came and Earl drove into the Gelenik yard around 5:30. He felt like a local high schooler. Certainly more awkward than the way he had felt when he'd called as a pastor. He visited briefly with Karl Gelenik while Gertrude was in Ella's bedroom helping her "to look her best," she'd declared. If the truth be known, Karl felt about as awkward as Earl. He did not share his wife's eagerness and seemed to sense that Earl didn't either.

Ella emerged and Earl ushered her out to his car as quickly as was proper. Thus began his first date since Lynn. They drove into Miles City without saying very much to each other besides the necessary niceties. As they drove into town they stopped at the Red Rocks Café on the east side of Miles City. They got settled in a booth and before they looked over the menu, Earl looked across the table to Ella. He was struck with her quizzical look and couldn't help but comment.

"Ella, you have such a curious expression."

"I'm sure I do. You've been bamboozled into taking me out by my dear mother. You and I both know that, don't we?"

This disarmed Earl making him speechless at first. "She's certainly been maneuvering things in that way. But what's to make you assume I wouldn't have asked you out on my own initiative?"

Ella looked even more quizzical when she offered this rejoinder. "If that's the case, it sure took you a long time!"

Earl was speechless again. Ella had seemed mousey when she was around her mother. Now, on her own she was anything but mousey. In fact—embarrassingly frank.

"I first had to check out all the many other eligible young maidens in the congregation. Of course that took time." Earl made sure she saw the mischief in his eyes. They both knew very well that she was the only one to check out.

"I deserved that."

The waitress came to their table. Ella said, "We're not ready, Can you come back in a minute or two?"

"Sure."

With that they each looked at a menu to make their selections.

"Now, my dear!" Earl spoke in mock formality. Then with another mischievous grin he went on. "I want you to order whatever you want, just so it costs plenty! I think we need to make the very most of this date, don't you?"

Ella pretended to look for the most high priced item.

The waitress returned and they ordered.

Ella ordered first. "I'll have the steak sandwich and fries. French dressing on my salad. Coffee with the meal."

"Make that two."

Earl switched moods and looking at Ella he sensed a certain sadness. "Ella, tell me about yourself. Up until today you have been Gertrude's daughter. Who is the real Ella Gelenik?"

She picked up on the serious nature of his question. "Well to begin with I was little when my folks moved to Saline from Minot, North Dakota. Dad was a hired man on a wheat farm there. But then he got a chance to buy a farm here from a cousin of his father's who made him an easy deal. The succession of people who had lived on our place here had been renters, and not too good at that. Anyway, when I got old enough to want to do things with other kids, I discovered that the neighbors treated my family like scum. I found out later that they treated us as if we were renting."

"Why was that? It must have been known that you folks had bought the place."

"I don't know. I think the reputation sort of attached itself to the farm itself." Ella went on "Anyway that put us a cut below everyone around. The kids picked up on this and teased my brother and me. It was cruel and it was awful for us, especially me. To make a long story short, I didn't have any, what you'd call close friends. My world was my brother, parents, my horse, and me. So far as the boys were concerned I didn't exist. So, as a result, I didn't date in high school."

Earl cut in at this point. "How about since school?" He dared to ask since she had brought up the subject herself.

"A little. After high school my dad offered me the job of 'hired man' for him. One of my jobs was to go to town for stuff. There was a young guy working at the feed store who asked me out a few times. It was ok, but I finally concluded that I'd rather be riding my horse."

"Your horse connection is serious business, isn't it?"

"It is. I've tried my hand at rodeo-ing, you know, women's barrel racing."

"Been in competition?"

"Not yet, but I'd like to enter the next time there's a rodeo comin' here to the county."

"What about long term? What do you want to do?

Earl noticed a blank expression void of enthusiasm when Ella replied.

"Oh, I don't know—maybe a vet."

When Earl tried to show encouragement, all she said was, "Too much school, though."

Earl switched the conversation to her brother. "You mentioned your brother. Where is he?"

"He quit high school and moved to Nevada. He works for a mining company there, driving one of those huge trucks."

"Does he have a family?"

"No, he's not married. . . . Makes a lot of money, though."

This left Earl without much to say. After the café, they made it to the movie theater in time for the feature. It turned out to be about as stimulating as their conversation had been. After the show there didn't seem much to do. Everything in town was closed for the night—except the bars. So they drove back to Saline.

When Earl dropped her off at her house she thanked him and went in.

Earl drove away saddened, not for himself, but for Ella.

When he asked her a couple of weeks later if she would like to try another movie she answered. "Thanks, Earl, but I need to spend a lot of time practicing with my horse for the rodeo. There's one comin' in a month."

Earl was not disappointed. In fact, if he really wanted to admit it to himself, he was relieved. As he thought about his feelings, he became aware of a deep misgiving which had begun to take shape in his consciousness, one of those feelings down deep to which you can't assign a name. *Much as I've come to like the folks here in Montana, there's a difference which is discomforting. I just don't feel like them. For the life of me I can't understand Ella's fascination with horses.* This undefined difference was something Gertrude had not understood, but Ella had. And now Earl was coming to acknowledge the culture gap between Earl Norris and the people of Saline. A gap which intensified his loneliness.

However, Earl would come to realize that to use the gap idea as an all encompassing explanation would be to oversimplify the social context of his new life in Montana. Not everyone was into rodeos, he would discover.

A partial answer to Earl's loneliness came in an unexpected form. In stark contrast to prevailing community interest in the western rodeo, Earl found one person interested in the game of chess. Earl had discovered chess in eighth grade when he and a neighbor boy had frequently played, but in recent years his playing of the game had been dormant. Here in Saline he found a chess enthusiast on a call at the Perry farm where he had been told bachelor twins lived. On his return visit the two men played a game of chess.

"Check." Martin announced. "Oh, I didn't see that," Earl acknowledged, deep in thought. Finally he moved his Queen diagonally three spaces to the right.

Martin immediately moved one of his Knights to a position which Earl hadn't seen. This move effectively blocked any escape for Earl's king. "Checkmate!"

The two men sitting across from each other at a small table smiled at each other while Earl admitted defeat.

"But you played very well. Keep that up and you'll have me one of these days."

"I'm not so sure, Mr. Perry." It had been their first game, only having recently met this unique man.

"Can you stay for a cup of tea?"

Earl looked at his watch. "Yes, I think so."

"Excuse me for a bit and I'll have some for us."

The older man got up and went into his kitchen leaving, Earl to his thoughts.

A couple of logs burned slowly in the fireplace illuminating the neatly kept living room of Martin Perry's log cabin. The books in a floor to ceiling book case were evenly placed. And numerous magazines were stacked in orderly piles here and there. Furthermore the place appeared much cleaner than one would imagine for a bachelor. Earl wasn't surprised after having driven up the lane a few months earlier on his first visit, a pastoral visit at that time. He saw none of the usual litter of discarded machinery. The lawn around the house had obviously been cut and cared for through the summer months. The logs of the cabin had apparently been recently seal coated and the other wood moldings painted a dark green. Earl had been impressed, and when he met Martin Perry, the man himself had impressed him. When Earl had visited Martin he found him wearing clean uncrumpled jeans, with a denim shirt over which he'd had on a woolen suit jacket. At around seventy Martin Perry still had a full head of graying hair, which was neatly trimmed.

In some ways, the most surprising aspect of the scene on Earl's initial call had been the small table with a chess board set with the chess pieces so arranged as to be the midst of a game in progress. Now, on his second visit with Martin Perry, the two had played a game of chess at the distinctive little table. As Earl waited for Martin to return to the living room with his tea things, he replayed in his mind his conversation with Martin on the first visit. Earl had asked Perry:

"Living alone as you do, I can't quite figure out the chess board set for two players. Some sort of solitaire?"

"Oh, that." Perry said with a grin. "I play correspondence chess and use the board to figure my moves.'

When Earl showed some question at this explanation, Martin went on. "I'm in the midst of six games right now. One in San Francisco, two in Illinois. Three in Georgia. We send our moves back and forth to each other on post cards." Martin opened a small drawer under the table and pulled out a stack of post cards. He took one and showed it to Earl. "Here is one."

> Mr. Perry:
> P-KR3
> Dr. Morgan

"Do you know what move that is?"

Earl thought about the letters and hesitantly said, "Pawn should move to the third square along the row of the rook on the king's side of the board . . . ?"

"Yes, 'pawn to king's rook 3.' Then when I determine my next move, I'll send him a similar card. Such as: Kt-KB3."

Earl thought a moment. "Knight to King's Bishop 3?"

"That's right."

"That must take a long time."

"It certainly does, but then I seem to have all the time in the world."

Earl's thoughts were interrupted when Martin returned to the living room with a tray of tea and cookies. "Let's take our tea over here in these chairs by the fire."

The two men sat in comfortable easy chairs by the fire, taking the opportunity to become better acquainted with each other. Earl began.

"Martin, tell me about yourself. I know about your chess playing now, but what about the rest of your life? I take it you have been in Saline a long time."

"Yes, I have. My father and mother were one of the earliest filers in this county. My father had been in the army and had been stationed at Ft. Keogh located where the Tongue River flows into the Yellowstone just west of where Miles City is today. That was back in the 80s." He served under General Nelson A. Miles. During that time he fell in love with a young woman in Miles City. When he was mustered out of the Army they were married. Father had been a friend of a nephew of the general who was George A. Miles. He was a banker in Miles City. So father went to work at the bank. Well, the upshot of all that after my father and mother had twin boys they filed on this place and then they moved here when my twin brother and I were three years old."

"So this was your childhood home?"

"Yes, and my brother, Marvin's, of course. Until he was killed in 1940 when a tractor rolled over him. The two of us were running this place at the time. Father and Mother had retired to Miles, where they have since died."

"You have lived here alone since then?"

"Neither Marvin nor I ever married, so, you're right. I've been alone."

Martin seemed not to want to say much more. "Here, Earl, have another cookie and I'll pour you some more tea."

"Thank you."

"Now tell me how things are at the church in Saline."

Earl didn't know how to respond to this surprising question coming from a person whom he thought had no connection with the church. "Well, everything is coming along quite well. Or at least I'm feeling good about my work and the people's response." Earl hesitated not knowing what else to say, but a bit uncomfortable with the question. "Or do you know something I don't and that's why you ask?"

"Oh no. I'm not a member and don't discuss church much. I gave up on church a long time ago. But I come from a church family. My grandmother was a charter member of the Miles City church, and my mother attended the first Sunday school class there. I guess that's why they keep me on the rolls. Every so often I get a letter telling me that they are about to put me on the inactive list, or worse yet, take me off the rolls. So, when I get the letter I send in a contribution and then they're ok for another year." Martin waited for Earl's reaction.

"Well, Martin, you're 'legal' so to speak, but it doesn't sound as though the church does you much good, does it?"

"No, no good at all. But now with Mother it was real."

"I'm impressed that your grandmother was a charter member."

"That was quite a story. One day in January of 1879—a very cold January it was—35 below zero it got for a day or two. Anyway, during this cold period a minister from Helena showed up ready to start a new congregation in Miles City. Rev. J.D. Hewitt arrived in a lumber wagon with no springs. He had crossed Indian country over which there were no roads. He'd come at the urging of the old Presbyterian missionary, Sheldon Jackson, who had founded quite a number of Presbyterian churches including Rev. Hewitt's church in Helena. Have you heard of Sheldon Jackson?"

Earl hesitated. "I think so, in an American Church History class, I believe."

"At any rate," Martin resumed his account. "J.D. Hewitt held the first service in an unfurnished room above a store at Main and Fourth Streets as soon as he arrived in January of 1879. My grandmother and her young daughter attended, and then Rev. Hewitt started a Sunday School for seven children including my mother. Soon after that he returned to Helena, I think. Anyway, a little over a year later Rev. W.L. Austin arrived and organized First Presbyterian Church with 13 members. Now the interesting thing about this group was that almost half of them were from Pontiac, Illinois, including my maternal grandmother's family."

"Interesting. That's how your family became Presbyterian."

"Well my grandparents had been Presbyterians back in Pontiac. Then after my parents were married and Marvin and I were born we were baptized in the Miles City church and later on joined. That was just before the family moved to this place."

"Did your parents transfer their membership to Saline then?"

"No, they didn't. As a matter of fact they never took much part here. They were so busy. As a result us boys didn't get much church, you might say." He seemed to review what he'd said. "But Mother taught us the Bible, and in fact we even had evening prayers on Sundays in our home." He thought some more. "But after Mother and Dad were gone Marvin and I let that go. I think we were too embarrassed."

"I think I can see what you mean."

"To use the term an old tent revival preacher used, 'Satan had won.' I guess I'd call it a *checkmate*."

Earl could see a troubled expression come over his new friend's face. He heard him mutter to himself something like "*but now . . . at my age . . . .*"

"No—only *Check*—Martin."

"What do you mean?"

"You still have a move!"

Martin shuffled in his chair as if to get up. "Some more tea?"

Earl could see that the offer was more out of courtesy than it was to prolong the conversation.

"No thank you. I really ought to be leaving. It has been a most enjoyable afternoon."

"We must do this again. Next time you might beat me!"

With that Earl took his leave. As he left Perry's lane and headed back to Saline he reflected on his visit, marveling at the difference in feeling he'd experienced with Martin in comparison to other calls he had been making on church folk. The fact that Martin was not a church member and had not participated in church, but nevertheless showed a great deal of openness to Earl seemed to take the pressure off. *I didn't have to represent the church, either by defending it or by promoting it. We could just be friends. That felt good.*

This visit and chess game would be the first of many for Earl and Martin. A growing relationship between the two men would provide each one not only with a chess partner, but with meaningful discussions of questions about life which each would raise. Earl would continue to be surprised at how well read Martin was and at what insights he would share.

CHAPTER 20

Sitka

The young woman pressed her forehead against the small window. She looked down onto the glistening Pacific. Slender and attractive, elegantly dressed in a black blazer over a white sweater and gray flannel slacks, she'd boarded the Boeing prop-jet at Sea-Tac, a stone's throw from the very spot where the aircraft had been manufactured in Seattle. After a brief landing at Ketchikan, her first touch down in Alaska, she soon began to feel the aircraft shuddering as it was slowing down, lowering itself for another landing. The aircraft banked first to the left, giving her a glimpse of stately Mt. Edgecomb as it came into view. Then banking to the right, the wing swung downward over a small city poised on the water's edge. Suddenly a narrow island came into view. Beneath her she spotted a landing strip on the island. It was steadily growing in size as the pilot was positioning the approach of the aircraft for a safe and comfortable landing. Moments later she was gently bounced in her seat when the commercial airliner eased itself onto the pavement. The cabin shuddered when the engines roared in reverse as the jet proceeded on the tarmac to the front of the small terminal. The plane came to a halt and the engines started to shut down. Inside the cabin people began getting up from their seats, reaching into the overhead compartments to gather their carry-on luggage. Soon the aisle was filled with passengers waiting to deplane through the exit at the rear.

The cabin door opened and the line of passengers began to move toward the rear. Lynette Ellerton carefully made her way down the steps onto the tarmac and walked toward the terminal building on Japonski Island. When all the passengers had deplaned they were directed to a boat dock on the bank of the narrow channel of water separating Japonski from the main island. Lynn stepped onto a waiting launch which took her to Baranof Island and her destination: Sitka, Alaska—at one time the capital of a Russian colony on the western shore of the North American continent.

As she disembarked and stepped up onto the wharf at Sitka, she spotted a young Native American man, with coal black hair and a strikingly bronzed complexion. He was facing the oncoming passengers holding a sign: *Sheldon Jackson College*. She strode over to him and introduced herself. "I'm Lynette Ellerton from Chicago. I've come as a volunteer in mission."

"Welcome, Miss Ellerton. I'm Ben. We have been expecting you. I'll to take you to the college."

With that he took Lynn's bags and loaded them into a station wagon bearing the college logo on its side. He opened the passenger door for her, took his place behind the wheel and began the short drive east on Lincoln, Sitka's main street. They drove past St. Michael's Cathedral with its Russian Orthodox onion dome. Literally in the middle of the street in downtown Sitka, it dominated the entire scene as Lynn eagerly looked out of the station wagon. The young newcomer was much impressed by the quaint old white and gray structure towering above nearby commercial buildings a few blocks in from the harbor.

The drive continued almost the entire length of Lincoln along the edge of a bay on her right. She saw that it was crowded with small boats of many varieties. They reached College Street where Ben turned left and up a slight rise. Thus Lynette Ellerton was brought onto the campus of Sheldon Jackson College. She felt a tingling sensation in her finger tips as her nervous anticipation heightened. She was finally arriving, over two thousand miles from her home far removed from the familiar surroundings of her childhood and youth. Here in Sitka she would live and work for the next twelve months. Here the course of her life would be changed.

Lynn was sent by the Board of National Missions of her denomination to the new state of Alaska as a volunteer. Sheldon Jackson College is dedicated to providing quality higher education to Alaskan youth, many of whom are from the native tribes of Alaska. To accomplish its mission it depends upon Christian volunteers from throughout the lower forty-eight. Such persons are brought to Sheldon Jackson College to fill support staff positions throughout the college. Lynette's assignment would be to work in the college library.

While this experience on which she was about to embark would bring significant changes in her perspective on her life, it would be unfair to attribute the new direction in her life solely to her work in Sitka. Significant changes had begun to occur in Lynette Ellerton's life during the six months prior to her flight to Alaska. Since college she had worked in the business office of Ellerton Manufacturing as a special assistant to her father. During those years of effective work for the family company her devotion and loyalty had been tested at times when she became privy to some of the ways her father operated. She discovered him to be ruthless toward his competition and a tyrant over his employees. When she was honest with herself she had to admit that this was indeed the father she had always known—only more so. When she had pondered her father's autocratic ways she had said to herself more than once, *No wonder Mother drinks so much.* She had often thought about how her life was leading nowhere, just as her mother's had led nowhere. She had frequently kicked herself for having let Don go. He'd wanted her to come to New Mexico, but when she refused she heard no more from him.

Lynn's disillusionment with her father was coupled with fearful disappointment with her mother. She found that it did her no good to try and talk about these things with her brother. He had become such an unquestioning follower of his father that she doubted that he saw any of the painful flaws she had come to recognize. In some ways it had been the same with Gail Abernathy. On a number of occasions she and Gail had discussed Lynn's father, but Gail had always seen him as the "Lord of the Manor" at Shore Crest, and had fallen under the spell of his strong personality. On the other hand, Gail had not taken kindly to the idea of Lynn's relationship with Don, and so never encouraged Lynn to re-establish contact with him in New Mexico.

For Lynn the break came at the time of her mother's death six months previous. Eleanor Ellerton died of cirrhosis of the liver. Alcohol had taken its ultimate toll. Gerald Ellerton alienated his daughter more deeply when he became even more tyrannical after his wife's death. So much so, that Lynn could no longer work for him, and found that she needed to stay away from him altogether. Her aversion to her father, and to her own brother as well, spelled the end of family life for Lynette Ellerton.

Her mother's funeral had been on a Wednesday. She had assumed that her father would remain home for the rest of the week and that they would spend time at home, recovering from the emotional trauma of Eleanor Ellerton's death and the services which followed. However, her father appeared at breakfast on Thursday morning in his usual suit and tie. When Lynn looked up in surprise his response was curt and demanding.

"Yes, of course, we'll return to the office this morning. I assume you'll be ready."

That was all he said. This was the breaking point for Lynn. Stifling her tears she went to her room to dress for work. The next day she gave her notice, and in a month left Ellerton Manufacturing. In many ways she left her father and brother as well.

She found a job in a small office just outside the Loop in Chicago, working for a manufacturer's representative, who had a few salesmen wholesaling sunglasses to drug stores throughout the Midwest. Lynn commuted to the office from the near north side where she had found a room in the McCormick YWCA on Dearborn and Oak. She became acquainted with some of the other young women staying at the "Y." Along with some of her new friends she joined a young business and professional group at Fourth Presbyterian Church nearby on Michigan Boulevard. It was in connection with this group that she found out about the opportunities to do mission volunteering for her denomination. She was touched by the stories of volunteers who were making a significant difference in the lives of people elsewhere in the world.

The transformation in Lynn ran much deeper than merely a change of job and moving to another location. In many ways she was experiencing a spiritual conversion, a turning from *the service of self to service to others,* as she would later understand it. She had come to recognize the self-absorption of her brother as well as that of her father and mother. Her mother's death from a self-destructive lifestyle heightened Lynn's introspection. She became terrified at the prospect of a life which would follow a similar downward spiral. Her father had wanted her to find a young man who could be groomed into following his footsteps into the company. A hope in which Earl had frustrated Ellerton earlier when he had rejected a career in the family business for a calling to the ministry. Lynn had shared in her father's hope for Earl, but now her mother's death had changed all that.

Lynn's change of perspective happened first as a negative. She came to know what she did not want. *No way!* became her motto. Developing a positive thrust for her life would take some help from one of the pastors at Fourth church, who helped her turn her focus to the needs of others. Through a series of conferences with the pastor as well as discussions in the young adult group, her own sense of mission began to emerge. She felt a call from God to do what she could to help make the world a better place.

In one such consultation the pastor challenged her. "Why don't you consider spending a year as a mission volunteer somewhere to see how God might be calling you to a life of service?"

Lynn was ready for this suggestion. As a result of that consultation, Lynn began the process which would send her to Sitka and put her in the library of Sheldon Jackson College. *To make my life count for something. To make a difference in the lives of others,* she thought as she pondered her decision to apply for a volunteer position.

One evening when visiting her father and her brother she told them of her plans to go to Alaska on a mission project. Her father's response was predictable. "What do you want to do that for? You'll be throwing your life away, girl!"

Her brother chimed in. "That's dumb."

That evening as she rode into the city on the elevated train she was sad. Alone and sad. But all the more determined.

Now as Lynette Ellerton introduced herself to Sheldon Jackson's Director of Volunteers, and as she was briefed on the arrangements for her work and life at the college, she was excited and eager to begin. It would be a life changing experience for her, more so than she could know at the outset. Perhaps her deepest anticipation was the meeting of new friends, and in a sense being adopted "into a new family" here in Sitka, Alaska, this family dedicated to service.

CHAPTER 21

Witch Hunt

The population of a community like Saline is usually quite homogenous. For the most part surnames will reflect a common northern European heritage. Minorities are absent or invisible. With the Crow and Northern Cheyenne reservations not far to the south of Saline, there is a trickle of folk from reservations passing through. But these neighbors are most always seen as not belonging in Saline. It follows that there is an almost 100% agreement on political issues—conservative—anti-government, except when it comes to federal agricultural assistance programs. And most agree on moral issues as well. Most folk want government agencies, especially school districts, to be the guardians of Christian morals. In Saline only few variations in this political monochrome were to be found. The Walter Norlands of the W Lazy N ranch, and some of the teachers in the local school. But then there was also Martin Perry, whom no one could figure out, making him fair game for those who liked to look for "enemies of the U. S. of A." as some of the local patriots liked to say. Given the average story of people in the community it would pretty well be judged that most of the men were veterans of World War II.

Because Perry was such a loner he was vulnerable to suspicion. Talk among the Conoco club members often revolved around "those subversive post cards he always gets and sends." This feeling intensified when it was reported by one of the members who saw Perry at the post office looking at his mail. "I looked over his shoulder and you'd never believe what was written on them cards!"

"What?"

"Stuff like: *Kt-KB3* Or *P-KR3*. Them's code words, I know!"

"Sounds like some kind of plot, if you ask me!"

134

The Saline School District has seven teachers, four for the elementary level, three in the high school. While there has been a fairly high turnover from year to year, a few teachers and their families have been in the community for a relatively long time. Michael Jankowski is one of the long termers, having been in Saline for eleven years. Mr. Jankowski teaches history and science in the high school. Unlike most of the other teachers, he never attends church.

Michael Jankowski is the kind of teacher who elicits loyalty in his students, creating something of a following. Sort of a "Pied Piper." Kids like him, and the better students are apt to become influenced by his opinions. This often leads to some heated discussions around the dinner tables in Saline. Most parents consider such alternative ideas which their kids have picked up from Mr. Jankowski "just a phase." Some are more troubled by Jankowski's influence. *Liberal views which don't fit in here*, many feel.

"School looks to be out in a couple of days." Dale Benson opened the serious part of "the meeting" of "the club" with this point of departure.

Most of the "reg'lars" were crowded in the Conoco on a very rainy morning in May. As each one had hastily "blown" into the door getting out of the swirling rain, the inevitable reference to weather was uttered. "Good weather for ducks." "Boy, we need it." "Them weather guys on KATL got it wrong. Said there'd be 10% chance of precip." "Looks more like 100% to me." "Still said to be a drought year, though."

Hank Hurlbutt picked up on Dale's comment about school. "Yeah, it'll be good to get the kid back—to do some good for me on the place. Instead of all that pinko stuff he's been spoutin.'"

"He been spreadin' that stuff again?"

"What stuff? Who's doing that?" Reisner acted as if he didn't know.

"Yeah, it's that Jankowski fella." Hank's snarl deepened. "S'posed ta teach American history and instead it's all that Commy trash. Over to Jake Munson's the other night we were shown proof."

"Proof of what?" Reisner sounded shocked.

"That he's a Communist—or sympathizer at least."

"What was that? The John Birch society?" Benson asked.

'That's right. They know what's up, I tell ya. And another thing. He likes the girls too much."

"Whad'ya mean. I thought teachers were supposed to like the kids." Wayne Swanson took secret delight in goading Hurlbutt. The rain had brought Wayne in. Usually he wouldn't take time off his farming for "the club."

"I mean—he always puts the girls with their skirts in the front row, my kid says." The snarl seemed to change to a leer. "The shorter the better."

"Aw, come on, Hank, you don't know what he's thinking." More goading from Wayne.

"I know. Myra Lou was in his class last year." Hurlbutt's daughter had graduated the year before and was working in Miles City. "She said so."

"Well, anyway, what's he been sayin' that's pinko?" Reisner wanted to get Hank back on the original complaint.

"To begin with he's always tellin' the class that there's poor people in the cities who haven't got enough to eat and that our system isn't helping them. And besides that he fills the kids with that atheistic propaganda that man came from monkeys." Hank thought about what he had just said and added his conclusion to the matter. "Yep, that Jankowski fella has got to go. He doesn't fit here in this God-fearing American community. This here's a Christian country. Doesn't Jankowski know that?"

Wayne took up this challenge. "As a matter of fact he says it isn't. According to what my kid said when he was in his class."

"I wouldn't be surprised," Hurlbutt added.

This reminded Dale Benson of the Memorial Day celebration. "Say, Claude, how are the plans for the Decoration Day service? Need any help?"

Both Dale and Claude were in the Miles City American Legion Post. Claude answered. "I think we are all set. Some of the men from Miles are coming, and we should be able to have a good showing. I've asked Rev. Norris to give the invocation and benediction. I'll let you know if I need any help."

"Good, that way he'll come to the services," Hank remarked.

"You mean he wouldn't come unless he has a part?" Wayne was goading again.

"Nah. He doesn't go for that patriotic stuff."

"How do you know that, now?" Wayne continued his interrogation of Hank's politics.

"He never preaches on patriotism. That's why."

"Well, we'll see how he prays!" Wayne ended this exchange.

"Club" members continued chatting about other things, mainly the weather and crops, until the rain abated and one by one the guys got up to leave.

Hank hoisted himself into his sugar beet truck. His pickup was in the shop. He fumed all the way home and at lunch continued his tirade, bombarding his wife, Louella, with his thoughts. "That Jankowski fella has to go—corrupting the minds of our kids with that commy stuff of his."

"Is he that bad, Henry?"

"Why certainly. With a name like *Jankowski*—he doesn't belong in these parts. Should go back to Chicago where he came from—or San Francisco where all those pinkos live. That's where. Not here. He gets the kids and they all start talking like he does. You heard how "the kid" was going on last night." That was how he often referred to his son, Delbert.

"Yes, I did, and I think he'll get over that once he's out of school."

"I hope so." He seemed to be reviewing his list of charges. "And then there's Myra Lou."

"What about Myra Lou?"

"It's that Jankowski that got her to go into town for that library job. And did you ever think of it?"

"Think of what, Henry."

"Librarians all talk like him—same twisted ideas. Anyhow, he's always in town at the library. And you know what's even worse?" He didn't wait for an answer. "He's always agoin into town to the library—just to see Myra Lou."

"You don't know that!"

He ignored that challenge and went on. "Who knows what them two are doing, especially when he goes in there of an evening."

"Oh, Henry, you're getting carried away. Myra's a good girl."

"I'm not so sure, when it comes to that hot hound, Jankowski." He changed his own subject. "Say, Louella, where's that Reverend been this week?"

"Over to Billings for a church meeting."

"Billings—Now there's trouble for a single guy like that, I'd say."

"How do you know, Henry?" There was a look of accusation in his wife's expression. "Don't you trust him?"

"I trust the Reverend when he's around here and we can see him . . . but Billings? Even Miles. No."

Hazel was tired of the harangue and wanted to move Hank off dead center, so to speak.

But Hank persisted, "When's the next session meeting"

"Week from this Tuesday night."

"I think I'll go along with you."

"Oh?"

"Yeah. I got some things to say." He'd save his remarks for the meeting.

CHAPTER 22

Out of Town

Earl re-read the pertinent paragraph of the invitation:

> *You are invited to be a representative from the Rocky Mountain Region at a Ministry Consultation April 24 to 28 at Menucha Conference Center in Corbett, Oregon, 22 miles east of Portland on the Columbia. All expenses will be paid out of national church funds. Your input is needed in the development of a Manual for Ministry. The purpose of this consultation is to pool experience and ideas from clergy and Christian educators who have been out of seminary for a minimum of two years.*

Checking his calendar Earl found that the dates for the consultation were clear. In fact this would come at a good time—after Easter and before summer scheduling. Besides, he was ready for a break. In a few months he'd be starting his fourth year in Saline. It would be good to get out of town. Out from under the spot light! He filled out the registration blank and hoped his church board would approve. He'd be traveling west. *Westbound! Westbound almost to the coast.* He exulted. *I wonder if I'll have time to see the Pacific?*

On April 24, Earl gathered with the forty or so delegates to the Ministry Consultation. They came not only from the Rocky Mountain Region, but from the Pacific Northwest Region as well. At first he had the impression that there was no one in the crowd with whom he had any prior acquaintance, until the group assembled in the Great Hall of the main building before dinner. He spotted Karen Collins from his seminary class. At the same moment she spotted Earl and they greeted each other with a hug. Not that they had known each other that well in seminary, but out here miles away from anyone familiar to either of them, it seemed like old times to find each other. An attraction which would grow during the four days of the consultation.

Earl considered her about his age. Some of the women in seminary were older, having had other careers, or families prior to their call to seminary and Christian education. Karen, however had come directly from college. She was a slender woman, a bit on the small side, lithe and pert. Her "dishwater blond" hair was relatively long but tied up into a loose swirl at the back. She wore an off white crew neck sweater over her form fitting slacks. Tiny peach colored ear rings accentuated her slightly tanned complexion and hazel eyes.

Earl noticed her ready soft smile. He was quite taken with her, which together with her greeting seemed so genuine and natural.

"Earl Norris! So good to see you. I haven't found anyone else here, have you?"

"No—you're the only one."

"We'll have to stick together. Us against all these San Anselmo people."

"Right. These all from that seminary, do you think?'

"Most of them, I think."

The opening dinner was announced and the two went into the dining room and found a space where they seated themselves. They ate dinner together, and in the time between dinner and the opening session at seven, they strolled around the grounds taking in all the unusual sights.

"Is this ever different from Saline, Montana!"

"How so?"

"Saline is dry country—semi-arid is the technical description. Only about 10-12 inches of rain a year. This lush green growth here so near the coast is something you don't see in eastern Montana. I can even smell the difference. The air seems heavy with humidity and the vegetation sparkles with droplets of moisture"

"I guess I see what you mean."

Earl realized he knew so little about Karen's location. "Tell me about your area."

"Moscow, Idaho is on what they call the Palouse, named for the formation of the gentle rolling hills in the region. We're not as dry as you. Good farming. But not like this region here. The congregation is barely big enough to have a Director of Christian Education."

Earl and Karen continued to discuss their two situations, finding a certain amount of similarity.

Then Karen remarked. "It's good to talk about this with someone in a similar region."

"I know what you mean. But, tell me, how are you really doing now after a couple of years?"

"Church or personal?"

"Both."

"Church is ok. I think I'm doing quite well, in fact. Better than the last DCE they had, I'm told." She paused to reshape her thoughts. "But personally—not good."

"Why?"

"I'm just plain lonesome, Earl. No singles in the church. If there were, that would probably be a bit precarious. So that's why I'm so glad you and I have gotten together here."

"I know what you mean. Out of town. Free! I've been in a fish bowl. They know my every move. There is a single woman in my congregation. I took her out once, mainly on her mothers's instigation. Neither of us could see any point of further dates. But you should have heard the rumors and all the talk that went around the whole community, until they got the message that there wasn't going to be any romance there for the preacher."

"I can imagine. I guess we are in the same boat. Do you feel lonely too?"

"Yes. That's why this is good, Karen."

The two were quiet as they continued to explore the grounds around the conference center. They had cut across a grassy area toward another gravel path. Coming to a fairly steep descent, Earl took Karen's hand to help her down. When they were on level ground again they continued to hold hands.

At seven o'clock the conferees gathered in the Great Hall. Some found overstuffed couches and chairs while others used the folding chairs set up in the center of the room. The conference leader introduced the featured lecturer.

"As announced, the resource leader is Dr. Rob Gilroy from the office of Congregational Resource of the Board of Christian Education in Philadelphia. He holds a Bachelor's degree from Temple University, his seminary degree from Yale Divinity, and a doctorate in sociology from Ohio State, where he served for a period of twelve years as the Presbyterian university pastor. This past year Rob came to the Board to bring his expertise and insights to the field of congregational development. We have asked him to provide us the theological and sociological base for our consultation. Dr. Gilroy."

Gilroy jumped up and stood before the group. His somewhat disheveled hair reached below his ears. His full beard had streaks of gray. He wore a faded maroon turtle neck shirt which fell loosely over his rumpled blue jeans.

"Thanks for that intro." He turned to the leader. "What've I got? Forty-five minutes?"

"That's right. Then there'll be ten or fifteen minutes for questions."

He turned to the group. "OK if I don"t use the microphone?" He then began his lecture:

> *Like Calvin's Institutes, at the outset I want to give you a summary of what I want to say under the general theme of "Getting Rid of Your Illusions."*

> 1. *America is not a Christian nation, nor should it be.*
> 2. *What is right and what is true depends upon who claims it.*
> 3. *Christian moral standards are neither moral nor standard. They are mores generated by the Christian group in compliance with the prevailing culture which the group finds itself.*
> 4. *Decisions made by national leaders are not necessarily the right ones.*
> 5. *The underlying principle of the human situation is self-interest. So what you believe to be true and right are based upon your answer to "What's best for me?"*

It was obvious that the speaker had caught the attention of the group. For the next forty minutes he expanded upon his five points, providing examples of what he considered proof for each of the five points. From the few questions which followed it was apparent that the audience was acquiescent, if not in agreement with Dr. Gilroy. What questions were asked were for clarification rather than to challenge what Gliroy had said.

The conference leader thanked Dr. Gilroy and then turned the attention of the group to their packets of materials for the consultation. "Take out the blue sheet entitled *Suggested Contents for a Manual of Ministry*. This will serve as a general outline of the work cut out for us during the next few days Now before we close for the day, Jerry McNare will lead us in our closing prayer."

After the prayer, at the close of the opening meeting of the consultation the group was divided into small working triads, three to a group. Each of the triads was given an assignment consisting of writing a draft of one or two sections of the manual for ministry which would result from the group's efforts. The triads would do their work on each of the three successive evenings after spending the mornings and afternoons in lecture presentations and discussions.

The leader formed the clusters of three according to the seating of the group. Earl and Karen had joined her roommate, Cora Lee, for the orientation meeting, and so were designated as one of the triads. Cora Lee Thomas, ten or twelve years older than Karen, had entered seminary after a short teaching career. She was now a Director of Christian Education in a Spokane church.

The balance of the evening was free, so the three spent the evening getting acquainted over pop and snacks in the canteen. Earl went to his room and found that his thoughts were more on Karen than on the meeting or what the lecturer had said.

The next morning Dr. Gilroy continued his series of talks which the conference planners hoped would provide input for the working groups which met for discussion during late morning and early afternoon sessions. The second half of the afternoon was free for individual study and contemplation. Earl spent a couple of hours in his room reading. Another lecture from Dr. Gilroy was given after dinner. Following the lecture the working groups were instructed to begin their writing of the proposed Manual. And so on the second evening they planned to gather in Karen and Cora Lee's room to begin their work

Earl went to his room after the lecture to relax before joining the other two. He found he couldn't relax. The first night's lecture had been upsetting to him. His initial reaction was to feel that if he accepted what Gilroy had said then his ministry would be undermined. Earl would need to think about all this. He changed into shorts and a tee shirt and went down the hall and knocked on Karen's door. When she opened to him he sensed a new warmth in her smile.

"M-m-m," he commented, "great minds . . . ." when he saw that Karen also had changed into shorts and a tee shirt. Cora Lee was wearing a terry cloth robe. Each of the women was parked on her own twin bed. Karen offered Earl an easy chair. "Why don't you take the chair? Pull it up to my bed for a desk."

After a preliminary exchange of reactions to what they had heard, Cora Lee concluded. "It seems to me that the speaker is a 'wild eyed' Eastern liberal. His ideas just don't fit the way we think out here." Without waiting for additional discussion she announced, "We better begin so it won't take us all. night." Earl, however, was still struggling with what Gilroy had said. He wondered if he could dismiss what he'd heard quite so easily as apparently Cora Lee had. But the little group had work to do for now. By ten o'clock they agreed that the assignment was as good as it was going to get, so they called it quits. Earl got up to leave. "You don't have to leave yet," Karen urged. But Earl could see from Cora Lee's reaction that he might just as well make his departure.

The next day during the afternoon coffee break, Earl found himself visiting with a most interesting pastor. A man in his forties who had come down from Alaska for the consultation. He looked the part, wearing what appeared to be logger's clothing—a heavy red and black woolen shirt, rough woolen pants and logging boots. He wore a full beard and talked with a Southern drawl.

"Where y'all from?"

"Montana—a little town called Saline. How about you?"

"I'm up in Skagway. I'm Pete Wills." He saw a curious look and added, "I'm originally from Alabama, but as a kid I felt the 'call of the wild.' I was a Southern Presbyterian, but I became intrigued with Alaska. So I turned

"Northern Presbyterian" when I became interested in the church in Skagway and and accepted a call to go there as pastor. Been there ever since. Ever been up to Alaska? By the way, what's your name?"

"Earl Norris—No, I haven't been to Alaska. Tell me about it."

"Well, we're at the north end of the inside passage in southeast Alaska—one of the few towns with road access. Everybody else is reached only by sea or air—like Sitka. Anyway Skagway was the gateway to the Klondike back in the 1890s. The miners outfitted there and then headed up the trail to the gold. Quite a trek at that—the Chilkoot. Some never made it. A lot of others made it to Dawson, but never got any gold. So it goes. Now we're a tourist town, with two or three cruise boats coming in every day in the summer. Pretty dead in winter, though. So the Presbyterian church is pretty small. I drive a school bus to help out. Great place, Alaska, I tell ya." Then he thought to ask. "What's Saline, Montana like?"

"It's dry land wheat and some cattle. Small town—small church. Just making it. I haven't taken on the school bus job—yet."

The conversation continued as the two men shared the coffee break, each telling more about his respective area. Earl was quite taken with Pete's stories about serving in Alaska. So much so that he found himself thinking about Alaska during the session that followed. He wondered what it would be like to accept a call to a church there. The truth of the matter is that Earl Norris had been thinking lately that perhaps his time in Saline was coming to an end. It seemed to him that he'd done about all the program expansion the little congregation could handle. The regulars were working pretty hard. A few were showing signs of fatigue. Besides that he thought he needed to grow, and growing while in the same position didn't seem too possible—to grow radically, not just a little at a time. This consultation was stimulating this sort of thinking in Earl's consideration of Saline and his own future.

On the third evening, after dinner, Dr. Gilroy's lecture was a continuation of the theme he'd begun in his first presentation. In this lecture he attacked the belief that morals were absolute and applicable to everyone. "Mores," he declared, "are relative to the basic value judgements of the group and the prevailing culture, and thus behavioral norms are subject to change if the basic values of the group change." He stunned many in the audience when he said. "Take sexual activity as an example. It used to be considered wrong for men and women to have sexual intercourse before marriage. That was believed to be so in a day when people took the Bible literally. They formed their basic value judgements on what they read in the Bible word for word. Now, however, many interpret the Bible more intelligently, thus they are able to relegate much of what the Bible says to its own culture, place and time. So they are free to adopt mores which are changing to fit the new value judgements of the culture. Thus, we find that an increasing number of couples have sex first and then subsequently become engaged and finally marry, oftentimes after having lived together in the meantime." He looked at his audience to judge their response. "And so sexual mores are changing."

This line of reasoning bothered Earl so greatly that he heard little else of the rest of the second lecture. He needed to process what he'd been hearing these past two nights. He determined to discuss this with Karen and Cora Lee, even though he realized such a conversation might be somewhat embarrassing.

When Earl knocked on Karen's door that evening she called out to him to come in. When he entered he again found her sitting cross legged on her bed with her clip board ready to continue collaboration on their section of the manual. On this night she wore her shorty bathrobe. Embarrassed, he said,

"Excuse me! I thought you said I should come in."

"I did. Cora Lee isn't here. She was called home for a funeral. It's just the two of us."

"I see . . . but . . . ."

"Oh, this?" She lifted her clip board in a gesture designed to display her state of undress." She explained. "I always study like this."

"But . . . ."

"It's OK. You're just like a brother, Earl. My bother and I always used to study like this together. He wouldn't have much on either. It doesn't bother me, if it doesn't offend you."

"Oh no, it's ok with me."

"So come on in. Lock the door in case anyone gets the wrong idea!"

Earl locked the door and took his place on the other bed. Earl got out his notebook and the two went to work on the assignment. They worked an hour or so and managed to develop the section of the report which had been assigned to them.

"Looks like we've got it." Earl thought a bit further. "But I'd like to know what you thought about Gilroy." he asked as he packed up his notebook.

Karen countered with "What did you think?"

Earl hesitated at first. He couldn't quite "read" Karen's view on the subject. But he decided to put his cards on the table. "Frankly, I have been quite upset by what the guy has been saying. Just about everything I stand for is under attack and I find that kind of scary. I've never heard this sort of thing before. Certainly not in seminary."

Karen agreed, "I know what you mean. But I'm not as upset as you are, I don't think, because some of this I've heard before."

"You have?"

"I have a certain amount of contact with people at both the University of Idaho and Washington State University. They are both quite close to where I live. The U. of I. is in Moscow and W.S.U. is only eight miles away. So I've gotten in on some public lectures and forums in which these ideas are frequently given. And in ministerial circles in the area, campus ministers from the two universities have helped the rest of us to update our ideas, so to speak." She could see that this might be shocking to Earl. "Of course I don't go along with all of it, but at least these are not new ideas for me . . . and I'd have to admit that I find his approach sort of appealing . . . I don't feel so uptight about sexual ideas anymore."

"Well, where I come from, anyone spouting off with these ideas would be ridden out of town." Earl didn't feel like getting into the matter any further at this point, so he began to get up to go back to his room.

Karen reached out a hand and took hold of his hand. "Earl, can't you stay for a little while longer? It would be good to talk some more."

"I guess I could." He returned to the spot on the other bed he'd been sitting on.

When he was settled Karen spoke. "I miss my brother, and it feels so good to have you here with me—sort of taking his place."

"Tell me about him."

"To begin with, we're twins and we have been very close."

Earl didn't know how to respond. "I have a sister, but maybe it's different with twins?"

"I think it might be." Karen wanted to say more. "I guess the thing I miss most about being with my brother is that we were so close. You know—there weren't any secrets between us. But now as a single woman in a parish, there isn't anyone that I can be close to."

"I know what you mean, Karen. You can't 'buddy up' to any one person or family. It'll get you in wrong with all the others."

"Yeah, and it's that fish bowl factor too—that everyone sees you and knows your business."

"Right. There is a regular column in the local paper devoted to the comings and goings of Saline people. Every so often there'll be sentence like this: *Rev. Norris was in Miles City for the day on Tuesday.* It certainly leaves a lot to the imagination. And imagine they will. If the reporter would just add *making hospital calls.*"

Karen agreed. "I know of a minister just out of seminary who moved to a church in a little town in our area with a red Plymouth convertible. There wasn't another car like it in the entire county. So everyone knew where he was all the time. He couldn't drop by the bar to pick up a coke without starting rumors that he was a lush."

"That's the way of the small town, I guess." Then Earl added, as if to put him back in the good graces of the Saline folk. "But, I like it."

"I do too, but I miss having close friends." She hesitated for a moment. "That's why it is so good having you here in the room, Earl. No one knows. And if this crowd did, they wouldn't care." She reached over and took Earl's hand.

"You're like having my twin brother here. I feel like I could share anything with you."

"I'm glad, Karen. I feel that way too, even though I don't know what it's like to have a twin." Her hand in his felt so good, and her openness was disarming.

They were both quiet, lost in thought. They got off on other subjects, family, seminary, and their present positions. There was never a lull in the conversation.

When Earl returned to his room around 11:30 he couldn't believe the ease with which he and Karen had come to relate to one another.

At the coffee break the next morning Earl sought out Pete. "Pete, how big a place is Skagway?"

"Oh, it's really small, man. Main Street's only a few blocks long and there are only about two streets on either side of it. The Church is on one of them on the west side. You don't need a car—just walk anywhere in five minutes."

"What's there to do?"

"Well, I help out at the Skagway Museum on Main Street—talk to tourists, explain some of the history of the Klondike—that sort of thing."

"I see. Are all the churches small like that?"

"Oh no, there's a big one in Anchorage and a few medium sized congregations like Juneau and in a few other cities like Haynes and Sitka."

"I guess I'd like to see Alaska some day. A lot of the guys in Saline either have driven the Alcan Highway or plan to."

"If you plan to drive, be sure and have a steel plate welded under your engine and transmission."

"Why's that?"

"The rocks on the gravel highway are somethin' else."

One of the leaders called out at this point, "Session II starting in three minutes."

The fourth and final evening, Earl joined Karen again in her room. They quickly got their concluding assignment done. When it was obvious that they had completed their work, Earl got up to leave Karen jumped off the bed and embraced him. They kissed. They let go, and when Earl was leaving to go into the hall Karen quipped, "Well, that wasn't like brother and sister, was it?"

"Hardly."

The next morning during coffee break while Earl and Karen were visiting, Pete came up abruptly and said, "Hi Earl. Say, would you want me to put your name in with our Presbytery people? They're always looking for possible candidates."

This took Earl by surprise, but he recovered and responded. "Sure, why not?"

"I'll do it, ol' buddy!" Pete went off to see some others.

"What was that all about?" Karen was curious.

"Oh, he's from up in Alaska, and was telling me all about it at break the last couple of days. And I guess he got the idea I might be open to moving."

"Are you?"

"I really don't know, Karen." He paused to think about what he really did feel. "Lots of first calls last three or four years in our area. It might be time."

"Have you got some opposition? The kind that won't quit and that drags you down?"

"Not really—I don't think. Only those few who didn't vote for me in the first place."

"What was their problem? Do you know?"

"The best I've been able to figure is that they don't like the fact that I'm a bachelor."

Kaye thought about this and pressed further. "Why should that be a problem?"

"I think there was an unmarried pastor in Saline some years ago that got sweet on someone in a nearby town. And that messed things up for him."

"Well, friend—all you have to do is find someone and get married!" she said with a grin. "Then you can stay forever. Any candidates?"

"Not a one—in Saline, that is." He looked knowingly at Karen. "The only single in the congregation loves her horses, but doesn't qualify on other counts."

That ended the discussion. The next session was about to begin.

The conference ended at noon and most of the participants took the bus to the airport provided by the conference planners. Karen and Earl rode together although Earl's flight was scheduled for the next morning. With barely enough time to reach her gate, Karen and Earl said a hasty goodbye before she boarded. They promised to write each other.

As soon as she boarded, Earl made his way to a car rental counter where he rented a Ford Fairlane. Using the map the rental agency provided he found his way through Portland to US 26. He then headed eighty or so miles northwest to Cannon Beach on the Pacific coast. *Westbound—all the way to the Pacific* he told himself as he caught his first view of the ocean stretching across the entire horizon. When he reached the state park, he found a spot to park his rental car and walked to the shore. As he saw the successive breaking waves roll onto shore and slosh up the sand, he was exultant. He found a water smoothed log dry enough on which to sit. He stared out onto the limitless sea remaining for as long as he could. He remembered having spent similar moments on the shores of Lake Michigan a few blocks east of the seminary. Also up at Saugatuck—*with Lynn*. And now he was on the shores of the Pacific Ocean. He had come west as far as you could go.

He could only remain for a few minutes, before having to tear himself away from the lure of the western sea. This was not his home. *Would it ever be*, he wondered. The consultation itself had been unsettling to Earl. The more Dr. Gilroy had expounded his ideas and the more people discussed his take on things the more Earl began to feel as though he did not belong in this group. The fact that Karen had been aware of some of this critical view of the relationship of Christian values to modern American culture, and had seemed somewhat favorable to such thinking had intensified Earl's "out of it" sort of feeling. He found himself yearning to be back in Saline. For now Montana was his home and by this time tomorrow he would be there.

As the plane veered on its course to the east over clouds and mountain peaks, Earl's mind darted back and forth between thoughts of Alaska and warm memories of Karen's embrace. And in between such intriguing thoughts, Saline and his work and life there kept intruding. And with these thoughts a vague sense of sin and guilt crept into Earl's consciousness. The very fact that he had entertained thoughts of moving to Alaska and becoming a pastor in that far off region made Earl feel a sense of betrayal, that he would be profoundly disloyal to Saline if he were to leave. Strangely similar, his thoughts of Karen pressed upon him a sense of betrayal. That he should have opened himself to "another woman." But when he thought about it rationally, he realized that his attraction to Karen did not compete with any other loyalties or commitments. There was no one else. But yet when he thought about Karen, he sensed that Lynn would not have approved. This realization of "two timing" Lynn surprised him. It made no sense. *This is a feeling I'm going to have get rid of, or I'll be single the rest of my life!*

The openness with which Karen had beckoned him to come in close both titillated and terrified Earl. Only four days and they had become close. Just as he had imagined how it would be if he lived in Alaska, he found himself imagining what it would be like to be married to Karen. How would she fit into Saline? What would his parents think of her? How about Anne? He felt himself becoming drowsy.

As always during his first years in Montana, Earl felt a vague premonition—unease—as he returned after an absence of a few days. Almost as if he would not find himself welcome to resume his duties. Returning like the "foreigner" he had been during his first months in Saline. The words of his rural church professor in seminary would sound in his mind's ear at times like this. "It takes, maybe, twenty-five years for a rural town to accept a newcomer as one of its own." Earl felt two conflicting responses well up in his consciousness. The one was to start planning to leave. The other was to win by staying in Saline for the next twenty years or so. He thought again of Pete and Skagway. And also of Karen. He dozed as the turbo prop jet churned its way east to Billings.

He was awakened by the announcement over the loud speaker. "Please make sure your seat belt is fastened, your seat is in the upright position and your tray table is folded up. We are making our descent into Logan International Airport in Billings, Montana.'" There would be no one to meet Earl. Instead he would pick up his car from the long term lot and begin his four hour drive home to Saline. He should reach home by nine at the latest.

CHAPTER 23

Settling In

Waking up in Saline was a jolt for Earl Norris. Always on the morning after returning from an out-of-town meeting, Earl would feel somewhat disoriented. After what he'd experienced and felt while out at Menucha, this feeling of disconnect was even more intense. After hearing Dr. Gilroy speak of the removal of Christian faith and morality from the American way of life, and after having lounged about with Karen Collins in her room, and then to have heard Pete exclaim the wonders of Alaska, Earl felt as though he'd returned from another world. Perhaps more than these experiences, having finally reached the western coast and having meditated there, Earl was not the same person as before this consultation. For one thing, he felt older. A certain boyish naivete had been taken away while in Oregon. But, strangely, instead of making him less content with Saline, his new perspective made him more willing to settle in. Almost as if he could say to himself that now he'd seen it all and home wasn't bad at all. Besides, if he were to admit it to himself, he felt safer in Saline. The world out there with people like Dr. Gilroy was becoming an alien place.

Now that he was home, he sensed that neither Karen nor Pete could ever fit into Saline as well as he was fitting in after only two years. A strong awareness that *this is where I should be* pervaded his consciousness on the morning after his west coast binge of sorts. This would be a conviction of which he would need to keep reminding himself. He sensed a great deal of agreement among his people and himself. Gilroy's ideas continued to trouble Earl. He was disturbed by the fact that quite a number of the others at the consultation—and to some extent, Karen—seemed to be taken with Gilroy's notions. Then that Alaska question. It made him feel like a two-timer every time he thought of Alaska with any degree of interest. *No, this is where I belong. These are my people.*

Such were his thoughts as he sat down to a simple breakfast. After breakfast he cleaned up the dishes and left the house to walk over to the post office on Main Street to see what mail had accumulated during his absence. He was struck by the clean quietness of the atmosphere in Saline as he sauntered along. He didn't see many people, but those whom he saw he greeted. It hadn't been that way the last few days.

Saline had the remnants of a Main Street. In an earlier day there had been a drug store and a small dry goods shop in addition to a bank and a grocery with a small post office attached, a café and of course a bar at the far end of the one and only business block. Now all that remained besides the bar were the combination grocery store and post office. People did their banking in Miles City and while there they could do all the shopping they needed to do. The café had closed after a small drive-in went up out on the highway near the Conoco. But Mabel and Karl Swensen had held onto the grocery with barely enough local business to keep going. Its main function was to stock sundry items folks may have run out of between trips into town. No fresh meat or produce anymore, mostly canned and boxed goods. One shelf provided incidental school supplies like pencils and paper clips. A greeting card rack for those who forgot while in town. It helped for Mabel to have retained the appointment as postmistress. Karl drove the rural deliveries daily. People in town had postal boxes in the little post office adjoining the grocery. When Mabel had gotten the postmistress position, Karl had cut a doorway between the grocery and the post office so that she could step over from the grocery counter into the postal area to distribute mail in the boxes and take care of postal customers. Others entered the post office through its own door onto the street.

The post office was one of four gathering places in Saline. Some years previous a former postmaster had found a discarded church pew and had put that in near the boxes, and had added some old spindle back chairs. The other three social centers were the bar, of course, the grain elevator out between the highway and the railroad tracks, and the Conoco. The drive-in never became a place to spend time except for high school kids after school.

The gathering place which Earl frequented by necessity, and grew to enjoy, was the grocery/post office. His daily walk over to get his mail became a pleasurable ritual for him. Usually his visits were around eleven each weekday morning. He tended to see the same people each day. Sometimes he would sit down to visit with church members who happened to be in for their mail at the same time. On the morning after his return from Oregon he walked over earlier than usual—around nine, long before the regular crowd. The first thing he noticed was a strange car parked in front of the post office, a late model Chevy sedan, cream colored. Having developed the local habit of recognizing people by the vehicles they drove, he now had no clue as to who might belong to this car. But the car was local with a county 14 plate, so he was curious as he entered to see who this might be. Somebody local, or maybe someone from Miles City?

When he walked in he saw a face he didn't think he'd noticed before. A pretty one at that. The bright morning sun streamed through the east facing window of the post office so that when Earl entered, he was struck by the sun shining upon the yellow and white western cut dress of a young woman who was just closing her mail box. He greeted her as he stepped up to his box. With an armful of mail, she smiled at him as she reached down to take the hand of a toddler boy. She urged him in a soft melodic voice, "Come along Davey, boy." The two walked outside into the full sunlight to the Chevy. A full mid calf length skirt and a loose fitting top with pearl snaps accentuated her somewhat tall stature. Her casually flowing chestnut hair spilled out beneath a cream colored cowboy hat. Around her neck she wore a pink bandana scarf. Earl was immediately attracted to this woman whom he'd not previously seen. It was her pleasant smile and soft expression which captured Earl. And the tender way she took the boy's hand was touching. He had never seen anyone quite like her. After she left the tiny building, he stared out the window and watched her gently lift her little boy into the car, carefully closing the door before going around to the driver's side. She started the engine and began backing out into Main Street. Then she drove down Main Street toward the tracks and the open country beyond. She was gone, but her gentle voice and warm smile remained with Earl.

He was tempted to ask Mabel who she was, but he thought better of it when he imagined what sort of talk such a question would stimulate. It had not taken Earl long to learn prudence in the face of small town talk. But it didn't keep him from thinking about this stunning woman, apparently living somewhere in the Saline community. She didn't appear at all like others in the community. Despite the western fashion of her dress and hat, she seemed strangely more urban to him. Western wear usually meant denim jeans, roughed up cowboy boots and well worn shirts and hats. The person he'd seen this morning was quite different. But her attractive appearance did not seem out of place. Rather, quite distinctive. *Perhaps I should make my post office visits every morning at nine!* he thought ruefully.

Fortunately at this early hour no one else was around to shatter his remembered image of this winsome stranger as he walked back to his office in the church. Unconsciously there was a buoyant lilt in his step and a question in his mind. *How can I see her again? I'm sure I haven't seen her in church, at least not yet!* To his disappointment, such a meeting would not be in church—at least not in the near future.

Earl spotted Homer Stein's vintage Dodge pickup at the church when he approached the parking area. Homer had been waiting for Earl. He got out to walk into the office with Earl.

"Mornin', Earl. Welcome home!"

Just the way Homer had said *home*, gave Earl a warm feeling inside.

"Good morning, Homer."

"I thought I'd drop this list off on my way into town."

"What list is that?"

"It's high time we did some roll trimming. Presbytery's 'head tax' is going up again."

By this time they were in Earl's study. "Have a seat."

Homer took a seat up against the desk on which he spread out a couple of sheets with names of Saline families. "Here's the list. I've got just about every family in the community. The one's with *M* are members. Those marked *X* haven't attended over the last few years and they aren't contributing financially."

Earl took the list and examined it carefully.

"If you think it's all right, I'm going to recommend that we drop the *X* names. Since they've been on the *INACTIVE* list for quite a while."

"Can we just do that?"

"Yes." At this point Homer hesitated, "But we're supposed to contact them first."

"Yeah, I guess that is what 'the book' says the session is supposed to do."

"There's the rub. It's not easy for us to go talk to neighbors like that. We're all friends, and we work together on each other's places every so often. But to bring up church attendance, and especially money—most of us just don't want to do that."

Earl was getting the drift. "So, what you're saying is—that the minister should do this?"

"Well, yes. I guess that's what it amounts to." Homer seemed reluctant to press this procedure. "The upshot is that this required visit with those to be dropped almost never gets done. And the list grows. It costs us more and more as Presbytery raises its per capita."

"I see what you mean."

"Why don't you have a look at the list, Earl. I've got to go now. We can look at this again before session meeting."

"OK." Earl took the list and Homer left.

When Earl tallied up the list he found thirty-six active families marked with an "*M*;" twelve with an *X* to be dropped from the role; One name he recognized on the list to be dropped was Norland. He remembered being intrigued by the view of the Norland ranch from its gate during that first drive-through tour Homer had given him. He felt a niggling desire to call on the Norlands, out of curiosity, mainly, he had to admit. At the same time he had to admit that he agreed with Homer. It wouldn't be much fun calling on back-sliders.

At the session meeting the following week, Homer passed out his list and brought up his recommendation to drop twelve families from membership. Earl could hardly believe the amount of discussion this aroused. As each name came up, there were numerous comments about that particular family—some relevant to the matter at hand, other comments and stories not relevant. The more prominent names in the community required more careful consideration.

These were four prominent families who were taken from the "*X*" list to be kept on the membership rolls by an action initiated by Mae Benson. "I move that these four be kept on the rolls—for the time being." The motion passed unanimously.

Then Hugh Baxter offered, "I move that the pastor call on the eight remaining families and report at the next meeting."

After there was a second to the motion, Homer stated, "I don't think we should put all this off on Earl. It's our responsibility."

Jane Moss cut in, "Yes, but it seems to me a call from the pastor might get them started back."

"Small chance," Sue Stark responded.

Homer resolved the question. "Why don't we wait until Earl has made routine calls—no mention of dropping from the rolls—and then he can tell us what he thinks. After that we can take action on the ones who are really uninterested."

There was agreement until Homer added, "But we are still going to have to call on them."

This raised more discussion. Finally it was decided to divide the eight names among Session members for follow-up calls. It was moved to table any further action until the pastor reported on his contacts. If the truth be known most everyone—except Homer—hoped this would be the last they'd hear of the matter.

After the meeting adjourned, Earl sat in his study looking at the list of eight families and realized he had his work cut out for him for the next few weeks. *But it's my job. With God's help I'll make these visits.* He'd gotten accustomed to coming up with a sermon each week. He and the session had worked out the kinks in what decisions the Session should be making and what were the proper responsibilities of the pastor in the Presbyterian system. The Sunday School and the Women's Association had been on their own so long that they needed little from Earl, excepting some ideas for the Sunday School teachers and Bible study for the women's group. There hadn't been a lot of pastoral emergencies like hospital calls, for which he was thankful. These would come, no doubt. And, he'd made his away around the parish to where he'd called in the homes of active members. *Now its time to reach out beyond the regulars!* he concluded.

CHAPTER 24

W lazy N

On a warm spring afternoon Earl drove through the massive gate with the wrought iron brand—W lazy N—hanging from the cross beam. On both sides of the lane leading to the house, Black Angus were grazing. The first thing he noticed as he drew near the buildings was their excellent condition, newly painted and well kept up. The yard surrounding the barn and sheds was neatly kept, unlike some of the other farms he'd visited, on which farm machinery and pieces of equipment were to be found nestling in the weeds everywhere one looked.

Earl pulled up to the front door of the ranch house and mounted the steps preparing to ring the doorbell. Before he reached the top step, the door opened and an attractive woman in her early fifties came out and called in a cheerful voice. "Come in, Mr. Norris. It is so good to have you come out to see us." She wore a pink and white western cut blouse with snap buttons and freshly washed and pressed jeans. Her graying hair was neatly trimmed and curled loosely just below her ears.

"It's good to see your place. You are Mrs. Norland?"

"Yes, call me Beth. Walter will be here shortly. Won't you come in?"

"Thank you, Beth. I'm Earl."

She ushered him into a large living room furnished with heavy oak and leather couches and chairs arranged around a Navajo rug done in earth tones. A massive stone fireplace was situated opposite the front door with a broad stairway next to it. Book cases were to be found at various places around the perimeter of the room. Oak end tables were located next to some of the chairs and a large coffee table also in oak was in front of one of the couches. These tables were strewn with various magazines including copies of the "The Smithsonian" as well as "Time" and "Life." Earl's overall impression of the room was one of warmth and gracious living, with a touch of comfortable affluence. Beth seated him in one of the overstuffed chairs, while she took her place on a couch at a right angle to him.

"As you know, I'm the minister in Saline and I just thought I'd like to get to know you folks, Earl began.

"Yes, I know. And Walter and I have looked forward to meeting you. By the way, he should be here any minute. He had to go into Miles City for something he needed from the farm equipment place. He knew you were coming, but had a slight breakdown this morning.'

"Sorry to hear that. I hope it wasn't anything too serious."

"No, it was on an older piece of equipment he's been meaning to replace."

"I'll look forward to his coming. Tell me about yourself."

"Well, we are both natives," She laughed. "Perhaps that says it all. My family had a ranch west of town, but it was sold after my retired. My brother had become a doctor and had moved away. By that time Walter and I were married and I was here with him. This had been the Norland place, which he took over from his father not too long after our marriage. We knew each other in high school."

"So you were married after high school and moved in here?"

"Not right away. Walter went to Dartmouth and I went to Hastings College in Nebraska. It was after we each got our bachelor's degree that we married. Our first couple of years together were over in Bozeman where Walter took a masters degree in Agricultural Economics. I taught school those two years."

"In Bozeman?"

"Near there, in a rural school called Monforton."

Just then they both heard Walter drive into the yard.

"That's Walter now."

"What was your degree in? Education?"

"Yes, but my major was in English."

Just then the back door opened and Earl surmised that Walter had come in.

"How about Walter's field?"

"At Dartmouth it was political science. He went on a full scholarship. Dartmouth had a program which made it possible for young people in rural areas to come to New Hampshire. He won such a scholarship."

Walter entered the living room and held out his hand to Earl. "You're Earl Norris?"

"Yes. Walter?"

"Yes. Welcome to the W lazy N."

"Mr. Norris and I have just been getting acquainted. You two talk and I'll get us some tea."

With that Beth rose and left for the kitchen. Just then another vehicle could be heard entering the yard.

"Your wife tells me that you are a Dartmouth graduate and that you have a masters degree from Montana State."

"Yes, I put off going to work as long as possible." He had a twinkle in his eye. "But both schools did me good. Bozeman, to help me farm. Dartmouth to get me in trouble around here politically!"

"Is that right?"

"Yes, I have, or rather, we both have some pretty liberal opinions which most of our neighbors don't share. You leave for a while, break out of the Saline box and you find that the rest of the country thinks differently. And when you return, soon the locals find out what you think and they put you on their list. In our case it's their list of 'Pinkos.' So we keep to ourselves."

Earl heard voices in the kitchen, that of another woman, and of a small child. Then Beth returned with a tray of goodies with a pot of tea and three cups. She turned to Walter, "They're back. I guess Davey has a slight viral infection in his throat."

"Serious?"

"No. I think he'll be over it in a couple of days." Then turning to Earl. "I've brought us some tea and cookies. Will you have some?"

"Yes, I'd enjoy that."

She poured three cups and passed the tray to Earl and to Walter.

"The preacher's been grilling me, Babes!" The twinkle in his eye returned. "I've told him how we have retreated from the hard hats who think we've been duped by the Communists."

"Did you tell him the bit about the county commission?"

"Oh, that! No. But he doesn't want all the dirt on the first visit."

Earl joined in the spirit of the occasion. ""I certainly do. Tell me."

It was Beth who revealed the story. "Walter used to be a county commissioner, but he resigned when one of the others had 'wangled' a deal to get a section of road out to his place paved without accepting any increased tax responsibility for it. Walter voted against it and wrote a letter to the paper telling what his position was. And that was the end of his county commissioner position at the next election!"

"Well, the reason was that this other commissioner was so well liked in the community that everyone sided with him, and more or less rode me out on a rail, so to speak. But what he did was wrong and I wasn't going to let that pass."

"Did he get it paved?"

"Yes, and some work seriously needing to be done on a county bridge had to be skipped. A young family of migrant workers hit that bridge soon after all this happened and it collapsed, causing one of the children in the car to be seriously injured. The worst of that was that the county refused to admit wrong doing so that the county's insurance wouldn't pay anything to the family. And the family didn't have any coverage."

Beth chimed in, "And Walter stepped up to the plate and paid the hospital bill for the child."

"From then on the community was done with us, I guess." Walter explained. "So we keep to ourselves. Raise our purebred Angus and the ranch keeps doing all right."

"That also gets everyone mad at us, doesn't it, Walt?"

"I guess so." He was done with the subject. "Now, Earl, tell us about yourself."

Earl told about his background in Illinois and his college and seminary experiences in the Chicago region, but didn't say much about his personal life or his experience in Saline.

"Are you married and have a family?" Beth wanted to know.

"No, I'm a single man—so far."

"But looking!" Beth smiled at him.

"Well, yes, but this is not the most hopeful place to look." Earl wished he hadn't said it quite like that, for it sounded critical of Saline.

But Beth agreed. "I'm sure that's so. But who knows what or who is in store for you, Earl?"

After this exchange Earl wanted to steer the conversation to the church. "I've been having a good time developing the program of the Saline church in ways I think best fit our congregation. I'm finding a responsive group. But we hope to grow in numbers now that our program is rolling." He was edging up to ask. "Do either of you have any interest in the church here, or are you involved elsewhere?"

This got Walter started. "Well, this used to be our church. Both of our parents were strong in the leadership. But, Beth and I have drifted away, I guess you'd say."

Beth added. "Not exactly 'drifted' Walter. More like 'left!'"

"Well, yes."

Earl felt this was a significant opening. "Was there some reason you left?"

Walter looked toward his wife, as if to gain her approval before getting into the story.

"When I returned from college and grad school, they asked me to teach the adult Bible class, which I did for a while. But it soon became apparent that I was too liberal for the class and they began to say things behind my back."

"Like what?" Earl dared to ask,

"Well, for one thing, they started saying that I didn't really believe. Some, who had become aware of my political leanings, even went so far as to say that the Communist ideology had made me an atheist." Walter showed some signs of lingering anger over this. "When Beth and I became aware of that attitude, we decided that the Saline Church was no longer for us. We quit then and there."

Earl could see the continuing pain over this. "What was the issue, do you think?"

"It was over how you interpret the Bible. I had come to see the Bible as a result of a complicated human process which involved a lot of writers from different times and with differing understandings of the world, and so the Bible has a lot of statements which on face value must be considered wrong or untrue. At the very least—outdated. God's word, I believe, is something beyond all the limited words and understanding of the Bible writers. They didn't like this, and thought that I didn't believe in the Bible anymore. So I thought that I'd better quit before the class disintegrated."

"Have you found a church since then that you are comfortable with?"

"No, we've just kept to ourselves."

"I'm sorry, Walter. I wish we could talk more about this, because, I think that I'm probably much closer to your thinking than your Bible class students were."

"I'd welcome such a discussion."

"I think that would be helpful." Beth offered.

"Let's plan on that. But now, I've stayed long enough. I know you have other things to do."

So Earl rose from his chair to leave, having had a significant get-acquainted session at the W lazy N. Walter walked Earl out to his car. Just as Earl was about to leave Norland leaned toward Earl's window. "But the way, I don't suppose you've met Jake Munson. He's not in the church, I don't think."

"No, I haven't. Why?"

"Well, he's someone to be careful with." Walter hesitated as if wondering if he should say more. "He's always looking for Communists . . . 'under every rock' . . . as he likes to put it."

"Thanks, Mr. Norland."

"Walter!"

With that Earl started his engine. As he began to leave he noticed that the other vehicle which he had heard enter the yard was a cream colored Chevy. *Where have I seen that before?* As he passed through the gate and onto the county road it came to him. *It was at the post office the morning after I got back from Menucha. That young woman and her little boy, whom I didn't know. She must be Norland's daughter. That must have been her voice I overheard coming from the kitchen!* He mused as he drove down the road.

That evening as Earl thought about his day, he brought back the words of Walter Norland. He wondered what the caution about Jake Munson meant. And he thought about the comments regarding Walter's interpretation of the Bible. He had referred to the fact that statements in the Bible might be untrue. *Factually untrue,* Earl pondered, *but carriers of truth nevertheless. I need to talk further with Walter Norland on this—and soon, while the "iron is hot."* He thought some more about his visit, and the cream colored Chevy. *Maybe I should pay them another call. And perhaps their daughter will be there! In fact, I'll phone in the morning and see what we might set up.*

The next morning Earl was unable to reach anyone at the W Lazy N by phone. But on the following day when he went for his mail he ran into Walter Norland in the post office. "Walter, I've been thinking about our conversation about Bible interpretation."

"Yes?"

"Well, there is something in that regard I'd like to talk about, which might add to your thinking. Would you like such a conversation?"

"Yes, I would, but I'm too busy this morning. I need to go into Miles today."

"I do too, as a matter of fact. I've got some hospital calls this afternoon. . . ."

Walter cut in at this point. "Can you come in early enough and join me for lunch?"

"I could do that."

"Good. How about the Olive at 12:30?"

"Great."

The two men sat in the café of the Olive Hotel and after ordering they exchanged small talk for a few moments. Walter Norland was curious about what Earl had in mind.

"You said that there were some things about my view of the Bible that you'd like to challenge?"

"Not challenge. In fact I feel that my view of interpreting the Bible and yours are fairly close. It's just that when you say that the Bible is complex in that it is made up of writing of many different people from various times and places, it seems to me that you are in danger of slipping off into a next logical step . . . ."

"What step is that?"

"To conclude that therefore the Bible is merely the thoughts of fallible human beings with limited minds and understanding."

"Well, that is more or less where I come out in this line of reasoning."

"Then the Bible loses its authority." Earl paused and saw that Walter wanted more here. "That it is not in any sense God's Word to humankind." He paused again. "And that you might just as well use the Declaration of Independence, or the latest philosophy as guides for your life—and the life of the world."

"Yes, I guess that is what I think. Why should we listen to some ancient people who thought the world was flat?"

Earl felt that it was time to declare what his theology was on this issue. "Walter, the missing piece in this puzzle is the Holy Spirit. It is the spirit of God who put insight into the truth of life in the minds of the old time writers and it is the same spirit who makes those words of human beings in the Bible come to life and reveal God's truths about Himself, about us, and how we should relate to God and each other."

"That's something I'll have to mull over, Earl. But it is interesting."

Their waitress brought their lunches at this point, which had the effect of bringing the discussion to an end—for the time being. As it turned out, this would be the first of many such discussions Earl would have with Walter Norland.

As they were concluding their meal a couple of men came into the café. Both Earl and Walter saw them and one of them saw Earl. One was Hank Hurlbutt. He looked away, but the only way to get to an empty table was to walk by Earl's table. Reluctantly Hurlbutt greeted Earl as he passed. "'lo Reverner."

"Hi, Hank.'

The second man was Dale Reisner who, not knowing Earl, walked on by.

Even though the two men did not acknowledge Walter, Norland said. "Howdy, men."

Reisner said, "Hello, Walt."

Walter and Earl rose and walked up to the counter to pay their bills.

The next day at the club Hank went on at great lengths about how he now knew for sure that the minister was a Commie.

Merle asked him how he was so sure.

"Tell him, Hank." Dale encouraged Hank.

"He was a-talkin' real serious-like with that Pinko, Norland."

CHAPTER 25

On the Inside Passage

The two women leaned against the railing on the forward portion of the deck of the Alaska Marine Highway Ferry. The sea breeze in the channel blew their hair and ruffled their jackets as this large vessel moved along northward. They were looking out across the bow of the boat as it made its way slowly up the narrow sea channel. It was plying the inside passage of southeast Alaska, sailing north from Juneau, Alaska's capital, toward Haines. Soon after Haines it would reach its northernmost point where it would dock at Skagway.

They watched the heavily forested shoreline slip by on both sides of the passage, a beautiful scene with the blue sky above reflecting upon the sparkling water below, beyond which was verdant green growth. Gulls swooped above the ship, while bald eagles could be seen over the shore. Occasionally whales surfaced, spewed water and flopped their forked tails into the water as they descended into the channel again. A more magnificent scene Lynette Ellerton had never before seen—or had she ever hoped to take in.

"Gerry, this is simply out of this world."

"Isn't it though," the older woman agreed.

Lynn and Gerry had struck up a friendship soon after Lynn had arrived at Sheldon Jackson some months previous. Gerry was a volunteer in the main office. The two often ate their noon meals together in the college cafeteria. Gerry, who was some years older than Lynn, had become something of a mentor and now was offering Lynn a tour of the Inside Passage.

"Thanks for talking me into taking this trip on my days off."

"I'm glad. I like to take this cruise at least once a summer. And you'll like Skagway."

"What's it like?"

"Oh, it's a tiny town, right on the shore with mountains behind it. It was the old supply town for miners heading for gold in the Klondike—the jumping off point." Geraldine Fischer looked at her watch. "It's almost noon. We'll have just enough time for lunch in the cafeteria before docking at Skagway."

"Good. This fresh sea air makes me hungry." Lynn eagerly anticipated each new experience on this trip with her friend and co-worker.

They left the railing and opened the heavy metal doors which brought them inside. They walked the length of the ship to the cafeteria, passing by passengers seated in lounge areas along the corridor, some sleeping, others reading. When they arrived at the entrance to the restaurant, they found that a lunch line had already begun to form. They took their places at the end of the line. The ship was crowded on this particular Saturday in July, with a mixture of tourists and Alaskans traveling from one town to another along the Inside Passage. Some of these, particularly tourists, had small staterooms, while many others had staked out comfortable chairs in the assortment of lounges.

Finally their turn came to pass through the cafeteria line. After loading their trays with an ample lunch they paid at the cash register and then made their way into the crowded dining area. At first they were hard put to find a spot to sit down.

"There's a couple leaving over to the left." Lynn noticed.

They worked their way to the vacated table with three chairs. Putting their trays down they got themselves situated in the midst of hundreds of lunch customers. After beginning to eat, a young man with a loaded lunch tray stepped up. Dressed in khaki pants and a white and tan woolen sweater, his appearance gave both a ruddy and refined impression. Something about him seemed to set him apart from other men in the crowd.

"G'dai, ladies. Might I sit here? There seems to be no other place to take my meal." His voice was pleasant and his demeanor courteous. He spoke with some sort of accent.

"Surely," Geraldine welcomed him. "Just sit right down."

"Thank you, ma'am." As he set his tray down and took a chair he introduced himself. "My name is John Lindsay."

"How do you do. I'm Geraldine Fischer and this is Lynn Ellerton." Gerry paused and resumed. "And I hear a bit of 'down under' in your voice. Australia?"

"No ma'am. I'm a Kiwi."

"Kiwi?" Lynn asked.

"New Zealander, ma'am. I'm on what we call 'the great Kiwi trip.'"

"What's that?" Lynn wanted to know.

"Oh, lots of us like to take off to see the world before we settle down. For many of the young men that means sheep shearing around the world." He thought about this and added. "Mum likes to tell visitors from America that 'when you live on an island your have to go somewhere.' That's what I'm up to."

"Is this custom just for the men?" Lynn asked.

"No. For the girls, their Kiwi trip often involves going to the UK as Nannies for a time."

"What brings you here on the Inside Passage? Not many sheep that I can see." Gerry gave him a wry glance.

"I've been shearing down in Wyoming and Montana, and I thought I'd see Alaska before I head for Saskatchewan. I hope to make my way east. Then when I run out of time or sheep—which ever is first, I'll be headed for home."

"Where in Montana have you been, John?" Geraldine asked. "I'm from Montana."

"Oh, you are? Big Timber is where I've been. A couple of sheep farmers there have been hiring New Zealand shearers for years."

Gerry explained. "I'm from quite a bit east of there. Around Miles City."

"Miles City?"

"Yes, about three hours east of Billings"

"I flew into Billings before getting over to the sheep ranch in Big Timber which had hired me—sight unseen, I might add." He turned to Lynn. "Are you from Montana as well?"

Lynn had been listening with rapt attention while she ate her lunch. She was quick to respond to this man's initial invitation to become acquainted.

"No, I'm from the Chicago area." She stopped at that, for a shy streak had hit Lynn—for reasons of being quite taken with this tall young man with such a romantic sounding accent.

"Ah yiss, (his short *e's* sounded more like short *i's*.) I'm in hopes of flying to Chicago on my journey to eastern U.S. if and when I run out of sheep to shear." He turned the conversation to the two women. "What brings both of you to Alaska? Are you related—family, I mean?"

"Actually, no." Gerry said. "We are both volunteers in Sitka at Sheldon Jackson College. This is my fourth year there. Lynn's first."

"Oh, what do you do at the college?"

"I work in the college library. Gerry is in the main office." Lynn said. "As for your question about family, Gerry is sort of family. She's been like a mother to me, helping me into the work at the college and into life in Sitka, which is so different from Chicago."

"I can imagine. Vast difference in size, isn't it?"

"Yes, and more. Sitka has a significant population of people of native tribes."

"Ah yiss. Like our Maori, is it?"

"Maori?"

"They were the people on our islands when the first Europeans arrived. Like your red Indians, except that Maoris weren't natives."

"They weren't?"

"No they came from Pacific islands a thousand years ago. They came south in their long boats—like canoes with many rowers. When they found the lush and beautiful island of what they called Aotearoa, they stayed and settled."

Gerry got into the conversation. "You know, now that you speak of the Maori in that way, that is the story of the native tribes of Alaska, and those further south as well. They came from elsewhere thousands of years ago."

"Is that right, Gerry?"

"Yes the native tribes on the American continents came across what was once a land bridge from Asia to Alaska, beginning, some say, 30,000 or so years ago. So, I guess ours aren't really native either!"

"Though more so than the Maori, I'd say," Lynn added.

"You mean that there were no native peoples on this continent, originally?"

"Not really," Gerry affirmed. "In fact some of the so called *native* Alaskan people are relatively recent with tribal relatives across the Bering straits in Siberia."

"I didn't know that," Lynn admitted.

"Nor I," the New Zealander declared. "A bit interesting, isn't it."

The conversation continued as the three ate their lunches. After all three had finished Gerry advised. "We better let others have our table."

The three rose and cleared their table for the next group of lunch customers. John started to take his leave. Lynn mustered her courage and intervened. "Would you like to join us up in the forward observation lounge?

He hesitated just long enough to be polite. "Ah yiss—that would be good."

The three left the cafeteria and passed along the corridor. They came to a lounge with writing desks. At this point Geraldine chose to give Lynn and the young New Zealander a chance to have time together. *Always the matchmaker,* her daughter in Montana would have observed.

"Lynn, I have some letters to write. I'd like to stop here at a writing desk and do that. You two go up to the lounge. I'll come along later."

Lynn was in favor of this and said perhaps too quickly, "That's fine, Gerry."

"I'll take care of your associate, Geraldine!" John quipped. "In fact, if we come across a sheep, I'll teach Lynn how to shear."

Lynn feigned naive shock, as Gerry headed into the writing lounge.

John and Lynn continued to the forward lounge and found a couple of seats and made themselves comfortable. They fell into conversation—nonstop.

Lynn soon got over her shyness. They shared their personal stories, feeling a mutual resonance as they felt themselves passing in a sweet and subtle way from strangers to friends. Each found this transition to be most intriguing and satisfying. And when Lynn thought about it later, she was shocked at the ease with which they had related, and so quickly.

"Tell me a bit more about your decision to volunteer at the college."

"After I quit working for my father, I struck out on my own. My ideas about life began to change. I saw my own father as money grubbing and ruthless. Doing no good for anyone except himself. I didn't want that. I wanted to live for something outside myself, something bigger."

"Ah yiss, Lynn. That's the way I feel sometimes."

"Well, I got involved in a great church near downtown Chicago. It had a strong young adult group. That's when the idea of giving time in some sort of mission activity came into focus. So that's how I came to be here."

John was very quiet as he pondered this. Finally he turned to Lynn, taking her hand. "You're showing me myself, especially my need to do something worthwhile."

Lynn made what she realized was an inane remark to keep him from feeling badly about himself—and from letting go of her hand. "Oh, shearing sheep does good for people."

"No, no. I need to examine my life. This great Kiwi trip is really quite self-centered, isn't it?"

"I wouldn't say that. Not if this is a time for you to re-think what you want to do when you get home. What will your life be like when you return home?"

"Father will want me to farm with him. In fact, if I were married he and Mum would move out of the house to a small house on the place, and I would move into their house and take over the farm."

Lynn pursued this line of thought with more than casual interest. "Any chance of that?"

"Of what? Being married, you mean?" He grinned.

Lynn was flustered. "Well, yes, I guess, that's what I mean."

"No prospects."

Lynn almost said *I'm glad*. But she thought better of it and said, "I see."

"What's good for the goose is good for the gander, isn't it?"

"What? I don't know what you mean, John."

"Don't you, now?"

Lynn thought about what he had said, and then it dawned on her. "Oh! You mean you want to know what my marriage plans are."

"Yes. I want to know if some big macho American is going to find me visiting so personally with 'his woman' and 'kick me out of the Longbranch' so to speak."

"You've been reading 'westerns' too much. No, there is no need to worry—no one to bother you." Lynn fell quiet and pensive.

John picked up on that. "What's wrong? Did I touch a nerve? I've gotten much too personal, have I?" John was sensitive and kind in the way he urged her on.

"No, no. It's just that there was a man in my life. But he went to theological school and became a minister. Or at least I think he became one. We have lost track completely—ever since we broke our engagement."

"Why should his taking up the ministry have been a problem?"

"My parents—and I have to admit I agreed with them at that time—said that such a life wasn't for me." She delved more deeply into her memory of her father. "'Wasted life' is the way my father put it."

"You agreed with them at the time?"

"Yes, I guess I did—at the time."

"You mean you would think differently now?"

"Yes, after I decided to try and do some good, like working here at Sheldon Jackson."

"I see, and now you are doing something similar to your friend's work. At least in the sense that you are working for the church."

"I know. It's ironic—and sad."

The two sat together in silence. He continued to hold her hand. The ever-so-gentle movement of the ship along the water seemed to lull them into a sort of hypnotic state. A warm settled feeling.

Eventually John asked. "Why does it make you feel sad to be doing some good work now in your life?" John was gentle with Lynn.

"I don't know. When we were 'in love'—puppy love, I guess, it was—we were on different wave lengths when it came to basic values in life. And now, when we are not together, we seem to have gotten on the same wave length after all . . . ."

"Yes?" John could feel that there was more which Lynn wanted to share.

"No, John, when I review that old history, it is more complicated." She thought about what was happening in this conversation. "But you don't want to hear all my life history."

"I do, Lynn. Please go on . . . if you want to, that is."

So courteous and gentle. Lynn thought. "Well, it's this way. We seemed to like all the same things in those days. By the time we were high school seniors everyone in our church group saw us—Earl and me—as a "couple" and assumed that some day we probably would marry."

"Did you and Earl assume that?"

"Well, not exactly. We were what we called 'going steady.'" Lynn paused and then continued. "Then our relationship developed further when he started coming up to the lake to be with me as much as he could in the summers."

"The lake?"

"Oh—Lake Michigan. My parents had a summer home on the east side of the lake. I spent my summers there with my family and with cousins and lots of friends. Earl fit into this scene. The more we spent time there the more we began to talk about how we would like to have a beach house someday after we were married."

"Was that a possibility?"

"It was, because by that time Daddy had persuaded Earl to get a business degree in college. He was grooming him for a high level job in the company—Ellerton Manufacturing."

"Is that what Earl wanted?"

"At that time, yes. But then something happened. He got the 'call of God' so to speak."

"Call of God?"

"To go into the ministry. That was the beginning of the end. My father, in effect dumped him, and any thought of marrying him was out of the question in my family."

"How did you feel?"

"Well to be honest, I came to feel the same way. But then later I guess you'd say, 'I got the call of God' too. And here I am." Lynn had told her story.

John was quiet for a few moments while both of them felt the hidden surge of the ship's engines propelling them onward. He then probed further. "Since each of you seems now to be on similar tracks . . ." He hesitated briefly. "If you were to meet him would you be interested?" He clarified his question. "In marriage, I mean?"

"I've thought so, but now I'm not so sure." Another silence. "No. I think that's too long ago. We were both kids . . . it was puppy love—I think."

"Ah!" There was a twinkle in John's eye. "Then I take it, that you are ready to dash off to New Zealand with the first Kiwi you come across!" This remark had the effect of lifting the conversation from the deeper level it had gone to.

Lynn joined in the mirth. "John Lindsay—you are a tease. Or is that the way they propose down under?"

"Ah yiss!" He grinned at her. "Strange—aren't we? The daily arc of the sun is in the wrong place. The stars are all different. We don't even have a North Star. We drive on the left side of the road, water swirls down our drains the opposite direction from the way yours does—and we have heavy glue on our shoes!"

"Why?"

"So that we don't drop down off the underside of the earth, silly!"

"You are a tease!"

"Come down with me, my new-found friend, and Father will give me the farm and the house as well."

"So that's it!" She looked him in the eye. Because he was from so far away, and because most likely she would never see him again, she felt daring about this exchange with her new Kiwi friend. "I'm to be your key to the farm and the farm house."

He looked her in the eye and winked. "Ah yiss!" He squeezed her hand and began to get out of his chair. "Let's go out on deck and have a look."

They went out and found a spot to lean on the railing together. In a most natural sort of way he put his arm around Lynn

He explained. "I must keep you from tumbling into the sea! Mustn't I?"

"Thank you, sir," she said facetiously.

They peered beyond the rippling waves made by the ship and to the shoreline. Suddenly there was a noticeable stir among the passengers along the railing. Someone shouted, "Bear!" and pointed to a clearing along the shore.

Lynn spotted it first and directed John to see it as well. "The first I've seen in the wild.' Lynn declared.

"For me as well."

They watched the bear in the distance foraging in the grass and shrubs along the edge of the forest. The ferry slowly moved past the lone bear.

Soon the ship entered a much broader expanse of water. They walked to the other side of the boat and there at the railing they found Geraldine. She made room for them to stand next to her. As she did she pointed to the shore. "We're coming in to Haines." They saw that the boat was drawing near to a small town near the banks of the channel. Slowly the ferry pulled up along side the dock and shuddered to a stop. The gang plank was lowered and a short stream of vehicles drove out of the hold and onto land. Ten or so passengers walked off on foot. A car and two trucks were waiting on the dock to drive up the plank and into the hold of the ship. Then a small group walked up the gangplank and onto the ferry.

After a very brief stop they began to move away from the dock.

Gerry announced. "Only an hour more before we are in Skagway."

"That's as far as we are going today, John. How about you?"

"I'm getting off there as well. I read stories about the Klondike when I was young. I'm eager to see this district for that reason."

Lynn shared John's anticipation. "I've been hearing about Skagway ever since coming to Alaska, and so I'm anxious to see it, too."

Geraldine thought to ask. "Have you arranged for a place to stay here, John?"

"No, I thought I'd find a hotel."

"There aren't many places. Why don't you go with us to the place we'll be staying ? Maybe there'll be a room." That was Gerry—always on the lookout for Lynn's interest!

"Where is that? Is it expensive?"

"No. It's just a small place—like a motel. It's called Sargent Preston's Hotel. Only a block off the main street."

"If you won't mind my tagging along, then?"

"Not at all," Lynn was a bit quick to reply.

Soon Skagway came into sight. By this time the ferry was moving cautiously into the harbor and slowly edging up to the dock. Gerry and Lynn, along with John, made their way to the stairway leading down to the main deck for disembarking. They heard the low toned whistle of the ferry and then within minutes the three, each with a travel bag, were on land again and walking north on Broadway passing the Golden North Hotel with its gleaming onion shaped cupola. It stood among other buildings from the 1890's, when Skagway was at its peak. According to the directions given them, they then turned a block west toward Sargent Preston's Hotel

When John asked the innkeeper about a room, he was offered one which he gladly accepted. They registered and prepared to retire to their respective rooms. Sensing a bit of awkwardness on John's part, Gerry offered. "John, unless you want to be on your own, you can certainly join us while we are all here. To see the sights and whatever."

"I should be very happy to, Geraldine. That is, if Lynn agrees."

"I'll think about it . . . Oh, certainly." The mischievous twinkle in his eye betrayed his assurance that she would surely agree.

CHAPTER 26

John Lindsay

"Gerry, I've never met anyone like him!" Lynn was bubbling over as she slipped out of her tee shirt and jeans getting ready for bed in the room they were sharing in Sargent Preston's Hotel.

Gerry beamed. "Ah yiss!" She mimicked the New Zealand accent.

"Oh Gerry, quit it!" Lynn disappeared into the bath room, but then turned around to share more of her feeling with her friend and surrogate mother. "Really, I have to admit that I'm quite taken with him."

"That was obvious."

"It was?"

"Yes, and it was also apparent that he feels the same about you."

"Do you really think he does?"

"Of course," Geraldine was in her pink cotton night gown, and pulling back the covers when the phone rang.

"Hello?"

"Geraldine, this is John Lindsay. I just wanted to tell you how much it means to me to have you and Lynn 'take me in' so to speak."

"Oh it's our pleasure, John."

Lynn heard her say "John" and came out in a night shirt and sat on the bed.

"When you are as far from home as I am, it finally gets to you that everyone around you is a stranger. It had gotten quite lonesome for me, really."

"I can imagine."

"Anyway, you both have dispelled the loneliness. I appreciate that."

"Don't forget, we'll meet you for breakfast at eight o'clock."

"By no means would I forget. So, good night to you both."

"Good night, John. Wait a minute. Don't you want to speak to Lynn?"

"Ah yiss. Put her on then."

Gerry handed the phone to Lynn. "John Lindsay wants to speak to you." Lynn said shyly. "Hello?"

"Just wanted to wish you a good night, Lynn. I'll be seeing you in the morning at eight for breakfast."

"That's sweet of you, John. Good night." Lynn put the phone down and with that crawled under the covers of her bed. An internal smile was radiating through her body.

Gerry switched off the light, apparently not wanting to say anything more. "Good night—sweet dreams!"

"Good night—I'm sure I will."

For the newly formed threesome a whirlwind three day tour of Skagway began with breakfast in the Sweet Tooth Café on Broadway just south of the Golden North Hotel. John talked his two new friends into ordering oatmeal—porridge, as he called it.

"It won't be a good day for you unless you start it with some good porridge."

"The only porridge I know about," Lynn confessed, "was in *Goldilocks and the Three Bears*."

"What?" Gerry cried.

"You know. 'Someone has eaten my porridge. Boo Hoo.'"

"Well," John replied. "This porridge will be for you ladies"

"What is porridge?" Lynn wanted to know.

"You mean you don't know, do you?" John was genuinely surprised. "It's cooked rolled oats."

"Oatmeal," Gerry added.

The waitress brought three bowls which they ate with abandon. And then they topped their porridge off with toast and marmalade.

"Also a Kiwi favorite," John announced.

After coffee for the two Americans and tea for John, they toured the town's original buildings with a National Park Service guide. They visited the Skagway Museum nestled among shops on Broadway and learned about Soapy Smith, the slick and not so legal boss of Skagway. In its glory days, Soapy ruled supreme until he was gunned down by Frank Reid, who thus became a hero after this celebrated Alaska gun-fight.

In the course of their tour of the town, the park service interpretive ranger told them of the Klondike and the history it spawned. In August of 1896 a drifter from California and his Yukon Indian friends hit upon gold in Klondike Creek in Canada. This discovery set off a world-wide rush of over 100,000 hopefuls who dropped their work and headed north in search of precious gold. Skagway became the starting point of the 600-mile expedition to the gold fields near Dawson. Many had to climb the arduous Chilkoot trail from Dyea, three miles from Skagway along the coast. Others took the White Pass Trail up from Skagway by foot until the railroad was built. A varied assortment of miners risked their lives trying to make it to Dawson City on the other side of the mountains to the golden treasure in the Klondike.

The second afternoon they took the White Pass & Yukon Route's narrow gauge railway up to the top where in the old days gold seekers left the rails to continue a wearisome overland trek to the Klondike. The much needed rail line was built in 1898 by courageous crews who scaled vertical cliffs and blasted a precarious right-of-way through granite to lay rails from sea level at Skagway 2,865 feet up to the summit where Canada borders Alaska.

On the third morning Geraldine suggested that they hike a little way up the Chilkoot Trail from Dyea. This climb up the mountain side gave them just a glimmer of what so many at the turn of the century endured in quest of fortune. They had learned from the park service ranger that the Chilkoot climb had been made many times more difficult because of the requirement of the Canadian government that each gold seeker carry with him enough food and supplies to keep him while he got established. This had made it necessary for most to make at least one trek additional with supplies to the top with provisions, before a final ascent.

Upon their return to Skagway, they freshened up for their last dinner in the quaint mining town before they were scheduled to board the ferry the next morning. They met outside the Sargent Preston and walked back to Broadway and again chose the Sweet Tooth Café.

As usual, and conveniently, after dinner in the evenings Gerry always seemed to have some reason to let Lynn and John take walks around town without her intrusion. The two could not have enjoyed one another more as they re-visited places in town each night walking hand in hand. And on this final night when they departed to their rooms, John very gently gave Lynn a good night kiss.

At noon on the fourth day they were scheduled to re-board the ferry which would take Lynn and Gerry back to Sitka. John's plan was to stay on the ferry all the way south to Prince Rupert from which he would make his way by bus to sheep ranches in British Columbia. But Lynn had a better idea, which she presented to John as the ferry approached Baranof Island, where Gerry and Lynn would disembark at Sitka.

"John, why don't you stop off here in Sitka for a few days. You could re-board after we've had a chance to show you around."

John pondered this. "I suppose I could. I'm not due to meet my next sheep farmer for another ten days. He is only a few miles east of Prince Rupert."

"We could get you a guest room at Sheldon Jackson College, and you could look around Sitka while I'm at work, and after work we could . . . ."

"I'll do it," John cut in.

Before long the ferry was drawing in close to the dock just north of Sitka. The three friends walked off the gangplank and into the terminal building. Gerry phoned the college for a ride. In minutes the station wagon arrived and they piled in for the ten minute drive to the college. Along the way, Lynn delighted in pointing out the sights to John, scenes over which she herself had only recently marveled. When they reached the college, Gerry arranged for a guest room for John.

For the next three days John played the tourist in Sitka. Most everything to see was in walking distance. He spent time at the Sitka National Historical Park with its display of totem polls and items from the Tlingits and other native tribes. He visited the state museum on the college campus, made up in large part of artifacts which Sheldon Jackson had collected while on his missionary journeys throughout Alaska for the Presbyterian church. John toured the Russian bishop's house and St. Michael's Cathedral. He found that although the cathedral is a replica of the original church building, the bishop's house still stands as it did in the 1700s. John reveled in the distinctive surroundings, so different from his usual environs in New Zealand—*excepting*, he thought, *places like the Maori village in Rotorua.*

In the evenings John and Lynn spent time together walking around town and just being together. Saturday evening was their last night before John had to leave for Prince Rupert. Lynn and John had dinner in the Sitka Hotel as a celebration of sorts. And then they meandered up Castle Hill for their last chance to be together alone before John's departure the next day. Walking arm in arm on a warm summer evening there was an obvious sadness enshrouding them. John was the first to speak of it.

"Lynn, I don't know how to say this, but I don't want to lose you. We've known one another for less than a fortnight, but my life has been profoundly affected." He paused and then went ahead and declared, "I love you and I don't want to leave you."

Lynn was moved to tears. "John. I've fallen in love with you too. And I don't know how I can let you go. But that's what we must do, I guess . . ." She thought *it's been so quick.*

They were quiet until Lynn spoke. "How could this have happened so suddenly, John?"

"We don't know, do we? But I know I don't want to let you go."

"I think it is because we are both so far from home. We've found a feeling of *home* in each other."

The two looked across the Sitka channel to Japonski Island and beyond. The sun was setting behind the majesty of Mt. Edgecomb. They embraced. Their tears mingled in this moment.

"Perhaps we can find a way." John said tentatively.

"But how?"

John was thinking. "How long are you committed to your work here at the college?"

"Through September first. Why?"

"I'm wondering . . ." as if to himself. "My visa runs out on September fifteenth. That gives us a two week gap." Then to Lynn. "What are your plans after Sitka?"

"I'm not at all sure. Chicago, I suppose, but I don't really want to go home. I'll really be at loose ends. I'll need to find a job. What happens when your visa ends?"

"I fly back to New Zealand."

"From where?"

"I fly out of Los Angeles."

Holding each other very close, they continued to watch the fading sun on Mt. Edgecombe.

An idea began to form in John's mind. "Is there any chance, Lynn, that you could join me in L.A.?"

Lynn thought about this. "My flight out of here will be to Seattle . . . I guess I could fly on to Los Angeles, before heading east."

Then John took another leap. "And fly home with me?"

After a lengthy pause Lynn looked at John and asked. "Is this the way a proposal is done in New Zealand, John?" She smiled softly.

John looked at her tenderly. "Not always, but it seems to fit our situation, doesn't it now?"

"Yes."

"You mean you are saying YES?"

"I meant yes, your proposal fits our situation."

"Oh." John was obviously disappointed—only to be retrieved.

Lynn was quiet for a moment, and then she declared. "Yes, John, I will fly to New Zealand with you. And if things work out, and you find that you want me to stay, I will!"

"Oh Lynn, darling! I couldn't be happier. It will work out, I know. And I'll want you to stay. Do you think you can be a sheep farmer's wife?"

"I'll try."

They sealed this with a deep and prolonged kiss.

The next morning, John and Lynn and Geraldine attended worship at the Presbyterian church a couple of blocks from the campus. John's departure would be in the early afternoon. At the close of the service, after the final hymn the minister pronounced the benediction. John took Lynn's hand as they heard his final words as if to them alone.

"May the Lord bless you and keep you this day and always."

John and Lynn walked out of the service hand in hand, greeted the minister and waited outside for Gerry, who had spotted someone she wanted to talk to for a moment. When she joined them they walked to the campus and the three ate Sunday dinner in the college cafeteria. This was a bittersweet occasion as they shared their remembered highlights of their brief time together and discussed what might lie ahead for each. Lynn was reluctant at this point to share her breathtaking news with Gerry. And then it was time for John to leave. She decided that it would be easier to tell Gerry while John was still with them, which meant that in a few minutes they would share their news.

The college station wagon took them to the ferry dock just north of downtown Sitka. On the way they told Gerry their personal news. She was ecstatic. Gerry hugged John.

"I'm so happy for your both." Then in an almost formal manner. "John, meeting you and having you travel with us made our trip so special. I wish you well now as you go on into Canada and home."

As the ferry approached the dock, John put his bag down and hugged Geraldine again. "Thank you, Gerry, for all that you have done for me."

"What have I done?"

"You've given me Lynn!"

She accepted this even though it didn't make sense to her. Then she thought to exclaim. "Providence, John, Providence."

"Ah, yiss!"

John added. "I shall always be grateful to you, Gerry Fischer, for a place at your table!"

And then John and Lynn embraced and kissed each other farewell. The deep and thunderous whistle of the ferry sounded and John was up the gang plank and in a few moments appeared on the deck where he gave them a final wave.

Lynn was in tears. And so was Gerry, for that matter, as the ferry eased itself away from the dock and began its slow departure from the shore of Baranof Island.

The two women climbed into the rear seat of the waiting station wagon and talked nonstop all the way back to their room at the college. There would be much to discuss in the remaining weeks of Lynn's stay in Sitka. Geraldine would be of incalculable help to Lynn as she prepared for a new life. More than ever, Gerry would be a surrogate mother to Lynn.

John remained at the railing on the dock side of the ferry as Sitka slowly faded into the distance. He reluctantly left the railing and found a reclining seat in one of the lounges. He put his bag there, staking out this place for his spot during the next twenty-four hours or so, the time it would take to reach Prince Rupert. He went back onto the aft deck and found a place at the railing from which he could watch Sitka receding as the ferry made its way north around Baranof Island and before turning south toward Petersburg. As the Sitka dock disappeared, his heart sang a farewell to his new found love. He could hardly fathom what had occurred in his life. But it had! The thought of it almost caused him to burst out with a shout of joy. He needed to tell someone, or he would burst. He went in and bought some stationery at the gift shop and found a writing desk and began to write. First his parents, and then the first of many letters to Lynn. His life would never be the same. All because the ship's cafeteria had been crowded on that fateful day, when he'd sat down at the table where Lynn Ellerton was having her lunch. Wow! *'Tis Providence. Isn't it?*

CHAPTER 27

Best Man

"I, Robert, take you, Anne . . . to be my wedded wife . . . and I promise . . . ."

Earl was standing next to his friend Bob Taggert, who was facing Earl's sister, Anne. The two families had come together in the church in which Earl's family were members. It was the wedding of Bob and Anne. Earl was the best man. *What surprising twists and unexpected turns life takes!* Earl thought as he stood there. Many friends from the old gang were in attendance for the ceremony.

As Earl stood beside Bob amid the familiarity of the church sanctuary with the sun sparkling through stained glass windows and casting colored rivulets onto the maroon carpeting, he reveled in the deep and sonorous sound of the three manual pipe organ, and in the mingled scents of perfume and recently polished pews. The comfortable sight of familiar faces bathed him in a misty nostalgia. But he was also struck with the incongruity of the moment. He realized he no longer belonged here. He was in some ways a different person now. His home was in Saline, Montana. His church was a small, white frame building without stained glass—amber frosted glass instead, a place where the upright piano reverberated against the bare wood floors and plaster walls. Good as it felt to be back home, he missed the now familiar faces of "his people" in Saline.

After the service Earl furtively looked around among the many faces at the reception. He was looking for Lynn Ellerton. But he did not see her. He was both disappointed and relieved. Then he saw a mutual friend, a girl who had been Lynn's buddy and also was a friend of Anne's, Judy Waymann. She had also been in the church youth group. "Judy! Good to see you."

"Great to see you, Earl."

She didn't waste any time with preliminaries. "I bet you've been looking for Lynn."

Earl felt himself blush. "Well, as a matter of fact . . ."

"I thought so. Sorry she's not here. She's up in Alaska this summer."

"What's she doing there?"

"It surprised all of us last spring when she announced that she was going up to Sitka to be a volunteer at some church college there. I forget the name of it."

"Sheldon Jackson College, right?"

"Yeah, that was it. You knew she was there?"

"Oh no, I'm just aware of that college up there." Earl was shocked. It wasn't at all like Lynn to do something like that.

Judy went on to say more about Lynn. "Her mother died, and I guess it didn't work out for Lynn to work in her father's business, or even to be at home anymore."

"Why's that?"

"I guess her father became a terrible tyrant after his wife died and Lynn couldn't stand him. And then when she told him what she was going to do, he practically disowned her. He said she was throwing her life away."

Sounds like her father, Earl thought to himself.

Just then some other friends stopped by and the conversation ended. Earl heard no more of Lynn Ellerton, but wondered about what he'd been told.

Judy turned back to Earl. "Where are they going for a honeymoon—do you know?"

"I've no idea. They are very secretive."

"I thought the best man would know. You know—making the arrangements, holding the car keys—that sort of thing."

"No, all I have on that list are the car keys."

"Oh, now that's interesting. Why don't you just tell us where the car is so that we can get it nice and ready for them!"

"Sorry—that's why I'm the *trusted* best man."

"OK for you. We'll find someone more willing." Judy thought about how that sounded. "But I understand, Earl. It's been good to see you." Judy went off with her friends.

"Tell Lynn 'hello' from me . . ." Earl realized that Judy hadn't heard him. He thought. *Just as well . . . I guess.*

The reception was drawing to an end. Earl got the pre-arranged signal from Bob for him to get the car. Earl brought Bob's car to the front of the church, where he waited for the couple to come running out of the church under a shower of rice and well wishes. He helped them into the car and drove off as quickly as possible. Earl drove a circuitous route to elude others in the wedding party who were trying to follow in their cars. As soon as he saw that he had shaken off the pursuers, he got onto Harlem Avenue and headed south to Washington Boulevard, onto which he turned east to Oak Park Avenue. He went around the block and brought the bride and groom to the entrance of the Oak Park Arms Hotel. He stopped in front and helped Anne and Bob out and walked under the canopy with them and into the lobby, to the elevator where he left them. The young man operating the elevator quickly ushered them in and closed the door. By pre-arrangement, Earl parked Bob's car a block north on Oak Park Avenue behind his own car. He locked Bob's and drove off in his car. Bob, of course, had a second set of keys.

Earl returned to the church, parked in the church lot, and found that many were still in the reception. However he found the church devoid of the excitement of the day. He felt a tinge of sadness—if not depression. In an irrational sort of reverie he felt as if he had just lost a sister and also a friend. *The classic bachelor best man.* He thought. Perhaps more devastating was that any chance of contacting Ellertons had been dispelled by Judy's account of Lynn's falling out of her tyrannical father's good graces. *A mission volunteer!* That wasn't the Lynn of the beach house in Michigan he had known. He certainly was curious. He could make some contact with Sheldon Jackson College, but unfortunately his reluctance would prevent him from trying to contact Lynn. *Lynn is past history.* He thought. *Regrettably. But who's in my present history?* The only person he could think of as coming near was Karen Collins. But he hadn't thought much about her since Menucha. *Like a summer camp girl friend. It's all over when you return home. It must be the same for her. She hasn't made any contact since Menucha. I haven't either. But then it's not been but a few months.*

With Bob and Anne gone, he felt that he did not belong to this group. *This is past history as well. My home is Saline, Montana.* Earl experienced in this moment a homesickness for his new home on the prairie and his new friends in Saline. With the exception of his own parents, Earl had no desire to renew any of his former relationships in the Chicago area—so long as Lynn was gone. In fact the old familiar streets and scenes had taken on a surreal quality, making him all the more eager to return to his home on the plains of Montana.

After spending the day after the wedding with his parents, Earl pushed himself to make it back to Montana in two days of driving U.S. 12. He pulled into a motel in Mobridge, South Dakota at ten o'clock in the evening and by seven the next morning he was on his way. He crossed the Missouri on the west edge of Mobridge and experienced exhilaration when he felt the effect of a bright blue cloudless sky. Towns were now further apart and traffic had thinned considerably. He remembered the essay he had read when he first drove out to take the job—*Where the Skies are Bluer and the People are Fewer.* He had learned the meaning of those words and now he was experiencing them again. Earl felt a surge of pleasure. He had to watch his accelerator foot. He wanted to be in Saline NOW.

His route took him through a corner of North Dakota. He entered Montana just east of Baker and almost wanted to get out and kiss the ground. He pulled into Glendive for a late supper at the Jordan Hotel. And then after the sun had set he reached Saline, turned off the highway and drove up to the manse. *Home at last!* he said to himself. The only feeling to reduce his euphoria was the emptiness of the house and the awareness that he was alone and unmarried.

After a good night's sleep and breakfast, Earl walked over to his office in the church. The first order of business was to look at his calendar and to begin planning what he should be doing. He found that he'd gotten back just in time for a presbytery meeting in Miles City, scheduled for the following Friday. This was Wednesday. The first day back also involved sorting through the mail which had accumulated during his Chicago trip. One piece of first class caught his eye. It had a W lazy N brand on the return address. He opened it and read:

> Dear Earl,
>
> Walter and I thoroughly enjoyed your brief visit. Not nearly long enough—we remarked to ourselves after you left. To remedy that, we would like to invite you to have a meal with us at your convenience. Might I suggest Saturday evening the twenty-third at six o'clock?
>
> If this will not work for you, perhaps another Saturday evening would be better. Please let us know if you can come out to the ranch.
>
> > Cordially,
> > Beth Norland

Earl checked his calendar and jotted off a note of acceptance. He looked forward to further contact with this intriguing couple.

Friday of the following week he attended a presbytery meeting held in the Miles City church. During one of the coffee breaks when the delegates went downstairs to the fellowship hall, Earl noticed a familiar, but unknown face, in the kitchen. The young woman whom he had seen in the Saline post office and whose car he had seen out at Norland's. Earl and Homer each took a cup of coffee and found a couple empty places at one of the tables. Earl sat facing the kitchen. When the young woman came out carrying a plate of cookies, he turned to Homer and asked.

"Who is that? I've seen her in Saline," he pointed discreetly.

"Oh, that's Walt Norland's daughter, Kaye."

"Does she live here in Miles City? She must be a member of the church if she is serving."

"I don't know. I find it surprising to see her here." He then added, "I heard she'd moved back. She had been living in Minnesota."

"I called out at Norlands recently, but didn't meet her."

Homer was interested in hearing about the call and further talk of Kaye ended.

Homer turned to visit with an acquaintance sitting next to him which gave Earl opportunity to go for a refill of coffee. He purposely timed this to coincide perfectly with one of Kaye's trips to the serving table.

"Oh, hello," he said brightly.

"Hello. Do I know you?"

"No, but I remember seeing you in the post office in Saline some time ago."

"Oh, that's where I saw you. I was trying to think."

She broke a moment of awkwardness by saying, "Anyway, welcome to Miles City." And she went about her work.

Earl went back to join Homer and to finish his coffee. The rest of the meeting was a blur for Earl. He couldn't keep his mind off the woman with the cream colored Chevy. The meeting broke for supper. Once again everyone filed downstairs to the church dining room where once again Earl kept his eye on Kaye Norland. The group enjoyed a few minutes of free time after the meal before returning to the sanctuary. Earl was pleased to see that Kaye and the other women who had served came up to the sanctuary for the Presbytery's evening worship. At the close of the service, Homer returned to Saline with another Saline member, while Earl stayed over, having checked into the Olive Hotel. Before going to sleep Earl told himself that he would speak with Kaye in the morning if she were involved again in serving the coffee hour.

The following day when the morning coffee hour was over and most of the members of Presbytery had gone upstairs, Earl held back to talk with Kaye. To his satisfaction she had come out into the dining room with a cup of coffee and a few cookies for herself. She took a place at an empty table. Earl came over to where she was sitting. "I'm Earl Norris, pastor of the church in Saline. May I join you?"

"Why, yes, of course. I'm Kaye Norland." The day before she had seemed a bit formal, but now she seemed to warm up to the idea of his joining her.

"I just felt that I wanted to ask you whether you live in Saline with your parents, or have you moved to Miles City? Forgive me if I sound nosey."

"No, not at all. For the time being I'm living with my parents, but I have joined this church and I come in to town on Sundays and at other times like for this meeting."

"I see. I guess that's why I saw you in the Saline post office." Earl thought it was a dumb remark, but he hadn't known what else to say. "But I'm interested in getting to know you."

Kaye sensed that she needed to explain further. "I was living in Minnesota, married to a man who dumped me and rejected the fact that I was to have his child. So I decided to come home—to people who loved me and would love little

Davey. Mother and Dad wanted me to be home with Davey, so they have helped me to do that. But, I'm feeling that I want to begin to work again. I'll see."

"I'm sorry, Kaye, that you had the bad marriage experience."

"Oh, it wasn't all bad. But it ended badly."

Earl felt that he'd spoken out of turn. "I didn't mean to write it all off for you . . . ."

"That's ok. I've sort of put you in an awkward position, telling you my life story right off the bat." She thought about this. "But your question seemed so real, that I felt I could tell you."

"I hope you still feel that way, Kaye."

She paused. "Yes, I do. You are really the first person besides my parents who seems to care enough about me to ask. The Saline people avoid the subject, and besides our family isn't on the best of terms in the community."

Earl wondered what more she could tell him about this, but felt that an explanation would come later if she wanted to follow up. "I called on your parents recently, and I thoroughly enjoyed meeting them. They struck me as folk I'd like to know better."

"I'm glad of that. They haven't wanted to be in the church, and so your visit is a nice surprise to me."

"In fact, I got a note from your mother just the other day inviting me out to dinner."

"You did!" Kaye seemed genuinely pleased about this. "When are you coming?"

"Saturday evening, the twenty-third."

"Oh, good. I'll be home that night." She was obviously happy about this prospect. Then she added with touch of fear. "You'll meet Davey."

"I'd like that, Kaye. I'm glad this will be at a time you both can be there. But I'd better get upstairs to the meeting. Good to talk."

"Yes. I'll see you."

Kaye returned to the kitchen to help clean up after the coffee break, musing over this exchange with the young Saline minister.

Earl returned to the meeting upstairs, but his thoughts remained downstairs.

CHAPTER 28

Family

As Earl's life in Saline progressed, he felt intuitively the social restriction inherent in the life of clergy. He was learning that the minister is in many ways a displaced person in a community, and to some extent "outside" of the congregation as well. Even more so when he is single. The minister who is not married is apt to feel this social isolation more intensely than one with a spouse and children. In the first "honeymoon" year this is not so obvious, when there are many invitations to dinner, and a constant adulation on the part of some members toward the new minister. Before the new minister has had a chance to step on any toes, or to fail to make a critical call, there is the illusion of being "in the family" of the entire congregation. But as relationships settle down and the reality of people's feelings and attitudes begins to surface the minister becomes pre-occupied with fulfilling various professional claims upon his time and effort in a way that causes the least amount of tension. What free time there is becomes a vacuum of sorts in which the minister can feel very much alone in this new world into which he has been called.

Earl felt this loneliness. For him it took the form of missing his family, or any family relationships for that matter. His parents were over a thousand miles away and opportunities to be with them would not ordinarily be more than a week or two each year. He had been fortunate in having enjoyed a good relationship with his parents and sister. The marriage of his sister had hit him hard. He experienced a profound loss when she and Bob were married. Of course it helped that they were only forty miles or so away. But Anne and Bob had their own life and work now. He did not feel free to intrude.

To draw too close to any particular family in the congregation was unwise. This he had been taught in seminary. Such "fraternization" is what might be termed *politically dangerous*. Earl did not spend a lot of time feeling sorry for himself along this line, but occasionally he became aware of his isolation

By contrast Earl's experience at the Norlands on the evening of August 23 was one of "family." Perhaps the fact that none of the Norlands were involved anymore in the Saline church put this visit in a different category. He remembered that an older minister had told once, *It's always nice to have a Catholic family nearby to be friends with*. When Earl had looked puzzled the older man had said, *They're not in your congregation—not even prospects*. The mood of Earl's earlier call at the W Lazy N had been as a call by the local pastor, so to speak. But his invited visit was different. On this evening he was included around the table of a delightfully congenial family, a family which incorporated Earl in a most gracious way.

Earl had been greeted at the door by Beth Norland. She ushered him into the living room where Walter greeted him. They had a pleasant conversation while the finishing touches were put on the dinner. Kaye entered the living room with Davey in hand.

"Hello, Reverend Norris. So good of you to join us tonight."

"Hello, Kaye. I'm honored . . . and by the way, it's *Earl*. Not *Reverend*."

"You have met?" Walter asked.

"Yes, Dad, I met him during the presbytery meeting in Miles." She then drew Davey toward Earl. "And this is Davey." She bent down to his level. "Davey. This is Mr. Norris."

Earl bent low and shook Davey's hand. "Hello, Davey."

At this point Beth reappeared and invited her husband and Earl to the table. The four went into the dining room. Walter sat at the head, and served the meal which Beth had prepared. She sat opposite with Earl on her right. Across from Earl sat Kaye, with little Davey in a high chair beside her.

Throughout the meal the conversation was easy with moments of laughter and periods of serious discussion. Earl felt so completely at home in this Norland family setting that he discovered that his guard was completely down. Later he reflected that he had not realized the way in which all of his contacts in his life in Saline had been guarded, always wanting to be sure that he was properly understood and accepted. But at Norlands he was himself. It felt as though he were back in the womb of his own family. He realized that the Norlands, including Kaye were accepting him as *one of their own*.

After the meal, Earl and Walter sat visiting in the living room while Kaye and her mother cleaned up. Davey climbed up on Earl's lap with a favorite nursery book wanting Earl to read to him. Earl enjoyed the feel of the little guy on his lap making appreciative gestures while Earl read. After the book he jumped down on the floor to play with some toys which he had on the floor. Without thinking, Earl called into the kitchen, "Won't you let me help with the dishes?"

"Sure." Beth replied. Anyone else in the parish would have refused to do him such a dishonor. Earl entered the kitchen and took a towel from Kaye and began to dry. Another nice sign of his acceptance was the fact that Beth and Kay continued with the conversation she and her mother had been carrying on. When appropriate, they included Earl. As he stood next to Kaye, each wiping a dish with no barrier between them, he thought it felt as though she were Anne. But then not! Kaye was attracting him more and more as a woman, and as a person with whom he felt he wanted to draw in close. *Family? Yes, but more like a spouse than a sister!*

By the time the dishes were done and the kitchen put to rest for another day, Walter was in the mud room beside the back door. He was putting on his overalls to do the chores. "Hey Earl, you helped the women, now come join me in my chores!" There was a chiding sort of grin in his voice.

Earl, however, took the invitation seriously. "Got some work clothes for me?"

"Sure. There are some hanging in here."

After Earl was decked out like a rancher, he and Walt went out to do the chores.

Beth and Kaye sat down in the living room watching Davey. Kaye opened up to her mother. "Mom, I never thought I wanted another man in my life after the fiasco . . . ."

"Yes, dear?"

"But Earl—I think he's the neatest man. So kind and gentle. So down to earth. He treats all of us with such respect. And I think he likes Davey. I saw him reading a book to him. It was so sweet."

"I agree with all that you say, Kaye." She seemed reluctant to say much more. "I'm glad you are feeling that way. You need not spend your life alone, you know."

"I know that now. But is it too soon to be interested in someone?"

"I don't think so. That is if you feel you have thoroughly given Buck up?"

"I have. If I saw him I'd look the other way."

"That's a start, but its when you see him and you have no particular reaction, as you would with a total stranger. That's when you are really ready."

They fell silent, each with her own thoughts.

The men returned from chores and joined in a pleasant conversation in the living room. Earl wanted to know about the early days on the ranch and about Saline's past history. "Tell me about the beginning of your ranch here."

"Well, it was my father, Kristian Norland, who filed on this homestead back in the late 1890's. He and his brother, Anton, and their wives, came out from

WESTBOUND 187

Minnesota as young newlyweds. My uncle and aunt went up and found a place in what was then Valley County. Now it's Sheridan, up around Plentywood. His place wasn't near as good as this one."

"How so?"

"The soil wasn't as good, but mainly it was so dry and windy, more inclined to droughts than here."

Earl had another question. "You spoke of a change of county where your uncle farmed. What was that about?"

"I'm not just sure when it was, sometime between 1910 and 1920, I think there were a whole lot of new counties formed when the original big ones split. We've got fifty six now, but back before 1910 there were only about half that number. The population was growing with so many sod busters coming in that the legislature saw fit to let counties divide like that." Walter thought about what he'd been saying and added, "Now we've got way too many."

"Why's that?"

"Well, for one thing the population has gone down. In the drought and depression in the 30s a lot of folks left the state. Couldn't make it. Now there's barely enough in some counties to support necessary services like law enforcement. But, as I said, my dad had a good place here and the drought and depression didn't knock him out like it did some. Oh, times got pretty tough but we made it. Back in the mid-20s we got as much as $1.42 per bushel of wheat. In 1932 we only got thirty-five cents."

"Wow, what a drop! How'd your uncle do?"

"Much worse. Already in the 20s he was having it hard, not so much the crop prices, but the poor yields. However, as it turned out my uncle became quite an influence on our family. It was the hard times that did it."

"How was that?"

"He got involved in the Nonpartisan League out of North Dakota. Eventually it became Farmer-Labor Party. Anyway this left wing outfit put out a newspaper in Plentywood called the *Producers News*. It was a populist sort of paper fighting the enemy which was industry and business interests on Main Street, so to speak, and county government. There was a man who had come from North Dakota to start the paper. His name was Charles Taylor and he was its editor for years. Much of what was in the paper he claimed was the voice of farmers, but it probably was mostly his own writings. But his ideas fed the anger and frustration of farmers in northeastern Montana during the tough times of the twenties and thirties. And what Taylor preached became their ideas. So much so that they even sent Taylor to the Montana Legislature as a senator for a term or two." Norland sensed that he'd been going on too long. "Anyway, the reason I'm bringing all this up is that my uncle kept sending copies of his *Producers News* down here to us, and eventually it had an influence on my father's thinking, and I guess I'd have to say on mine as well."

Earl dared to comment, "It's why you are one of the few Democrats in a heavily Republican area!"

"That's right, Earl. But the movement up there went too far. It even got allied with the Communist Party in those days. That's when my father quit reading the rag."

Beth took over. "Walter, I think Earl's probably heard more than he wants to know about the Norland political saga."

Earl demurred. Walter agreed, "Certainly, Beth."

Turning to Earl, Beth asked. "So, tell us your story."

Given the cue, all three Norlands quizzed Earl about his background in the Chicago area.

"Well, as you know, I was a city boy—suburbs, actually. At first, during high school and college I thought I'd probably stay in the area, go into some kind of business. In fact for a while I thought I had a future in a manufacturing firm. That's why I majored in business. But then I felt the call of God to ministry, and went to seminary."

Kaye interjected. "Whatever made you come out here? There must have been lots of churches needing ministers back there."

"I don't know exactly . . . ." Earl thought a moment. "When you grow up in the midwest like I did there is a sort of romantic ring to images of the *WEST*."

Beth Norland chimed in, "'Go west, young man!' Wasn't it Horace Greeley who said that?"

"Yes, Mother," Kaye agreed. "Is that what got in your blood, Earl?"

"To some extent. I remember the morning I boarded the *westbound* North Coast Limited. I felt the pull of the west. Anyhow here I am and I like it."

"I'm glad you do." Kaye seemed especially interested in Earl's story. "I know when I went back to Minnesota, it seemed like I was going backwards."

"What did you do in Minnesota?"

"I had a job with a local government agency. That's when Davey was born. But after my husband left me I wanted to come back to Montana. I guess you'd say I too wanted to go west."

There was an awkward silence which Walter broke. "Kaye was married. They lived in the Twin Cities, but her husband left her when the baby was born."

"I'm sorry, Kaye." Earl didn't want to reveal that Kaye had told him some of her story when they'd gotten acquainted in Miles City.

"You needn't be. That's all over, and I don't think there was a future for me in Minnesota. I'd much rather be here."

Earl felt that it was a subject which needed changing. "Talk about going west. I can't believe it, that my sister is just forty miles away from me." Walter expressed surprise.

"She was out here for my ordination and met Bob Taggert, the Presbyterian minister in Terry who was single, and they fell in love and married!"

"Do you get to see her very often?" Kaye asked.

"Not very often. We each have our own reasons to keep busy. I'm hoping that at least on holidays we'll get together." Then Earl announced, "It's after nine. I must let you get to bed. I have some polishing to do on tomorrow's sermon."

When Earl got up to leave, Walter stopped him long enough to make a suggestion. "Speaking of holidays, we usually celebrate Labor Day with a family barbeque outside in our yard. I'm the chef and maitre d' so I'd like to include you this year, Earl—and your sister and her husband as well. Do you think you all could come?"

Earl stammered, not wanting to wear out his new welcome into the Norland family.

Walter sensed this. "Besides, Davey needs someone to read him stories!"

"OK—for Davey." Earl grinned. "And I'll check with the Bob and Anne."

With warmth Kaye added, "Thank you, Earl."

As Earl reached the door in a spontaneous show of affection Beth hugged him. Perhaps to excuse this display she said. "You seem like family, Earl."

On the night of the Norland barbeque, Anne and Bob stayed at Earl's before driving home the next morning. At breakfast Anne said of the celebration, "Earl, we had a perfectly happy day at Norlands. They're great people. And Kaye!" She gave a knowing glance at Earl. "Something there?"

Earl felt himself blush, which Bob could see. For all Bob's bluster he is a sensitive person, able to key into other people's feelings. "That's ok, buddy. Anne's a bit nosey, and we need to hit the road . . . gotta feed the cat."

After the Taggerts drove off, Earl walked over to his office. There was a new spring to his step, and a smile down deep. When he sat down behind his desk and leaned back he clasped his hands behind his head and thought. *Family: Anne and Bob, Walter and Beth, little Davey, and Kaye.* Little did he know how these "family" relationships would develop. But for now it was all good. On this September morning he didn't feel so lonesome anymore.

A few days later Earl got a phone call from Bob Taggert. "Hello, brother-in-law!"

"Hello, Bob. How are you and my favorite sister these days?"

"Great, but I've got some startling news."

"What is it?"

"Well, ol' buddy, I got a letter from a special friend of yours . . . ." Bob waited for Earl to ask.

"Who?"

"Kaye Norland."

"Kaye Norland? What on earth does she want—writing you . . ."

"She is on the pulpit committee at Miles City. The committee asked her to write me, because she told the other members that she had met me." Bob was stringing this out for as long as it could take.

"Yeah—what for?" Then Earl decided to play along with the delaying action. "I know, she wants a recommendation from you about me, whether I would be a good selection for Miles City!"

"No, as a matter of fact what she wanted to know was, whether I would be willing to be considered for pastor of Miles City."

There was a long pause. "Really? Are you going to say *yes*?"

"I don't know, Earl." Bob turned serious. "That's what I'd like to visit with you about. I need some perspective from someone else before I reply to your new friend."

"I can't say what you should do, but I'd be happy to let you bounce your ideas off of me."

"That's what I mean. Might I come over and visit with you tomorrow afternoon? I'll talk Anne into coming over and fixing us supper while we talk."

"I'll have something ready. Tell her to come and relax."

The next day the two talked while Anne read a book. After considering all the ins and outs Bob concluded, "I've felt that my effectiveness at Terry would soon be over. And I believe God is calling me, at least to allow my name to be considered."

"Great. But there's one thing."

'What's that?"

"If you do go to Miles City and become Kaye Norland's pastor, don't let that change the fact that we both agree that the Norlands are 'family.'"

"I see what you mean." Then Bob put on a fiendish grin. "Of course, if you were to take certain actions she might find herself in a different congregation and really in the family!"

CHAPTER 29

At Home in Southland

Trevor came through the door into the mud room. He'd been working out in his shop for most of the morning.

"We've only got an hour and a half, dear. You'll be changing your clothes. There's a sandwich in the fridge."

Slipping off his gum boots, he replied, "Thank you, Meg. I'll be ready." With that he went to wash up. After that he headed for his closet in their bedroom and selected his best woolen trousers and his newest jersey, also wool. His wife, Margaret, was in the kitchen when he got his sandwich out of the fridge and sat down with her. "A special day, isn't it?"

"Ah yiss. Almost a year, love."

"You're looking spiffy, dear."

Meg had on her newest woolen skirt and knit sweater combination. She'd also spent more than her usual time fixing her hair. Attractively set, it was auburn speckled with gray.

"Thank you. I want John to be proud of his Mum!"

"And to make a good impression on his friend."

"Shouldn't I, though? And look at you. Like Sunday, Trev!"

"Right! It is a special day, isn't it."

They finished their sandwiches, cleared the table and hurried with last minute details before going out the back door to their car. Trevor climbed into the driver's right door and started up his Mitsubishi sedan. They headed out the lane, off to Invercargill.

Trevor and Margaret Lindsay drove into the car park at the air terminal fifteen minutes before the scheduled arrival of their son's flight from Christchurch.

John and his new American friend, Lynn, had flown into Christchurch from Los Angeles earlier that morning.

The terminal waiting area was crowded with people, some meeting family and friends, others waiting to board for the return flight to Christchurch. The Lindsays sat on the dark blue vinyl seats facing the large plate glass window looking out to the tarmac—expectantly.

"'twill be very good to see John again. Besides, I need him on the farm."

"Is that the only reason, dear?"

"Of course not. I want to see him—farm or no farm."

"So do I, it's been a long time. But I know he's had a great trip, hasn't he?"

"I'm sure, especially bringing a friend back."

Meg had a troubled look. "Trev, I wonder what she'll be like. She's from Chicago."

"Like the Mafia, I suppose," Trevor grinned.

"Oh no. I don't mean that. But an American. I think she'll be tall, and she'll have a perfect complexion with lots of make-up . . . ."

"And self-confident, just a bit brash, perhaps. Like the Americans . . . ."

"A bit distant, I imagine, don't you, Trev?"

"No, I think of them as casual and folksy. Maybe a bit artificial. We don't know, do we? I think we're going on a bit."

Meg wouldn't be stopped. "A city girl. How will she do as a sheep farmer's wife?"

"Wife—is she? What are you saying?"

"Well, when your son brings a young woman all the way from Alaska to see New Zealand and to meet his family—what else does that mean?"

"Oh, I think she might just be a tourist. One of those rich American kids wanting to see the world."

"Ah yiss, the world and John Lindsay's parents!"

Trevor turned serious. "You may be right. That would be something now, wouldn't it?"

"Think of the adjustments—to a new country—to the farm—to small town life."

"Maybe they plan to live in the U.S."

"Oh!" Meg was taken aback. "I hadn't thought of that. Do you suppose?"

"Can't tell, can we?"

"But then, perhaps just a tourist." She seemed to be assuring herself.

Trevor added. "However, dear, we must face it that John's old enough to be married, and this might be . . . ."

Their conversation was brought to an end with the announcement over the loud speaker, "AIR NEW ZEALAND, FLIGHT NUMBER 1304 IS ON THE GROUND AND WILL BE ARRIVING AT GATE #1 SHORTLY." Just then they heard the sound of the turbo jet engines slowing down while the airliner rumbled as it cautiously taxied toward the terminal.

The Lindsays got up and took a position next to the entry door of Gate #1, standing to the side to allow incoming passengers room to pass. They could see through the window that the plane was slowly arriving and now coming to a stop. The propellers continued to rotate a bit after the engine had been shut down. First one and then the other came to a complete stop. The ground crew rolled a stairway to the cabin door, and after one of the ground attendants went up to open the door, the stewardess appeared in the opening. Then the passengers began to de-plane. Trevor and Meg watched intently.

"There he is, Meg."

"I see him, and that must be his friend right behind him."

They saw John reach the tarmac and turn around to give the young woman a hand as she too stepped onto the pavement. They came walking toward the terminal doorway. And then they were inside.

"Mum! Dad!" John hugged his mother and then threw an arm around his father.

"John!" they both acknowledged in unison.

Then turning to Lynn, "My parents, Trevor and Margaret Lindsay, Lynn," and facing his parents and smiling, "Mum and Dad, meet Lynette Ellerton."

After a brief moment of hesitation, Margaret Lindsay offered her arms to Lynette in a hug, and after that Trevor extended his hand to her. "Miss Ellerton, welcome to New Zealand."

"Oh, thank you, Mr. Lindsay."

"Such formality." John exclaimed, turning to his parents. "She is Lynn." And to Lynn he advised. "These two Kiwis are Mum and Dad."

The awkward moment seemed to be dispersed by this invitation to familiarity. Then John said, "Let's go over to the baggage window and I'll fetch our two bags." Trevor took the cue and excused himself. "I'll bring the car up."

The two women engaged in courteous small talk about the flight while John retrieved the luggage. The three walked out of the terminal building to the curb where Trevor was waiting outside the car with the boot open. John put the bags in while Trevor took Lynn's arm. "Lynn, won't you sit in the front, so that you can have a good look at New Zealand as we drive home?"

"I'd like that very much."

She started to move toward the right front door.

"No. The passenger side is on the left . . . I told you things were strange here!" He gave her a sly look.

"Ah, *yiss*, the water drains the other way too," she joined in the fun.

John and his mother got in the back and the four were off. They drove through Invercargill quickly and soon were heading west on Highway 99. A few miles past Wallacetown, Trevor turned north on a secondary road to Drummond.

The three Lindsays began pointing out familiar sights. John especially exuded enthusiastic pride as he named one sight after another. When they reached the southern edge of Drummond, John pointed out the Golf Club House and then, "There's my old school, Lynn, and over to the right you can see the steeple of our church."

"Not much to Drummond, I'm afraid." Trevor's mother said apologetically.

"Oh no, Mrs. Lindsay, I'm finding everything I see so very fascinating." Trevor announced. "We'll soon be coming to Glen Mor."

Lynn seemed perplexed. "Is that the name of the village you live in?"

"Oh, no. That's the name of our farm," Trevor corrected her with a sense of satisfaction.

"I didn't realize that farms had names here. But I guess I did see names at the gateways of farms as we've been driving along." Then she asked, "What does Glen Mor mean?"

This was enough to start Trevor off on some family history. He seemed to slow down the car in order to give Lynn the full story. "The farm was named by my grandfather when he and grandmother first came here to New Zealand from their native Scotland. He had his work cut out for him when he first arrived. It was a gigantic effort to get things started here, clearing trees and the like."

"His young wife, my grandmother, was most unhappy so very far from her home and her family in the northwest of Scotland—the Ross-Cromarty area. Her people were of the Ross clan. Grandfather did all he could to cheer her up. One of the things he did was to name their farm for her home region. Glen Mor is along the Carron River which runs to the east into the Dorroch Firth. That was near the village of Kincardine where Grandmum grew up . . . ."

Margaret interrupted. "Trevor, Lynn doesn't want to know all that." She addressed Lynn. "He'll go on and on and I won't blame you if you're bored with it."

John responded too quickly. "Mother, she will need to have this family background." In the pause that followed, John realized what he had hinted at. He tried to recover. "If she is interested in what it's like here in New Zealand."

"Yes, I want to hear it all," Lynn helped to smooth over the subject.

Trevor continued. "Anyway, that's how the farm came to be called Glen Mor. It's a name which has stuck over the generations. I'm the third generation of Lindsays to farm here. And we're hoping—aren't we, Mother—that John will be the fourth."

"Oh, Father, you sound as if you are in doubts." John was quick to assure his parents of his intention.

"Well, we thought perhaps you'd fallen in love with the U.S. And that you would move there."

"Doesn't sound like the John I know," Lynn remarked.

"No—I've had my 'Great Kiwi' trip. I'm ready to settle down right here at Glen Mor."

Trevor gave a knowing look into the rear view mirror catching Meg's eye. By this time they had reached the entry to the lane into the Lindsay farm. Trevor pointed out. "There's the sign."

"*Glen Mor!*" Lynn intoned when she observed the wrought iron name on the curved masonry wall to the left of the lane entrance. On the right was a simple metal plate announcing, *The Lindsays.*

Trevor entered through the left gate into the circular drive which took them to the front of the house. He stopped in front of the steps leading to the front entrance. He hurried around to Lynn's side, opened the door, and offered her his hand as she stepped out. "Welcome, lass, to Glen Mor," he stated formally, as he rolled the "r" affecting a Scottish brogue.

Lynn smiled and responded in a similar tone. "Thank you, Trevor Lindsay, Lord of Glen Mor!"

"'tis *laird* if we're going to give it the Highland touch," John corrected. Everyone laughed politely.

"Anyway, Lynn, we are so very glad you are here with us." Meg put her arm around her.

"Thank you, so much."

With that they all went into the entry hall. "Trevor, show Lynn her room, while John gets the bags and I start tea." She turned to Lynn. "You can freshen up a bit and have yourself a bit of a 'relax.' I'll call you when I have our tea ready."

Trevor showed her to her room. "The bathroom and water closet are down the hallway. They are yours exclusively. Ours are downstairs." Trevor returned downstairs passing John as he carried Lynn's bag.

Alone for a moment John and Lynn gave each other a warm hug and a kiss.

"It is so very good to be here, John. Your parents are such neat people."

"Thank you. I think so too. I can tell they both like you." He turned to go downstairs. "I'll see you at tea."

Lynn opened her bag and took out some of her things to hang, and took her toilet kit and headed down the hall. Later when they would be alone she'd tell John how surprised she was to find the water closet so cold. "The seat was made of ice!" she would tell him mirthfully. The bathroom was warm and she lingered to wash and "pretty-up" for her first meal at Glen Mor. Back in her room she pushed aside the lace curtain on the northwest window and looked out across the yard to the field beyond which was speckled with sheep grazing. She would learn to call it a "paddock." Still further to the northwest she gazed upon bright shining snow capped mountain ridges in the distance which she would learn were the Takitimu Mountains between Mossburn and TeAnau. Turning from the window, she sat down in a cloth covered chair to 'catch her breath.' She became aware of a stillness and a silence as she sat. The drone of the airliner was no longer lingered in her head and the slight sensation of motion no longer tingled throughout her body. On the ground in New Zealand. *I can't believe it,* She thought. *Half a world away.*

The sun shone into the window through the lace which had fallen back in place. There was a scent of lavender perfume and freshly laundered bed clothes. Her bed, higher than she'd been accustomed to because of its feather mattress, looked so inviting. *After supper I hope I can turn in. What a comfy room this is. And this house and John's family! I feel so at home.* She experienced the bittersweet realization that her own home had never been so good as she felt it here, nor her parents as warm to her.

"Lynn! Tea is ready." It was Margaret calling.

"I'll be just a moment." Lynn responded as she quickly changed into a fresh skirt and blouse *Don't know what they wear for tea, but this should be better.*

Lynn came down and found John's mother putting the last few dishes of food on the table. She heard the men washing up in the lavatory off of the mud room. They'd been out in the shop together. When John entered the dining room he went to Lynn's side and gave her a sideways hug and helped her to her chair. Trevor and Margaret beamed. Soon all four were seated around the table enjoying a cold supper of roast beef, bread and cheese, as well as a side salad of tomatoes and cucumbers. Meg then retired to the kitchen and soon brought a tray with a teapot of steaming tea with four cups and saucers, sugar and cream. Next she brought a tray filled with delicious looking sweets.

The conversation darted back and forth between items of interest at Glen Mor and bits and pieces of John's year abroad. Every so often one of the Lindsays would turn to Lynn and ask her a question or two about her time in Sitka or in the lower 48, as well as other questions about her life in the U.S.

When dessert was over and the conversation had gone on for a while, Meg looked at Lynn. "Babes, you look so tired. I think you should go upstairs and give yourself a good night's sleep."

"I am tired, Mum. I'll do that, if you say so."

"I do. And sleep in if you want in the morning. Breakfast whenever you come down."

John rose as she got up to leave, and gave her a sisterly pat on her arm.

Upstairs, Lynn stripped and put on her long tee shirt which she used as a nightgown, folded back the covers and slipped between the sheets into a luxurious womb of bedclothes. *At home—ready for a new life,* she thought. She was very quickly overcome with sleep.

Downstairs the three Lindsays lingered over their second cup of tea. It didn't have to be said for John to realize how quickly Lynette had won over the hearts of both of his parents.

"Just the way she called me 'Mum' melted my heart."

"It almost made me weep," John admitted.

"What do you mean?" Trevor asked.

"Well, she had a very tragic home life, so much so that she really has no home anymore in Chicago or anywhere else. And I guess in many ways never had much of a Mum."

"How so?" His mother wanted to know more of this.

John shared with his parents what he knew of Lynn's background and concluded with an explanation of the present circumstance. "Her mother died a few years ago of liver failure due to alcohol. Her father turned into an insufferable tyrant. And Lynn left home forever. I can imagine that what you both have been to her in just a few short hours is what she's missed all her life."

"Oh my—what a sad story."

"It is that, Mum."

"I'm glad you've told us, Son."

Trevor nodded in agreement.

Everyone was quiet. The ticking of the kitchen clock took over.

"Let's call it quits for today," Trevor suggested. "You are home, John Lindsay. Mother and I couldn't be more pleased. And I need you on the farm, Son."

Agreement was total and before long the entire household at Glen Mor was asleep.

The next morning Lynn opened her eyes to see the sunlight beginning to break through the curtain of her bedroom window. She heard sounds of breakfast preparation downstairs. The aroma of toast wafted upward. Lynn jumped out of bed and exchanged her night shirt for her clothes for the day, putting on a new pair of slacks and a Sheldon Jackson sweater. After a very brief touch up in the bathroom she came down the steps and into the kitchen. "Good morning, Mum."

"Good morning, Dear."

"How can I help?"

Meg put Lynn to work setting the table, and finally had her bring the bowls of porridge and the stack of toast into the dining room, while John's mother brought the tea to the table. The two men had been outside doing chores, and by this time had washed up and were seated at the table.

Lynn addressed John's father. "Good morning, Laird of Glen Mor!" she grinned.

"And top o' the mornin'to ye, me lass! 'tis a day that's good as gold, isn't it?"

Lynn went around to John's chair and bent down to give him a slight kiss on the cheek.

And it was the first day for Lynette Ellerton at home in Southland.

CHAPTER 30

A Cold Wind Blowing

"Close that big door, Merle. It's freezing in here."

"Sorry, boys." Merle pushed the button and the garage door began its rumbling descent to a foot above the floor where Merle stopped it, to allow exhaust fumes out. This set up a whistle through the ill fitting door into the service station counter area, the frigid whistling sound of a cold wind blowing through Saline in late November.

What leaves had remained on the few trees in Saline had now blown off. No snow yet. But the cold wind through the naked trees and on the dry dead grass made for an inhospitable outdoors. As a result the Club was well attended. All the available ancient steel folding chairs were occupied by "members" while others sat on the floor propped up against the counter. Merle had made a second urn of coffee.

"Well, what's the latest on your preacher, Hank?" Darrel opened with his favorite conversation starter.

"Plenty!" Hank stopped, waiting to be encouraged. This was Hank's favorite way of maximizing the effect of his information.

"Plenty what?" Claude played into the game.

"He's taken up with that divorcee over ta' Norlands."

"Divorcee?" Merle called in from under the hood of a pickup.

"Yeah." Hank called back more loudly now. "Her and her kid came back from 'the cities' a couple of years ago. Heard she was kicked out."

Claude broke in. "The way I heard it, she walked out on Buck."

"Well, whichever it was." Hank wanted to say more. "She's been sponging off her old man ever since. Them Norlands—high and mighty. Probably don't want no one to know."

"She go to your church, Hank?" Darrell knew she didn't but thought that might be part of the problem.

"That's just it. He oughtn't ta go runnin' after some outsider like that."

Karl Gelenik was one of the non-regulars who was seated on the floor. This remark made him give his opinion. "That's right. It causes trouble when them preachers go hootin' after some pagan like that."

"What kind of trouble?" This topic was going better than Darrell had dreamed it would.

"Trouble like makin' people quit the church."

"Like who?" Claude wanted to know.

"Well, the wife for one thing?" Karl reported.

Hank gave his opinion. "He should have gone after your daughter, Ella, Karl."

"He started to, but I don't know what happened."

"So that's it!" Merle was out from under the hood and appeared in the doorway to the garage bay, wiping the dirt and grease off his hands.

"Whad'ya mean—*that's it*?" Darrell goaded.

Karl somewhat sheepishly admitted. "We were hoping he'd like Ella. But that didn't work out. To make matters worse he took up with that Kaye Norland. Gertrude just couldn't take that. Sort of a blow to her pride, I guess."

The crowd was quiet. The subject had turned from mere banter to serious sharing by Karl.

Trying to help out, Merle asked. "How does Ella feel about him takin' up with that Norland woman, Karl."

"The funny thing is, she thinks its fine, and she still goes to church."

"Strange," Hank said. "Well, that kid never did get it right."

"Maybe not so strange." Darrell gave another perspective.

One of the other non-regulars was Homer Stein. He thought the subject needed changing and tried to steer the "club" off of Earl. "What did you guys think of the Bobcats last night?"

However, Hank Hurlbutt had more on his mind. "And another thing—that there ad in the paper . . . ."

"What ad, Hank?" Reisner asked.

"You know. The one about Communist China and all that other stuff. Signed by all them 'socialists' . . . ."

Merle hadn't seen it. "What did it say?"

Hank took out a crumpled newspaper clipping from the pocket in his bib overalls. "Here I've got it. Read it for yourself." He handed the ad to Merle. "Lemme read it out loud so's we can all hear it."

A Statement of Concern
IN VIEW OF RECENT STATEMENTS BY MEMBERS OF THE LEGISLATURE: that no sale of surplus wheat should be made to people in Eastern Europe because they are in the Soviet bloc; and that this country should not recognize Red China; and that there is no need for a Civil Rights Bill because if those who are allegedly discriminated against improve themselves discrimination will cease to exist.

As members of the clergy of Montana we make clear and relevant the basic ethical implications of the Christian Faith for the decisions which are being made in our day. THEREFORE:

WE AFFIRM our duty as Christians to feed the hungry no matter their politics.

WE AFFIRM in the interest of world peace the need to give diplomatic recognition to China.

AND WE AFFIRM the need for legislation to ensure the civil rights of those in our society who are victims of discrimination.

"And it is signed by twelve preachers, including *The Rev. Earl Norris!*"

"Yeah, I read that. It didn't bother me. They have a right to their opinion." Homer felt that it wasn't so bad.

"I don't like our preacher gettin' political and being critical of our country's policies. He's got no business signing a thing like that. Should stick to preachin'. Me and Jake Munson was at a patriotic meeting the other night and the subject came up, and we don't like it one bit. And another thing . . . always talkin' about the hungry."

There seemed to be general agreement among "club" members. Homer, however, took another position. "Now wait a minute, Hank. Suppose a preacher comes out in favor of the president and says what a good job he's doing and supports his policies, whatever they are?"

"That's different. I mean politics. Politics like what that there Norland talks about—Commie stuff, I say. That's what's bad. Preachers should stay out of politics. Their job's the Bible." The more Hurlbutt went on the more angered he became. "In fact, you just wait, Homer. I'm going to go to the church board about this."

The cold wind blowing through the loose door kept on whistling as the conversation shifted to the weather.

Winter on the plains of eastern Montana that year was bitter cold. The wind seemed never to tire. Snow was scarce, and most of the locals feared that this would be a drought year. Only 60% in the streams the experts reported. Not enough for summer irrigating. It worried people.

However, over the months of that winter the warmth of relationship between Earl and Kaye deepened. They spent more and more time together. They often included Davey who adored Earl. Earl turned out to have a knack for relating to Davey. Nothing had yet been said, but Earl and Kaye each had begun to imagine what life would be like if they were to marry. *Would I be a very good pastor's wife?* Kaye often wondered. Earl found himself asking. *If we should marry, would we have to move to another church somewhere?*

Gertrtude Gelenik hadn't been to church all winter, though she still went to the monthly circle meetings of the women's group. However, Ella was in church every Sunday and Karl attended with some regularity. This did not escape the attention of church folk. Gertrude's absence and Ella's attendance was perplexing to some. But there were those who saw this as a confirmation of what they had always thought—that it had been Gertrude who had her eye on Earl as a husband for her daughter, but that Ella, apparently couldn't care less. On the surface, Earl's courtship of Kaye didn't seem to bother most of the church members. However, Earl felt that some were rather cool to the idea of his friendship with Kaye. This seemed unreasonable to Earl.

On one of his trips into Miles City to make a hospital call Earl had a helpful conversation with Homer. They met by accident in the Red Rocks Café in Miles City. After the usual small talk, Earl asked Homer, "Why is it that my dating Kaye Norland seems to be a problem to some people in the church?" He modified a bit. "Besides Gertrude, I mean."

Homer took a sip of his coffee, thought for a moment and then offered his perspective. "At first there was a sort of sympathetic support for Gertrude. Everybody knew how she felt and why. But then, as they saw that Ella kept coming and didn't seem to care what your personal choices might be, folks settled down to accepting you and Kaye. But still not liking it."

"Why not?"

"Well, I think it has to do with how they felt about Norlands in the first place."

"Which is something I've never quite understood."

"It's a long story. I've never really discussed this with anyone, but if you have time I'll try and explain, at least what I think."

"I wish you would, Homer."

Homer took a drink of coffee and began. "In the first place, Walter Norland is very successful. He's on a good piece of land. The original homestead was probably the best slice of eastern Montana anyone could claim. Down in the river bottom, the soil has always been rich, and there seems to be more moisture on his place than on those higher up. Beyond that the Norlands have been good farmers. The W lazy N is known all around the state. When he takes cattle to the auction yards in Billings, all the auctioneer has to say is that the critter is from the W lazy N and the bids start higher. People like that are not appreciated, Earl. Their wealth is resented by those who are just getting by. So there are small minded people in the community who hate the Norlands for that reason." He added reluctantly, "And some in the church feel that way."

"I see, but I find that unreasonable."

"Maybe so. There's another reason why people in this community have turned against Walter. He and his wife went to college in the east somewhere. Not only college, but each got a masters degree—not in agriculture, but in cultural subjects—English and history, I think. That makes them seem to *put on airs* people will tell you. But I don't think so. Education sets you apart, but it doesn't have to make you stuck on yourself. I've worked with Walter. He's just as common as the next one. But you can't tell people that. But there is one thing about their particular education."

"What's that?"

"Well, around here everyone is pretty conservative politically. Not Norlands. They are pretty far to the left, which gets them in trouble whenever they speak out on some issue. In fact some folks are sure that Walter and his wife are Communists." He added. "And atheists."

"What do you think, Homer?"

"Absolutely not. Quite liberal in their views, but they are Americans. And I say they are Christians. Just have had a bit of set-to with the church, that's all. But you can't convince people of that. They'll believe—and spout—what they want to."

"No wonder they seem quite distant from the community."

"But there's more. The most hurtful reason church people oppose your becoming friends with Kaye Norland is that the Norlands don't go to church—not only don't go, but they definitely spurn the church."

"Why is that? Do you know?"

"Yes I do. They used to be in church all the time, and in Sunday School. One Sunday morning when Kaye was a mere infant, Walter was teaching the adult Bible class. It was about Genesis 1. He told the class that he didn't believe creation happened the way the Bible said. He said he favored evolution. Well, it caused a near riot. Before the hullabaloo was over, two or three of the other members said that his teaching was *of the devil* and that he was an unbeliever, and *you know where they go*, some said. Then there were one or two who called him a Communist with such ideas in his head. *He must have gotten those ideas from Stalin,* they said."

"What did Walter do?"

"He didn't get mad. He just packed up his books and left. I know he was hurt."

"What did the preacher at the time do?"

"That's just it. We were without a pastor at that time. Norlands never came back. Nor have they gone anywhere else, so far as I know."

Earl told Homer about the degree of Kaye's relationship to the Miles City church.

"That's good to know. Perhaps if our folks knew that, and got acquainted with Kaye on her own, not just as a Norland . . . . then it might go better for you, Earl."

"You've been helpful, Homer. But now I guess we'd both better get back to whatever we are doing today!"

As Earl drove back to Saline, he had a lot to mull over. If only his congregation could know the Kaye whom he had come to know. Fortunately that day would come.

CHAPTER 31

Firestorm

When Earl put his signature on the advertisement for the newspaper he had no idea it would be so inflammatory. He had been one of seven clergymen who had signed the ad, which was circulated among the members of the county ministerial association. Only two had refused to sign. The ad was written as a result of a talk the ministers had heard the month previous when a political science professor from the University of Montana in Missoula had spoken to the group. The gist of the talk had been that it would be better to recognize a country with whom we disagree, so that dialogue could be established and thus the danger of attack from such a country could thereby be reduced. This point of view was stated in the ad, and reference was also made to the National Council of Churches, which had come out in favor of the recognition of Red China. When Earl signed the ad he agreed with its message but did not think much about it.

The statement made public by the ministers ignited a firestorm throughout the region covered by the local newspaper. Letters to the editor began appearing immediately, most of which expressed strong opposition to the recognition of China. For Earl and other ministers the most disturbing letters concerned the relationship of the church to politics. Among the most scathing was one written by a church member of a conservative church in Rapid City.

> To the Editor:
> Attention all Christians!
> The time has come to rid your congregations of Communist preachers. The recent advertisement signed by so-called ministers in

Montana proves that Satan is at work in your midst. Satan's strategy is to put Communist atheists in our pulpits who are trying to lead us away from the Lord.

The United States is a Christian nation. It's time we stand up for Jesus. If your preacher is one of the signers of this despicable Communist ad, go to your church board and demand that your preacher be removed. Withhold your offering money until he is gone.

"If thy right eye offend thee, pluck it out, and cast it from thee: for it is profitable for thee that one of thy members should perish, and not that thy whole body should be cast into hell." Matthew 5:29

Signed:

A servant sent to purify Christ's body.

Rapid City, South Dakota

When Earl read this letter in the paper, he thought of the reference Dr. Gilroy had made to the illusion of a Christian nation, which he had said was simply not true. At the time Earl had not been particularly impressed with this argument, but now he saw the danger of a too-easy alliance of religion with national politics. Before this issue simmered down he would find himself immersed in the argument. Strangely, he would find that sometimes those who believe most fervently that theirs is a Christian nation are least willing to have their pastors make political judgments.

Two weeks after the infamous ad had appeared, the session of the Community Church of Saline met for its regular May meeting. During those two weeks Hank Hurlbutt had spoken privately with every member of the session beginning with his own wife who was serving a term on the church board. He had then asked Earl for permission to attend the next meeting.

"Certainly, Hank. We'd be glad to have you come. Nothing coming up of a confidential nature. Could you tell me what you'd like to present—so that I know where to place you on the docket?"

"No, Reverner. I'd rather wait and present it to the whole group, if you don't mind."

"That's ok. Just come and we'll give you a spot on the agenda." Earl had no idea what Hank had in mind. No one had said anything about this matter to Earl. The fact of the matter is that Hank had asked each member to keep it quiet until he had a chance to speak. Even Homer complied with Hurlbutt's wish, until the night of the meeting.

. Earl had turned a small corner room off the front of the sanctuary into an office. He was in his office before the session meeting gathering his papers for the meeting when Homer appeared at the door.

"Earl, I don't like what I see developing."

"What's that, Homer?"

"Hank Hurlbutt has been gaining support for his strong opposition to your signature on that ad. He's going to bring that up tonight."

"How much support do you suppose he has?"

"I think he has enough for a majority vote, but I don't know what he wants voted."

"I'm surprised. I haven't had much comment on the ad. It seemed to me that most folks were comfortable with it, or at least with my signing it, even if they didn't agree with what it said."

"At first they were ok with it, but all those letters in the paper, especially that one claiming Satan put you here, have had an effect, and then Hank's been going around to everyone—that has made it worse."

"I see. Well, we'll just have to see what he wants."

"Just thought you might need a bit of an advance warning."

"Thanks, Homer. That helps—I think."

Homer left to go down stairs. The session met around tables in the basement dining room of the church. Earl waited a few minutes and went down to the meeting. As he came down the stairs, he heard a steady buzz of conversation. When he appeared the talk stopped. This sudden silence was unusual and signaled some trouble ahead. He greeted Hank, who gave him a perfunctory "hello." Earl took his seat and opened the meeting with prayer. He turned to Homer and asked for the minutes of the last meeting. Homer read these and they were approved as read. The routine items of business and committee reports were handled smoothly in what appeared to Earl to be a somewhat subdued atmosphere.

Finally Earl asked, "Are there any new items or matters of miscellaneous business?"

At this point Hank Hurlbutt raised his hand. Earl recognized him. "Hank is here to present something. Is there a motion to grant him the privilege of the floor?"

"I so move." It was Homer.

"Second." Hank's wife did the seconding.

Hank looked a little baffled by this introduction, but he forged ahead. "All of you know about the ad . . . ." There was a noticeable sound coming from the members of session. Slight coughing. Hard breathing. "Well our pastor signed that. We need to take some steps."

"What steps are you talking about?" Sue Stark had not been supportive of Hank.

"Yes, are you here to suggest some session action?" Earl pushed.

"Now I'm not sayin', Reverner, that you're not Christian. But anyone to think like that ad is either a Communist or duped by the Commies. But either way. It's not right to have your Commie ideas in this church . . . ." Hank seemed to hesitate before moving ahead. Everyone sensed that this was going to be the crucial action. "So I have the following action."

"Since you're not on the session, Hank, can you give your motion to one of the members—for them to make?" Earl pointed out proper procedure.

Hank turned to his wife seated next to his chair. "Here, you take it."

"I should make this motion?"

'That's right."

Earl offered her the chance to make it.

Hank's wife, Louella, took a deep breath. "I move that the Session ask the minister to resign." She had looked down while she spoke and seemed embarrassed.

You could hear a pin drop. Earl broke the silence. "Is there a second to the motion? Before you discuss it?"

Apparently no one was willing to speak.

"If not, the motion will die for a lack of a second," Earl advised.

Then Archibald Steadman, a new member of the session and a new resident of Saline said, "I second the motion." He explained, 'I don't necessarily agree, but it's gotta be handled."

"Any discussion?" Earl didn't know what else to do at this point. Then he said. "I believe we need to hear Hank's reasons."

Hank spoke. "Everyone knows that an ad like that one is Communist because Red China is Communist. So them what signs such an ad is duped by the atheist Commies. And me and the wife don't want no atheist dupes in our pulpit—and teaching our children. Them's the reasons."

"Thank you, Hank. Any discussion of the motion before you?"

Archibald Steadman raised his hand again.

"Archibald?"

"The reason I seconded the motion was to be sure that we take care of this matter, and don't just sweep it under the rug. Now I don't happen to agree with Hank. But what I think we need to know is what happens next if this motion should pass. Is it like firing an employee—here today and gone tomorrow?"

Earl turned to Homer. "As clerk can you tell the session what the proper procedure is?"

"Well, sort of. Since something like this has never happened here before I have to say what I think *The Book of Order* says to do." He paused. "In the first place the Session can merely recommend such an action to the congregation. However, it can't hire and fire, so to speak, on its own . . . ."

"Why's that?" More than one member shouted.

"There's the congregation and then the presbytery. Congregation has to vote. They have to approve. So the session's first step is to call a congregational meeting, and present a recommendation to the congregation. If it should pass then it is sent to the presbytery that the pastoral relationship between Earl Norris and the Community Church of Saline be terminated. Prior to that we would have to go to presbytery and inform them, asking them to provide a moderator for the congregational meeting. Because Earl shouldn't have to do that. So they send another pastor to moderate. Then if the congregation approves the recommendation we ask the presbytery to concur in our request. Of course they will have to call a special meeting to act on our request to terminate."

"That's a lot of mish-mash," somebody said.

"Presbytery's full of Commies too," Hank said under his breath.

"Mr Moderator." It was Steadman.

"Yes, Archibald."

"I think we need time to think about what we are doing, and to pray about it, so I move to table the motion for three weeks and that a special meeting of session be called to handle the motion before us."

Homer seconded.

Earl declared,. "A motion to table is non-debatable, so I will call for the vote. All in favor answer with an 'aye.'"

There were quite a few "ayes".

"All not in favor?"

A number voted against placing the motion to table.

"The motion passes," Earl stated. "We will meet one week from tonight to take this motion off the table." He added sternly, with just an edge of anger in his voice, "And, Mr. Clerk, will you see to it that presbytery provides you a moderator for that special meeting of the session?"

"Yes."

"I plan to absent myself. Now I call for a motion to adjourn."

The session voted to adjourn. Earl closed with a terse prayer, and left the room immediately. There were those who wanted to talk to him, but he was gone. Hank Hurlbutt and his wife left in silence. The others left murmuring to each other. Homer folded up his papers, locking the building as he left.

Earl let himself into the darkened manse and decided not to turn any lights on. He was hurt and angry and did not want to talk to anyone. Except to Kaye. He felt like he was being swept away in a firestorm. And he wanted only to find Kaye and to be with her. But it was too late to talk to her now.

This is it. I'm not going to give them the satisfaction. I'll do the terminating. I'll go further west as I've always wanted to. He thought of Phil Otis, his friend from seminary days who had taken an assistantship in a Spokane church, and resolved to phone him in the morning to see if there might be a vacant church out his way.

CHAPTER 32

Looking West Again

"Sleeping on it" did not change Earl's resolve to look west with an eye to moving to another congregation. After a hasty breakfast he phoned Phil Otis.

"Hello, Phil. This is Earl Norris . . . . Well, pretty good, but actually things have gotten a bit shaky here . . . Some people are out to get rid of me . . . because I signed an ad urging the recognition of Red China . . . . The real reason? I don't know of any other, but you raise an interesting question. But, Phil, what I'm calling you about is to see if there might be some vacant congregations out your way—something I might be interested in."

This got Phil's attention. "Really? It would be great to have you in this area. But I can't think of any places right off hand. Let me to do some checking around. I'll call you back. What's your number? I'll call you back later when and if I find something—ok?"

"I'll be waiting. When we have a little more time I'll clue you in on the situation here."

"Right. So long for now, though."

After hanging up Earl thought about Phil's question, "Are you sure that's the real reason?" *Hank Hurlbutt is the one who brought this up. So if there's a underlying reason it would have to be something in Hank's head.* Earl thought about Hank and Louella. He'd called on them early in his time in Saline. They had not been particularly friendly. They were fairly regular in worship. Louella was currently on the session and active in the women's organization, but Hank wasn't doing anything else in the church. *About the only time I see the guy—other than on Sundays—is at the Conoco—or at least I see his pick up.* Earl knew what he ought to do. But the idea was not a pleasant one. But then, he could drop by Kaye's on his way back.

Earl heard someone walking through the sanctuary toward his office. In a moment Homer Stein was at his door.

"Come in, Homer. Good to see you."

"I came to see how you're doing after the meeting last night."

"Frankly, pretty dismal. If Hurlbutt's motion goes through, I don't know what I'll do." He paused to see what Homer's reaction might be. Seeing none, he went on. "And you know, Homer, even if it doesn't pass and there is still a group voting to send me out on the Westbound, my effectiveness is gone."

Homer couldn't help but agree. "You are probably close to right on that," but he couldn't let the matter remain on such a negative conclusion. "But I think there is still time to patch this one up."

"How so?"

"To begin with we need to watch that we don't end up with a church split right down the middle. If we let this go until the special meeting, and then take the vote we're going to have two sides, each mad at the other. Then when it goes to the congregation, we've got a church split. I've seen this happen before."

"Not a pretty picture, is it, Homer? But what can be done in the next few days?"

"I'm going to talk to the other session members in the next few days and see what can be done."

"That's good, Homer, but a lot of running around for you."

"It's what we've got to do."

Earl thought he'd share some of his own thinking. "Homer, I've been trying to figure if this Red China thing is the real reason." He waited to get Homer's reaction, but he didn't see any.

"Hank has never been friendly to me, and I wonder if there's something else, deeper maybe."

"Could be. He's not an easy person to get close to. Never has been."

"Anyway, I've made the decision to go out and call on Hank and Louella in the next day or two, just to see if I can understand better what's going on with him—and just maybe help to soften him."

"More power to you, but I'm not too hopeful, if you really want to know."

"What can you tell me about the Hurlbutts?"

"Well, he inherited the place from his father who died suddenly of a heart attack when Hank was in his teens. It never has been a good piece of ground. His father could barely make it. So after Jake Hurlbutt died, Hank and his mother were farming the place until Hank was old enough to go it alone. His mother moved back to Iowa to her people. Hank and Louella had to get married after he got her pregnant while she was still in high school. This about broke his mother's heart. That's why she moved away, they say. She had been raised very strict and that's the way she taught Hank. His father went along with that, I guess. He'd been in the war. Lost an eye and got a bum leg out of it. Turned bitter after coming home, they used to say. Old man Hurlbutt wasn't much for church but he sure was into his lodge and a veterans organization. Used to fly an American flag day and night on his gate. I guess Hank let that go, but he was in the same lodge his father had been."

Earl was picking up some significant background, he thought. "About that pregnancy. I've not been aware of any children in that family."

"No, the baby was a stillborn. Louella never got over that. And they never had any other children." Homer looked at his watch. "I've really got to go now, Earl, but let's talk later in the week—after you've called on Hank, and after I've done some 'repair work'—you might say."

No sooner had Homer left than the phone rang. It was Phil Otis.

"Earl, I did some phoning around and I was told about a church here in Spokane which might be just the thing for you."

"Tell me about it."

"It's Bethany Church on Freya Street. Its small, but I assume bigger than Saline. Around a hundred and forty members, I think. It might be just the place for you."

'Where are they in the process of getting a minister?"

"I understand that they are looking over dossiers right now and that soon they'll select a few to interview. Want me to put your name in?"

Earl thought fora moment.

"You can think it over and call me back."

"No—put my name in, Phil. I'm interested."

"OK, I'll call you back if something develops that I know about."

After Phil's call, Earl phoned Kaye to see if she would be home that afternoon.

"I'm making a call out your way. I'd like to drop by after that. OK?"

"You know it's OK!"

"I know, but I wanted to be sure you'd be there. I've got some church stuff to tell you about."

"Good or bad?" Kaye had a way of cutting to the heart of things.

"Bad."

"I'll be here."

Hurlbutts lived up on some bench land south of the river. To get to their farm Earl took the road past Norlands, which winds along the river for a while and then veers upward to the north. Their lane was closed with a sagging barbed wire gate, which Earl maneuvered open to pass through and shut again before driving up the rutted lane. The surrounding land didn't look too good to Earl (worse to those who knew the land). Theirs was an older two-story house, quite small. Unlike so many houses in the area, Hurlbutts' showed no signs of having been added onto. Two sheds across the farm yard behind the house were in need of paint as well as a few well placed nails to hold them together.

Earl parked his car at the back door and mounted the eroded concrete step to knock. Louella came to the door.

"Hello, Reverend?" She said this more as a question than a warm greeting.

Earl responded by taking the bull by the horns. "I wanted to talk to you and Hank about the meeting last night."

"Oh—" Louella looked ashamed. "Hank didn't mean no harm."

"I'm sure—but I'd just like to have a word with him. Is he around?"

Louella hesitated. "No—I don't believe so. Probably out on one of the far pastures."

Earl was still standing at the door. Louella seemed to feel that her answer took care of the matter.

Earl wanted to retrieve this visit from the "scrap heap." "Perhaps I could talk to you, Louella?"

"Well, maybe for a little bit. There's a couple of chairs on the glazed front porch. I think it'll be warm enough there."

Earl walked around the house, while Louella went through the house and came out onto the porch. When they were seated, Louella explained. "Henry would be angry if he found me entertaining a man in his house." She appeared nervous, sitting stiffly in her chair.

"Well, I won't stay long. I'd just like to have your opinion of the meeting last night."

"I thought it was a good meeting—got a lot done."

"Yes, but what about the motion to terminate my pastorate?"

Louella looked embarrassed, "Oh, that—well, Henry says it will be for the good of the congregation and for your good as well . . . ." She stopped short as Hank's pickup came toward the house. She was obviously fearful of his coming. But then, it stopped and turned around and headed away. She observed, "Must have forgotten something." She sat back in her chair muttering under her breath, "Or seen the reverend's car."

Earl had the distinct impression that when Hank had spotted Earl's Chevy he had turned around in order to avoid him. But the net effect of this dodging was for Louella to relax and to become more willing to talk. Taking advantage of this more open mood, Earl asked her how things were going for them here on the ranch.

She didn't seem to hear the question and spoke of Hank instead. "Henry's very patriotic. He was just a boy when his father went off to war—World War I. And when he returned from France with his wounds, Henry had a hard time with that."

"How was his father wounded?"

"He lost an eye and his left leg was shot up pretty bad, and healed stiff. Henry's reaction after World War II was to hate the Germans and the Japs, and later on the Communists. Most of all it seems now that he is angry with anyone who would dare to criticize the U.S."

"That's why he is down on me for signing the ad?"

"I'm sorry, but I guess so, Reverend."

There was a silence for a few moments until Earl pressed further. "How do you feel about it, Louella?"

She was noticeably embarrassed. "Oh I don't know anything about world affairs, so I just go along with my husband on those things."

"What's important to you, then? Are you active in the county Extension Club?

"No, I'm not a joiner, you might say."

"How about family. Any family in the area . . . brothers, sisters . . . . ?"

Louella stiffened. "No I'm afraid we don't have anyone . . . ."

Earl started to say something, but she continued in a very soft voice. "We were re going to have a little girl—but she died."

"How old was she, may I ask?"

"Stillborn." There was a look of stark horror in the eyes of the mother, still bereaved years after.

"I'm sorry . . . ." At this point Earl didn't know quite how to go on with this subject so obviously painful to Louella. But she had more to say.

"Reverend," she appealed. "The Lord took her away from me—to punish me. I know He did."

"Louella, God doesn't do things like that to punish us."

Then she became very quiet and spoke as if only to herself, "But I deserved his punishment—Henry and I weren't even married when . . . ." She began to weep.

Earl had the sense to let her cry and to wait in silence for her to continue.

"And not only did He take little Louise from me, he struck me barren. Henry blames me, and that makes it all the worse." She suddenly shifted in her chair, a movement which denoted a conclusion to the matter. "So how are you these days, Reverend?"

Earl could see that there would be no point in any further discussion, at least at this time. Louella's question was more of a statement which he acknowledged in perfunctory manner. "Oh, quite well, thanks. I really must be going now. It's been good to visit." and then he thought to add. "And, Louella, please don't chastise yourself so much. God is a forgiving God, not a tyrant who punishes."

Eart started to get up. He noticed that Louella had something else to say.

"When my father found out, he took the belt to me. And I always think of him when I think of God—and also sometimes when I think of Henry, especially when he gives me the silent treatment."

"You mustn't. God does not take the whip. Nor does God reject you in silence."

Louella didn't seem to hear. It was as if she was talking to herself. "And when he's silent like that, the look on his face, I think he's remembering . . . ."

"Remembering what, Louella?"

This startled Louella. "Oh—Reverend . . . I forgot . . . that other time—The girl was just an eighth grader. She went to Helena to have the baby . . . and never came back . . . I think Henry must wonder about her and the baby sometimes."

Earl felt like an intruder, unable to comment. "Louella, I must go now. Will you be all right?

"Yes. When Henry comes back it'll be like it always is." She sighed quietly. "I'm sorry about the meeting, Reverend," she said as Earl took his leave.

As Earl drove away he thought about what he'd heard. *The poor woman has Hank and God and her father confused. It's Hank who has been punishing her all these years! And Hank—what a load of guilt he must be carrying. Both Louella and that eighth grade girl . . . .*

Earl reached the Hurlbutt's gate and hassled it open, drove through and stretched it closed again. Not far along the road he met Hank returning. Both men waved. *Well so much for patching things up with Hank,* Earl thought. He turned his attention to Phil Otis' call and Bethany Church in Spokane. *Westbound again?* Meanwhile, his next stop would be Norlands. *What will Kaye think?*

From the very beginning Beth and Walter Norland had treated Earl like one of the family. And he was moving closer and closer to making that literally true. It wasn't at all unusual for Earl to finish his afternoon calling with a "call" on Norlands, and that often included staying for supper. While *the question* hadn't actually been popped, Earl and Kaye had begun to assume that some day they would be married. And little Davey would be Earl's son in almost every way. That would be much to the delight of both Davey and Earl. And for that, Kaye would be most grateful.

Thus it was quite natural for Earl to share the recent session action with the Norlands while they ate together. "Hank Hurlbutt got his wife to make a motion to oust me from the church for having signed the Red China ad."

Shock reverberated around the table. "Oh, Earl!" Kaye reached to comfort him by taking his hand.

"They can't be serious!" Beth concluded.

Walter pondered this news for a few moments. "Earl, Hank's my neighbor. Lives down the road, but that's the only aspect of neighbor there is between us.

He's got an anger in him that erupts every so often. Now you're getting the brunt of it. And if somebody doesn't call him on this, it will ruin your church."

"I know, and I'm at a loss to know how to deal with this."

"Did the session vote on the motion?"

"They tabled it until a special meeting in three weeks."

"Good. I think I'll talk to some people before then."

"Walter, we're not even in the church," Beth cautioned.

"Yes, but we're part of Saline, and what happens to the church affects us all in this community. You know that, Beth. Remember the last time something like this happened." He turned to Earl. "Tell me who's on session right now."

Earl named off the members while Walter jotted them down. He looked at the list and commented. "There's three here I'm going to see. The others think I'm as much a Communist as you are, Earl, so it'd do no good to talk to them."

"You mentioned the last time?"

"Quite a number of years ago, Hank got crossways with the minister and forced him out."

"What was the issue that time?"

"No one really knew, but I have my ideas about that."

"Now, Walter—" Beth was concerned that he might say too much.

"Tell him what you think, Dad." Kaye urged.

"It was when Hurlbutts had been married only a few years. The parents of one of the high school girls came to the preacher to complain about Hank hanging around the school in the afternoons. I guess a couple of times he gave their daughter a ride home, instead of her taking the school bus. Well nothing was ever really discovered about this business. But at the very least it looked bad. I'm told that the preacher confronted Hank. He got mad and soon he began to stir up trouble in the congregation."

"What was the official reason for sending him on his way?" Earl wondered.

"Well, certainly not the business about Hank. But it was something about the preacher not calling on people enough. It was Hank who had probably started that complaint going around, until finally it forced the preacher to move."

"And you mean that the real reason was Hank's anger at him for bringing up the matter about the young girl."

"Right. So my question now is, 'What's the real reason this time?'"

"I've wondered that too, but I don't have any idea, except to look at his anger and to see if anything in me has triggered that."

Kaye wanted to rescue Earl. "Oh, Earl, I'm sure you haven't done anything."

"Not that I know of."

"Give me a chance to talk to some folks." Walter dismissed the matter in this way. The table conversation turned to other, less weighty, matters.

After the meal Earl volunteered to help Kaye with the dishes. Beth and Walter took Davey into the living room—conveniently.

"Kaye, I want you to know that I phoned a friend in Spokane to ask him if he knows of any vacant churches."

"You mean, you are considering leaving Saline?"

"Yes, this whole mess makes me wonder if my time here is over."

Kaye was taken aback. "Oh, Earl! Is it really that bad?"

"Yes, I think so. After that special meeting I may very well have my 'walking papers' if Hurlbutt gets his way. So it's just simply prudent on my part to take some initiative."

"But what will happen to us?"

"Who is the 'us?'" Earl knew the answer but wanted Kaye to say it.

"Davey and me."

"How about the 'us' meaning you and me and Davey?"

"You mean . . . . ?"

"Yes, that's what I mean."

Kaye took her hands out of the dish pan, and with her wet hands she threw her arms around Earl and kissed him and she said, "Yes!"

They embraced with a kiss.

CHAPTER 33

Becoming a Proper Kiwi

A glorious day had begun. The New Zealand sun had risen in the northeast illuminating Glen Mor with delicious golden rays. Lynn was coming down to breakfast. It was Sunday morning and Trevor and Meg were at the table when Lynn arrived. John was not yet at the table. She was met with a heavily Scottish brogue when Trevor greeted her, rolling his "r."

"Aye and a guid mahrnin' to ye, Lassie"

Lynn joined in the fun. "And a delightful mahrnin' to you, Laird." She turned to Beth. "And to ye, as well, Lady Beth Lindsay!" Then she asked. "What is all this Scottish business about?"

"'Tis the Sabbath, and we're about to get ready for worship at the local parish kirk. And, as you know, we're Church of Scotland here," Trevor replied.

"Presbyterian," Meg clarified with a smile.

John appeared and his father turned to him. "Divine services this morning, Son."

"I know, Father. And I have been looking forward to bringing Lynn and introducing her to everyone." He sat down to his porridge.

A brief wave of shyness wafted through Lynn's consciousness, but was quickly replaced by a nervous excitement as she anticipated meeting John's old friends.

"I've got a few more chores, so I better let you eat in peace," Trevor said with a twinkle.

Lynn turned to Beth. "Mum, what should I wear? What do you plan to wear?"

"The women wear skirts, and usually a jersey over their blouse. That's what I plan, Lynn."

"Good, I can match that pretty well, I think. I don't want to stand out anymore than I have to."

"Oh, there'll be lots of interest, I'm sure," Beth commented as she rose from the table and took her dishes to the kitchen.

"I hope you're not worried over being the center of attention," John commented.

"Oh, no, I think I can take that. I better get used to it, huh?"

"Ah, yiss, mustn't you?"

Soon Lynn and John were finished and each left to get ready.

At 10:30, Trevor had the car waiting for the family. Lynn noticed that John's father also was wearing a jersey. Under it he wore a white shirt with a plaid tie. The Lindsay tartan, she would learn. Soon they were on their way to church.

Lynn found Lindsays' church to be a small picturesque frame building on Drummond's divided main street. Many others had arrived by the time Trevor drove up. He parked on the grass near the building. Soon Lynn was thrust into the midst of a cluster of new friends. John was polite about introducing her to everyone who came near. She felt a genuine warmth in their greetings.

After worship on the way back to Glen Mor, Trevor asked,. "Well, now, how was that experience, Lynn?"

"It was really quite pleasant. I feel as if I have become part of your community, as well as of your own home." Then she added, "And I thought your pastor made some good points in his sermon."

John and his mother joined Trevor in expressing satisfaction over Lynn's response. Soon they were at home and they got out of the car and walked into the house. A most delicious aroma met them as they entered. Lynn exclaimed, "What a wonderful smell!"

"Ah! It's the corned beef roast in the oven!" Beth was quick to acknowledge.

Everyone remained in their church clothes for a meal which followed. When all were seated, Trevor asked the blessing. Beth brought out pumpkin soup. After trying some, Lynn turned to Beth. "This is scrumptious ! I've never had soup like this. What is it?"

"It's pumpkin, dear."

Along with the roast, Beth had prepared both mashed potatoes and what Lynn assumed was a sweet potato dish. "It's swedes, dear," Beth corrected.

"Swedes?" Lynn asked. "I've not heard of them."

John answered proudly. "Southland is famous for the best swedes for the table." He explained. "They are grown mostly as food for sheep. They love to eat them right out of the paddock where they've been planted. They are a type of turnip."

"I see." Lynn tried some. "M-m-m. I like them."

There were three different vegetables and freshly baked rolls. For dessert, Beth brought out a large bowl filled with scoops of vanilla ice cream, as well as a type of brownie. When dessert was finished Beth announced, "We'll take our coffee in the lounge." There she offered each one a wrapped chocolate truffle with the coffee.

"Oh, Mum, this has been such a good dinner." She became quiet. "I can't remember when ever my mother fixed a Sunday dinner. Sometimes we ate out, but the rest of the time we had to fix our own."

Meg patted Lynn's hand and looked at her with sympathy. "I'm sorry, dear. But for now you're ours."

"Well, what are you two up to this afternoon?" Trevor felt a bit uncomfortable with the mood of sadness.

Lynn showed signs of not knowing how to answer.

John announced, "I thought I might show Lynn some local sights. I thought we might drive down through Tuatapere to Te Waewae, and then on through Riverton to Invercargill, maybe down to Bluff." He turned to Lynn. "Would you like that?"

"Why . . . yes. I'm not aware of these places . . . except Invercargill . . . but I'd love to get acquainted with the area . . . especially the ocean!"

"That's what we'll do. Let's change into something more casual."

"Let me help Mum with the dishes before we leave, John."

Meg intervened. "Oh no, dear, you go right away. We want you to have a proper tour."

"You sure?"

"Certainly."

The light rain which had fallen during the night left the ground wet under foot. But above, the bright sun was out in all its glory. Lynn felt a surge of enthusiasm as she and John drove out of the gate and onto the country road going north to Heddon Bush. They crossed the Waiau River at Clifden and again at Tuatapere. Both are small typical New Zealand towns. A few minutes later they came to the ocean shore on Te Waewae Bay.

"Oh, John, the ocean! Let's stop. I want to walk out to the water."

John found a lay-by near Wiahoaka where he could park the car. They walked down to the shoreline hand in hand to a strip of sand onto which the water sloshed up intermittently. Lynn took off her shoes and went down as far as she dared, letting the wet sand ooze over her feet. Now and then she stopped to scoop up a shell which had just washed up. John enjoyed her child-like appreciation. When she returned to him he threw his arms around her and lifted her off her feet planting a kiss on her lips. She regained her footing and they continued their embrace with a long and passionate kiss.

"Ah! My Alaskan mermaid."

"Oh, John, you've turned my life around, sweetheart. I couldn't be happier."

"And my life as well, don't forget."

"I don't want to go back to America." She kissed him again. "I'm so very happy here, John."

John looked pensive. "Must you go back?"

"Remember, customs wanted to see my return ticket . . . to be sure I had one."

"That was just a formality."

"But yet, I assume I must return . . . ." Her reply sounded a bit like a question. "At least to tie things up . . . before coming back . . . that is, if you want me here . . . ."

John was quick to reply. "I want you here, Lynn—forever. Now, let's be on with our tour."

They continued their Sunday jaunt.

John noticed that whenever the road took them along the shore, Lynn seemed especially thrilled.

"You're so taken with the sea, Lynn, that I think we should go down to Bluff. That's the very southern tip of the South Island."

They reached Invercargill, turned south through town and onto the Bluff road.

At Land's End they found a car park and walked to the very edge of the South Island. "Oh, John, this is gorgeous."

"What is it about the sea?"

"You'll think it strange, but it reminds me of my childhood at our summer home."

"You are right. It is strange. Chicago is hundreds of miles from any ocean!"

"Thousands. But our summer place was on the east shore of Lake Michigan. It was called *Shore Crest.*"

"Just a lake, though."

"But large enough that you couldn't see across. That's why the ocean reminds me of our view from Shore Crest." She looked downcast for a moment. "Some of my better days as a kid were there." She became pensive.

"Now you're sad, Lynn. Why?"

Lynn looked embarrassed, but then recovered. "So many of my memories of my parents are not good." But it was a fleeting thought of Earl which occupied her mind.

John interrupted, "Tell me more about your parents."

For a moment Lynn felt a jumble of emotions before she blurted out. "Mother was a drunk and my father was a money-grubbing tyrant." She seemed angered. "I've already told you that."

John could see that it was an unpleasant topic. He turned their attention to a tall post, loaded with yellow signs. "Look, Lynn, the sign will tell you where in the world we are." He began to read. *"Bluff—New Zealand—latitude: 46.36 minutes, 54 seconds South."* John could see that the numbers didn't mean much to Lynn. "That's really south. Antarctica is only 28 more minutes south." He turned her head gently to the right a bit. "There—do you see it?" He grinned.

"Ah yiss!" She feigned a New Zealand accent.

She took up the game and read some of the distance markers. *"15008 km NEW YORK—LONDON 18958 km."*

John read one more. *"1401 km CAPE REINGA*—That's the northernmost point in New Zealand. Some day I'll take you there."

"I'd like that. How far in miles?"

"Only between eight and nine hundred miles. We're a small country . . . We'd best go now. time for tea."

He helped her up and they turned toward one another and kissed before going back to the car and headed back to Invercargill, only a little over fifteen miles.

"I know a place where we can have tea."

"Where's that?

"It's called Zookeeper's Café. It's on Tay street. A laid-back sort of place. You'll like it."

"You're my tour guide—carry on, McDuff."

When they finished their meal at Zookeeper's and were leaving, Lynn took John's hand. "You were right. I did enjoy the meal and the atmosphere."

"Great! What don't you like about New Zealand!" More of an exclamation than a serious question.

"Haven't found a thing."

It was dark before they drove back to Glen Mor. Lynn snuggled close to John. "This was a perfect day. I liked everything you showed me and supper was delicious. And what a zany place!"

"Tea! If you're going to be a proper Kiwi."

"Yes, TEA."

"Then will I be a proper Kiwi—if I say *tea* instead of dinner?"

"That's part of it. It's a whole lot different now for you, Lynn, isn't it?"

"Very, very different."

John caught an ominous tone in her voice. "You mean New Zealand, don't you?"

"Yes, John, it is all so new to me. Sometimes I wonder who I am and what I'm doing here. My return flight is in two weeks. I get very sad thinking about leaving you."

"We have to talk, Lynn."

"About my leaving?"

"Or staying." John then launched into an important discussion, he'd been anticipating since their arrival in New Zealand. "You have had a bit of an introduction to New Zealand. You have seen what it's like at Glen Mor. You have helped Mum with so many different tasks, that I think you must have a pretty good idea of what life on a New Zealand sheep farm would be like. Am I right?"

"I think so, unless there are some things I haven't experienced yet."

"When I asked you to marry me, you spoke about seeing if you thought you could be the wife of a sheep farmer. Now, can you answer that?" There was an anxious expression on John's face.

"Oh, John, I've thought so often about that. And I feel that I was being totally unfair to you in giving you that answer."

"How so?"

"My saying yes to marrying you ought not rest on whether or not I can be a certain kind of wife. If it is any kind of answer to such a big question it ought to be unconditional." She paused. "Then after that we can talk about sheep farming."

"Before you get me confused, let's hear your answer, Lynn?"

"Yes, John, I want to marry you—very much!" She took his hand. "I think we have both known that all along—ever since Alaska."

"Yes, Lynn. The die was cast on the Inside Passage."

"Not die—providence."

"That is a better word for it . . . God has had a hand in this from the moment I found a seat at your table."

"Ah yes. Led by the hand of God . . . ." She responded thoughtfully. Then brightly. "And we'll be sheep farmers, John, if that's what you want to do."

"It is."

"End of subject." Lynn's eye twinkled.

Meanwhile on Sunday evening Trevor and Margaret were alone in their dining room for tea after John and Lynn had left for an afternoon tour.

"Have either of them said anything to you about marriage, Meg?"

"No, but I can't believe they don't have plans."

The next morning when Trevor and John came in for breakfast after chores they joined John's mother and Lynn at the table. Lynn was bubbling with her report of the tour of New Zealand. John was obviously pleased. But he finally cut her off.

"But before we bore you with more travelogue, we have an announcement."

Trevor and Meg looked up with anticipation.

"Mum and Dad, Lynn and I plan to get married!"

"Oh John, I'm so happy for you both!" John's mother was ecstatic.

Trevor was more reserved but also pleased. "When will that be, Son?"

"We are not quite sure. Lynn needs to go back to the U.S. to close out some things there and then she'll be back." He looked at Lynn.

She smiled and said, "As soon as possible!"

CHAPTER 34

Decently and in Order

Sitting alone in his office in the church, Earl felt torn between the loyalty he had developed for Saline and a new enticing attraction to Spokane. It didn't feel right to him to run, merely because he was confronted with some opposition. But on the other hand, the matter had become serious enough for some church members to want him to leave. *How many? That's the question.* His thoughts were interrupted when Homer Stein came into the church and walked into Earl's office.

"Homer. Good to see you."

"Hello, Earl. How're you doing?"

"Oh, pretty good. I'll be glad when this special meeting is over . . . I guess no matter which way it goes."

Homer didn't seem to know what to say to this declaration. "Well, I'm working on the matter. I've got Rev. Baxter coming to moderate the session meeting tomorrow evening. He'll also lay out to the session the full implication of the situation they may be creating. That may scare a few into voting down the motion." Homer had taken a seat across from Earl in the office.

"Thanks for doing that, Homer." Earl then gathered his courage. "And I have another request of you."

"What's that?"

"Well since I am not to be around for tomorrow's meeting, I would like to be gone through Sunday. Could you get a supply preacher for Sunday? I know it's late in the game, but this whole affair has muddled everything up, so far as I'm concerned."

"I think I can do that, Earl. If nothing else I'll do the service myself."

"Thanks."

"I can see where you might feel quite awkward on Sunday if the votes goes against you, Earl."

"Well, that's right."

"Where are you going, may I ask?"

"Spokane. I have an old seminary friend in First Church there. I'd like to visit him." Earl left it at that—true, but there was a great deal more to this Spokane trip than Earl could reveal. He felt a tinge of guilt when he thought about his going to Spokane.

A few days earlier, Earl had received a phone call from the Bethany committee asking if he would be willing to come to Spokane. "We are very interested in you, Mr. Norris. We would like to meet you, and if you are willing, we want you to preach in a neutral pulpit for our committee."

"A neutral pulpit?" Earl had not heard this term before.

"Yes, in a different church where only our committee will be there to hear you."

"I see. This is sudden, let me think a moment; and give me time to look at my calendar. I'll call you back as soon as I can. The special meeting which Earl would not attend provided a break in his calendar into which he felt he could fit a quick trip to Spokane. Almost on impulse Earl returned the call the next day." I will accept your invitation, so long as there is nothing binding either way on this—no obligation."

"Of course not. Just a 'look-see' you might say. We are delighted that you can come."

Specific arrangements had then been made which would put Earl out on a limb until Homer could get someone to cover for him. To Earl's relief, now with Homer's help, he was free to make a quick trip to Spokane.

By the Thursday morning of the special meeting, Earl was on the road driving toward Spokane. He left at 5 AM before anyone could notice his departure. He had been with Kaye the night before and they had discussed the implications of his trip. Phil had sent him a packet of Chamber of Commerce maps and brochures about Spokane and the state of Washington which he had shared with Kaye. These enticed Earl more than they did Kaye.

"I don't know whether I hope you win their hearts and get invited to Bethany, or hope that you are not offered the church."

"We've got to leave this in God's hands, Kaye, and hope that we hear God's direction!"

"I know, darling. I will pray for that, the whole time you are gone."

"I'll phone you if there is any news at all."

"Please do."

Now, as he sailed along westbound, the further he drove the less significant the meeting in Saline seemed, and the more important his interview with Bethany became. He kept imagining himself living in Spokane. *It will be like Chicago again.* He imagined a city apartment where he and Kaye and Davey would set up housekeeping. He thought of all the delights of a big city which the little family of three could enjoy. Parks, concerts, shopping, going to the movies, sports events and lots of people. Maybe they could get a dog for a family pet. Davey would like that. And they wouldn't be living in a fish bowl. Anonymity! Something he admitted to himself that he had missed in Saline.

About two-thirty he drove over Lookout Pass and down the mountain into the mining towns of northern Idaho—Mullan, Wallace, Kellogg, and the rest. Then Lake Coeur d'Alene. His excitement rose after passing through Coeur D'alene and across the state line into Washington. Traffic was becoming much thicker now, the closer he got to Spokane. *This may be home for us someday soon,* he thought as he looked to the north across the outlying areas of the city. Earl found his way to the motel which the Bethany committee had reserved for him, carefully following their map. He walked into the very nicely appointed lobby and checked in. His got his bag and walked on plush carpet along an interior corridor to his room on the first floor. They had reserved a room which was considerably more upscale than the motel rooms he'd been accustomed to booking on his own. Not only did it have the usual items of furniture, but it included a very comfortable sitting area with a writing table which occupied the window end of the large room.

His arrangements were to meet a member of the committee who would call for him at his motel the next morning at nine. He would be taken to the church where the committee would meet with him during the morning. His evening arrival was early enough for a brief visit with Phil Otis.

"Phil, I've just arrived at the Red Lion River Inn. It's downtown on Division. Do you have time to drop in tonight yet? . . . Good."

"I know where it is."

"I'll see you here in about twenty minutes then."

Earl was eager to have someone to talk to about the Bethany possibility before seeing the church and the committee. Soon the phone rang. It was the desk clerk.

"Hello, Mr. Norris. There is a Mr. Otis here to see you."

"Send him to my room, would you?"

Earl and Phil spent the better part of a couple hours talking. About old times in Seminary, about Saline as well as Phil's work in First church. Finally they discussed Bethany and Earl's upcoming interview.

"It sounds like you might be just what Bethany is looking for."

"What mainly do you see as my qualifications for them?"

"Well, to begin with you are middle-of-the road theologically. That's where Bethany is. The trouble with their former pastor was that he was way too conservative for them. And then the fact that you grew up in a big city. They see themselves as very urban and would not want someone whose only experience was rural. Even though they are small, they want to attract urban dwellers in the area."

"I can relate to that. Just the few hours I've been here makes me feel like I'm back home in Chicago. This experience is making me see Saline for what it is—small, rural, struggling." Earl thought about how this felt to him. "It's like going to a shoe store and trying on a new pair of shoes."

"What do you mean?"

"Whether you buy them or not, the experience in the store makes your own shoes seem pretty shabby."

"Yeah, I see what you mean. What do they have planned for you this weekend?"

"Tomorrow noon there's a committee luncheon at a downtown hotel. That's when I'll meet the whole committee. Two of the committee members are meeting me here tomorrow morning and they are going to show me around. I'll see the church and they want me to see the surrounding community which they consider their parish, so to speak. They want me to relax here in the afternoon. Tomorrow evening is a dinner at the home of one of the committee members. The entire committee and their spouses will be present."

"Wow, they have you occupied! What about Saturday? Patricia and I were hoping there'd be a time when you could come out to our place, possibly for a meal."

"I'd like that. So far as I can see, Saturday evening is free. One of the committee members is a realtor and she is going to show me some housing possibilities on Saturday morning, and I think that will include lunch with her. They want to give me Saturday afternoon and evening to prepare for my big debut—so to speak—on Sunday morning when I'm to preach for the committee at Emmanuel Church."

"Let's plan on Saturday evening. I'll pick you up here at five-thirty."

'Great."

"What happens after the service on Sunday?"

"I'm not sure. The committee will meet in the early afternoon, and then at a four o'clock meeting I'm to be there to find out if they will want me to candidate. Monday, I drive back to Saline."

"The big question, Earl—if they invite you to candidate, do you think you will?"

Earl took a few moments to ponder Phil's question. "I need to meet the committee and find out all I can about their church and the position, terms of call and all the details. But if I feel like I do tonight, on Sunday, I'd accept!"

"I'm glad."

"Of course that's just on the basis of my feeling now and my anticipation."

"Sure."

Earl changed the direction of their conversation. "So tell me about your life and times, Phil."

"I'm having the time of my life. I like Spokane and the church is doing great."

"How about the Presbytery?"

"Oh, it's O.K. A few too many conservatives for my blood. One church recently hired a new Director of Christian Education and after only a few months fired her, because she was too liberal. Seems to me they should have known her better than that, since she only came from Moscow, Idaho."

"Karen Collins?"

"Yeah, do you know her?"

"I was at a conference with her at Menucha."

"We knew her in seminary, but now she seems to have gone off the deep end theologically. She sort of got off into the sixties social revolution."

"Is that right?" Earl did not show surprise.

"Almost unitarian in her views and otherwise a bit on the wild side, I think."

And with that tentative conclusion the two ministers parted until Saturday evening. As Earl prepared for bed he thought about Karen and could see why he'd not heard from her. *No longer would we have much in in common.*

The next evening Earl phoned Kaye. "Kaye, this has been a thrilling day . . . Yes, I had a very good meeting with the committee. They are an impressive group. We had a luncheon in a fancy downtown hotel. The three men on the committee were all in suits with ties. The three women were smartly dressed . . . . Yes, very different from session meetings in Saline . . . . No, they're not rich, just urban, I guess you'd say. Two of the committee members showed me the church . . . very nice . . . brick . . . small but very well kept up. The sanctuary is quite worshipful and they have a very good organ for their size room. There's a really nice office for the pastor which they have recently remodeled. I could just see me in there. It has a telephone on the desk—not on the opposite wall like mine in Saline."

Kaye feigned chagrin. "Earl . . . . We do our best here in Montana!"

Earl's enthusiasm was suddenly quelled by a lurking thought of Saline. He interrupted his account of the day to ask. "What have you heard of the Saline session meeting?"

"I don't know, Earl. But Daddy is asking around and he hasn't said yet. I'll ask him tomorrow and let you know what, if anything, he has learned."

"Whatever you can find out." Earl continued his report to Kaye.

"Then they took me around the community this morning and showed me the region of the city they consider their parish . . . . Other things too—what you might call the amenities . . . . You know, museums, parks, shopping areas—that sort of thing . . . . Yes, I found these all very attractive . . . . Yes, Kaye, I can't help but admit that it all looks very good to me—at this point. But of course we don't know about the Sunday service and what they decide. But I believe my interview with them went very well . . . . Thanks! I'll phone you again, tomorrow evening . . . . Good bye—I love you."

Earl's call on Saturday evening was even more enthusiastic. "Hi, Kaye . . . . Another good day . . . . I had only part of the afternoon to prepare for my service and sermon tomorrow morning. I found out that the Ministerial Relations Committee of Presbytery wanted to interview me . . . They came here to the motel café and we had lunch together. We met until around two thirty . . . that went fine. They just wanted to be sure I wasn't some kook! . . . . Thanks a bunch. I found them to be a congenial group of ministers and elders. People I could work with, I'm sure. This evening I had dinner out at Phil's. I met his wife, Patricia, and we had a good time together . . . . very nice, but no children yet. I'm sure you'll like them, especially Pat. We could really be good friends with them. Then this morning one of the committee—she's a realtor—took me around showing me possible housing . . . . Some to buy, others for rent . . . . Yes, there was one which I was particularly taken with. A small two bedroom brick house—single story, on a nice shady street. That's another thing. There are lots of trees in Spokane—unlike Saline and all of eastern Montana. When she took me into the house I could just imagine us living there! . . . Yes *us!* . . . . You're teasing, I hope . . . . That's better . . . . The big day is tomorrow. If I do well when I conduct the service at Emmanuel Church, and if the committee invites me to candidate, then the ball is in my court to decide whether or not to accept the invitation to preach before the entire congregation with the hope that they would vote to call me to be their pastor . . . . I don't know, Kaye. The way I feel right now is positive . . . . Yes it is a complicated process. *Decently and in order,* that's us Presbyterians for you . . . . No, I'm glad they're doing it right."

Then Earl thought about Kaye and her feelings. "But, I need to hear how you feel about moving to Spokane . . . . I know you can't say now . . . after I return on Monday, you and I will have a long heart to heart talk before I give them my answer, OK? Now, you were going to find out from your dad about the Session meeting?"

"I guess it's not for sure yet. It was such a close vote that Rev. Baxter from Presbytery advised that the congregation needed more time before taking a vote. So he got them to table the motion. What do you think of that?"

"I frankly don't know what to think. I guess I wish it had been decided one way or the other. When's the congregation going to re-consider?"

"In two or three weeks, I think."

"Oh great. So I won't know about Saline before I have to answer Bethany. Well, I better get some sleep so that I'm coherent in the pulpit. I'll talk to you tomorrow night, Kaye."

When Earl phoned Kaye on Sunday evening, she was the first to ask. "How did it go, Earl?"

"I felt very good about it. The sermon went well and the service too. It had been arranged for one of the elders at Emmanuel to have me in his home for Sunday dinner. He and his family live in a nicely kept up large older home on a tree-lined street. He and his wife were most gracious to me, and their two kids seemed to enjoy having an extra "uncle" in for dinner. A girl—eight and a boy—six. It turns out that the elder owns a butcher shop and really knows meat."

"What did they serve?"

"Well as he began to serve the meat he began with saying, 'Most people don't realize this, but beef and pork together in the same meal complement each other.' It was delicious, with mashed potatoes, asparagus, and tossed salad. For desert they served baked Alaska!"

"Sounds good."

"It made me wish that they were in Bethany church instead of Emmanuel."

"Don't tell me one thing more, Earl, until you tell me how the committee voted."

"Unanimously to invite me to candidate in three weeks."

There was a moment of silence. "Oh, Earl, I'm so happy for you."

"Wait a minute. I didn't say I was going to accept."

"I know, but just the fact that you were given so full an affirmation—especially after the despicable way Saline is treating you."

"Yeah, you're right. It does make me feel good." Then Earl thought of her response. "Happy for *me?* How about *happy for us?*"

"Remember? We're going to have the heart to heart talk before I'm sure, Earl."

This dampened Earl's spirits a bit. "I know, we will do that as soon as I get back."

"How long before you have to answer the committee?"

"I told them I would get back to them on this coming Wednesday. That way you and I can have time to talk this over, Kaye."

"It's a big question for you, Earl. And for me! What are your thoughts right now?"

"I have to admit that I am strongly drawn to accepting. There is so much here that is appealing to me, both in the church and in Spokane itself."

"I can understand that. Like going back home to Chicago, isn't it?"

"Yes. All this has made me realize what I've been missing since living in Saline—like trees."

"I remember how thrilling it was to me when I first moved to the twin cities . . . ." Kaye didn't want to continue that thought, since her experience there had turned bad.

"We both need really to pray—that God shows me His will." *But I hope He wants me here in Spokane,* Earl thought as he prepared to end his conversation with Kaye. "I'm leaving first thing in the morning, so I should be back sometime tomorrow evening. If it's not too late I'll phone. Otherwise Tuesday morning."

"I'll be waiting. Plan to come out Tuesday so that we can talk."

"Right. Well, It's goodbye for now. I love you."

"Love you too—Goodbye."

CHAPTER 35

Eastbound

Earl's windshield wipers were beating mightily against the heavy rain which was pelting the streets as he made his way out of Spokane to the highway. The gray skies draped the city in semi-darkness causing most vehicles to use headlights which cast silver streaks on the glistening wet pavement. He had not been in rain like this since his Chicago days. In Saline, when it did rain, and that was rare, it was a mere light sprinkling, only enough to put tiny dark spots on the dusty streets.

Once onto the highway he sat back and relaxed for his twelve hour eastward journey to Saline. Relaxed, but with a mind filled with thoughts of Bethany Church and of Spokane. The further away from Spokane he got, the more thoughts of Saline and of Kaye crowded into his consciousness.

Earl found himself wishing the unthinkable. *If only the session had clearly voted me out. Then I could think my way into Bethany with a clear conscience.*

By mid-morning he was climbing the Idaho side of the mountains to Lookout Pass, still driving in light rain. On Lookout he passed the "*Welcome to Montana—Big Sky Country*" sign. A sudden surge of a warm good feeling swept through Earl's consciousness, taking him by surprise. Not too far down the Montana side, Earl drove out of the rain. By the time he reached St. Regis the clouds had parted considerably, allowing for a sky which was partly blue, with intermittent gray clouds. He pulled into town, found a local café on Main Street and stopped for lunch. There was something comfortable about seeing a number of the locals sitting at the counter in their scuffed cowboy boots and wearing hats, some broad brimmed western, others of the baseball cap variety. These people were at home, as he would soon be. After a hamburger and fries,

Earl gassed up at the local service station. When he went inside to pay, he found three local men sitting around with coffee mugs. They gave him a friendly greeting. *Just like Saline. I'm still miles from there and I feel as though I'm home. There's something about Montana that does that to a person. But in time that's the way Spokane will feel—maybe.*

Five hours later Earl passed through Laurel and soon was slowing down as he entered Billings on Highway 10 from the West. An oblique turn brought him onto 1st Avenue North. In a moment he was downtown in time for a late supper at the Belknapp Broiler. Eager to get home, he ate rapidly, paid his bill, and was on his way, stopping for gas and then eastward again on Highway 10.

By the time he drove through Miles City around 10 o'clock, his mind was in a sort of lock down—no more free ranging thoughts about Spokane, Bethany and all the rest of his musings of the day-long drive. Darkness had overtaken him. All he thought of now was his own bed in the manse in Saline.

He pulled into Saline and drove along the darkened and deserted streets which led him quickly to the manse. He felt like a run-away secretly returning. The town was asleep, allowing him to slip into the house unnoticed. The closed up house emitted a not unpleasant odor of recently varnished wood mixed with a variety of the usual household smells. He opened his bedroom window. The fresh aroma of the native grasses gently swept into the room on a very subtle night breeze.

He wasted no time getting ready for bed from which he soon turned off his bedside lamp. *I've returned home to Saline. But for how long?* He lay his head on his pillow and in the dark he "listened to" the utter quiet of the world outside his window. So different from the incessant noises of the city he'd experienced in Spokane. He had almost gotten accustomed to the swoosh of cars driving past, the occasional siren sounding in the distance, car horns, and a mixed blur of indistinguishable noises in the background. Earl had been in Montana long enough to have forgotten the night sounds of Chicago. Now, in his familiar surroundings of his home in Saline he heard nothing. Utter peaceful silence. He slept the night through like a lost kitten who'd found its way home.

The brilliant eastern Montana sun illuminating a cloudless blue sky shone into Earl's bedroom window awakening him. He heard the melodic song of a meadowlark somewhere in the field beyond the manse. Otherwise the silence of the night before persisted even after dawn. He got up, went to the window and stared at the yellow-green grassland stretching to the east of town as far as he could see. Above it the blue horizon. There welled upon within him a sense of ease and *rightness. This is my country. I belong here,* he thought as he gazed out of his open window. Finally he withdrew and quickly dressed. He went into his kitchen and fixed himself a cup of coffee and a piece of toast. He spread a generous gob of some locally made chokecherry jam he'd been given. It was so quiet as he sat alone at his dining room table. *Not at all like Spokane,* he thought. All the questions of the day before seemed to be "on hold." He needed to break the spell with two phone calls: one to Kaye, the other to Homer. He decided to phone Homer first before he left his house.

"Hello, Homer. This is Earl. I just got back last night."

"Earl, it is good to hear your voice. Did you have a good trip?"

"Yes, I did. But I want to hear how things are here."

"Well, there's a lot of development. I'd like to come over and talk to you about it."

Homer's response jabbed him with a disturbing feeling. "Would around nine be OK?"

"That'll be fine. I'll see you then."

Earl felt some guilt pangs when he thought of Homer's innocent question about his trip. *Little does he know what I was doing.* Then Earl thought about the members of the Bethany committee. *They are really strangers who live far away in a place I hardly know. And they are trying to claim my life.* Earl felt uneasy. *To take me away from friends like Homer.*

He phoned Kaye, but he was reluctant to say much on the three party line in the manse. "Kaye, I've got an appointment this morning, but I could come out to your place by eleven."

"Oh, Earl, please do. I'll have some lunch for us. Mother and Dad are in Miles City today, so we can talk."

"Good, I'll see you at eleven."

Earl left the manse and walked down to the post office where he picked up his accumulated mail on his walk to the church. While emptying his box, Hank Hurlbutt came in. Hurlbutt gave him an icy greeting."'Lo Reverner."

"Hi, Hank."

That was all that was exchanged between the two men.

Earl walked to his office and sat down to look over the mail before Homer's visit. The significant piece of mail was a letter from Hugh Baxter, who had moderated the session meeting. Earl opened it warily.

> Dear Earl,
>
> You'll have the minutes of the special session meeting which your clerk will have taken, but I thought I'd give you my account of the meeting.
>
> All nine members were present. In the course of the discussion I made sure that each member expressed himself. In this discussion I could see that the session was pretty evenly divided. I was about to advise against taking a vote at this time, when the question was called for and the session clearly wanted to go ahead with the motion. However, when I found that the session was nearly evenly divided with a one vote tilt toward passing the motion to dissolve the pastoral

relationship, I took a moderator's privilege—and then some—and advised against concluding the matter in this way. I strongly cautioned against allowing a vote at this time which would have the potential of splitting the congregation right down the middle—which Saline can't afford. I more or less forced the issue by directing the session to table the motion for two weeks and to invite the presbytery to conduct a congregational consultation before taking any action.

The up-shot of all this is that next week on Wednesday evening, representatives of the presbytery will come to Saline and consult with church members individually or in family groups. The following week they will meet with the session to report and advise before allowing the vote to be re-taken. Once again I will be the moderator of this next meeting.

It is my hope that in this way we will find a way to resolve this issue without splitting the congregation down the middle—which is where it is now, I fear.

Give me a call if you want to discuss this further, Earl.

> Sincerely yours,
> Hugh Baxter
> for Yellowstone Presbytery
> cc Homer Stein, Clerk of Session

This left Earl feeling dismal about the prospects of any further ministry in Saline, and angry. *Baxter's concern seems to be for the congregation. Nothing having to do with my welfare or future. This is a sign that I ought to head west!* He fumed as he sat alone in his office tucked behind the chancel in the church building. In the distance the church door opened and he heard Homer walking through the sanctuary to his office.

After the preliminaries, Homer began. "I see you have Hugh Baxter's report of the meeting."

"Yes, I just got through reading it. Is that a fair evaluation of the meeting, Homer?"

"It is—as far as it goes."

"What do you mean?"

"Well, as I see it, there is just one element in the congregation upset enough with the ad, to vote you out, and that is a relatively small group. The problem is that the longer we stew over this the more that little group will rile up others. For that reason I was not in favor of Hugh's advice to delay."

"You weren't?"

"No, and this is why. The session vote was four in favor and three opposed. Two abstained The four are Hurlbutt's bunch. The motion is to call a congregational meeting for the congregation to vote up or down on whether to recommend to presbytery to dissolve the pastoral relationship. In my opinion Hurlbutt's four votes won't increase much in the entire voting membership. That means that what will come of a congregational meeting is something like six in favor of dissolution, and twenty-nine opposed. The majority want you here, Earl."

"That's a helpful perspective—if true." Earl felt unsure, but he trusted Homer's knowledge of the community and the church. "What happens to the six or so who vote me out?"

"Well, Hurlbutt and one or two others may quit the church. But that's not a split. I firmly believe the majority will be appalled at the idea of ousting their preacher."

In a perverse way this opinion was disconcerting to Earl. *So, that leaves me with the question of Bethany. If Saline would kick me out I'd know I should take Bethany!* "So will this delay mess up your prediction?"

"It could, but I think if the presbytery people do it right they can hear from members that they are for you, by and large. And it would be just like Hurlbutt not to show up."

"Well we'll wait and see. Anything you think I should be doing in the meantime?"

"No, just keep doing the good job you've been doing." Homer was getting ready to leave. "How was your Spokane trip? Did you enjoy seeing your old friend?"

"I certainly did." Earl hesitated to say more.

"It just wasn't the same around here with you gone." Homer gave Earl a knowing look, and picked up on Earl's reticent answer, catching Earl short with an embarrassing question. "Do you wish you lived in Spokane or some big city like it? Saline must seem pretty small to you."

"No question about Saline seeming small after my having grown up in Chicago. But I have no desire to move back to Chicago. And driving back into our state yesterday gave me a good feeling after having been in Spokane for the weekend. Phil is an assistant pastor of the big First Church there, and I can't see myself doing that."

If Homer had been listening closely, he would have realized that Earl had not really answered the question. Whether he caught that or not he chose to end the conversation. "Well, that's good. I've got to be moving on."

"Thanks for coming by, and bringing me up to date, Homer."

"No problem. We'll be in touch."

After Homer left, Earl pondered the question "Do you wish you lived in Spokane?"

Earl thought about the question. On this he would need to be evasive. *At this point, even to myself.* He needed to put the Spokane question aside, and the congregational vote issue as well so that he could get at some of the immediate tasks as he got back in the routine of pastoral duties. But by noon he'd be with Kaye. He wanted to tell her about Spokane and also about his conversation with Homer.

Earl put away some of his papers in his desk drawer before leaving the office for Norlands. As he was getting up to leave, his phone rang. He stepped over to the wall to answer. "Earl Norris, here."

"Hello, this is Phil. Just thought I'd bring you up to date."

"'Lo, Phil. What's up?"

"Well, I was talking to one of my church members, who is a friend of one of the search committee members at Bethany. Earl . . . ."

"Wait a minute, Phil . . . ." Earl cut in. "I'm on a party line. Let me call you back on a pay phone in just a few minutes."

"O.K. I'll be waiting."

Earl left his office and stopped by a pay phone outside the post office on his way to Kaye's house.

"Hello, Phil, I just didn't want to risk someone listening in. I don't think I heard anyone, but you can't always tell."

"Well, anyway, Earl, they really want you to come. According to this person, you are what they have been looking for and were afraid they wouldn't be able to find." Earl found this both affirming and strangely disconcerting. "Is that right? They must be talking about someone else," he quipped.

"No way. You're their man. Say, how did things go at your session meeting?"

Earl told Phil about the delay in taking action. "And so, I'm going to have to respond to Bethany before I know what Saline says."

Phil latched onto this. "There you are, buddy. Beat 'em to it and tell them you're out of there, before they can give you the ax."

"That's tempting." Earl thought about this. "You'll be the first to know, Phil . . . after the committee."

"Wednesday, is it?"

"Wednesday. But I have a noon appointment, so I'll be in touch. Thanks for the information."

"No problem. I just want to have you in Spokane, friend!"

"Thanks, and good bye for now."

The number of "members" present at the Conoco on any given morning varied greatly, depending upon weather and work. Jake Munson and Hank Hurlbutt were the only two present on the morning after the John Birch Society had met at Munson's the night before. Merle was tied up with a major overhaul in the garage.

"Whadya think about the meetin' last night?"

Hank thought about it and then said., "Well I don't know. I don't think he's as bad as that."

"You said yourself he's always talkin about feeding the hungry and how our society has overlooked some folks; and you know yourself, he signed that ad. What more do ya want?"

"I know, but to say he's a card-carrying Commie. I think it's just that he's been duped."

"I dunno. I still think we ought to 'take steps.' Know what I mean?"

"Yeah, but not yet, Jake.

The phone rang, bringing Merle into the office. That ended the conversation— for the time being.

CHAPTER 36

Decisions

After his phone conversation with Phil in the pay booth, Earl stopped in the post office to pick up his mail. Among the people picking up mail was Marabell Malone, a long time church member and active in the women's association. When she spotted Earl she came up to him.

"Rev. Norris, I'm so sorry about all this bickering going on."

Earl looked at her with a puzzled expression. *"Oh, hello, Marabell."*

"Please don't take this to heart. There's just a few people who like to stir things up. But the rest of us want you to stay."

"Well, thank you . . . ."

"In fact we took a straw vote at women's association yesterday, and it was unanimous!"

"Unanimous?" Earl looked as if he could not determine what she meant.

"That you stay, Reverend." There was a look of pleading sincerity in her expression.

"Thank you, Marabell, for your support. It is heart-warming to me." Earl proceeded to unload his box.

She smiled with a look of satisfaction.

Earl dumped his mail onto the passenger front seat of his car and drove off. *That was nice of her to say that . . . and it took courage . . . A lot of good people I'd be letting down if I left.* As he drove out toward Kaye's, he turned the matter over and over in his mind. One minute thinking about his ties to Saline. The next minute visualizing the house in Spokane the realtor had shown him. And when he thought about the fact that he had to decide by Wednesday, a feeling of panic filled him.

He felt distracted during lunch with Kaye as these conflicting ideas and images kept circulating through his mind. After lunch he and Kaye sat together in the living room. Earl took up the Spokane question. "If I decide to take the Spokane church will you still marry me, Kaye?"

Earl and Kaye had been discussing his Spokane trip and the Bethany Church on and off a number of times. Now he was no closer to a decision than when he had arrived at the Norlands.

Kaye was rather short in her answer. "Earl, don't try to make marriage a factor in your deciding."

"I'm not—I don't think."

"In a sense, what you are doing is making me decide for you!"

"OK, I see what you mean."

Kay softened. "Earl, darling, I'm yours no matter what you decide, I love you and want you. Davey wants you for a dad as well."

"I want you too, Sweetheart. And I want to be Davey's dad."

"And we will be very happy with you in Spokane, Saline, or wherever else."

"Let's set a date, Kaye. How about June?" Earl was glad to put the Spokane question on hold.

"I'd like that. Mom and I will need a bit of time, and by then all this other stuff will be washed out of your system, regardless of where you are pastor."

"June it is. Where?"

"Saline, of course. Saline is Davey's and my home. Here is where our family is! You can come back for the wedding."

Earl was very quiet for a long time before announcing. "I don't want to come back!"

"You mean you want to have the wedding in Spokane?"

"No. Now as we talk about our wedding and being a family, I don't want to live in Spokane. I want to live here—at home—in Saline, darling."

"You're very sure, dear?"

"Very sure. I think when I drove over Lookout Pass and down the mountain into Montana that I became sure and didn't know it."

"What about the church vote?"

"I'm convinced now that this is where God wants me. And that means we need to see to it that things work out that way." Earl thought about what he was feeling. "In fact, Kaye, you know I think if I should decide to leave I would in some way cause the vote to be against me. I know that's not rational. But I sense that by my deciding to remain here I am casting my vote in favor of staying and in some mysterious way persuading the church to vote for me. Somehow marrying you is the vote that keeps me here."

"Oh Earl, I love you so much!"

"I love you, Kaye!" Then Earl grinned. "I have two loves."

"What?"

"Kaye Norland—and Saline, Montana."

"Three."

"Three loves?"

"Christ."

"Yeah, you're right."

"But realistically, Earl, where does the Saline church fit into all this? All good and well to say that Christ is your first love, but how does that play out in your ministry in a congregation which has some dissenters in it? How do the people feel about you, Earl?"

Earl was quiet for a time. Kaye's question raised the pertinent issue. Finally he shared with her. "I spoke with Homer this morning." He didn't know exactly how to tell her of the conversation.

"And what did he say?"

"He told me that some representatives of Presbytery are coming to interview people in the congregation to see how I stand."

"Is that good or bad, Earl?"

"Homer seems to think that they will find a lot of support for me, and that the negative vote isn't all that big—but . . . ."

"But what?"

"If," he said, "Hurlbutt gets around to enough people he could sway more negative votes. Hurlbutt, apparently, is the root of the opposition."

Kaye wasn't surprised. "It figures. He's done that before, I think."

"Is that so?"

"Dad says that every so often over the years when a pastor left the church here, it was because of Hank Hurlbutt."

"Well, he's at it again, I guess."

"Dad also says that what it will take is for a pastor to stick it out—stand up to him, or else this sort of thing will go on and on in the life of the Saline congregation." Kaye paused and looked into Earl's eyes. "Earl, with God's help, you can be the one to stay!"

"Thank you, darling. I'll do all I can."

Unforeseen events in Saline would radically affect the outcome.

The relationship of a pastor to a congregation has frequently been seen as something similar to a marriage. Usually this comparison is seen in the selection process through which a congregation and a prospective pastor must decide whether they are "meant for each other" as couples must determine before setting the wedding date. There are other similarities. The so called "seven year itch" seems to plague some marriages and some church-pastor relations as well.

Earl Norris could now be said to have survived the seven year itch. The seductive attraction of Spokane had been due to a sort of "seven year doldrums." But it lost its appeal, the wander-lust had quelled, and he had returned to Saline with new enthusiasm and commitment. And so at the end of his eighth year, his forthcoming marriage to a woman from Saline sealed his relationship to Saline and set the stage for "growing old together!"

When Earl drove up into the church parking lot after his lunch with Kaye, he was shocked to see Hank Hurlbutt's pickup. And Hank walking into the church. Earl hurried into the building and found Hank at his office door. "Hank, I'm not in."

"Oh, I thought you might be, Revener." Hank was obviously distraught. "Can I see you?"

"Yes, of course."

The two entered the office and as soon as Hank was seated he spoke. "I'm on my way into the hospital in Miles City. The wife had a heart attack this morning and the ambulance has just taken her."

"I'm sorry, Hank. Can you tell me about it?"

"I was in the kitchen. She got up and went into the bathroom. I thought she'd be out in a minute. But she didn't come out to the kitchen. So finally I went and rapped on the door. No reply. So I went in and found her slumped on the floor." There was a trip in Hank's voice. Emotion he couldn't help but feel, which he wanted to hide.

"I'm so sorry, Hank. You called the ambulance then?"

"They came right away. Took her into Miles. I'm on my way there right now."

"You need to hurry. But let's have a prayer first. And then I'll follow you in."

"You will?"

"Certainly. I'm your pastor and God wants us to give her all the support we can."

Both men kneeled while Earl prayed.

"We'll go to the Emergency entrance first. If she's already in a room they'll tell us." Earl could see that Hank was in no shape to figure things out. "So we'll meet there—OK?"

Hank grunted an assent.

Earl dared to warn Hank. "Drive extra carefully, Hank. In your distress you could miss something."

Then they both were on their way to Miles City. Earl was careful to follow Hank.

Earl and Hank entered the hospital together and Earl went up to the counter to ask for Louella Hurlbutt.

The ward clerk in E.R. told them, "She's with a doctor right now. In a moment you can go in to see her. Are you her husband?"

"He is." Earl pointed to Hank. "I'm her pastor."

The two men sat down in the little waiting room across from the E.R. counter. They didn't speak.

The doctor came out of Louella's enclosure, spoke briefly with the ward clerk, made some notations on Louella's chart and was off down the hall, his white smock flying. The clerk immediately made a phone call and then summoned Hank. "She is to be taken to Billings, to Deaconess hospital. If you want to accompany your wife in the ambulance you may. Hank said he would do that.

"You both may go in to see her until she is prepped for the trip."

Earl and Hank went through the curtain and approached the gurney. Her eyes were closed. She was under an oxygen mask and had other tubes and wires connected to her.

"Ellie, it's me, Hank."

She did not respond.

Earl put his arm on Hanks shoulder. "Hank, she's unconscious right now. But I'm sure she can hear you."

"Ellie, don't leave me." Hank was almost weeping.

The nurse came in to prepare Louella for the journey.

Earl asked for a moment for prayer.

"Certainly, Reverend."

He gathered Hank close to the bed. "Hold her hand, Hank." Earl took the other hand and had a brief prayer.

He took Hank's arm. "We better go now so that they can get her ready."

The nurse turned to Earl, while Hank leaned over close to his wife's face. "I'll let him know when he can follow her to the ambulance. It should only be five or ten minutes. Perhaps he'd like to use the rest room. It's on your left down the hall."

Earl thanked the nurse and led Hank to the men's room. They returned to the E.R. The two then sat in chairs near the E.R. desk.

"Are you all right to go to Billings without me, Hank?"

"That's fine, Reverner."

"I'll phone the chaplain at Deaconess. He'll see you there, I'm sure."

Hank nodded, but didn't say anything.

"Anything I can do on this end?"

He didn't seem to know how to answer, and then he thought. "Would you tell Darrell? He'll know what to do."

"I can do that as soon as I get back home. Anything else?"

Hank Hurlbutt's face clouded up and it appeared that he might weep. "Reverner Norris, if Ellie doesn't make it, I know it's my fault."

"No, Hank. It can't be like that."

"I just know it. He's punishing us."

Earl could hear the tense struggle in his voice and saw in Hank's face a look of abject misery. "Hank, God doesn't do that—no matter what."

"He does to us. That's why the baby never made it, and that's why we never could have kids. And now this."

In a moment of deep insight Earl realized that he ought not deny Hank's desire to unload. "Is there something you need to say to God, Hank? Or to me as your pastor—in some ways a representative of God?"

Hank became very quiet. Earl could barely hear.

"No."

Earl realized that he probably should not have added *or to me as your pastor.*

The nurse came at this point. "Mr. Hurlbutt, we are ready for you. And thank you, Reverend, for staying with him."

Earl realized this was a gentle dismissal and so he said to Hank. "I wish you well. Please phone me when you have any news about Louella."

Hank grunted an answer. He seemed to Earl to be miles away at this point.

On his way back to Saline, Earl thought, *He's carrying a load of guilt. He needs to dump it. I don't know if I can help him do that. But I've got to try.*

The next day Hank phoned. "She's had some tests, and they think she has some heart damage. They will give her some medication and keep her on oxygen."

"I can come, if you want me to, Hank."

"Don't come, Reverner."

Earl was shocked at the short negative answer.

Hank must have realized how he had sounded. "The hospital chaplain is real good and will see the wife each day." Hank hung up.

Earl was perplexed. However, he remembered other times in his ministry with people, that when he had come in too close, they had pulled away, and sometimes had broken off communication completely. *I guess I hit a raw nerve where that load of guilt is.*

The call came the next afternoon. "Hello, this is Darrell Reisner, Hank Hurlbutt's neighbor. You called me the other day about Louella."

"Yes, I know."

"She died in the Billings hospital this morning."

"I thought Hank said that she was making it, but with heart damage."

"At first, but they think she had another heart attack."

"Oh I am so sorry. For Hank especially. How is he?"

"He's pretty shaken up. My wife and I are leaving in a couple minutes to get him and bring him back."

"That's very good, Darrell. He'll need you, I know. By the way, his car is in the E.R. parking lot at the Miles City hospital."

"One of us can drive it back on our way home from Billings. We're going to keep him with us for a while. He and Louella don't have any close family. We'll be in touch with you Reverend."

"Do that. I'll keep you in my prayers for a safe trip."

"Thanks, Reverend."

The next morning Darrell and Hazel Reisner brought Hank in to see Earl about the service. They stayed out in the sanctuary while Hank went into the office.

"Reverner, could you do the service for the wife?' He acted sheepish. "I really don't deserve it . . . ."

Earl broke in. "You certainly do. Yes, I'll conduct Louella's funeral services . . . ."

Hank wanted to say more. "Because I wanted to vote you out. I didn't know this was going to happen." He added an ominous word. "I still feel the same, Reverner, mind you."

"That has nothing to do with deserving or not deserving, Hank. When do you want the service?"

"The undertaker said Thursday at two would be fine."

"That'll be ok."

Hank began to get up. "By the way, it's gonna be in the church."

"Good. We can talk about the service sometime tomorrow. I'll drop out to the house, Hank."

"No. I gotta see the undertaker tomorrow morning. I'll see you here after that." Hank insisted before getting up to leave.

When Hank left, Hazel stuck her head in. "Earl, you need to talk to Hank."

"He's coming in tomorrow to discuss the service."

"He needs to talk about himself and Louella and not just the service—know what I mean?"

"Thanks for the tip, Hazel."

Earl's conference with Hank regarding the service didn't amount to much. He just wanted the regular service and had no suggestions. He didn't want any special music, nor very much said about Louella. Earl got the impression that Hank was making every effort to keep the lid on his feelings, and was very reluctant to say anything about his wife, or their relationship. It was almost as if he was hiding some unsavory information. This made it impossible for Earl to get anywhere with what Hazel had suggested Hank needed.

After Hank left with Reisners, Earl wondered what Hazel had referred to.

In Earl's experience it was rare for a funeral to be held in the Saline church building. The preferred location was the chapel in the funeral home in Miles City.

In fact Hank's insistence on the church would cost him for the extra travel and trouble which a Saline location would cause the undertaker. But that seemed to be the one thing Hank wanted for "the wife." As it turned out, having it in Saline cost the mortuary and their insurance company far more that anticipated.

At two o'clock the Community Church in Saline was about half full of people who had come for Louella Hurlbutt's funeral. The usual sadness of such occasions was intensified in this case by the fact that Hank had no family. The Reisners accompanied him into the front pew while the pianist played an assortment of funeral hymns. Ordinarily when the mourners were seated the pianist would know to bring her preliminary music to an end. However on this afternoon she was advised by the mortician's assistant to continue playing. The casket had not yet arrived from town. This delay persisted for at least forty-five minutes. The congregation became restless, to say nothing about how Hank must have felt.

Outside the building the mortician paced, looking nervously for the hearse to arrive. Earl stood outside with him and was equally disturbed by this unusual delay. Finally they saw a station wagon from the funeral home speed down the street to the church. As soon as it arrived the mortician rushed to the driver's window. "What on earth?"

"I've got the casket. The hearse had a wreck a couple of miles out of Miles, and we had to come and transfer the remains to the station wagon."

"Tell me about it later. We need to get going on the service." He went inside and summoned the pall bearers.

Earl walked down the aisle and whispered to the pianist, and to Hank. Hank whispered something back to Earl, who then mounted the platform and took his seat behind the pulpit. Soon the pall bearers brought Louella to the front of the sanctuary. The pianist stopped her playing and Earl proceeded with the service. Hank wore a downcast expression throughout the service, refusing to look up at Earl.

When the service concluded with a benediction, the mortician came forward, opened the casket, rearranged the flowers and then invited the mourners to come forward. The congregation filed by, while Hank and the Reisners sat quietly. Hank stared at an imaginary spot on the floor the whole time as the mourners passed by. When all had filed by and left the sanctuary, the mortician invited Hank to come forward to the casket. He looked only briefly and then accompanied the mortician to the waiting limousine to go to the local cemetery. The Reisners followed.

After a brief committal service at the cemetery, the small crowd disbursed while Darrell and Hazel ushered Hank into their car. Earl stepped over and announced to Hank. "I'll be out tomorrow afternoon to talk with you, Hank."

Hank gave him a reluctant and almost inaudible, "All right."

The next afternoon Earl kept his promise. "Let's sit here at the kitchen table, Hank."

". . . . but I don't have anything much to say."

"You've said a lot already and I'd like to help you." Earl took a breath and began. "Twice now you have told me that you think God is punishing you. You talked about how your baby girl died before she was born and that you and Louella couldn't have any more children. And then yesterday when I told you it was time for the service, you said that the delay was another case of God punishing you."

"And Louella and I deserved it."

Ordinarily this first day after the funeral would be considered an inappropriate time to do any serious counseling with the bereaved. But Earl sensed that it was now or never. Now when Hank was vulnerable. So he pressed on.

"Hank, I don't think God punishes us like that, but if you do, you need to come clean and tell me why you deserve punishment from God . . . or this thing will plague you the rest of your life."

Hank retained a "put-upon" expression and didn't reply to Earl.

"Hank, you've got to get this off our chest, or you'll wind up with a bleeding ulcer or worse."

Both men were silent for a very long minute or two. Earl felt that Hank was seriously assessing his situation. *If I can just wait him out, maybe Hank will share his distress.* Earl silently prayed for Hank. He spoke to Hank. "What you have in your heart is not for me but for God to hear. God wants each of us to come to Him and confess to Him our sins. If we do that God is ready to forgive. God doesn't want to punish us. He wants to forgive us."

Earl waited. Finally Hank began talking in a way that seemed to be an utterance to God. "It was wrong. We never should have done it."

Very softly, Earl encouraged Hank. "Say to God what it was you did."

"I made Ellie pregnant. We weren't married. That was terrible. So bad that we could never do it again—never in all those years . . ." His face became extremely contorted and he burst into sobs, soul and body wrenching sobs which wouldn't quit.

Earl realized that Hank also might be carrying a load of guilt in connection with his affair long ago with the young girl. "Hank. Is that all? If you have more to confess, perhaps that's what you might say to God silently. Hank—tell God. Get rid of it after all these years. Tell God now." He could sense that Hank was locked in a struggle with himself.

All the while Earl prayed out loud. "Gracious God, hear your child, Henry's, confession. Take note of his sorrow for what he's done. Purge him of every thought of it. Scrape the terrible crud out of his mind and heart. Wash him clean—clean-CLEAN!" Earl was nearly shouting by this time, so intense was the emotion of these moments. He stepped over to Hank, and put his arms around his trembling body and prayed some more. "Oh yes, Lord. Your child, Henry, is clean. The blood of his Savior, Christ, has washed him. The old sinful, dirty soul is washed whiter than snow. Now, Lord RELEASE HIM FROM HIS SLAVERY TO HIS FORMER GUILT! Through our loving forgiving Lord Jesus Christ. AMEN!"

Earl felt Hank's body relax. The two men held each other in a firm embrace. Earl let go. Hank said in new and softer voice. "Thank you, Lord. Thank you, Earl."

Earl felt that it was time to leave. "Will you be all right, friend?"

"Yes, pastor, better than I have been for years."

As he returned home Earl could not fathom the change in Hank's attitude toward him. From cold and resentful to warm and vulnerable.

At the special session meeting a few days later, Homer reported. "Regarding our intended vote on the motion which was made by Louella Hurlbutt, Hank has been to see me and has asked me if there might be some way that the matter could be dropped. I said that I would speak to the session about it. When a motion is brought off the table and you discuss it for a re-vote, a substitute motion can be made which would in effect cancel the proposed action."

When the matter came up for discussion Sue Stark raised her hand. "Sue?"

"Mr. Moderator, I move a substitute motion as follows: *that the session commend Earl Norris for his courageous stand, and affirm its satisfaction in having him as our pastor.*"

It was seconded. No discussion followed. It passed unanimously. The session went on to other business scheduled for the meeting. After these items were disposed of there was a motion to adjourn, followed by an affirmative vote.

Earl phoned Kaye after the last session member had left the building. "I know it's late, but I want to see you, darling."

"Come on out right away, sweet."

When Earl walked into the Norland house, Kaye was in the living room with Walter and Beth. Davey was asleep in his room. He went to Kaye and they embraced. He announced. "The motion was dropped. Instead they took a vote of affirmation and support for me."

"What happened to bring that about?" Walter asked.

"Hank Hurlbutt had asked Homer to drop the motion. Homer suggested the proper way for this matter to be dropped."

Kaye exclaimed. "We've won, haven't we, Sweetheart."

"God has won all of our hearts, beginning with Hank."

"We are so glad that you decided to stay in Saline, Earl," Beth declared. And Walter and Kaye agreed, of course.

The phone call to the Bethany committee would not be easy. Nor the one to Phil Otis.

CHAPTER 37

Seasons of the Years

When the session had acted to affirm his ministry, Earl had felt he had been given a new lease on life—a renewal of his call to ministry in Saline, Montana. In the weeks following the resolution of that crisis Earl felt that he was beginning to hit his stride. The congregation had been growing a bit with a few new members having joined the church. He felt good about what seemed to be a deepening of people's understanding of the implications of Christian faith for their lives and for their church. Kaye Norland had joined the women's association, to the satisfaction of older women who had frequently complained, "Why don't the younger women come?" Earl noticed that they were rallying around Kaye. Her participation had been the catalyst for other younger women to join, including Ella Gelenik.

Quite gratifying to Earl personally was the fact that Kaye and Ella had "hit it off," as they say, and were becoming good friends. This left Gertrude with little recourse but to start coming back to church.

Spring arrived in early March, allowing Saline farmers to get into their fields. Earl was exhilarated with the thaw in the weather and in the warmth he'd been experiencing in his ministry. When Easter dawned on the last Sunday in March, Earl felt its message of new life permeating the congregation. Earl himself certainly had been enjoying new life as his relationship with Kaye had been intensifying. He'd become a weekly dinner guest at the Norlands. As June approached more and more of the conversation revolved around the forthcoming wedding. He and Kaye spent most of their Saturdays together. Occasionally they spent the day in Billings, or in good weather in outdoor activities, exploring the countryside surrounding Saline, especially along the river. These times together were also devoted to wedding and honeymoon plans. However, Earl had been reluctant to share with the congregation his intention to marry, but it was a reticence which would soon need to give way to revelation.

One day, Homer came to the office to check on some session business and to chat with Earl. "Earl, I think that the congregation is accepting Kaye. What we'd hoped for is happening."

"Like what?"

"People are getting to know Kaye, and they like her. She is no longer *one of those Norlands* so to speak. She's *Kaye, the preacher's friend.*"

"Very good to hear. How would they take to *Kaye, the preacher's wife?*"

Homer showed some surprise. "Well, now—are congratulations in order?"

"Well, yes, but not out loud quite yet."

"I think they'll accept your decision, Earl."

"Even the boys at the Conoco?"

"Let's not ask too much. You'll give them quite a bit to talk about. But after the dust settles they'll find other topics." Homer thought for a moment and added. "And—surprisingly—Hank seems to have mellowed."

Earl nodded, knowing more about the change in Hank's mental state than he was at liberty to share. "Homer, now as they say in presbytery *if the way be clear* an important action is pending, I would say *the way be clear!* Kaye and I will be setting the date—most likely sometime in June."

"I'm pleased for you both . . . and for us as a congregation."

On June fourteenth, Earl's parents arrived. Anne spent most of the next few days at Earl's, and by Saturday all was ready. After the rehearsal they had been treated to a joyous dinner at Bensons. Now it was Saturday and at a minute or two after three in the afternoon, Bob Taggert took his place in the center aisle facing a packed sanctuary as the pianist played the traditional wedding march. The best man, Homer Stein, came next, and then Earl Norris, the groom, appeared, and walked to the center, positioning himself so that he could see the procession assembling in the rear of the sanctuary. Then he watched intently as the bride's procession began coming down the aisle to join Bob Taggert and him in the front of the congregation. Davey came down first bearing an embroidered pillow on which the rings were tied. Then the maid of honor, Ella Gelenik. When she reached her position in the front of the congregation, Bob motioned for the congregation to stand. The piano shifted into *forte* and Kaye Norland gracefully walked down the center on the arm of her father, Walter Norland. She joined Earl and they faced Bob Taggert, with Walter a step behind. The music came to an end. The congregation was seated and the wedding was underway.

"Dearly beloved, we are assembled here in the presence of God to join Kaye and Earl in holy marriage . . . ."

To the minister's right in the first pew, Beth Norland brought a lace handkerchief to her eye. Seated next to his mother was Kaye's brother, Ken. He had flown in from Cleveland the day before. Ken had recently joined the faculty at Oberlin as an assistant professor of political science. In a moment Walter would join his wife and son in the pew after "giving away" his daughter. Then as soon as the rings were taken from his pillow, Davey would come and join his grandparents. To Bob's left in the first row sat the groom's parents, Esther and Robert Norris, and their daughter, Anne Taggert.

In a matter of minutes, the words *I pronounce you husband and wife* would be heard, followed almost immediately by the benediction which would be closed with the words, *both now and in the life everlasting. Amen.* At that instant the pianist would begin the wedding recessional, the bride and groom would kiss. As the congregation would rise, Earl would escort Kaye as his wife down the aisle.

And so the Rev. Mr. Earl Norris and Kaye Norland were now married. Turning to face the congregation they descended the three steps and began their recessional. In a sensitive gesture the couple paused briefly at the first pew to invite Davey to join them in walking out. The three would now be the manse family in Saline.

As is sometimes the case, weddings bring families together as well as individuals. In the reception which followed Kaye and Earl's wedding it was gratifying to observe how Bob Taggert and Ken Norland "hit it off." That night Bob remarked to Anne, "Ken is a person I'd like to spend more time with."

"I noticed you two seemed to enjoy some deep conversation. What was all that about?"

"I found his ideas on the politics of what is happening in America in the '60s most intriguing. Political science is his field and he, himself, has been caught up in some of the social revolution happening on campuses back east."

"I take it he wouldn't fit in too well on Main Street in Saline!"

"No, you're right on that. He told me that's one reason he hardly ever comes back to Montana."

"Too bad. You'd like to have him in Miles City, I bet." Anne thought further. "He could teach at Miles Community College!" She grinned.

"That would be the day."

A year earlier, and many thousands of miles to the south, another wedding had taken place in a tiny rural church building not many miles from the sea. It was a pleasant autumn Saturday afternoon. Cars were parked all over the lawn outside the white frame church building in Drummond. Inside, friends and neighbors from the entire district were celebrating with the Lindsay family the marriage of their son, John. Of course it had been big news in the community that John Lindsay was marrying the young woman from the U.S. whom he had met while in Alaska.

In the months since Lynette Ellerton had come to Glen Mor, she had become increasingly a part of the family. So eager to learn all she could about the ways of both the household and the farm, she had given a hand to John in some of his farm work, as well as to Margaret Lindsay around the house. Lynn routinely helped John's mother to a far greater extent than Meg had dreamed. During the brief time Lynn had been back in the U.S. to close up loose ends before moving to New Zealand permanently, all three Lindsays had missed her sorely. Everyone in the district who knew the Lindsays were pleased that John had found such a "perfect" mate, and a girl from an American city at that. And so it was that on their wedding day the little church was packed with well wishers.

A passerby on Drummond's only street would have seen the doors of the tiny church burst open and an exuberant bride and groom come running out onto the lawn and over to the Sunday School building next door for a joyous reception.

If Lynn hadn't been fully accepted as part of the community before the wedding, now she certainly had become *"one of us"* as an appreciative neighbor was heard to say. The life of a respected New Zealand sheep farming family was in store for Lynette and John Lindsay.

Before digging into their new life, they allowed themselves a four-day honeymoon. As friends gathered outside the church and Sunday school hall, John and Lynn made their official exit, running out to John's car. After John bundled his wife into the car they sped off to Invercargill where they had reserved a room in the Coachman's Inn.

The next morning they parked their car at the airport and boarded a South Seas Air flight to Stewart Island where they had reservations at the South Seas Hotel until Thursday morning when they returned to Invercargill and then to Glen Mor.

By the time John and Lynn returned from their honeymoon, the elder Lindsays had moved out of the main house and into what on some other places was called a "Granny Crib." This was Trevor's first step in turning Glen Mor over to his son.

After sunset on the first night of their residence in the main house, John led Lynn out beyond house and sheds to a little rise in the landscape. He turned his wife's head toward the dark sky and pointed.

"There's the Southern Cross. Your life is under it now, as mine has been. May God's blessing through that cross be with us now and always."

"Amen," Lynn said. Then as they embraced, she sensed that she was now the mistress of Glen Mor. When they separated to return to their house she gave a slight bow and formally addressed her husband. "John Lindsay, Laird of Glen Mor!"

"Yes, and Lynette Lindsay—Lady of Glen Mor!" John said with a formal bow as well.

"Oh John, I'm so very very happy." They embraced again.

In the coming years, the inevitable cycling of the seasons in both hemispheres kept Earl and Kaye Norris busy in their life and ministry in Saline, Montana. John and Lynn, of Glen Mor were both active in Oreti parish and on their farm in Southland. While each season had its vagaries of unpredictable weather, the Lindsays enjoyed overall prosperous years in sheep farming. New Zealand politics and changing markets in Europe made for some ups and downs in the financial side of the production of lambs and wool over the years. So deeply in love were John and Lynn that none of these outside influences could dampen their enthusiasm for their life together as their marriage matured and Lynn became more and more of a "Kiwi." While her neighbors could still hear "American" in her voice, tourists whom she met from time to time mistook her accent for that of a native New Zealander.

"Ah yiss," she would say when introduced to someone from overseas.

Family life became exciting and meaningful as their blissful marriage brought them two children, a boy, and a girl. Ian was their first born, arriving in the fall of 1966, and Amanda the next year, graced their home with her infectious smile about a year later. Now Glen Mor once again was alive with new life. It would not be long before Lynn found herself a leader of Amanda's Girl Guides troop, and John would be teaching Ian the age old mysteries of sheep farming. His time of full responsibility would come.

Far to the north, in a curious way, marriage to Earl brought Kaye into the center of the life of the church while at the same time Earl's marriage to a Saline native made him a part of the community as no preacher had ever been. Through what remained of the turbulent 60s Earl steered a steady course, helping the congregation to accept some of the changes which were occurring in American society and to reflect upon contemporary life from a Christian perspective.

The fact that Earl had married a local woman, even though the marriage was opposed at first, had a way of solidifying Earl's standing as *one of them*, a full fledged part of the community. This was a level of acceptance many pastors never attain, always and ever considered outsiders. Add to the effect of a local marriage the fact that Earl was staying in Saline.

The longest pastorate in the past for Saline had been seven years. By 1974 Earl's pastorate in Saline was going on fifteen years. His place in Saline and in the church began to be taken for granted. It was commonly agreed that he was not planning to move away. A most unusual feeling for a small congregation like Saline, so accustomed to losing their pastors after a few short years. Earl and Kaye themselves did not feel inclined to move. *In for the long haul* Earl had begun to tell himself.

In many ways theirs was a typical Saline family. In addition to her membership in the church women's association, Kaye became an active participant in the local county extension club. Davey spent many hours with his grandparents on the Norland ranch and was an enthusiastic member of 4-H, winning blue ribbons two years in a row for his calf projects.

For the most part the 1970s were good years for Saline and the church. The economy was holding up. The price of wheat had jumped up to $5 a bushel in the early '70s when the Russians had started buying U.S. wheat. Loans were easy and relatively low cost. Many farmers were expanding their operations by borrowing from the Federal Land Bank for additional land. The good times enabled the church to add a modest Christian education wing onto the church building.

Roy and Judy Malone were church members who expanded their farming operation in the '70s. Roy had been very active in Earl's first high school youth group. After graduation Roy had married Judy Dahlquist, a daughter of one of the town families. Earl had performed their marriage and in the years following had baptized their three children. Roy and Judy took over the Malone place after his father died. They raised their family on the farm and did fairly well financially. So well that they began to think of expanding in the early '70s.

One evening a neighbor from an adjoining farm came over to visit with Roy. He was retiring, without having any children to take over. After telling of his plans to retire he put the question to Roy. "Would you be interested in buying some or all of my land.? You know what it can produce as well as I do."

"That's a pretty big question . . . but one that interests me. What are we talking about in the way of money?"

The two talked about the price, and about the availability of loans as well as about the neighbor's long term plans until finally Roy said. "Give me a week. I need to do some figuring and see my banker. I'll get back to you."

"Sure, that's fine. I'm not in that big of a hurry."

Roy found that through the Federal Land Bank he could borrow $600,000 to purchase his neighbor's land with the equity in his own property sufficient to sustain this amount of loan. For a few years he managed fairly well with a heavy mortgage on the farm. With the increased size of his operation, Roy had to buy new and larger equipment, and in peak seasons he needed to hire extra help. The Malones and others in the Saline community were experiencing what might be called boom times. But in some ways they were living on artificial stilts in so far as their mortgage depended upon inflated land values, and the sale of their wheat to the Russians.

As the years went by Earl was called upon more and more often to conduct funeral services for church members as well as for others in the Saline community. Each one affected him but none as much as Homer Stein's.

One night in the late 70's his bedside telephone rang.

"Hello, Earl Norris, here."

"Earl, this is Tom Stein. I'm sorry I'm calling you in the middle of the night . . ." He sounded distraught.

"Quite alright, Tom. What is it?"

"It's Dad. I'm calling from his house. He's very very sick. Could you come?"

"Yes, of course. As soon as possible, Tom. Is he conscious?"

"Just barely. I think you better hurry. I'm afraid we are going to lose him."

"Hang on. Be right there."

Earl hung up. By this time Kaye was sitting up in bed.

"Who?" was all she asked.

"Tom Stein. About Homer. It sounds as though he may be dying."

Earl dressed as fast as he could and got in his car and sped to Homer's house. He went to the door where Tom met him and brought him into the living room where Jenny, Tom's wife, and his brother Ray, were seated.

After Earl greeted them Tom spoke. "He's failing. He's going to be taken to Miles City. But I think he wants to talk to you first. Come this way."

Tom tiptoed down the hall and very quietly opened Homer's bedroom door and beckoned Earl to step into his room with him. He then closed the door. The room had a stuffy medicinal smell, testifying to the sickness which permeated the space. In the semi-darkness of this bedroom Homer lay under a stack of blankets. When the two came close to the bed, he opened his eyes and saw Earl with his son.

In a subdued voice he spoke to Earl. "Earl. Thank you for coming."

"Of course, Homer. I'm sorry you're having a difficult time of it. Can I help you in any way?'

"Yes. They're going to take me into the hospital in Miles. But, before they take me into town I want you to know that there is an insurance policy on my life, which will go to the church. I have it here and I want you to take it with you now."

Earl was hard put to know how to respond adequately. "Homer, I hadn't realized. This is very generous of you."

"It's not much, but enough to tide the church over after I'm no longer here to meet my pledge." He then turned to Tom. "Would you open the drawer of my bed table here. In it you'll find the policy. Would you take it out and give it to Earl?"

"Certainly, Dad." He opened the little drawer and found the policy and handed it to Earl.

Earl took it and when he saw the amount he turned to his friend. "Homer, $10,000! That will make a big difference. The congregation will always be indebted to you. Thank you so much."

"I have always loved my church, and I want it to thrive. I know that thriving will be difficult during hard times. I hope this insurance will help the church over such times."

This testimony coupled with Homer's condition brought tears to Earl's eyes. "And it's clear to me, that you love Christ, my good friend."

Just then the front doorbell rang, and Tom left the bedside to attend to it. Earl could see that Homer's energy had been sapped by this exchange and he was beginning to drift into sleep again.

He returned, "The ambulance is here and they are ready to take him to town." He said this to Earl realizing that Homer had fallen asleep, but when his voice awakened Homer, Tom repeated. "They are ready to take you into the hospital now."

At this point Earl intervened and asked to have a prayer with the family before letting the E.M.T.s take Homer. Tom brought Jenny and Fay into Homer's bedroom and the family members held hands while Earl asked God's blessing on His child, Homer.

After the prayer Earl bid him goodbye and promised to come into town in the morning to see him. The attendants brought in a gurney. Earl waited in the hall until they had him carefully placed and wrapped for the trip into Miles City. Tom rode with him.

As Earl waved them off before turning to his car, he had a premonition. *I don't think I'll see Homer again.* Earl's feelings were accurate. Homer was pronounced "dead on arrival."

Conducting's Homer's funeral was difficult for Earl, largely because he had allowed himself a personal friendship with Homer Stein and he had become quite dependent upon Homer for advice and counsel over the years. The only person in Earl's life—excepting Kaye, of course—who came close to being a friend as Homer had been was Martin.

The morning after the Stein funeral, Kaye and Earl discussed the plans for the day.

"I think I'll run out to see Martin this afternoon."

Kay understood her husband's sense of loss over Homer's death and could see that Martin would be good for Earl. "That's a good idea, darling."

By three o'clock Earl and Martin were at the chess table engrossed in esoteric strategies only chess players understand. In seemingly no time, the clock on Martin's mantle clock struck four and almost immediately thereafter Earl announced, "Checkmate!"

"Well, my friend, you beat me. First time at that!"

As the two players set the chessmen back in their original positions, Martin asked. "What's going on in your life? . . . Besides Homer's funeral, I mean." "Not much. Kaye is out for the day and evening, so I'm 'batching' for supper." As soon as he said it, Earl wished he hadn't used the term with Martin, who was a full time bachelor.

"So? I'm 'batching' all the time." Martin grinned. "Which means you can stay for a bite here, right?"

"I suppose. But I don't want to put you out."

"Not at all. I've got a couple antelope steaks."

Earl was glad for the invitation. He didn't have much in the house for supper, and it would give him a longer time to visit with Martin. Earl had found conversations with Martin easy, non threatening and often quite penetrating. He could be himself, not having to remember constantly that he was "the preacher." Earl also sensed Martin's hunger for meaningful dialogue with another human being. Not only was he a bachelor, but something of a recluse as well.

After they had finished their steaks and had taken a second cup of coffee, Earl opened up a subject which had been on his mind lately. "You know, Martin, I've been plagued in the past few months with troubling questions." He hesitated. "And I guess I wonder how you would answer these."

"You mean questions you have, or some that people come to you with?"

"From people. After that tragic death of the little boy in the house fire out on the Perkins place. Remember?"

"Oh yes, one doesn't forget such a thing."

"Well the first question that I got—from lots of folks—was *Why did God do that?* Or a milder form of it: *Why did God let that happen?*"

"Yes, that is a tough question."

"How would you answer, Martin?"

"I'd say that God didn't do it. The faulty wiring caused the fire, and smoke kept anyone from going upstairs to rescue the child."

"That's more or less what I said, but then there was a person who came back at me and said. *If a God of love is all powerful, things like that shouldn't happen. So God's will isn't done, after all, is it?* Frankly, I was stumped. Oh, I said something, but not very convincing, I don't think."

Martin gave Earl a knowing look. "I was stumped, too, some years ago after Marvin was killed, I went through the same contortion of logic. It finally came to me that even though God eventually wins, there's a lot that happens along the way that God doesn't will."

"Yeah, I guess it's just the way it is."

PART III

The 1980s

CHAPTER 38

Bed & Breakfast

Lynn picked up the kitchen phone after the familiar two rings. "Hello, Mrs. Lindsay, here . . . . Yes, this is Glen Mor . . . Yes, we do, what do you require? . . . . Certainly. A room for two for three nights, beginning tomorrow evening. Your name?"

"Charles and Janet Johnson from the United States . . . Arlington Heights, Illinois."

"I have you down for tomorrow, Mr. Johnson." Lynn's curiosity was perked.

"Can you give me directions on how to find your B & B?"

"Where are you now? . . . Queenstown, ah yiss. Take No. 6 east to Frankton, then south through Lumsden toward Winton. Just a bit before you come to Winton take No. 96 a little over three kilometers west 'til you come to the road on your left to Oreti, then west to Drummond. Then in Drummond you'll come to our sign which will direct you to Glen Mor. . . . How much time? Give yourself about three and half hours driving time . . . Yes, we shall be expecting you and Mrs. Johnson. Cheerio!" Lynn hung up the phone and went upstairs to check on the room she planned for the Johnsons.

After their children had moved out, Lynn and John had opened a B&B in their home. Not so much for the extra income. Times had been good on the farm. But as something interesting for Lynn to do since the children had both left home, to pursue their own dreams. Ian was their first born and was now an engineering student at Otago University in Dunedin. Just about ready to graduate. Amanda was in London working as a nanny. She had seemed a little young to Lynn for such a trip, but John had persuaded Lynn that it would be all right. So Glen Mor had become empty of their youthful exuberance. A friend of Lynn's had moved to TeAnau and had opened a bed & breakfast. On a visit Lynn had become intrigued with the idea of running a B&B. It took some convincing, but John finally gave in, and now he seemed to enjoy this expansion of their lives.

The Johnsons arrived in the early evening having taken their supper in Winton. Lynn saw the car coming onto the circular drive and went out to meet them as they got out of their car.

"G'day! Welcome to Glen Mor! I'm Lynette Lindsay."

"Hello. I'm Charles Johnson, and this is my wife, Janet."

"I'll have my husband help you with your bags."

Lynn summoned John from the lounge where he was reading. John assisted Charles in bringing their four suitcases upstairs.

"When you are settled, do come down to the lounge. I'll have a cuppa ready for you there."

"Cuppa?" Janet asked.

"Ah, yiss, that's our way of referring to a cup of tea! If I had said come down for tea, you might have expected a full supper."

"I see," Janet replied. "We'll be glad to come down—for *a cuppa*."

With that the guests were shown into the house and taken upstairs to their room.

A bit later, when Lynn heard them coming down the stairs, she brought a tray with the tea things into the lounge and put them on a small table by the sofa. She showed them in and offered them seats. John put down his paper and got up to greet the guests, joining them for the evening refreshment.

After a brief conversation about Johnson's tour of New Zealand and their trip down from Queenstown, Lynn was eager to ask. "Now, I've been dying to know about your life and home in Illinois." She had a twinkle in her eye.

"Well," Charles began. "We are both high school teachers in Arlington Heights and that's the suburb in which we live. That's in the Chicago area."

"I know," Lynn was quick to affirm.

"You do?" Janet picked up on this without waiting for an explanation and continued. "Chuck teaches history and I am a math teacher."

Charles asked John about his farm while Janet spoke with Lynn.

"You say, you know where Arlington Heights is? Have you been in that area?"

"Yes. As a matter of fact I grew up in the Chicago area."

"You didn't! . . . . Charles, did you hear that?"

"What?"

"Mrs. Lindsay is from Illinois!"

Charles was as shocked as his wife. "But you sound like a New Zealander! I just assumed this to be your home."

John stepped in. "Not to my ears. Ever since I met her on the ferry in Alaska she has sounded like somebody from the U.S. Can't take the Midwestern twang out of a native, I've always said!" He grinned.

"John! I don't twang anymore, you know that."

"No, but to the ear of a true Kiwi the sound of a Yank comes through!"

Janet couldn't wait to hear. "But what brought you here . . . How did you meet . . . do you ever go back?"

Lynn began. "Well, to begin with, I've lived here for over twenty years. It's my home. In some ways more than Illinois ever was. John and I met in Alaska. We were both sort of on a youthful excursion away from home. We met on a ferry on the inside passage."

"I barged in on a table in the cafeteria with two Yanks sitting there innocent as can be. I wound up marrying the younger one! I brought her home."

"And I've been a sheep farmer ever since." Then she thought of another of Janet's questions. "And no, I've not returned to the U.S."

"Sounds romantic!" Janet put in.

"It is, isn't it?" John agreed.

Lynn then changed the subject. "What more do you plan to see and do while you're here in New Zealand?"

Charles launched forth with a complete itinerary of the balance of their trip, beginning with the drive up the east coast to Dunedin and northward to Christchurch.

John offered some tourist advice. "After Dunedin, before you come to Oamaru be sure and stop at the Moeraki Boulders a few kilometers this side of Hampden."

"What are they?" Charles asked with interest.

"Perfectly round large boulders strewn along Hampden Beach. They are concretions."

"Concretions?" Janet asked.

"Yes," John explained. "Some sixty million years ago lime salts gradually accumulated around a live crystal core. And now they are not doing anything except lying around to be looked at!"

Lynn looked at the clock on the mantel. "My sakes, we are keeping you two up. We better let you go."

The Johnsons agreed and asked about the time for breakfast.

"Unless you want to get away quite early it would be ready any time after eight. Will that be suitable?"

"Yes, that will be fine." Charles was quick to say.

With that, the surprised foursome broke up for the night.

While Lynn and John were preparing for bed John remembered Lynn's reaction to the Johnsons. "Lynn, you seemed sort of subdued with the guests."

John's question took Lynn by surprise. On and off she had been thinking about Earl since hearing of Johnson's location in the Chicago area. She was reluctant to share much more than, "Oh, I guess I got caught up in memories of my days back home, and not all those memories were pleasant."

John gave a knowing look.

"As you well know, John. Mother, the drunk, and Dad the tyrant!" Lynn said with an edge of anger. That seemed to satisfy John's curiosity.

But later, after Lynn was aware of John's deep breathing, she lay next to him wide awake, thinking of Earl Norris. *I wonder where he is . . . did he ever marry . . . if so, what sort of woman . . . does he have children . . . what's he like now ?* Sleep came finally, but she was restless through the night. If she had dreams, they were lost in her subconscious when she awoke, but she had a vague feeling that Earl had been in her dreams that night. Once into the chores for the day she put him out of her mind where he remained—for a time.

Her first chore was breakfast for the Johnsons. By eight when they came to the table in the dining room, Lynn had bowls of steaming porridge to put before them. And after that she brought out eggs and bacon along with toast and marmalade. And, of course, coffee.

After expressing their appreciation for the "excellent breakfast" and a "good night's sleep" the couple brought their suitcases down and Charles put them in the car. As they said "good bye" Janet added. "Now, remember, if you return to Illinois, be sure to look us up."

"I'll certainly try to do that. But I can't promise such a trip."

And then they were off. Lynn stood at her front door and watched as the Johnsons' car left the circular drive and headed down the lane toward the road. *A few more days and they will be in the air going home to the US—back to Illinois.* For one brief, fleeting moment she felt some remorse—*or is it envy?* she wondered.

Lynn returned to the dining room to begin clearing the table—with thoughts of Illinois and Michigan—and Earl—fueling her reverie.

CHAPTER 39

Home is where the heart is.

"The B& B is keeping you quite busy, isn't it?" John had come in from his shop for morning tea. He found Lynn scurrying through the kitchen with a load of soiled bed linen.

"Oh yiss, but I enjoy it."

"You mean meeting all the folk, but all this laundry and housework. What about that?"

"I just like the whole business, so that I don't mind the work, even doing the dishes. I guess there's something of the *innkeeper mentality* in me." By this time she had put two cups of tea on the kitchen table and was now bringing a plate of lemon squares. John took his seat and Lynn joined him.

"It's fun to visit with folks from all over New Zealand and the world. And to share in their delight over their touring of New Zealand. I like to imagine the places they come from. And you know, John, wherever the guest might be from it always seems to confirm that right here in Glen Mor is where I want to be."

"That pleases me. You are the one I want to be with here at Glen Mor, I might add. I need to get back to work".

A few mornings later Lynn was working at her sink which looks out over the paddock closest to the yard. She was especially drawn to the sight of John and his two dogs as they worked the sheep toward the gate on the far end of the paddock. She could see him whistling to the dogs and their quick response as they raced toward the moving sheep to guide them toward the opening into the next paddock. Holding their heads down and swerving this way and that to bring them where John wanted them. She knew how happy he was in his work and also how well things had been going the last few years. She had come to love Glen Mor as much as John did. There was nowhere else she'd rather live. This was home.

She thought about the children. Ian had already been offered a job in an engineering firm in Dunedin. In fact he was to start in a month as soon as he would graduate. A little short on social life, but perhaps after getting into a job, he would meet someone. She was not as pleased with Amanda, however. Since she had left for London they had very seldom heard from her. They had phoned her a few months ago. But the call left Lynn with an uneasy feeling. She just hadn't sounded as pleased to hear from them as Lynn had thought she would. John had said that it was just her age, but that had failed to satisfy Lynn. But she put the matter out of her mind as she always did, after thinking about the way she herself had left her own family. It was just too painful to think of Amanda mirroring that same attitude.

The time came for Ian's commencement. John and Lynn drove up to Dunedin and stayed for a few nights in the Magnolia House, a bed and breakfast not far from the Octagon, which is at the center of the downtown area where the streets come together to form an octagon. Ian showed them the firm he would be working for and the apartment he'd found near his work.

After the ceremonies the three found a four star restaurant for a dinner to celebrate Ian's accomplishment, The Terrace Café on Moray Place. After the meal and before they separated Ian said, "Mum, this was a near perfect day. Thank you for coming."

"We wouldn't have missed it," she replied. And then she questioned Ian. "Near perfect?"

"Oh, I wish Amanda could have come. I invited her . . . but I never heard from her."

This hit Lynn like a block of concrete.

"I even told her that I could help her on her airfare."

This prompted John to ask. "Do you hear from her regularly?"

"That's just it. I haven't heard from her since she went to London. I assume you have heard, though."

John and Lynn gave each other a somber look before John replied. "Not very often."

"It's been months," Lynn interjected.

"Well now, this is supposed to be a celebration. Let's not get mired down." John was obviously uncomfortable with this discussion.

"Ian, we can help you shift into your new apartment tomorrow, if you would like us to."

"That would be great, Mum."

By noon, Ian was completely shifted and John and Lynn were on their way back to Glen Mor.

Lynn was unusually quiet until she expressed her feelings. "John, it's like we've lost both our children. Ian will be on a full schedule of work. No more school holidays when he can come home. And Amanda . . . ."

John didn't know what to say. "Do we have the name of the people she's been working for?"

"Yes. Do you suppose we should write them?"

"Telephone! Then we'll find out right away."

"I wonder why she hasn't written . . . ."

John cut her off, "Now, Lynn, let's just put this subject away until we phone London. Then we will know what to worry about, if anything."

"But . . . ."

"Wait for the phone call." John surprised her with a sharp firmness.

Most of the rest of the drive home was in silence. Once they were home and each involved in their work the subject of Amanda didn't come up, not that they didn't think about her frequently.

One day some weeks later on returning from Winton, when they drove in the gate, Lynn, got out to pick up what mail had arrived in their post box. She jumped back into her seat. "John! There's something here from London."

"From Amanda?"

"No . . . let me see . . . from S. Winters . . . her employer!" Lynn opened the letter while John drove up to the house, where he stopped and turned off the engine.

Lynn read:

> Dear Mr. & Mrs. Lindsay,
>
> It is very troubling for me to write this to you. In fact I have waited for further information. But, receiving none, I felt it best to write you.
>
> A few days ago I awakened at the crying of the children. I thought that at any moment Amanda would go in to comfort them. But they continued, until I thought I had better see what the trouble might be. When I entered their room they were alone. Amanda was not there. After comforting the children I went to Amanda's room. She was not there. In fact all of her things were gone. It was apparent to me that she had left us. Not a trace could I find.
>
> Later in the morning I rang up the agency from which I had obtained her services. They had no knowledge of her whereabouts, and had not known that she had departed. In the days following I hoped I would hear something, but I did not. Consequently I felt that I should notify you.
>
> However, I am in hopes that by this time you have heard from your daughter.
>
> The children miss their nanny. She was indeed very suitable.
>
> Regretfully,
> Mrs. Sarah Winters

Amanda's parents sat in stunned silence, until John announced. "I guess we better go into the house and determine what to do next."

Once inside, Lynn suggested. "John, I think we should call Mrs. Winters. Perhaps by this time she has heard something."

"Yes, but let us not get our hopes up."

"What time is it there, John? I want to call."

John looked at his watch and figured in his mind. "A little before 7 PM yesterday."

"Will you get me the number? I've never quite gotten the hang of that."

John took the phone and obtained the number. He wrote it down for Lynn.

She took the phone and dialed the number. She waited through the necessary succession of clicks and buzzes as the connection spanned the globe. She heard the double ring on the other end.

"Hello. Mrs. Winters, here."

Lynn was suddenly overcome with emotion, and could barely speak.

"Mrs. Winters, here." The voice repeated.

"Yes, Mrs. Winters. Hello. I'm ringing you up from New Zealand. . . . ."

"Oh, my . . . you are Amanda's mother?"

"Yes. Have you had any word from her or contact since writing me?"

Lynn heard a dog bark on the other end of the line. "Down, Perkins, down . . . excuse me a moment." Sarah Winters left the phone long enough, apparently to put the dog in another room. Lynn waited nervously.

"Sorry. He's such a baby. Doesn't want me talking to someone else." Mrs. Winters paused and seemed to catch her breath, and then went on. "Mrs. Lindsay, I am so sorry to have to tell you that I have heard nothing. And I simply do not know where to turn to look for her."

"Can you tell me whether you noticed anything about Amanda in the few days before she disappeared?"

"Yes, now that I think of it, she seemed . . . Oh I don't know . . . distracted, I guess you'd say. Perhaps even distraught. But certainly nothing she herself mentioned."

"I see." Lynn thought about this. "Do you think it would help if I came to England?"

"I can't think what you could do, Mrs. Lindsay." She seemed to ponder this and added. "But, of course, you are welcome to come up. You would be most welcome here."

"That is very kind of you. I shall need to think about this. I'll talk with my husband and let you know if and when I come."

John was trying to tell Lynn something.

"Just a moment, my husband has a message for me."

John handed Lynn a slip of paper with Glen Mor's phone number.

"Oh yes, he wants you to have our phone number." Lynn read it off to Sarah Winters. "Please ring us up if you get any information at all . . . yes, thank you . . . Cheerio."

Lynn hung up and burst into tears. She haltingly told John everything she'd gotten from Mrs. Winters, which wasn't much.

John and Lynn spent the rest of the evening wrestling with the question of whether or not she should fly to London. By morning it was clear to both John and Lynn that she would go to England.

CHAPTER 40

Cabin in the Mountains

The Montana farm economy in the 1980's took its toll on many small farming communities because of a resulting decline in population and the closing of retail businesses. The church in Saline felt the impact of dwindling population. During this period some of the younger supporters of the church had to cut back financially. Other members were forced to move away. The frequent farm sales in the community were the source of sadness for Earl as well as for the congregation. More than a few farms had to be placed on the auction block to bail out farm families who had been hit by plummeting cattle and grain prices together with markedly higher fuel and energy costs which increased the cost of production. Some years costs equaled or exceeded income from the sale of wheat and barley. For those farm operators who had over extended themselves when land values were high and government loans had been cheap and easy to obtain, the economic crises of the 80's spelled doom. When the farm economy experienced a sharp down turn, in the mid 80s with the value of land dropping significantly, farms which were heavily mortgaged were in serious trouble. For some the only way out was to put the farm up for auction and to move off the land. Roy and Judy Malone were among those who were thus forced to sell.

When the victim of such economic collapse was a church member, Earl made it a point to attend the sale and to offer moral support to the family during the emotionally draining day of the sale. Roy and Judy were among those in the community who were forced to sell. The day of the Malone auction arrived and Earl drove out to their place. The farm yard was filled with farm implements and equipment arranged in neat rows by the auctioneer. Pickups and cars from all over the county began arriving early in the day. Soon vehicles were parked every which way along the road and around the house and sheds. Earl recognized some of the farmers who were walking among the items put out for auction examining each piece. Others milling about were unknown to Earl. Near the back door of the house tables had been set up on which various household items were on display. Some of the women were clustered at these tables. A platform had been erected between the barn and the house.

At sale time the auctioneer and a couple of assistants mounted the platform and were getting ready to start the auction, making sure that the microphone was working "ONE—TWO—THREE—TESTING" came over the sound system. Everyone stopped what they were doing and turned toward the platform Soon the auction was under way. One item after another was described, put up for auction, and sold. Everyone was in dead earnest as this ritual proceeded.

Earl looked around for Roy and Judy, but did not see them. He entered the kitchen of the farm house and inquired of the group of women who were their getting the lunch ready. "Have you seen Judy, or Roy?"

"They're in the living room," one of the women pointed.

Earl went in and found Judy in tears and Roy comforting her. It was a tender but embarrassing moment for both Earl and the Malones. Earl didn't know what to say. "I came to see how you're doing."

"Not good, Reverend," Roy admitted. "Especially for Judy here."

Judy turned to Earl. "Oh Earl. I can't bear to see our whole life out there on the tables and in the yard."

"I know how sad this must make you, Judy."

"I was going to help with the lunch, but I just can't . . . and I know Roy should be out there in case there's a question."

Earl looked at Roy. Roy gave a slight nod. "Judy," Earl offered. "Why don't you let me take you to our house where Kaye can be with you?" Judy hesitated. Earl looked at Roy.

"That would be a good idea, Reverend." Roy added, "No need for you to come back. I'll be OK."

"Judy, let's you and me go into town. I'll bring you back to the farm after supper. Or better yet, Roy, why don't you come in for supper with us?"

"All right. Thank you." He turned to Judy. "Now you go in with the Reverend and I'll come to supper with you there." He kissed his distraught wife and left for the proceedings outside. Earl took Judy home to Kaye.

Two days later Earl went out to Malones again for the last time. Their car was loaded with only space enough for Judy to drive. Roy would drive their pickup, also overloaded. They were ready to leave.

"Come into the kitchen, Reverend. Have a last cup of coffee with us."

The three sat around the old kitchen table each with a cup of leftover morning coffee. Judy shared some of her feelings. "I woke up this morning and the dead silence hit me. No more sounds from the livestock. No sounds of farm machinery running. Nothing. The yard was empty. The last of it was hauled off yesterday. I felt so alone . . . except for Roy."

"Yeah it's like a silent death."

"What's next?"

"Billings." Roy answered.

Earl waited for more about their plans.

Judy added, "We're renting a mobile home in Lockwood. Roy's got a school janitor job. I'm going to cook at the school."

Earl acknowledged this, but little else was said. The three left the kitchen and Earl offered his final condolences and offered, "Please come visit us when you get a chance."

"And you come see us, Reverend."

With that Earl got in his car and drove off. When he got back to his office he checked a few things and then walked over to the post office. As he did he saw the two Malone vehicles driving through town on their way to the interstate and then to Billings. Earl was saddened.

Not only were farms for sale, but other properties as well. It was not uncommon to find FOR SALE signs on fence posts and in front of houses in town.

However, while the size and attendance of the Saline church had been decreasing, some of the financial support continued due to the financial stability of its older members, and also it became apparent that there were those staunch members who had raised their level of support to make up for membership losses. So for the time being, things were going along relatively well for Earl's ministry. Davey was now married and had moved onto the Norland place. He was now farming in partnership with his grandfather, whose retirement would soon be complete.

One day while on vacation during the summer of 1986, Earl and Kaye came across a FOR SALE sign at the mouth of a lane leading to a mountain hideaway which caught their eye. This discovery came near the end of their vacation during which they had been touring by car.

Instead of a trip to the Midwest to visit Earl's family, this year they had decided to explore Montana. After an overnight and leisurely breakfast at the Dude Rancher Lodge in Billings they drove up to Red Lodge, an hour or so south of Billings on the road leading to Yellowstone Park. They stopped to amble up and down the three block business street finally entering the historic Red Lodge Café for buffalo burgers. After lunch they continued on U.S. 212

and came to Westminster Spires Camp where Earl had been a camp counselor. Kaye had never seen the camp.

"Would you like to stop and see the camp?" Earl suggested.

Kaye agreed and they drove in and got out of the car. There was something subtly romantic about being in the camp alone. They held each other's hands as they walked from building to building. Earl explained each one as they came to it. They walked out past the craft hall and into the sage brush dotted open space beneath the tall rock peaks named "Westminster Spires." They both felt a magical moment as they looked up to the spires which were reflecting the afternoon sun. Instinctively they turned to each other and embraced. In the kiss they exchanged under the sky their love soared.

"I hate to admit it, Kaye, but there is something so special being here without any camp responsibilities, and with you, without anyone else. You know—church members or family."

"Yes, just us, darling!"

"And on vacation without any cares! No meetings . . . No sermon to prepare or people to see . . . ."

"Just us, sweetheart!"

"In the midst of all this mountain beauty—a bit different from Saline!"

They continued up the Beartooth Highway. The magnificence of this drive over the mountains into Wyoming and back into Montana at Cooke City was simply overwhelming. The road carried them over a number of switchbacks until they reached the "top of the world." They found themselves above timberline which gave them unobstructed views of the western slopes leading toward the eastern border of Yellowstone National Park. They looked down upon small alpine lakes of crystal blue, beside which they would soon be driving as they made their way downward toward Cooke City and then on further for another five miles to Silver Gate at the northeast entrance to Yellowstone.

In order to be fresh for their excursion through this large and diverse national park, the first ever—in the world—they pulled into Grizzly Lodge on the park end of Silver Gate for the night. They were assigned a small log cabin overlooking Soda Butte Creek. After washing up, they walked a few hundred feet along the road—Silver Gate's main street—back to the Log Cabin Café for a steak dinner before turning in for the night. After coming out of the quaint café rewarded with a fine meal, they felt the refreshingly cool breeze as they walked toward their motel. There was a pine scent in the air. The sky of early evening was deep blue, and only a few white clouds were to be seen.

"Let's walk for a bit," Kaye suggested.

They sauntered along the highway toward the park entrance. This late in the day there were few cars, almost none going into the park, a few coming out. They turned around at the sign announcing Yellowstone National Park. As they re-entered Silver Gate and came to the Grizzly Lodge, Earl looked at his watch, but asked anyway,

"Ready for bed, Kaye? Even though it's only 9 o'clock?"

"Yes . . . I'm for that . . . ."

Something about the way she answered gave Earl's heart a leap.

When they entered their cabin they found it still warm from the day's temperatures. They'd been wearing light jackets which they took off. When they did they were drawn to each other and embraced as they had at the camp.

After kissing her husband, Kaye said, "I'd like to shower first."

Earl read to the background music of Kaye's shower. When she came out in her bathrobe, Earl went in. After a quick shower Earl dried off and emerged in his bathrobe to find that Kaye had drawn all the shades and drapes, making the room moderately dark. She was in bed with the sheet drawn up. Earl tossed his robe over hers and got in bed next to Kaye.

"Oh, darling Earl, what better way to celebrate the grandeur of nature which we've been seeing all day . . . ."

"Than to fulfill our part in the nature of things!"

The digital clock on the night stand read 10:13. Earl was still awake, lying on his back. He listened to Kaye's deep breathing. She was nestled against his side with her arm resting on his chest and her head against his shoulder. The word for tonight, and for all day was *bliss* he thought. Kaye's coming into his life had made such a profound difference. He felt as though he'd come into his stride, so to speak. Her loving support had boosted his self confidence and made him feel adequate to the tasks set before him in his ministry in Saline. He'd noticed a change in how the church members seemed to view him in the years since their marriage—as an adult. While he was still single, some seemed to regard him as a kid. Even though there were some who liked to put him on a ministerial pedestal, for the most part he now felt that he was treated as an equal. *That feels good*, he thought. *I'm finally seen as someone from Saline and not Chicago. All this and so much more Kaye has brought me. I hope I've brought as much into her life.*

At this point she shifted her leg over his, as if to lay claim to him and to assure him that he'd given her so much as well. As Earl exulted in the stimulating warmth of Kaye's unclothed body against his, he whispered out loud, "Thank you, dear God! Life is good." Sleep finally overtook Earl bringing dreams.

He'd set the alarm for seven. When it rang Earl was in a deep sleep. It had rung for a minute or so until Earl was jolted awake. He switched off the alarm and opened his eyes. He felt a vague uneasiness bordering on guilt. Yet there was a smile down deep inside somewhere. Kaye had rolled over and was facing away from him when he reached over to touch her cheeks as he gently spoke. "Kaye, darling. It's seven and we need to get rolling."

She turned his way, opened her eyes and with her lips invited a kiss.

Bacon and eggs at the Log Cabin Café concluded their Silver Gate experience and they were now on their way through the northern tier of Yellowstone Park, an area neither of them had seen before. After driving through the Lamar Valley, they came to Tower Junction and Roosevelt Lodge. Then west to Mammoth Hot Springs where they stopped for lunch in the Mammoth Hotel. From there they decided to leave the park at Gardiner and drive down the Yellowstone River valley to Livingston and over to Bozeman by evening. While driving down the broad Yellowstone valley, Kaye nodded off to sleep, leaving Earl alone with his own thoughts. Thoughts which were both intriguing and disturbing.

His dream of the night before surfaced in his mind. He was in a cabin in the mountains with a woman. At first he hadn't known who she was. Then she began to seem familiar to him. She didn't say anything, but merely went about her household chores in the cabin. It seemed like it was a century ago. The woman wore a long dress, maroon with a ivory floral design. He was lying in a bed with a straw mattress, and was covered with a woolen blanket. Then he was up and sitting in a straight back chair at a rough hewn table. Someone came over and kissed him on the forehead. He stood. There was no one in the room. The scene shifted radically. He was now standing on a sandy beach. Someone wearing a white bathing suit was waving at him. He had awakened at that point. The alarm had been ringing. After awakening he wasn't entirely sure who it was he had seen in the dream.

Now, while driving along U.S. 89 toward Livingston Earl re-lived the last scene of the dream and concluded that it had been at Shore Crest. His mind remained focused on the girl in the white bathing suit. *Was that Kaye?*

Kaye awakened. "Where are we?"

This jolted Earl away from his reverie. "Ten or so miles south of Livingston." With that the woman in the white bathing suit faded into the barren places where there is no memory. In fact it would be years before Earl would think about this night vision again.

After a quick supper at Martin's Café at the Northern Pacific Depot in Livingston, Kaye and Earl took the interstate over the Bozeman Pass to Bozeman where they found a room for the night at the Baxter Hotel on Main and Willson in the heart of the business district. As they were getting ready to go down to breakfast, Kaye suggested. "I'd like to get into some more mountain scenery, now that we are over this way."

Earl thought about this and decided to ask around. After they ate Earl took his bill to the cashier to pay and asked. "What's the closest way to the mountains?"

"I'd suggest Hyalite Canyon just south of town. Just take Willson here on the corner and drive south as far as you can and angle to the west, and finally you'll come out on a road going west. You'll see a sign for Hyalite Canyon. Turn left and soon you'll be in one of the most beautiful mountain canyons around."

They followed her directions and in a short time came to the sign she'd mentioned. They turned, and in a short mile they were in the canyon with the mountain stream to their right and the mountains forming canyon walls on both sides of the curving gravel road.

"This is gorgeous, isn't it, Earl?"

"The best we've seen, and so close. We're right in the mountains."

About a mile from the mouth of the canyon, they came to a bend in the road with a wooden bridge to the right built across the river. Just this side of the bridge was a "FOR SALE" sign.

"I wonder what's for sale." Earl slowed the car and then suggested. "Let's go across the bridge and see."

Immediately on the other side of the bridge the lane entered a thick forest of pine and aspen. The dirt road wound to the left along the creek and then up a slight hill to a clearing. In the midst of the open area was a small single story cabin with dark wood siding and a asphalt shingle roof. Not at all fancy but in a superb location. An ample stack of cut logs for the fireplace was arranged between two trees near the back door of the cabin. No power lines led to the cabin. A hand pump and an outhouse along a short path from the back door proclaimed that the cabin had no water or plumbing. They walked around the building peering in the windows. They found it to be simply furnished with rag rugs on the floors of what appeared to be two rooms. They could see no sign of occupancy. Surrounding the cabin was a thicket of bushes of a number of varieties and a generous amount of trees, mostly pine and aspen. The sunlight filtered through the leaves creating a light and shadow pattern on the ground. With no wind, the only sound was that of a chorus of birds in the trees and bushes nearby.

Kaye was ecstatic. "This has gotta be ours, Earl. I could spend my life here."

"You're joking, aren't you?"

"No, I'm very serious. I would like very much to own this. Wouldn't you?"

"Well, yes, I guess so." Earl thought some more and restated himself. "The fact of the matter is that I'd love to be up here for an extended time, and this cabin would make that possible, wouldn't it?"

"That's right. Oh, Earl, let's go and see the realtor."

"Alright, that's what we'll do. Can't hurt to find out if it's possible."

When Earl and Kaye returned to Bozeman they found the realtor who had listed the cabin in Hyalite Canyon, and before they left town they signed a buy-sell. The price and terms had been so favorable that they were afraid it would be snatched up by another buyer if they didn't act fast.

From Bozeman they began their trip home—almost three hundred miles. All they could talk about while they drove was "their" cabin. When they drove into Miles City, they immediately made a stop at the bank to consult their banker. As a result, the mountain hideaway became theirs. By the end of the summer they had brought furniture of their own to supplement what had been left in the cabin.

On a Sunday afternoon, the day before Labor Day, Earl and Kaye drove over to the cabin to spend a few days there before closing it up before winter. After an idyllic few days, they left it reluctantly on Tuesday morning. On the way home Earl shared a "dream" he'd had. "Kaye, what would you think of coming up to the cabin during the Christmas holidays?"

"You mean, you think we could use it in winter?"

"I think it's close enough to the road for us to walk in on snowshoes, and the fireplace would heat up the entire cabin. I think we could do it. I've always had a dream of spending Christmas out in the woods like that—a 'Courier and Ives' sort of image."

"We could try it this year the day after Christmas!"

Their family celebration was at the Norland ranch with Davey and Barbara and their children as well as the senior Norlands and Ken. Bob and Ann Taggert also celebrated at the ranch since Bob could not be away from church to spend Christmas with either of their own families.

The next day Kaye and Earl left for Hyalite Canyon. The driving lane of the highway was clear of snow and ice. They arrived at the bridge leading to their cabin by sunset. Fortunately the lane was passable a few feet beyond the bridge and the remaining distance on foot was not long. Earl started a fire in the fireplace while Kaye put the food away and put out some Christmas cookies. Earl had brought a portable tape player and put on some Christmas music. They would begin their Christmas cabin experience with music to accompany hot cocoa and cookies before the roaring fire.

When the music shifted from "Joy to the World" to Bing Crosby singing "White Christmas," Earl was momentarily transported to the fellowship hall of the church of his youth, They were singing "I'm dreaming of a white Christmas, just like the ones we used to know." Earl was transfixed as he was overcome with memories of his high school days, and of the girl in blue and yellow.

Kaye must have noticed something different about Earl's demeanor. "Earl. What's wrong?"

"What! . . . Oh! . . ." He thought quickly. "I must have been mesmerized by the flickering flames." He turned his attention to Kaye, forcing his memories from his mind. But the images lingered for a while until they faded.

By the end of the time they had allotted for their Christmas hideaway Kaye summed up their feelings, "We must do this every year. It was everything I'd hoped for."

"It was." Earl replied. *And more.*

CHAPTER 41

Heathrow

The bright sky-blue glare outside the cabin window quickly sloughed away when the giant 747 pierced the sunlit clouds on its descent over Heathrow west of London. Suddenly the cabin windows revealed only a heavy gray impenetrable shield. Lynn gripped her armrests, bowed her head and prayed . . . as she had never prayed before—not so much for a safe landing as for an amicable reunion with her missing daughter. In a few moments the grass alongside the runway came into view, seeming to tilt downward at first and then as the aircraft neared the ground, the runway leveled. With a massive double thud, the heavy aircraft touched down on its multiple landing wheels. The cabin vibrated as the reversing of the engines forced the aircraft to slow down while it moved cautiously onto the tarmac beneath the designated gate.

The excitement among the passengers in the cabin around her was palpable. She, on the other hand, had no desire to be in London, even though this would be her first time. She wanted only to find Amanda and to bring her home as soon as possible. Of this she had no assurance. Her last contact with Sarah Winters had yielded no new information, though there had been something evasive in Mrs. Winters' demeanor on the phone. The only thing she could think to do was to notify the police in hopes that a missing persons search would help her find her daughter.

The Winters had not offered to meet her plane. Instead they had given her explicit directions as to how to find a taxi and where the taxi should take her. She only slightly heard the almost inaudible intrusion of an announcement over the sound system concerning the arrival and instructions about deplaning, so concentrated were Lynn's thoughts about Amanda. The aircraft had now come to a complete stop and passengers were in the aisles excitedly retrieving their personal items from the overhead bins. Lynn stood up clutching her purse, took down her top coat, and began to move toward the nearest cabin door.

Since their phone conversation, Sarah Winters had decided to come to Heathrow to meet Lynn Lindsay, after a fateful phone call she had received from the lie-in clinic.

Air New Zealand, flight 3369 from Auckland is now deplaning at gate 31.

Sarah hurried to gate 31 and arrived in time to see the first of the line of passengers coming into the terminal from the ramp—most with carry-on bags slung over their shoulders. Meeting someone whom you have never seen is always an awkward procedure in an air terminal. She watched for a woman about ten or so years older than she, and traveling alone. Sarah hoped that Mrs. Lindsay would bear some resemblance to Amanda. She spotted a woman her age walking alone. "How do you do—are you Mrs. Lindsay?"

The woman smiled. "No, I'm afraid not."

Embarrassed, Sarah Winters continued to stare at the faces of those coming toward her. Finally she saw another woman whose expression was obviously strained. Sarah was certain. "Lynn Lindsay! I am Sarah Winters."

Immediately she was rewarded. "Oh, Sarah, I didn't know you were coming to meet me."

"I decided to come to meet you, just this morning."

The two women moved along with the stream of passengers bound for the baggage retrieval area. Lynn was quick to ask. "Any news from my Amanda?"

"Ah . . . . but . . . ."

"Yes?"

"Let's get your luggage and find a place to talk."

Lynn reluctantly agreed as they swept along with the other passengers hurrying down the concourse.

After an impatient wait, Lynn saw her bag coming around and quickly picked it up.

Sarah guided her to a pair of seats away from the crowd.

"Now, Lynn, I do have some news. I'm not sure how you will take it."

"Tell me, please."

"Yesterday morning I got a phone call from a small clinic not far from my house. It was a nurse who called to tell me that they had an Amanda in the lie-in ward. And did I know her."

"Oh Sarah! Was it our Amanda?"

"At the time I didn't know. She had not given a surname. So I went to the clinic and asked to see 'Amanda.' When I entered her ward I could see that it was Amanda!"

"Oh, thank God."

"She was in a deep sleep, and the nurse asked me to not to awaken her. So I asked the nurse what her problem was. I was told that such information was private—only available to family members."

"Of course. Can you take me there as soon as possible?"

"Yes, but I have to tell you that I returned yesterday afternoon and found her awake . . . ." Sarah hesitated, taking a moment to phrase what she had to say. She leaned over and put her hand on Lynn's arm. "When I told her that you were coming to London, she began to weep and said to me, 'Please don't let her come to see me.'"

Lynn was devastated.

"I tried to persuade her, but she was adamant."

Lynn's eyes glassed over with tears. "Did you find out why she is in the clinic ward?"

"Yes, I did . . ."

"What is her trouble?"

Sarah hesitated. "She's pregnant."

"Oh!" Lynn was completely taken aback, and speechless.

Sarah saved her from having to comment. "And apparently she was having difficulty and the doctor wanted her in bed."

"Oh my, I hope she will be all right . . . all the more reason I wish I could see her."

"Yes, of course."

Both women were quiet for a time.

Sensing an unspoken question, Sarah Winters declared. "I knew nothing of this. Except now, as I look back, that may have been what seemed to preoccupy Amanda in the time before she left." She thought further. "I was not aware that she had been seeing anyone."

"And she was?"

"Not really. And apparently no one has come forward. I believe this is a case of some bloke taking advantage of a naive girl and then melting away into the crowd. Get my meaning?"

"Yes, I'm afraid I do . . . How far along?"

"Five or six months, I think."

"I'd like to go there now."

"Of course."

Instead of driving Lynn to the Winters' house, Sarah drove directly to the small hospital. She parked in the car park next to the building and both got out of the car. "I think I should go in first, and see if Amanda might be willing to see you, now that you are here."

Lynn sat in a small waiting room located along the main corridor while Sarah went down the hall to see Amanda. It seemed to Lynn to take a very long time.

After forty minutes she wondered if she should go ahead and walk down the hall, but considering what Sarah had said, she thought better of it and continued to wait. It was almost an hour by the time Sarah returned to the waiting room.

"I tried. But I couldn't get anywhere with Amanda. She refuses to let you see her. I think she is so deeply ashamed that she can't face seeing you, Lynn. They were about to take her down for an ultrasound. I think you should talk to her nurse. Let's go down the hall to the nurses' station."

"Yes, I thought of that."

They began to walk toward the nurses' station when they had to make room for two aides rolling a bed with a patient toward them. When the bed began to pass them, Lynn exclaimed, "It's Amanda!" She stopped the bed and leaned over so that Amanda saw her.

"Mother!" Her voice betrayed devastating shock.

Before either had a chance to say more the aide warned, "Excuse me, but the patient is to have an ultrasound. We are late already." With that, Amanda was pushed out of reach. And the bed was rolled down the corridor.

Sarah, uncertain how to handle this situation, suggested, "We might go down to her room and wait . . . now that the ice has been broken."

The two waited in Amanda's room until she was returned, at which point Sarah discreetly removed herself. It would be up to Amanda and her mother to come together. During this first visit Amanda was painfully silent. What questions Lynn asked were perfunctory, but even these were met with only slight nods. Wisely, Lynn did not push her daughter into conversation. Instead she tried to communicate her love and acceptance of Amanda. She also shared with her daughter news of Southland and talk of Glen Mor. She told about Ian's graduation and about John's farming. After about an hour of this sort of monologue, Lynn could see that Amanda was becoming tired. But she also sensed a slight easing up. When she got up to leave, she kissed Amanda and promised to be back later in the day. Amanda showed no particular reaction, but at least did not resist the idea of her mother's return.

Sarah was waiting in the reception area. "How did you get on?"

"Fairly well, under the circumstances. She still is not saying much—hardly anything."

"I imagine this is hard on both of you, isn't it?"

"Yes. But it is a start. I'll come back as often as they'll let me."

Over the next four days Lynn continued her visits. Each morning she took a taxi to the hospital and spent her day either in Amanda's room or in a little tea shop nearby where she took her meals. Each evening Sarah was at home waiting for Lynn to get a report before each went to bed. Gradually as the week progressed, the miracle of renewing relationship began to come about. Much would remain to be worked out, but the healing power of love was evident.

Lynn's London visit would be seven days, time enough for Amanda to be dismissed from the hospital and re-installed with Winters. By mutual agreement with Amanda, Lynn would return when the baby was due.

Once again at the gate at Heathrow, this time with Amanda as well as Sarah Winters, Lynn was prepared to return to New Zealand. Mother and daughter hugged as the door to the ramp opened. Lynn boarded and found her seat for her homeward journey.

CHAPTER 42

Tragedy

John was at the gate when Lynn came down the steps onto the tarmac in Invercargill. They reached for each other and embraced with a prolonged kiss.

"How is she?" John wanted to know right away.

"She seems to be ok now. Healthwise. She came to the airport with me—along with Sarah Winters. She'll be with her now, and I feel good about that. Sarah is a very kind and loving person. Amanda is still wrestling with herself, but at least she has allowed me in, and we were able to talk things over together."

"Good." John continued his questioning. "What will happen when it's time for the birth?"

"I'd like to return to be with her. I don't know how I'll time it, but at least right afterward, I should think."

By this time they were waiting at the baggage gate. "And then . . . . ?"

Lynn's demeanor became serious and somewhat downcast. "I don't know, John . . . I just don't know what will happen. We didn't talk about that. It was enough that Amanda became willing to talk to me."

Lynn's bag arrived. John picked it up and they walked out of the terminal building to the car park and got in. They drove off to Glen Mor.

"Well," John ruminated. "We've got five or six weeks, don't we?"

With that, by silent mutual consent they began to talk about other things. Lynn was happy to be home. John had a lot to say about how things had been going.

After her return, life at Glen Mor resumed its normal routines.

Between the sheep business and the bed and breakfast the Lindsays kept very busy. During this time of anxiety over Amanda they drew support from their church and community relationships. It was good to know that Ian was well placed in a good firm, and that his career as an engineer showed much promise. When either of them thought of Amanda, it was with a mixed feeling. They were glad that there had been a reconciliation of sorts and that contact had been re-established. In fact their correspondence was about once a fortnight. But what was ahead for Amanda, and for them, posed a serious question which John was reluctant to face, and Lynn did not know how to think about it. All the while, the days on the calendar moved on inexorably.

One evening John announced. "I would like to go with you to England when Amanda is due."

"Oh John, I'd like that!"

"Then maybe we could both bring our little girl home."

"And a grand baby."

John's expression clouded. "Yes."

"That could be in a few weeks. Do you suppose we should get reservations?"

Some time later the call came. "Hello, Lynn. This is Sarah." She sounded hesitant.

"Yes, Sarah . . . do you have news?" Lynn was excited.

"Yes, but it is not good news. The baby came early . . ."

Lynn cut her off. "It did? A boy or a girl? How's Amanda?"

"Amanda is fine, considering . . . ."

"What do you mean?"

"The baby didn't make it."

Lynn could hardly take in what she was hearing.

"Mrs. Lindsay, I think you should come. Amanda needs you." Sarah added. "She wouldn't say it, but I feel strongly that you should come."

"Yes, of course, John and I will try to get a flight as soon as possible."

"Good. Meanwhile here is the phone number where you can reach her in the clinic ward."

Lynn took down the number. "I'll call immediately. And we will let you know when we have a flight. Thank you for your call and for being there with Amanda." The call to Amanda wasn't very satisfactory. She resisted the idea of her parents coming, but Lynn insisted.

The sound of the jet engines changed pitch to a lower drone. John and Lynn could feel the huge aircraft descending slightly at first and then more sharply. Soon the gray clouds out of their window gave way to a misty view of the city spread out beneath them. Rain spattered on the glass and soon they could see that the tiny streets below them glistened wet with rain. Here and there multi-storied buildings extended above the heavy foliage which covered residential neighborhoods and small shops.

John took his wife's hand, squeezed it and spoke. "London!" He paused to savor the thought. "I always wanted to bring you here on holiday. To show you the sights and to soak in the centuries of history still evident here."

"That would have been good, John. You were here as a youngster?"

"Ah, yiss. I was twelve. Mum and Dad took me. It was great fun. But this must be a quick trip, and not for fun—for serious family business, I guess—isn't it?"

"Yes, John, for Amanda."

"To bring her home."

"I'm not sure. What Amanda wants, Amanda does. That's our Amanda. Always has been head-strong."

John thought about this, but didn't say anything. They watched as the streets and the trees grew in size. Suddenly the runway was underneath. In a moment they were on the ground.

Sarah Winters met them as they came through customs and after retrieving their bags they were on the way to the clinic and to Amanda. They found her dressed and sitting in a chair.

Over the next few days no amount of urging could change Amanda's determination to remain in England. The pregnancy and the baby's death seemed to have taken away any desire to return to New Zealand—ever.

At least for the time being she would stay on at the Winters. John and Lynn had found a bed & breakfast near Sarah's house. Fortunately for Lynn and John, Amanda's rejection of New Zealand did not include her parents. In fact; Amanda seemed to have returned to her childhood dependence. One morning shortly before Lynn and John were scheduled to return to New Zealand, Lynn was visiting Amanda alone. "Oh, Mother, what will happen to me? I feel so anxious. Everything in my life revolved around the coming of my baby. Now it's like I'm floating over a bottomless black hole. Help me!"

The anguish in her voice and demeanor left Lynn with feeling of helplessness. *How can I help my little girl? I've never experienced what she has been going through.* In tearful silence; Lynn reached for Amanda and caught her up in her arms, as a mother would her baby.

After a prolonged embrace Amanda separated herself. "I want to lie down . . . and sleep."

Lynn helped her onto her bed and covered her with a blanket. She remained fully dressed. Lynn saw that she almost immediately was asleep. Lynn quietly closed her door as she left Amanda and sought out Sarah. "Mrs. Winters, I don't know how to help her. Her condition scares me."

"I've been concerned too, but not knowing Amanda so well I thought perhaps this reaction was somewhat normal for her."

"No. I have never seen her like this before."

"Then I think I should ring up her doctor."

Later in the day the doctor saw Amanda and prescribed some medication to calm her. But then he added, "I really feel that you should take her to a psychotherapist. She needs someone professional to talk her through this crisis period in her life."

As a result of the doctor's recommendation Amanda began seeing a therapist while Lynn made the decision to remain in London for a while to support her daughter in this time of emotional stress. It was necessary, however, for John to return to the farm.

"I guess one thing that can be said of our trip to London is that we have restored communication," John concluded as they waited at the gate where John would board his return flight.

Lynn added, "And we have found something concrete we can do for her—my staying with her for a while, that is."

"Ah yiss, I'm glad you can do that for her. How long do you suppose?"

"I should think two or three weeks, from what the doctor told me. That holiday in London you've dreamed of, John, will have to be put off 'til Amanda is better, but perhaps in a few months she could join us for a tour of England as well as London."

"Good thought."

At that point John's flight was called and they sorrowfully kissed goodbye.

Amanda's progress was encouraging and the break-through came after three weeks of counseling when she was taken off her medication and continued to feel upbeat, like her old self. Lynn obtained reservations and prepared to leave. "Are you sure you don't want to return to New Zealand with me?"

"No, Mum. This is my home. I plan to find an apartment and a job. But I have to do this on my own, my therapist advises . . . but this time I promise to stay in touch with you and Dad."

Lynn took her leave regretfully, but glad for the renewal of relationship with Amanda which had come about through these difficult circumstances. Once again Lynn experienced a sorrowful parting at the gate at Heathrow. This time she boarded the flight to Christchurch while her daughter remained behind.

Over the years each spring after the summer farm work was done, John and Lynn would think about a holiday trip of some kind. Now after leaving Amanda,

London was the favored destination. Finally it appeared that John and Lynn would make it to London.

One Saturday in May, John announced that he would free himself of his farm responsibilities for a special celebration of their twenty-fifth wedding anniversary that year. "Lynn, how about that trip to London? this year?"

"Oh John, can we?"

"Yes, I think we can, and let's include Alaska on our way to the UK and really celebrate our marriage where it all began Would you like that?"

"Oh, John, you know I would."

"Well then, I'll see what I can do at the travel agency in Invercargill next week, when I go in on business."

It was all the two talked about for the rest of the weekend. On Monday John obtained the required reservations, and during the next couple of weeks they got things ready for the anniversary trip.

But a grim intruder would cancel their plans. It came to Lynn a month before they were to leave for Alaska and Britain, when a neighbor rushed into her yard, sprang from his pickup and raced to her back door. "Mrs. Lindsay, John has been hit and they're taking him in to the hospital in Invercargill!"

"What happened?" Lynn cried out.

"A truck hit him while he was driving his tractor along the road to his field further up the road."

"Oh Dear God . . . ."

"Let me drive you into town to see him."

With that Lynn gathered a few things, closed up the house and climbed into her neighbor's truck.

They sped off to town.

It is the essence of an accident to be unexpected and unprepared for. Serious accidents leave no options. This was Lynn's experience. She and John had not had the chance in the past few days to speak with one another on any level but superficial. The rapid drive to Invercargill was in silence for most of the distance. Lynn's mind was anything but silent. An amalgam of thoughts and feelings clamored for attention in her mind. *How is he? If I had just kept him home a few more minutes, I could have started a conversation—any conversation, he wouldn't have been at the wrong place. Oh God, don't let him die. What have I done? I must call Ian and Amanda. Oh John, I hope you are all right. I hope someone has reached his mother.*

Finally they reached the hospital and hurriedly entered by the emergency door. He was in one of the emergency room enclosures. At last she was at her husband's side. But she found him unconscious. She held his hand, hoping for some sign of recognition. She drew up a chair so that she could keep physical contact.

Nurses were in an out checking vital signs and adjusting his position. The doctor came in, lifted up John's eyelid, and checked other places on his body. He then turned to Lynn.

"You are Mrs. Lindsay?"

"Yes, doctor. How is he?"

"We need to take him into surgery as soon as possible. There are some broken bones and we need to check some other things. We'll assign him a room and you can wait for him there."

At that point two nurses aides came in and began rolling John out of E.R. and to surgery. A nurse came up to Lynn. "Mrs. Lindsay, your husband will be returned to room No. 214. You can wait there. And by the way, we have reached his parents. They are on their way."

Lynn found the room and tried to relax, but her racing mind wouldn't let her. *Hopefully he'll be awake when he comes back.* Finally the door opened and John was being wheeled in. Lynn's heart sank when she found that he was still unconscious. Moments later Trevor and Meg arrived. The three held each other, sharing their anxiety.

They took up a vigil next to his bed speaking with each other in hushed voices while Lynn held John's hand. His parents took up their watch from chairs near the bed. They were awake with John most of the night, but drifted off to restless sleep every now and then. He remained unconscious through the night while his family stayed close. As the earliest rays of dawn crept through the heavy curtains on the window, Lynn felt John twitch. He opened his eyes for a moment. Then they closed forever. The nurse monitoring vital signs came in and gently covered John Lindsay completely with a sheet.

Lynn and Meg wept silently and each woman bent low over John's chest in a futile attempt to hug him once more. After a moment Trevor stepped over to the bed and gently lifted Meg up and held her in his arms, allowing Lynn to remain on John's chest. In time Lynn rose and turned to John's parents. Trevor and Meg gathered Lynn to themselves. They embraced tearfully in the silence of death, holding each other tightly.

"Oh, Mum . . . ."

"Oh, God . . . ." Trevor uttered desperately.

When a nurse came into the room they asked her to uncover John's head.

The Reverend Mr. Edmonds, the Lindsays' pastor, had been called by the nursing staff when it had seemed evident that John had taken a turn for the worse. Thus, soon after John's passing Mr. Edmonds entered John's room where Lynn and John's parents remained seated. Lynn looked up at her pastor.

"Oh—thank you for coming. I don't want to leave him . . . ."

Glenn Edmonds looked at Lynn and nodded his assent.

"I know he's gone, but . . . ."

"You don't have to leave just yet, Lynn." For a few minutes he sat in the room with the mourning family without saying anything.

The nurse peeked in and Edmonds nodded to her, and turned to Lynn and John's parents. "Let's have a prayer now before the nurses take him." He rose and helped Lynn up so that they could stand by the bed. By this time the nurse had come in and joined them. The five held each others' hands in a circle around John's body while the pastor offered a prayer.

He ended his prayer ". . . In the name of our Heavenly Father, the Holy Spirit, our comforter, and Jesus Christ, our Savior, Amen."

Lynn leaned over the bed and gave her husband a final kiss on his cold and motionless forehead. The pastor and the nurse then led the grieving family out of the room. As they walked down the barren corridor. Mr. Edmonds asked, "Are there people whom you would like me to contact?"

Margaret Lindsay was the first to reply. "Contact my brother, Ken immediately, but Trevor and I will want to do that. All my other people are here in Southland, and they will be here soon enough I'm sure."

"How about you, Lynn? Anyone in the U.S.?"

"No, not really . . . I will want to contact Ian in Dunedin and Amanda in London myself . . . ." She thought further. "But you could perhaps drop a line to the folks on our Christmas list."

"I'll be glad to, if you have it handy"

"Yes, it is in John's desk."

Trevor turned to Lynn. "Let's find a phone and try to reach Ken."

Mr Edmonds then offered, "As soon as you make your call let me drive you three back to Glen Mor," when he noticed some reluctance. "My two sons came to town with me and they can drive your vehicles back, if that is suitable."

It was agreed.

Trevor made the call to Ken. After a sad and poignant exchange Ken said. "I will come on the earliest flight I can book, Trevor."

Lynn and John's parents returned to Glen Mor in Mr. Edmond's car. When they arrived Lynn got the address list for the pastor.

"Thank you. I'll make contact immediately. Now you both stick together. The church women will be bringing you some food dishes. And in the morning I'll be by to help make arrangements."

The two Edmonds boys drove in with both the Lindsay cars, and joined their father as he made his departure.

Ian arrived home the next day. Amanda had not committed herself to return, leaving Lynn with a deepening gnawing emptiness. "I don't believe she will come, Mum." With more tears, she and John's mother hugged. The next day Ken flew into Invercargill. Trevor was at the terminal to meet him.

On the morning of the day of the funeral, an unfamiliar car drove into the drive at Glen Mor. Lynn heard it and went to the front door to greet the caller.

The door burst open and Lynn was overwhelmed when she heard, "Mum! I'm home!" Amanda and her mother locked in a tearful embrace. It was only after she let go of Amanda that she saw to her surprise that Sarah Winters had come with Amanda. "Sarah! You've come too. That is so touching to me."

"I wanted to help Amanda and I found that I'd come to feel in some small way a part of your family."

"I'm so glad you came."

The Drummond church was filled to capacity. The shiny black funeral coach stood outside as if in solemn attention, surrounded by what appeared to be every car in the community. Inside the mood could be described as a faithful sadness—humble resignation—unseeing hope.

Most poignant for Lynn, at the memorial service for her husband was the singing of a hymn which would become her favorite in succeeding years.

> *Time, like an ever-rolling stream,*
> *Bears all its sons away;*
> *They fly forgotten as a dream*
> *Dies at the opening day.*
>
> *O God, our Help in ages past,*
> *Our Hope for years to come,*
> *Be Thou our Guardian while life shall last,*
> *And our eternal Home.*

Lynette stood with John's parents as well as with Ian and Amanda. Surrounded by their family and neighbors at the grave which had received John's body, the words of the hymn echoed in Lynn's mind. But in her heart she uttered a correction. *Fly as a dream, but not forgotten.* And then, as if from Heaven itself, the words of an old song, long since unsung popped in to her mind.

> *In the consecrate silence know*
> *That the challenge still holds today.*
> *Follow, follow the gleam*
> *Of the light that shall bring the dawn.*

A few days later Ken had to return to Auckland. Within a fortnight Ian had driven back to Dunedin, needing to return to his work, and Amanda and Sarah had flown back to England, leaving Lynn completely alone, except for John's parents. A few years earlier Trevor had been forced to give up farming with John due to severe arthritis coupled with a precarious heart condition. He and Meg had moved to Winton in order to be closer to medical assistance. After John's accident, Trevor had wanted to move back to the farm to do the necessary work, but his doctor, aware of Trevor's heart condition, had strenuously objected. Lynn also discouraged him from returning. "I'll do what I can and hire help as well." She had assured Trevor, who was forced reluctantly to give in.

In the weeks immediately following John's death, neighbors were quick to drop by and to give Lynn a hand at the farm work. But this, everyone knew, would be only temporary. Lynn determined to hold on to the management but she would need hands-on help. This much needed help came from within the family. In a most fortuitous turn of events, the engineering firm for which Ian worked in Dunedin had opened up a branch in Invercargill just a year previous.

One month after John's death Ian was called into his boss' office. When he took a seat across from the firm's senior partner he was given a most attractive offer. "Ian, our Invercargill office is understaffed at the moment. Too much work for the two engineers we have there. But then not enough for a third. I am aware of the situation your mother faces on the farm just now—your father's death and all . . . ."

"Yes, she is very nearly overwhelmed, I am afraid. But she does not want to sell."

"Yes, I see. Which brings me to an offer I am prepared to make, Ian."

"What is that, sir?"

"I am prepared to offer you a three-quarters time position in Invercargill, which I would assume would allow you time to give to your family farm."

Ian was stunned. As he thought about it for a moment he could see that this offer could very well be the answer to his question of how to help his mother and at the same time keep his engineering position. "I accept your offer! It will help me greatly in fulfilling my family responsibilities, at least for the time being."

"Good. I've spoken to our folks there and they will work with you to arrange time commitments at the office to best accommodate your farm schedule."

"When does this begin?"

"As soon as you can arrange to shift to Invercargill."

As soon as Ian returned to his office he rang up his mother. "Mum! I have some very good news."

"You do? I need some good news, Ian."

"I've been offered the chance to join our people in Invercargill on a part-time basis. They need extra engineering help but don't have enough for a full-timer. So, that means I can spend the balance of my time on the farm. I'm sure you and I can keep it going, Mum."

"That sounds very good. But are you sure you want to give up some of your work to come back to farming?"

"Absolutely! The truth of it is that I've missed Glen Mor."

"When will this happen? Where will you live? Invercargill?"

"Right away. No later than a fortnight, I should think, and about where I would live, I think I could live at Glen Mor and drive back and forth to the office. That way I'm on the farm for the early and late chores."

"Ian, that sounds wonderful. Perhaps I can hang on to the B.&B. That gives me some people contact, which I need now that your father's gone."

"I don't see why you can't keep it going. This shift will give me lots to do in the next few days. So I must hang up and get busy, Mum."

"And you've given me so much to think about."

Ian moved to Drummond and made the house at Glen Mor his home once again. With his help, Lynn would be able to continue the management of the farm and to keep the B.&B. open much of the time. While these pieces of her life were falling into place, there would continue to be one very big void in her life. She grieved the loss of John sorely. She would be lonely for some time to come.

Life's reordered routine began to establish itself for Lynn after Ian returned and began to take over the responsibilities on the farm. Lynn's B & B was in some sense a Godsend, in that it kept her busy.

One day some month's after John's death she got a phone call while she was making beds in one of the guest rooms.

"Hello. Glen Mor Inn."

"Hi Lynette. This is Gerry Culbertson!"

"Geraldine—what a surprise. Where are you calling from?"

"You won't believe this. I'm in the air terminal in Auckland!"

"Here in New Zealand?"

"Yes. Howard has been asked to speak to the New Zealand Wool Board tomorrow in Wellington."

Lynn and John had been aware of Geraldine Fischer's marriage to Howard Culbertson and his position with Montana State University in Bozeman in the Wool Lab. She was eager to hear more. "Gerry, is there any way I can see you? How long is Howard involved in Wellington? You don't have to return to the U.S. right away, do you?"

"Howard's conference is for a week. But I'm free to see you, Lynn. Tell me how I can arrange that."

"See if you can get a flight to Invercargill. That's close to where I am, so I can meet you and come to Glen Mor for as long as you can. Call me back as soon as you know the flight time."

It was arranged, and later that day the two old friends met at Invercargill. Lynn's cloak of loneliness was lifted for four days as Lynn and Gerry shared their memories of Sitka, especially as she re-lived her meeting John and the romance which had developed so quickly, a love which was right and deep. Before the week had flown by, they talked of sheep farming and wool production, the specialty in which Howard was working. In fact the two old friends ended their rendevous by plotting a return visit.

"Since Howard is a wool expert and has been with our wool board, I think you should arrange with his *powers that be* to send him on a tour of Southland to see how Kiwi sheep farmers do. And especially here at Glen Mor!"

"Lynn, that's a perfectly marvelous idea. I'll get to work on that as soon as I hear him say something like *I wish I'd had more time in New Zealand*. It would be just like him to say that in a couple of weeks."

After Geraldine's flight to Auckland lifted off, Lynn returned to Glen Mor with thoughts of Alaska, and John, thoughts which evoked sadness as well as nostalgic memories. *A very good life it was . . . all because of Alaska and the ferry boat . . . they say I should look ahead to a new era in my life, whatever that might be, but it's too soon . . . I 'll cling to John as long as I possibly can.*

Lynn's loneliness was assuaged only by her deepening relationship with Margaret and Trevor Lindsay, who shared her grief. But this did not last. The time came when Trevor was hit with a severe heart attack, which turned fatal after a hospitalization of eight days. Within the year following Margaret Lindsay died in her sleep. Many saw this as *dying of a broken heart.*

However, with Ian on the farm and her B.& B., Lynn settled into a routine, pleasant, if not joyous. The fellowship of the church in Drummond provided her emotional and spiritual support. Life seemed to be turning gray along with her hair, as she found associations with other widows in the church and community. In a mellow mood she took pleasure in volunteering again, this time in the local school as a teacher's aide and the local library in Winton once a week. These weekly afternoons in Winton had a way of transporting her to Sitka and her summer in the college library there. Rarely, however, did Lynn think of Illinois except at those times when she received a letter from her old high school friend, Judy Waymann, usually at Christmas. Judy had never married and was a nurse at West Suburban Hospital. Lynn often thought about how differently their lives had turned out.

PART IV

The 1990s

CHAPTER 43

Bittersweet

Yellowstone National Park—1990

He looked across the white table cloth into his wife's tender eyes, each reflecting the candle flame on their table in the Mammoth Hotel dining room. She returned his look with a soft smile. She extended her hand to place it over his. Her graying hair so carefully done for the occasion and the self assured countenance of a mature woman gave her a regal appearance, dressed "to the nines" as she was. His hair, speckled with gray, had thinned a bit and his face, somewhat more wrinkled than hers, exuded a gentle joy. Dressed for the celebration, in a blue blazer over a white shirt with a mellow red tie, Earl spoke quietly.

"Twenty-five years! Can you believe it, Kaye? Twenty-five good years, very happy years, darling."

"Very happy years, Earl, dear." She gave his hand a squeeze. "It seems like only a few years."

The waitress appeared and took their order of prime rib for each. She left and returned shortly with green salads. An attendant standing nearby stepped over and offered each freshly ground pepper. Soon their waitress appeared bearing a tray over her shoulder with two dinner plates with aluminum covers. She placed the tray carefully on a folding rack, removed the covers and placed an entree before each of the celebrants. After the main course, they selected desserts from a sample tray brought by the waitress who then returned with their selections and poured coffee. They conversed easily as they had during dinner. More serious talk would follow.

Soon they were walking across the hotel drive and into the lounge. Before going to their cabin, they sat together before a pine log fire in the massive lounge fireplace. They shared their feeling about the celebration given them after worship by the Saline congregation the day before.

In a mellow mood Earl reflected, "The celebration at church could not have made me feel happier. For the congregation, which at first had been so tentative about our marriage, to join with us in celebrating our 25th. And the speech which David gave at the reception. Not only as clerk of session but as our son!"

"O sweetheart, for you to say *our son* always means so much to me. That still touches me, even after all the years."

"He has been my son as much as yours from the very start of our relationship, Kaye. And now to have David and his wife and children so active in the church . . . ."

"And to have him on the ranch," Kaye added.

"After your father's death, your mother was so alone, until he moved to the ranch not only to run the ranch, but to care for her."

"I am so proud of him." She looked troubled and sad and added. "I'm so sorry that we were not able to have other children together."

"I know, but I have always felt fulfilled in having Davey and then bringing into our family Barbara as his wife and now little Jenny and Josh."

Kaye looked more serious when she asked. "Do you think you stayed on as pastor longer than you might have in Saline because it was my home?"

"I suppose that was part of it, but really, I have continued to feel energized. Not going stale like I have seen some pastors who have remained too long. For one thing, the congregation, especially the leadership, has changed quite a bit over the years."

"Yes, you have had a lot of funerals. Now the adult children of those old timers have taken over—some of them."

"You're right. Only some of them. So many have had to move away to find adequate work. I recently called the county extension office and found that the population in the county has fallen by a third in the last twenty years."

"And that's not Miles City. It's all the little surrounding communities."

Kaye added. "The few businesses that were in Saline when I was a kid are almost all gone."

"Except the bar—and of course the Conoco."

"Where would the club be without the Conoco."

"Well, there isn't much club left. They probably meet now in the nursing home in Miles City!"

"Seriously, Earl, what is going to happen to the Saline church? There are barely enough to pay your salary anymore."

"I'm not sure, Kaye. The last two years the finances have been in the red—as you well know. If it hadn't been for Homer Stein's insurance policy, we'd be dead in the water—broke."

"Tell me again about that policy. I don't remember how that worked."

"Well, after Homer died, his estate provided the church with the insurance which he had taken out with the church as beneficiary. So the church received the $50,000 for which the policy had been written!"

"Good old Homer. Even after his death he was a strong supporter of the church—and of you, Earl."

"Yes. I know. What a solid Christian he was and a great friend."

"But his money has run out, has it?"

"Yes, and that really brings the church to a crossroads." Earl thought for a few moments and then shocked his wife with a question. "How would you like to move to Miles City?"

"What? Miles City, what are you talking about?"

"Well Bob Taggert and I had a conversation last week—and came up with an idea—that is for our two churches to merge."

"So, what would you do in Miles City?"

"Bob has accepted a call to a church in Spokane. This is not for public knowledge yet. He's got a session meeting tonight. He's going to tell them."

"Oh, I'm sorry to hear that. I've enjoyed Anne so much, and of course Bob has always been a lot of fun."

"I'll miss them too, of course. They made holiday celebrations so special for us over the years. But I guess he feels it is time for him to move on. It will leave the pulpit vacant when and if we should merge."

Kaye considered the matter. "But there are some very big questions," Kaye cautioned. "Could we ever get the two churches to merge? And if they did, how do you know you'd be called as pastor in Miles City? And then too, if they decided not to merge what will happen to Saline—and to us?"

"Big questions, Kaye. You are absolutely right to ask them. And, furthermore, I don't have an answer to those questions."

"I wouldn't think so."

"But I'm working on them. In fact I've been lining up a consultation on the issue of Saline's future. Next Friday we are going to sit down with a few people to see what's what."

"Who's coming to this?"

"Bob, the county agent, a couple of elders from both of our churches, and an agricultural economist from Montana State."

"Which elders?"

"Carol Rogers and Wayne Culver."

"Why the county agent and the university professor?"

"Because one of issues here is community development . . . or redevelopment, and the university person we are asking has special interest and expertise in community development. My hope is that out of this meeting they will be able to come up with a recommendation to our session for next steps." Earl changed the subject. "But, Kaye, we're not here to talk business. This is our anniversary."

"Well then, we'd better get out to our cabin," she said with a sly grin.

Hand in hand the two walked out of the hotel lounge and took a moment to look at the dark shadows of five or six elk silently feeding in the grass across the road. An almost full moon had risen over the mountain valleys to the east of Mammoth Hot Springs, reflecting slightly on the backs of the elk. To their right on the south edge of town they could see in the moonlight the steam rising from the hot springs terraces. They stopped to take in the silent beauty of this night high up on the Yellowstone plateau.

"Look at the elk, Kaye. So content. They and their ancestors have been grazing like that for centuries. While people and nations all over the earth are forever engaged in warring madness. Why can't life be like it is here tonight?"

"Oh Earl, I feel what you are saying—that's life, and besides, you have been devoting your life to trying to get people to be more like the elk . . . and the Saline congregation is sort of like it is here—peaceful, I mean."

"I know, and you're right . . . this is what our work is about." Earl expressed a feeling which had been growing in his consciousness. "But, Kaye. The church nationally isn't peaceful and that bothers me. Wrangling over sexuality issues when we ought to be proclaiming God's love to people in need of it all over the world."

"I know."

"And then I think about myself and how I feel at odds with the world around me. It's not a Christian culture anymore, and I feel like my voice is often drowned out by the noise of a consumer society with its bottom line always money, instead of how to make people's lives better."

Kaye was disturbed and countered. "Earl, you are making a difference. It's not all bad. And this serene picture of the elk in the moonlight . . . That's how God created them to be, and it is how God created us and wants us to be . . . and God will some day bring this scene to all the world. You've preached and taught that, Earl. You call it *the Kingdom of God.*"

"You're right, dear. Sorry I got so glum."

"We have a right to be downcast once in a while—as long as it is temporary." She looked into his eyes and grinned, reminding him. "Where was it we were going?"

With hands clasped, Earl and Kaye Norris turned. onto the lane which took them to their hotel cabin.

Saline, Montana—1992

The special meeting of the Saline church session had been called. Word had gotten out about the consultation, and so almost all the members showed up for the special meeting. As they gathered, Earl braced himself for controversy because of what the proposal would recommend. Wayne Culver presented it after both he and Carol Rogers had given a full report of the consultation. It was a simply stated recommendation, but with momentous implications.

As moderator of the meeting, Earl recognized Culver. "Wayne, I believe you have a recommendation."

"Yes, Mr. Moderator. I move that the session take necessary and prudent steps toward the goal of merger of the Presbyterian churches of Saline and Miles City."

You could hear a pin drop. For a long moment no one said anything. Then there was a flurry of questions beginning with,

"Does Miles City know about this?"

Carol answered quickly, "Yes, they will be acting on a similar recommendation from their two elders who attended the consultation."

"Would we still have church here?"

"No," Wayne replied, "We'd be going into Miles for worship."

There was an audible murmur.

"Well, then, what would we do with our church building?"

Wayne continued, "That's just it. Part of the reason for this merger would be that we wouldn't have the expense of the upkeep of a building."

"Yeah, this old church is an albatross . . . . costs us more than it's worth."

There seemed to be some agreement.

There were more frequent questions about details. Most of these were answered with the reply, "It is too early to know, but later discussions will be about such questions."

Earl kept quiet during most of the discussion, surprised that there wasn't more negative response. He hadn't yet heard the question he most feared.

Eventually someone asked, "What is the first step?"

Earl answered. "It seems to me that the first thing needed is a joint meeting of the two sessions. To discuss the ramifications of this proposal."

Dwight Benson then raised his hand.

"Yes, Dwight?" Earl recognized him.

"I move an amendment to the recommendation before us, as follows. Instead of *take necessary and prudent steps toward the goal* we substitute, *arrange to meet with the Miles City session to discuss the possibility of—*."

Someone seconded the motion to amend.

After a brief discussion of the amendment, the question was called for. The amendment passed and the amended motion was then passed by a narrow margin.

Earl concluded the business. "We shall have our clerk contact their clerk, and see what develops. That's all we can do at this meeting. Is there a motion to adjourn?"

Then someone asked the question which was on more than one mind. "Who would be the pastor?"

Earl had feared this point. He turned to Wayne for an answer.

"Well, we talked about that and didn't come to any conclusion. It would depend, at least in part, upon what Earl decides to do."

"What does that mean?"

"Well, since Miles City's pastor has moved and they don't have a regular pastor right now, it means that Earl's first in line, you might say, and we don't know, he might decide that this would be a good time to move on, or perhaps to retire." There was an awkward silence. "But, of course we believe Earl should stay."

"And be pastor of the combined congregation?"

"If the new congregation voted on him and called him."

Another silence.

Someone broke the ice. "Earl, what do you think?"

"Well, frankly I'd like to stay. As you know, I am near retirement age. But I would be interested in helping both churches through the transition period."

Carol added to the discussion another piece of the discussion in the consultation group. "Some on the task force feel as Earl has just suggested, but others felt that an entirely new leadership might be more effective—someone with no ties to either congregation. So I guess we would just have to let the new congregation decide."

"And I'm certainly comfortable with that." Earl assured the session.

From the nearly non-verbal reaction in the group one could sense relief on the part of session members.

This left the future unknown, but the necessity to take the first step was still before the session. Dwight Benson made the motion to meet with the Miles City session, after saying. "This is indeed a sad day. To think that this church which has been here since the 1900s is considering closing. But I do not see how we can avoid some form of closure. Perhaps merger is the best of a few very painful options for us."

The meeting adjourned. Everyone went home to tell their families about what they had discussed and done. For those, like Hugh Stark, who had come from Miles City, and those who had close associations with Miles City, like Jane Moss and Kaye Norris, this process which had been launched was a bittersweet reality. A reality which most were facing with a quiet acceptance. "Only a matter of time," many were saying. *Time and many long meetings.* Earl thought as he entered the manse to share with Kaye news of the session meeting.

"I've always wanted to move further west, Kaye. Now it looks like you and I will be westbound, even if only a few miles."

"What are you talking about?"

"You and I will be moving to Miles City before all this is over."

"You don't know that the merged church will want you as its pastor."

Earl looked at his wife. "I don't know why they wouldn't!" He grinned.

Miles City, Montana—1992

It had been years since the Presbyterian church in Miles City had held regular Sunday evening services. And so Earl Norris wondered what kind of a turn-out there would be. He sat behind the desk in the pastor's office looking over the order of service for the evening. Under the heading, THE PRESBYTERY OF YELLOWSTONE, the title of the service was long and official:

Service of Organization of the Presbyterian Church of Custer County
and the Installation of The Rev. Earl Norris as its Pastor

Earlier in the day, during the morning services of the Presbyterian churches in both Miles City and Saline, the Presbytery had taken action to dissolve each church in preparation for the merger of the two congregations into one. Earl was excited about the actions soon to be taken. They represented the culmination of two years filled with meetings of both congregations and of the Presbytery, most of which had been fairly amicable.

It was almost 7 P.M. and Earl could hear the organist beginning her preliminary music. He joined the other participants from each congregation and from presbytery in the fellowship room adjoining the sanctuary. The moderator of presbytery offered a brief prayer and they filed in and seated themselves in the front pew of the empty sanctuary. At seven o'clock sharp, the organist pushed down the "swell pedal" and with the full organ began to play, "The Church's One Foundation." As Earl looked toward the rear of the room he saw two processions of people emerge, one from each side. They met in the middle. The congregation from Saline had entered on the left and the congregation from Miles City had entered from the right. Now as they came forward, two by two, each pair consisted of one person from Saline and one person from Miles City. They stayed together as they found seats in the sanctuary beginning in the front, symbolizing the merger of two congregations on an equal basis. Earl found this procession especially moving. Thus a new congregation was formed, and an hour and a half later after the service during a spirited fellowship hour and reception in the dining room in the basement, Earl was greeted as the newly installed first pastor of the Presbyterian Church of Custer County.

Earl and Kaye moved their household from Saline to Miles City in the days following the merger service, because the Saline manse was now rented and the new occupants wanted to move in as soon as possible.

In the months following the merger, Earl found himself spending two or three days a week visiting members of the former Saline church. These were the folk who had a more marked adjustment to a new church experience in a different location and in a much larger congregation. He also recognized the need to acquaint himself with the Miles City members in order to establish himself as their new pastor. The transition from two congregations to one did not always go smoothly, giving Earl an occasional misgiving about the future of the newly merged church.

Kaye felt at home in the new setting, since she had been a member in Miles City in the months following her return to Montana as a young single mother. Because of her former Miles City experience Kaye was able to help Earl in his understanding of the subtleties of this blending process.

On the one year anniversary of the merger, Kaye and Earl spent an evening together at home assessing the progress so far. Earl introduced the subject. "Kaye, how do you feel about the merger so far?"

"Overall I think you and the session have made the transition about as smooth as one could expect, but . . . ."

"But what?"

"I worry about some of the older widows in Saline. They are not as able to go back and forth to Miles for church on Sundays or for other events."

Earl thought about this for a while and offered a thought. "I wonder if we might be able to provide some transportation . . . perhaps a church bus . . . ."

"That's something we might look into."

"Meanwhile, we have the anniversary service next Sunday. That should help us move forward."

The anniversary service was a time of celebration. Especially significant was Earl's sharing of the transportation idea with folks in the reception which followed. He discovered good support for this project among session members with whom he discussed the idea.

Despite excitement and joy of the occasion for his congregation, Earl was troubled by he fact that Kaye had become ill the day before. She came to the service but by the time she and Earl got home her condition had worsened.

Sunday during the night she awakened Earl. "Earl, I think I need to see a doctor."

"Right now?"

"I'm afraid so."

Earl took her into the emergency room of the Miles City hospital. She was given some relief, but the doctor wasn't sure of the diagnosis. She was admitted to a hospital room and after she was settled Earl was advised that he could go to her room.

When Earl got to her room, he found Kaye asleep. Not wanting to awaken her, he settled down in an easy chair in her room, where he spent the night. Sometime after 4 AM, she awakened. Earl slept only lightly and was at her side immediately.

"It would have been so good to be with you for another year in the new church."

"Yes, but you will, as soon as you're well enough . . ."

"I don't think so, precious . . ." Her voice trailed off. She moved herself to a more comfortable position in the bed and began to talk. "These have been good years, Earl—when you came to Davey and me to form a new little family—and then during Davey's growing up years, you were such a good father . . . ."

Earl felt a chill in the back of his neck. He was hearing a sort of eulogy *her life review . . . at the end?* He wanted to respond but she seemed to want to continue undisturbed.

"All those beautiful Christmas Eves we had together, at home after the service—Davey and his new toys. We kissed long and tenderly after he went to bed, didn't we, dear? Then there were those wonderful Christmas dinners at Mother and Dad's the next morning . . . Oh Earl, so many good years. Remember when I teased you about the first streaks of gray hair, and the bit of a paunch you began to sport? Then you'd help me in my flower garden each spring. I made you dig. I claimed it was too hard for me. And the vacations we took, camping in a tent that leaked, driving up into the mountains. And our cabin these last few years. I wish I could go back to it one last time . . . So many good years, Earl."

He noticed that her eyes were moist, and when he saw that and considered what she had been saying and the bittersweet nostalgia of her expression, he felt his eyes moisten. He leaned over the bed rail and kissed her and then put his face against hers, feeling each other's tears. When he felt her body loosen, and lifted himself up and saw that she had fallen back to sleep.

Years later he would often remember this poignant moment, this final loving tryst holding her in his memory as long as he could. *Kaye must have had a premonition that her life would soon be over. God gave us that one last moment.* He would so often say to himself as he felt his eyes moisten as he remembered Kaye and their many years of love.

The next day Kaye was sent to Deaconess Medical Center in Billings where she was diagnosed with an aggressive pancreatic cancer. Tragically after only a few days of struggle during which she was unconscious Kaye Norris died in the hospital in Billings. She was only 57.

Earl would have to continue his ministry in the new church alone, without Kaye's helpful support, upon which he had relied since their marriage early in his years of ministry in Saline. Though he now lived in Miles City, Saline would remain home to him. Davey and Barbara remained in Saline on the ranch. Earl spent holidays, as well as many Sunday afternoons at the ranch with his family. And he made frequent "visits" to Kaye in the Saline cemetery in the months and years following her death.

Fortunately Earl's involvement in the newly merged congregation kept him busy and very much engaged in the progress the church was making. After the first year and a half the old timers from the Saline congregation seemed to be adjusting to the new surroundings, and the Miles City folk had moved over, so to speak, in order to include their neighbors from Saline. Enhancing this blending was the fact that many had known one another in other contexts such as banking and farm machinery and supply businesses as well as county-wide social and political organizations.

On evenings when Earl was at home without a meeting to attend, he felt his loss of Kaye most acutely. Thus, for the first time in his ministry he actually wanted more evening meetings. Vacation periods were difficult. He and Kaye had reveled in each other when together on vacations, both on trips and at home. This had been especially true at their cabin in their later years. During the first few years after her death Earl stayed away from the cabin. Instead he encouraged Davey and Barbara to use it as often as they could. He joined them on a couple such trips to the cabin. Not until Kaye had been gone three years did Earl allow himself to try going to the cabin alone.

Hyalite Canyon 1996

It was dusk before he rattled across the bridge and wound his way up the slight hill to the back door of the dark cabin. He turned off the engine and stepped up to the door and unlocked it. He pushed it open and stepped into a dark and cold cabin. In late August the days begin to feel short and the evening temperatures seem lower each successive night, especially in the mountains. He lit the coal oil lantern over the kitchen table and set about making a fire in the cook stove first, and then in the fireplace. After each was burning nicely he put some water from the pump at the sink in a coffee pot and put it on the stove. He opened a can of spaghetti and after heating it up, he buttered a piece of bread and sat down to make fast work of his simple supper. Then after the coffee pot had begun to boil he put in a small amount of coffee to let it boil cowboy fashion. After cleaning up his dishes he poured a mug of coffee for himself and took it to one of the two chairs positioned in front of the fireplace. Night had come and the windows were now black. The only sound besides an occasional crackle of the fire was the faint sloshing of Hyalite Creek down the hill. A dark pall of loneliness fell around Earl as he watched the remaining embers of the fire burn out.

Earl was tired. He had no particular thoughts. As was his custom at such times at the end of the day, he said to himself, *I've got nothing more to give.* He got up, banked the fire for the night, turned back the covers on his side and went to bed.

The next morning he made sure both the fireplace and cook stove were cold. He locked the cabin door and drove away under a cloud-covered sky and a slight drizzle coming down. That evening at the ranch he told Barbara, "I just couldn't stay there. Too much of Kaye was all around me, and she wasn't there . . . too soon, I guess." He added to himself *if ever.*

The Cabin 1998

High clouds kept the cabin quite dark until around eight when Earl was seated at his kitchen table with a steaming bowl of oatmeal and mug of coffee. He had re-started the fire in the fireplace and the cabin was warming up nicely. After cleaning up his breakfast dishes he put on his wool jacket and went to the wood shed where he planned to spend an hour or so splitting logs into useable sizes for the stove. It wasn't long before he shed his jacket. Not only had he warmed himself, but a strip of blue sky was letting some sunshine into the canyon. Each morning he'd been splitting logs so that when Davey and family arrived on Friday there would be enough for a week, during which they planned to use the cabin. Two more afternoons of hiking and two more evenings of reading and lounging around remained of Earl's vacation. Not at all like the last time he'd attempted the cabin, this year he felt exultant in this beautiful natural surroundings. In fact he hated to think of having to leave on Friday morning to return to Miles City for the Sunday service.

On Thursday evening sitting by the fire Earl took stock. *Kaye's been here with me but in a different way than two years ago, when she was felt in her absence. Now, in a mystical way, she's been keeping me company, not so much making me lonely as before. In fact, come to think of it, that's sort of the way it's been at home as well. It's like she has her own life she's living—in heaven, I guess—and she looks in on me and seems to encourage me to live my own life . . . happily now. It's like she is freeing me to plan my own life without her, something I used to think was being disloyal.* He marveled at the change. *The popular wisdom is right—time heals.*

It had gotten late, so Earl took care of the fire and went to bed. During this visit to the cabin he'd been enjoying sprawling out on the whole bed. In the morning he would be heading back to Miles City and work. This year for the first time he contemplated his return to Saline with reluctance. In the past Earl had always ended his vacations with a sense of exhilaration as he anticipated getting back to work for another year. That up beat feeling was missing this year. In its place was a much more negative feeling—almost dread. *Maybe that's God's way of calling me to consider retiring,* he thought as sleep began to overcome him.

CHAPTER 44

Honorably Retired

Saline, Montana—1999

The church building in Saline had been closed since the congregation had merged with the Miles City congregation. Now someone had lettered a poster board and nailed it to the locked wooden door of what had once been *The Community Presbyterian Church of Saline, Montana*. It contained a simple message, but one which spoke volumes:

RETIREMENT RECEPTION
For THE REV. EARL NORRIS
Sunday at 3 PM—May 2nd, 1999
EVERYONE WELCOME

Posting this sign was the final step of a work day which David Norris had organized. It had taken a good bit of cleaning to spruce up the abandoned church building. Fortunately, one of the stipulations in the merger agreement had been that the session of the the Presbyterian Church of Custer County would appoint a sub-committee to serve as trustees of the Saline property. It was their job to maintain the building. *Or if deemed prudent, to negotiate the sale of the property,* the agreement had stated.

As he left the building after the clean-up had been done, he looked at the sign and commented to the others who had been helping. "Mother would have enjoyed being with Dad for this occasion . . ." David choked up.

"But she'll be with us in spirit, Davey . . . . watching from above," one of the others assured David.

Another of the workers wanted to get onto a more comfortable subject. "Who do you suppose the church will get to replace your dad?"

"We don't know, of course, but the presbytery wants to give us an interim for a year, before we call a new pastor."

"Why is that?"

"After a long and successful pastorate they feel it helps to give a transition to someone else's ministry."

"But it won't be the same, will it?"

The Custer County Presbyterian Church was fully attended on Sunday morning, May 2, 1999. It was Earl Norris' final service, the day of his retirement. Earl rose to make an announcement before the singing of the hymn preceding the sermon. "Will you rise to sing Hymn Number 147. I have chosen *O Come, O Come, Emmanuel* as the hymn of preparation for what I want to say on this day of my retirement in this last sermon here. We have most likely never sung this hymn in May. It is an Advent hymn, usually sung only in December in preparation for Christmas. But it is appropriate today as I look ahead into retirement. Sing it with me, will you!"

The organ began in a wistful minor key of the ancient 13th century plain song. The congregation began to sing—

> *O come, O come, Emmanuel,*
> *And ransom captive Israel,*
> *That mourns in lonely exile here,*
> *Until the Son of God appear.*
> *Rejoice! Rejoice! Emmanuel*
> *Shall come to thee, O Israel.*
>
> *O come thou Dayspring, come and cheer*
> *Our spirits by thine advent here;*
> *Disperse the gloomy clouds of night*
> *And death's dark shadows put to flight.*
> *Rejoice, rejoice, Emmanuel*
> *Shall come to thee, O Israel!*
>
> *O come desire of nations, bind*
> *All peoples in one heart and mind;*
> *Bid envy strife, and quarrels cease;*
> *Fill the whole world with heaven's peace.*
> *Rejoice! Rejoice! Emmanuel*
> *Shall come to thee, O Israel!*
> *—Latin 12th Century*

The organ concluded the lingering line of the hymn tune after which the congregation was seated. Earl began his sermon. "Friends, this morning I leave you with the hope of Advent. The sure and certain hope that one day God will release us from our captivity within a culture which is driven by values and desires contrary to God's intention for the world, that one day God will remove us from our exile in a foreign land, as it were . . . ." Earl went on to single out phrases from the hymn which he lifted up as descriptions of the human condition and of the problems facing the world. Then he repeated the Advent hope for the binding of heart and mind of all peoples and the ceasing of envy, strife, and quarrels, and the Advent hope that the coming of God—Emmanuel—will "fill the whole world with heaven's peace." He concluded his sermon with these words. "Advent isn't just four weeks prior to Christmas every year. It is a season of the Christian heart all the year long. So long as we must live as a captive Israel in some form of exile, we must hold on to the Advent hope of God's coming kingdom. And so I leave urging you to *Rejoice! Rejoice! Emmanuel shall come to us and ransom captive Israel.*"

That afternoon by one o'clock, members of the reception committee began arriving to prepare for Earl's retirement party. They decorated both the basement fellowship room and the sanctuary upstairs. And of course they laid out a most festive table of goodies to accompany the coffee and tea for the reception. By a quarter to three, others started to arrive, not only coming from Saline, but from communities nearby, including many from Miles City. The guest of honor arrived a little before three and stood ready to "receive" his well-wishers.

Everyone, including Earl, agreed that his retirement celebration was a huge success. The worship in the morning in Miles City with Earl's final sermon was a moving experience for many. At the close of the service the moderator of presbytery conducted a meeting of presbytery in which Earl Norris was conferred the status of *HONORABLY RETIRED.* The reception in the afternoon in Saline was *the best we ever put on,* according to the women who had planned and served it.

When the reception ended and most everyone had gone, those who had hosted it gathered up their things and mounted the steps and walked outside to their vehicles. Earl watched as the last car drove away and then turned to Davey who was waiting to lock up, and then went upstairs and walked through the empty sanctuary. At the back he stopped to turn around and looked up to the pulpit on the platform, imagining himself standing there before the congregation he had come to love, so many Sundays over the years. An image emblazoned on his memory reappeared from the day forty years before when he'd given his candidating sermon hoping for the approval of the Saline Church. He could almost hear the horn of the Northcoast Limited as its engines came to life to take him back to Chicago after his first success in Saline, Montana. Earl paused a moment, deep in thought, while Davey waited very quietly by the door thinking how his dad must feel. Then Earl turned and left the building through the main door. The last one to leave, as he had been thousands of times before. This time except for Davey who locked the building before the two made their way back to Miles City.

By six o'clock Earl was settled in his living room in the manse in Miles City. He had carefully placed his retirement gift against a wall in the living room so that it could be seen and enjoyed. The congregation had presented him with a watercolor they had commissioned for him. It was a scene looking westward from the edge of Saline. In the foreground was prairie land with the Yellowstone River flowing beyond it. In the distance were the rolling hills. By special request the artist had placed in the far distance a snow capped mountain range, typical of what would be found further west in Montana. The painting was appropriately entitled *WESTBOUND*.

Now in the living room Earl was surrounded by his family. Anne and Bob had flown in from Spokane, where Bob had recently retired from a large congregation. David and his family were also gathered around Earl in the living room, for *a debriefing* as Bob had put it. The mood was mellow, with a tinge of sadness as David announced. "We have another gift to present to you, Dad . . . ."

"Oh!" Earl looked startled.

Davey bought forth a small gift-wrapped box, no more than six or eight inches square and presented it to Earl.

Earl accepted it and opened it up, revealing a small oak picture frame, this time without a painting, but with a gold plated key fastened to a sky blue felt backing. Earl read the engraving on the key: *KEY TO THE SALINE CHURCH.* "What a thoughtful and appropriate gift!" Earl exclaimed. "This I will certainly cherish. Thank you so much." With that he hugged Davey and Barbara. After the key was passed around the *debriefing,* as Bob had called it, began.

"Mom would have enjoyed today," Davey remarked. It had been long enough since her untimely death that the family felt comfortable speaking of her. In fact Earl had assured the family on a number of occasions during the last year, "I like it when we talk of Kaye, now that I've come to accept her passing. It sort of brings her back with us, I feel sometimes."

"Yes," Anne said. "One of the drawbacks for me when we moved away was losing the regular contact which Kaye and I had come to enjoy so much. I had always wished for a sister, and Kaye was an answer to my wish."

"But times have a way of changing. Life has its twists and turns." Earl had often said this.

"Which brings up the number one question, Ol' Buddy," Bob still used this term of endearment. "What are your plans?"

"Well, I've got a couple of weeks in the manse before the interim minister comes."

"Is that all?" Anne was concerned. "Can you be ready to vacate so soon?"

"I think so, I've done a lot of packing and a little tossing. I've rented one of those new storage units in town and I've already put quite a bit in it—may have to rent a second one. I'm not too good at throwing stuff out. Kaye used to call me a pack rat."

"What will you do with your books?" Barbara asked.

"Oh, they're all pretty old. Stuff used in seminary years ago and other books from bygone days, I guess," Earl answered.

"Wouldn't other ministers want them?" Davey wondered.

"No. I've seen lots of times how retiring pastors put their precious libraries out on a table at presbytery meetings for pastors to take . . . and you know what? Nobody wants 'em and they go in the trash."

"Sort of sad," Anne remarked. "All that wisdom gone to waste."

Bob offered a more upbeat conclusion. "The wisdom in those books has been coming forth each Sunday that Earl has preached, and every time he teaches a class . . . and even in the wise remarks he offers to people."

Earl gave a quizzical look. "So I've just been a pipeline from the professors who wrote the books to the parishioners who sat in my pews?"

"No . . . ." Bob turned more serious, "A conduit from God to his people by way of the Holy Spirit."

Such a statement as that has a way of terminating the discussion. Or so Anne felt. She wanted to know more of Earl's plans. "Then what?"

Barbara was quick to say, "We've asked Dad to come out and stay with us until he decides where he wants to settle."

David added, "We have talked of building a small house on the ranch for Dad."

"And, I might add, Davey." Earl smiled at his son, "That idea appeals to me more and more. I've enjoyed living in Miles City . . . as much as one can—alone . . . but Saline has been home for me ever since that day when the old westbound Northcoast Limited dropped me off on the platform—a dressed up kid from Chicago still wet behind the ears!"

The family gathering laughed, genuinely joining Earl in his nostalgic memory. The little group went on to discuss the idea of Earl moving onto the ranch.

Then Earl changed the subject when he announced, "I got an invitation the other day from my seminary alumni office announcing a 40th reunion of our class in June. I'm strongly tempted to go."

"Oh, Earl, you should." Anne was enthusiastic, partly as a projection of her own desires. "I'd envy you going back and seeing some of the old haunts—like the house where we grew up, the church where we had such a great youth group. And you could even go up to Saugatuck and see Westminster Lodge."

When his sister mentioned Saugatuck, Earl became pensive. Almost as if to himself. "And the beach house."

"The beach house?" Davey had never heard of it.

"That was a house at the beach on the east shore of Lake Michigan where some of our high school friends visited on summer vacations." He didn't say more. Anne looked at him knowingly.

"You should go, Earl. But we also want you to come out to Spokane to visit us."

"Whatever I do, it will surely be a new phase of life—retirement. I'll tell you in a year what it's like."

With that, David and his family got up to leave. "We need to get back to the ranch. I've got chores."

Later that evening after Anne and Bob had gone to the guest bedroom, Earl lay in his bed, too keyed up to sleep. He relived the day's events. He thought about his having to move in the next few weeks. And about staying with Davey, and the possibility of a little house on the ranch.

And he imagined himself on a trip west to Anne and Bob's and perhaps even a drive to the West Coast. But his last thought before sleep was Chicago. He remembered the first time he had come to Montana from Chicago on the westbound North Coast Limited, and stepping off onto the platform at Saline. *It all began that day. So long ago . . . yet only yesterday . . . yet the world has changed so.* He'd come out from Chicago alone. On a passenger train which no longer runs. He would be returning alone. This time he would fly.

CHAPTER 45

Return

Monday morning, the dark red Explorer with the W lazy N brand on the door over the name, **NORLAND RANCH, Saline, Montana**, was parked in front of the little church building. David Norris had come by to check on things on his way into town. After coming out and locking the front doors, he paused to read the sign once more. There was no one around to watch him carefully take down the poster announcing the retirement party. He put the cardboard in his vehicle and drove down the deserted main street with its abandoned buildings. He passed the old Northern Pacific Depot, boarded up and surrounded by mangy weeds. On his way out of Saline he saw that the local bar had its usual assortment of pickups parked outside. And the Conoco—still open, but here it was ten fifteen in the morning and there were no vehicles about. Kenny Johnson, Merle's son, was in the garage bay servicing his own pickup. *Saline, too, has retired*, David pondered on his way into Miles City.

Chicago—1999

High up over the heavy shroud of gray clouds of early June, Earl felt the jet engines of the 727 vibrate as they began to labor at slowing down while the aircraft descended for its landing at O'Hare in Chicago. He was returning to McCormick Seminary after forty years. To the Chicago area forty-seven years after high school graduation. In the midst of his mellow nostalgic thoughts, he pondered how everything was so different now. He was coming in by air to the terminal of the busiest airport in the country. He'd left the city years ago on a train from Union Station downtown. The seminary had moved from its hallowed buildings up on Fullerton and Halstead, miles south to Hyde Park with a single

314

headquarters building on Woodlawn Avenue—McGaw Hall. The Alumni Banquet was scheduled for the cafeteria in the Lutheran School of Theology building a block north which his seminary now used on a rental arrangement. He would not be returning to the Commons on the old campus, to that beloved Gothic Oxford-like dining hall.

An hour and a half after he had walked into the concourse at O'Hare, he was getting close to his destination. "International House on 55th," he instructed the driver of the Airport Shuttle after it had plunged into the bustling Hyde Park district of south Chicago. In a few minutes Earl Norris stood at the registration desk of this University of Chicago accommodation dedicated to housing guests from around the world. He took his bag up to his assigned room and returned on the elevator to the main lobby, where he passed through the cafeteria line and found a place at a small table in the dining room where he took his supper alone on this first evening in Chicago before his seminary reunion would begin the next morning. Around him he observed men and women of varying ages whose appearance and dress identified them as having come from many parts of the globe, Asians, Latin Americans, Africans as well as others whose conversations revealed accents from many areas of Europe. He sat in the multi-cultural environment of one of the great universities of the world. Earl Norris, retired, of Saline on the lonely plains of Montana, thrust into what seemed to him to be a bustling center of the world during the final few months of the twentieth century! This first night in Chicago, while exciting, was vaguely threatening to Earl. *It's not my world anymore. Others have taken over. My place is back on the old campus, in the comfort and familiarity of dining with my classmates in the Commons there.*

For three days in June, Earl enjoyed getting reacquainted with his former classmates. They traded stories of the old days in seminary, and exchanged information about each other's careers, and where each was now located. Roughly half of the class was retired. A few had lost their spouses. Earl found himself somewhat disappointed with the planned activities He had hoped that there would be time for a sharing of each other's impressions of the state of affairs in the world and in the church. But few seemed interested in serious discussion. *I guess we're all just school kids again.* However, during one of the coffee breaks he fell into a discussion with Arnold Larson, whom he had not known too well when they were in seminary. But now they seemed to "click."

Arnold had opened with a serious question. "Theologically speaking, Earl, who have been your opponents over the years?"

"That's an interesting question. I guess I'd have to say that at first the opposing ideas came from the very conservative folks who wanted every word of the Bible to be true. They didn't want me to do much interpreting, so to speak. You know—Jonah was swallowed by a whale and that was it."

"Oh, I know!

"How about you?"

"Well, I found that sort of opposition at first when I was pastor of a rural church in southern Illinois. But then when I moved to Urbana and had a lot of university people in my congregation, I found opposition coming from an ultra-liberal position, almost unitarian, I'd say."

"I never had that . . . Oh, a little more in later years in Miles City, but not much, really." Then Earl added, "Now the problem comes in the area of worship, people who want what they call *praise music*. They seem to be influenced by these mega-churches with rock music and the words to the songs projected on the wall."

"Yeah, I know what you mean. They say this new style of worship will bring in the younger generation, but I'm not so sure."

Earl shifted the discussion. "How have your own views changed, Arnold?"

"Well, I'm much more tolerant of other positions . . . even non-Christian ideas. I used to think that if you weren't Christian you were all wrong. Now I see that people of other faiths have a lot to offer this messed up world of ours." Arnold seemed to be lost in thought for a moment, and then went on. "I attended a conference on world affairs a few years ago and the Dalai Lama spoke. He seemed to be saying all the things I thought were exclusively Christian—things about peace on the world scale and in one's own life. It shook me up until I began to make room for other faith positions in my judgements."

"Yeah, I remember we used to explain Gandhi's thoughts and actions on peace as coming from his contact with Christianity. We couldn't admit that he could have developed such an approach on the basis of his Hindu faith . . . Now we are more open to other faiths, I guess."

Arnold turned the question to Earl. "How about you?"

"I've moved in that same direction . . . somewhat, but not as far as you. But I have met people who aren't in the church who have some very worthwhile ideas. I think of one older man with whom I used to play chess. He had what I would call some very Christian thoughts and values, but he never darkened the door of the church . . . although he had Christian roots."

"There a lot of people out there like that. We live in a pluralistic society, Earl. Our way is just one among many . . . not like it was when we left seminary and everybody assumed America was a Christian nation!"

"I think you're right, Arnold. Things have changed." Earl thought about this. "You seem to have adjusted to the new scene, but I don't think I have been able to adjust to the same extent as you."

With that their conversation seemed to come to an end.

"Well anyway, good talking to you, Earl."

"Right." As Arnold moved on, Earl felt alone.

The last evening after the banquet Earl's aloneness intensified when a group of his classmates, including Arnold Larson, invited him to go out with them "to find a place where we can have a few drinks." Earl demurred and afterward wondered why. Instead he walked back to his room. He thought to himself. *I feel as if I'm living on an island that is shrinking. Most of the others seem to have jumped over to the mainland, leaving just a few of us where we were when we lived back on the old campus.* Earl pondered some more. *I guess I'm sort of a theological liberal . . . or maybe middle of the road . . . but an old fashioned conservative socially—in terms of behavior.*

The conversation with Arnold Larson and his turning down the invitation to find "some drinks" left Earl with some deep and troubling thoughts—some self doubt among other feelings. But as it turned out he would have another contact which would upstage Arnold's thoughts before the Chicago trip was over.

The next morning Earl found an Enterprise car rental agency next to Illinois Central tracks and rented a compact car, and so he was able to do some exploring on his own after the alumni days had ended. He took a morning drive through his old neighborhood and passed the house in which he and Anne had grown up. He took a look at his high school and stopped in at the church which had meant so much to him as a young person. That, too, was disappointing. He knew no one. The secretary was pleasant but formal, allowing him to look around. Things looked pretty much the same in the sanctuary. The same familiar smell of furniture oils mixed with many perfume scents. He walked around elsewhere in the building remembering a classroom here and a fellowship meeting there. But he soon found he had nothing more to do at the church, so he thanked the secretary and left.

He found a McDonald's and stopped in for a quick lunch. It was here that he decided he needed to drive to Michigan to visit Saugatuck and Westminster Lodge—perhaps to see the beach house again. Thoughts of the old high school crowd began to fill his consciousness as he found his way onto the Dan Ryan Expressway and began his trip around the southern end of Lake Michigan and up the eastern shore to the haunts of his high school days. The temperature was warm. In the bright sunlight it felt even warmer. Earl rolled down his window as he drove northward near the east shore of Lake Michigan

When he got to Saugutuck, he looked for the motel where he had worked and found it under a different name, and fortunately it had been considerably remodeled. They had a room available and so he checked in. He had told himself that it was Westminster Lodge which he was eager to visit. But now that he was here, he felt impelled to drive out to the beach and look for Shore Crest, the house on the beach which Ellertons had owned. *Will it still be there? Will Lynn's family still own it? What—and who—will I find there?* These questions crowded his mind as he drove toward the beach. Earl hadn't taken time to stop for supper. Daylight would remain until after eight. He could eat then. He did not want to waste sunlight in a restaurant.

He remembered the way to Shore Crest, and soon was driving up the lane remembering his first visit as a high schooler "in love" with Lynn. He drove up to the entrance, but found that it was owned by strangers. Under the words SHORE CREST were the names strangers—of the new owners—family members: Hugh, Polly, Debbie and Ron Howland. He entered the property, hoping no one was home. Fortunately the beach house showed no signs of occupants. There were no cars around. So Earl parked his rental car. And after walking around the house, he started down to the beach. The first streaks of pink and orange had appeared over the calm water of the lake. Dusk was fast approaching as the sun slipped behind a bank of clouds. *"Day is dying in the west,"* popped into his mind from days long gone. As he came nearer to the beach, he saw a person walking along the shore line. The indistinct figure moved slowly, keeping pretty well in front of the beach house on what had been the Ellerton property along the shore. Looking toward the still light sky, the personage appeared a dark silhouette.

Earl emerged from the trees between the house and the beach and started walking on the sand toward the water. By this time he observed that the person was a woman, apparently about his age. As he turned in a direction away from her, she spotted him and called. "G'diahy!"

"Hello." He judged her to be British from her accent. He continued to walk away from her until he reached a fence marking the southern boundary of Shore Crest. Nothing to do but turn and walk toward the woman. By this time she had seated herself on a bench placed near the water. Again when he came close she called to him, "Sir, am I on your property?"

"No, I'm just a tourist."

"I am also. I don't want to trespass, but I wanted to see this particular stretch of the lake shore."

"The same here." By this time Earl had walked over to the woman on the bench.

"Sit down, if you want to," she invited.

"Thank you. I believe I will." By this time the daylight was fading, and it was difficult to get a good view of the person he was talking with. But he was curious. "Are you from England? Your accent . . ."

"No, but can you guess?" There was a certain playfulness in her voice.

"Not really. Where I come from everyone sounds the same as everyone else." Then he thought to add. "Except me. You just can't lose your Midwestern twang, I guess."

"Apparently I have lost mine."

"Lost what?"

"My Illinois accent—but I asked you to guess my accent."

"Sorry, I can't."

"It's a New Zealand accent."

"You're from New Zealand?"

"Ah yiss," she emphasized.

"What was that about losing the sound of Illinois?" As he asked this he was vaguely aware of something familiar in this woman's playfulness. But he couldn't put his finger on it.

"I'm sorry, forgive me. I've been stringing you along, haven't I? Let me come clean."

"Please do."

"I live in New Zealand, but I'm not a Kiwi by birth. I was born in West Suburban Hospital on the west side of Chicago—sixty-three years ago. But I've lived in New Zealand the last thirty-five years."

"Well, that does explain your speech. But not quite why you are here on this beach at this particular spot."

"Oh that? My parents used to own this place—SHORE CREST. And I wanted to come back and see the beach house once more, and the lake shore."

It can't be! Earl was stunned and took a moment before turning to the "stranger" and looked her straight in the eye with a twinkle in his own. "Lynette Ellerton!"

After a momentary look of perplexity Lynn's face broke into a smile. "Earl Norris!"

Involuntarily they reached out for each other and embraced. An embrace which had been withheld for over forty years.

They stood up and kissed. Then dropping their arms both broke forth into a slurry of questions.

"Lynn, what's a misplaced New Zealander doing here? Have you been visiting family?"

Lynn's face clouded. "No," she answered with a touch of resentment in her voice. "I've lost touch with family. I'm visiting my old high school buddy, Judy Waymann. You remember her, don't you?"

"Sure, in fact I saw her some years ago when my sister Anne was married in our old church." Earl added "And her first word to me was to ask if I was looking for Lynn!"

"She did? What did you say?" Again the playful look.

"I sort of admitted that I did wonder if you might be there!"

"That was sweet." She continued, "Well anyway, she's been wanting me to visit her for a long time. And since I have the time now, I thought I'd come up to the U.S."

She then asked, "Why are you here, Earl?"

"I was at my 40th year seminary reunion, which just ended. I thought I'd come here and have a look around before leaving the area. Am I ever glad I did!"

"Ah yiss, and so am I!"

Then they laughed heartily knowing that they needed to start at the beginning, in order to catch up on a lifetime apart.

Earl broke the dead lock. "Have you had your dinner?"

"No, I came right here when I arrived in Saugatuck."

"So did I, and I suggest that we go back, find a good place to eat where we can take all the time we need to catch up."

"A good idea."

Earl followed Lynn, who said she knew of a place. They drove to Saugatuck and the two cars pulled into the parking lot of a supper club on the edge of town. They walked into the restaurant hand in hand like teenagers, which in a sense they were again. After they ordered Earl couldn't wait to hear Lynn's story. "How did you get to New Zealand?"

"I spent a summer in Alaska, as a volunteer in mission at Sheldon Jackson College in Sitka."

Earl cut in. "Actually I heard about that. When I met Judy at Anne's wedding she mentioned your being in Alaska at the time."

"Strange that she never told me . . . ." Lynn seemed to say to herself. Then she continued her account. "Anyway toward the end of the summer, I had a few days off and spent them on the Alaska Marine Highway ferry going around to different towns on the Inside Passage. One noon in the cafeteria on board—the place was so crowded—a young man with what I thought at the time was a British accent asked if he could take an empty seat at a table my friend and I were occupying. My friend was the librarian at the college. I had been assigned to the library. Well, anyway, the upshot of this chance meeting was that I married the guy!"

"Wow!"

Lynn enjoyed the shock value of the way she was telling her story. She grinned, "Not then and there, but miles from there on the South Island of New Zealand, and some months later. John's family had a sheep farm there, and after John's 'great Kiwi trip' as he called it, was over he returned to New Zealand to take over the farm. By the end of the summer we had become good friends, and I had nowhere else to go, so I booked a seat on the same flight he had to Christchurch. His family 'took me in' so to speak and it wasn't long before John and I were married. And we had a wonderful twenty-two years together. Fifteen years ago he was killed in a farming accident. By that time his father was in poor health, and this left our son and me to run the farm. Our daughter had moved to England. Ian is on the farm now. He's married to Kirsty and they have a little boy, Nevin, who is two. Amanda is a teacher in London and is not married. I still live on the farm, in the little house where John's parents had lived. So that's my story."

"Remarkable! But you didn't tell me about your life between the time we knew each other and when you went to Alaska."

"Those were not good years. My mother died an alcoholic. My father became even more of a tyrant after that. I was working for him, but couldn't stand it any longer. Then I found a young adult church group in Chicago in which I found a new life, so to speak. I saw the old values of money and status which motivated my family for what they were. I recognized my brother's addiction to a monied status as well and found I no longer could stand being with him. I believe God turned my life around and sent me to Sitka. Earl, I believe that I was converted into viewing life more as you did, and as I guess you still do now. So how about you?"

"Not nearly as exciting, Lynn. It was more or less as you could have expected. After seminary I accepted a call to a little rural church in eastern Montana. I married a woman with a small son, who was from that community. Her first husband had left her. I adopted her son. Her father had a cattle ranch, which our son now owns and operates. Kaye and I had a good marriage, but she died six years ago—a cancer death. She was only fifty-seven. And, like you, I'll be living in a little house on David's farm."

"You mean you stayed in the same church?"

"Yes, except that a few years ago it merged with a larger congregation in a nearby town, and we moved there until my retirement."

By this time their meals had arrived, and they brought their stories to a close in order to eat dinner while it was still hot. They spent the rest of their time that evening sharing impressions of how things had changed around Chicago and in Saugatuck. Lynn also had a room in a motel and so they arranged to have breakfast together the next morning. Earl escorted Lynn to her room and before separating for the night they embraced again, giving each other a good night kiss.

As Earl lay in his bed he reflected on his return to Chicago, to the beach, and to Lynn. He had no idea what was ahead. He knew nothing yet of Lynn's long range plans, and he himself certainly had none, except that in two days time he was scheduled on a return flight to Montana. But he had an overwhelming feeling that he did not want to let Lynn go, as he had done once long ago.

The conversation the night before had been about the past. Now over breakfast they were eager to hear about present circumstances and what might lie ahead for each of these old friends. Earl declared. "I'm scheduled on a flight out of O'Hare Thursday morning."

"Where to?"

"Back to Montana, but I can't say to what I'm returning exactly. If I were to predict, my future is something like this. I'll live with my son and his family until we get a small house built on the ranch. Then I'd move in there."

"Granny cribs, we call them in New Zealand."

"And I haven't a clue as to what might be next in my life." Earl paused and asked Lynn. "What's next for you, Lynn?"

"I'll be returning to Judy Waymann's where I've been staying this week, then Friday I'll go home."

"Home?"

"Yes—to New Zealand."

"I thought maybe you were going to stay here in America."

"No, New Zealand is my home. It has been better to me that the U.S. ever was, Earl."

"Even when we were kids?"

"Well, those were good days . . ." She seemed to hesitate and then her tone became somber. "Until you and I split up. After that it sort of went from bad to worse, until I went to Alaska. That was the beginning of a new life for me."

Earl was taking this in and thinking ahead at the same time. "Lynn—I don't want to lose track of you again."

Lynn was pensive. "I guess I don't either . . . ." She seemed reflective. "But you 'can't go home again' as they say."

"How do you mean that?"

"That my new life as Lynette Lindsay, of Drummond, New Zealand cancels out the old Lynn Ellerton and her crowd."

"Including Earl Norris?"

She hesitated. "Yes . . . . at least in the old sense."

Earl let it go at that, to ponder later. He then presented an idea which he'd been forming. "What would you say to our getting the old TUXIS gang together this week while you're at Judy's?"

Lynn hesitated at first and then admitted. "I guess I could get Judy to round up the ones that still live in the area . . . ."

"You don't sound too enthused. What's wrong?"

"Oh, I guess I think it just wouldn't be the same. So much has changed since then."

"I think it would be great. Let's do it."

"O.K. I suppose . . . Where will you be, Earl?"

"I'm at the International House near the Seminary, but I could get a room out at the Carlton That's not too far from Judy's, I don't think."

They agreed and Lynn promised to get something arranged They rose from the booth. Earl left a tip and prepared to pay the breakfast tab.

As they left the restaurant, Lynn turned to Earl with a quizzical look. "You didn't happen to bring a bathing suit?"

"I sure didn't!"

"Well, I did. For years I've wanted to take another swim in Lake Michigan. And, so I decided to do that."

"You did? You're going down to the lake now?"

"Yes, come with me to Shore Crest. I'll only be in the water for a short swim."

Earl drove Lynn to Shore Crest in his rental car. Before he could get out of the car she was running down to the beach where she stripped off her street clothes. As Earl followed he was shocked until he saw that she had her bathing suit on underneath. She ran into the water in her white swimsuit, waving to Earl and shouting. "I'll only be a minute, Earl."

Earl stood watching her and he remembered a dream he had had. After Lynn came out of the water and dried herself, Earl suggested. "Before we go let's just sit here on the shore . . . for old times' sake."

The two who had been friends at another time at this very spot sat for a while in mutual silence. Lynn was the first to break the spell. "Do you remember when you and I used to sit looking out at Lake Michigan?"

"I remember," Earl admitted.

"Is it like that for you now—I mean being together and sharing the view?"

"Sort of . . . ."

"I know. For me it's both the same as it was and different."

"Why is it different? . . . I mean besides the obvious."

"Well, I'm a different person now. My experience after my mother's death really changed me. It made me grow up in a hurry. Revolutionized my values. Ironically my values came closer to yours, I think. And then my move to another country and becoming a sheep farmer's wife. A city girl that I was! Imagine . . . ."

"I can't, frankly."

Lynn went on in a form of monologue. "A wife, and a mother, and now a widow—so I look out at the water and I have thoughts different from those of long ago, Earl."

"I don't know what to say. My life hasn't been all that different from what it was beginning to be in high school. But it was a good life. Good marriage, I would say. We were sorry we didn't have children of our own. But David became so much my son as well as Kaye's, that it made up for it. He and his family are a great blessing to me, especially now after Kaye's death. No, this seems pretty much like it did when we sat together on the beach. Maybe I didn't think about it deeply enough then—or now."

"Maybe it doesn't matter. In a couple of days I'll be going home, and so will you."

Earl was disturbed by this thought. "And that will be that?"

"I guess so. What else?"

"Well we could stay in touch. Or . . ." Earl interrupted his own train of thought." "Lynn, are you homesick for New Zealand?"

"Yes, not just for the country, but for my home and family, friends there and familiar scenes. This is gorgeous here, but it's not where I belong. The U.S. isn't my home anymore, Earl. Can you understand the weight of what I'm saying?"

"I think so. So you wouldn't want to move back to the U.S—or to Chicago—or to the beach house?"

"Heavens no! There's no one there for me anymore."

"Come to think of it, what you say of New Zealand must be much the same as how I feel about Montana. I wouldn't want to go back to Chicago."

"But it's the same country for you."

"Yes, but in a way Montana is a whole other world from what I'd known before. Like a new country, I think."

If what Earl had said registered in Lynn's mind, she certainly didn't show it. In fact the subject had run its course for Lynn.

She stirred. "Well, I think I'd like to get back to Judy's."

"O.K." Earl stood up and took Lynn by the hand to help her up. If he had thought about a kiss, her demeanor certainly discouraged such thoughts. They walked up to the car. Earl felt somehow cheated. "Sorry, all good things come to an end."

"Yes, Earl," she said very seriously.

"A few days and then it's goodbye again."

"I know . . . but we'll see each other if the TUXIS bunch gets together before I go back to New Zealand."

With that, they got up and prepared to part ways temporarily—Lynn to Judy's house and Earl back to Hyde Park. They exchanged phone numbers for the International House and Judy's home.

"I'll phone you when I get to the Carlton, and by that time maybe you'll know what the plans are."

"Right, I'll see what I can arrange."

Each had a rental car and so they went their separate ways, planning to see each other in a day or two.

When Earl got back to the International House he discovered that there had been an urgent phone call from David for him. He dialed David. "Hello, Davey. You called?"

"Yes, Dad, I hate to cut your vacation short but we have some bad news."

"What's that?" Earl was worried about what he might hear.

"Barbara's been in a serious car accident and she's in the hospital in Miles City in critical condition. Dad, I really need you here to help out with Jenny and Josh. I'll have to be in town pretty much of the time . . . ."

"Yes, of course. I'll get a flight as quickly as I can. Tell me about her condition."

"We don't know at this point. She is still in a coma with a broken leg and ribs. The doctor said that if she doesn't come out of it by tomorrow night he'd get the HELP helicopter to fly her to Billings."

"I see . . . Davey? Hold on. My prayers are with you both, and I'll be there as soon as I can."

They hung up, leaving Earl stunned. Earl phoned Lynn.

"I got a phone call last night which means that I'm going to have to leave as soon as I can get a flight to get back home as soon as possible." He went on to explain.

"That means we won't be seeing each other again."

"I guess not. It has been so good to be with you again, Lynn."

"Ah yiss. It truly has, Earl."

They exchanged their home addresses and promised to correspond. And then they said good bye. He hung up and Earl prepared for his return to O'Hare and a flight back to Montana as soon as possible.

CHAPTER 46

In Touch

It was a month to the day when Earl finally received a letter from Lynn. He picked up the mail from the box at the road as he returned from an errand in town. Most of the mail was for David and his family. But one piece stood out. It was a light blue onion skin aerogram from New Zealand. The left hand corner bore the return address:

Sender: L. Lindsay
RD #4 Winton
Southland,
New Zealand

Earl was surprised at how excited and nervous he became as he realized this letter was from Lynn. By this time he had settled into a routine which provided him a modicum of happiness day to day. He had pretty well blocked out thoughts of Lynn relegating her to ancient memories of his youth. *After all I shall always belong to Kaye.* But such resolve melted as he took her letter to himself. He didn't want to be disturbed while reading this at the house, so he pulled off the lane and opened the letter.

Dear Earl,

We agreed to keep in touch so I thought I'd write you to tell you about my return home. But first, how is your daughter-in-law? I hope she has recovered. and I trust that you are now safely tucked away in Saline, Montana! I still can't quite get over thinking of you as a Chicago boy living there! But I take it that you must like it, or you would have gone back to the Midwest to retire. Right?

Judy gathered some of the old gang, but without you there I felt sort of disappointed, especially since you had been the one to suggest it.

My flight home was uneventful, but long. Everything was fine here at GLEN MOR when I got back. It was wonderful to see Ian again.

Everything is going fine here. I hope the same for you.

Sincerely yours,
Lynette

Earl read the letter a second time before folding it and putting it in his pocket. He continued his drive up to the house. He couldn't help to feel a bit of disappointment. *Why do I feel like there should be more to the letter?* As he thought about it, he concluded that when he opened the letter he had hoped for more warmth, and more indication that she wanted to hear from him and to keep in touch.

That evening after retiring to his room Earl wrote a letter in reply to Lynn.

Earl Norris
W Lazy N
Box 31
Saline, MT 59338
U. S. A.

Dear Lynn,

It was good hearing from you. I'm glad your trip went well and that you are safely home. Home in New Zealand! How different from what you probably used to imagine when you said—"home in Chicago." But life has its twists and turns. One of the most surprising twists was running into you in Michigan. What a coincidence that we were both there at the exact same time. Was that Providence?

Years ago I fell in love with Montana and with Saline. I wouldn't move back to Chicago if you paid me. So I was very glad to arrive in Billings, and to drive here to Saline.

When I got here I discovered that Barbara had been flown by helicopter to Billings for further treatment. I was much needed here and kept the children while David spent as much time as he could in Billings. It is fortunate that his farming operation is big enough for him to have a hired man, who could keep things going while he was away. Five days after she was hospitalized in Billings she woke up without any apparent brain damage. She is better now, and resting at home. Still a ways to go. I am still needed to pitch in.

I wish you could have had the opportunity to visit here and see what my life is like on the W lazy N! Some different from a house on a narrow lot on a city block in the Chicago suburbs! It is quite interesting that both you and I have gone rural since our high school days. Tell me more about Glen Mor.

That's about all for now. But I hope we will keep in touch. My best to you in the coming days, Lynn.

As ever,
Earl

The next letter from Lynn arrived only a few days after he had sent his to her. The fact that the two letters had crossed in the mail encouraged Earl. She had written on her own initiative, not merely as a polite reply.

Dear Earl,

I'm looking forward to hearing from you. Ever since seeing you so many of the old memories have been coming back. Especially of the times we spent together in Michigan at Shore Crest. How different our lives would have been had we remained in that "culture!" We would have married and had kids. You would have gone into my father's business. And I would have been a suburban wife and mother. But not like my mother, I would hope. And yet, to be honest that style of life might have led me down the same path. Perish the thought. And maybe you would have become business-like and severe like my father. Now that imagined scenario isn't so good, is it? The truth is—I like you better the way you are.

And I would have to admit that I'm glad that a change came over me, leading me away from a selfish life to one of service. When I moved to NZ and married John, I wondered about service in this setting. Well, I found that living here in Drummond, there were lots of ways for me to be of service. Helping John with his work, of course, and also raising the children. These were "service projects" in a way. But more than that I did a great deal of volunteer work in the Drummond School. I loved working with children. Later on I put my Sheldon Jackson College library experience to work as a volunteer in the library in Invercargill. Through the years there were many church and APW activities which were service to others. That's *Association of Presbyterian Women.*

That brings me to the subject of our parish. It is made up of two churches: one here in Drummond and other in Oreti, around five miles east of here. The pastors who were here held services at both places each Sunday. Drummond has a manse, so the pastor always lived here. But changes have come. There are fewer people in the church, too few to support a full time minister. There is talk in Southland Presbytery of merging the Oreti parish with Winton, about ten miles away. It is a small town, but much bigger than Drummond. The high school age young people go to school in Winton. We call it "college." Anyway, we don't have a pastor right now, and some of us wonder if we will ever be able to have one again. It's sad. The whole area is changing. So many North Island dairy farmers are moving down here and buying up sheep farms and turning them into dairy farms. We are not finding many of these families interested in our parish. So-o-o-o—what to do?

I've gone on long enough. What is happening in your life, Earl? What do you think would have been the case if we had both stayed in Illinois?

Love from the old days!
Lynn

Yes! Earl thought. *Love from the old days.* There was a warmth in Lynn's letter, which made his heart sing. *What would have happened? I don't know. There are so many variables.*

Over the next few months, Earl and Lynn exchanged correspondence, but nothing very substantive passed between them. More like international pen pals telling each other about the things they were doing. Always eager to read her letters, Earl usually found himself slightly disappointed after each letter. What warmth he discerned was usually the remembered feelings of their experience as young people.

Then in March a letter from New Zealand arrived, but it wasn't from Lynn. Nevertheless, it brought a touch of excitement to Earl.

13 March 2000
Graham Patterson
RD #3 Invercargill
Southland,
New Zealand

The Rev. Mr. Earl Norris
P.O. Box 31
Saline, Montana
U.S.A.

Dear Mr. Norris:

Your name has come to my attention as a retired Presbyterian clergyman, who might have an interest in serving our parish for a limited period of time. Three to six months, I should anticipate.

Our parish has been without a regular pastor for over a year. We are in need of a pastor, but the Presbytrerian Church of New Zealand is in short supply of ministers. Those few who are seeking places to go, do not ordinarily want to come this far south, and to such a small parish as ours. They think it is too cold here.

If you have any interest in coming to New Zealand and to our parish, please inform me by return post. We can discuss details if you indicate your interest.

Cordially yours,
Graham Patterson
Session Clerk, Oreti Parish

The letter shocked Earl. Before the day was over he would read it over many times. One thought which warmed his heart more than any other was this: *Surely it was Lynn who gave him my name.*

The following Saturday evening when Earl was at David's for supper he shared the letter with them.

"Are you going to accept the offer?" David asked.

"I don't know." Earl couldn't help but smile as he thought about this idea. "If you don't need me, maybe I will."

"Oh, Dad, we'll do fine." Barbara was enthusiastic. "I think you should take them up on it."

"Well, I just might! But now I need to get back home. I've got some things to do before bed time."

After Earl had gone Barbara turned to David and commented on Earl's demeanor. "Did you notice your dad when he talked about going to New Zealand?"

"No, what do you mean?"

"He looked so alive and excited. We haven't seen him like that since your mother was alive." She continued. "If I didn't know otherwise, I'd say there is someone there he is interested in. The woman he met when he was in Chicago at the time of his reunion, I think was to return to New Zealand, wasn't she?"

"I think you're right. I believe her name was Lynette Lindsay." David thought about what Barbara had said. "But, no, I can't see Dad getting interested in anyone."

"I don't know. You think that way because he's your father. But I think I saw a glint in his eye!"

PART V

Into a New Century

CHAPTER 47

Starting Over

A delegation of three had come to the terminal to meet Air New Zealand Flight #1304. After its arrival was announced they got up and stood next to the gate to welcome one of its incoming passengers. Their official errand was to meet the Rev. Earl Norris on behalf of the Oreti Parish. The contact person in correspondence with the Rev. Mr. Norris had been Graham Patterson, and so it was natural for Graham and his wife, Patricia, to be on hand to meet the pastor from the U.S. who was coming to their parish as its pastor for six months. Also Lynn Lindsay had been asked to be the third member of the delegation—since she knew Mr. Norris.

The usual lengthy wait between the time the flight is announced and the moment the person one is meeting actually steps into the terminal had the effect on Lynn of making her quite nervous. She hoped it wouldn't be obvious to Tricia and Graham. She knew she would recognize Earl, but that was all she knew. What was it going to be like having him close by over the next six months? She felt drawn to him, but *that's only because of our close relationship when we were kids—or have I really been attracted to him as he is now?* And at the same time she did not want to establish a close relationship with Earl or any other man. *Alone is the way I want it. I'll always belong to John.* Her thoughts were put on hold when she heard the decreasing drone of his incoming flight overhead.

Soon the Boeing 737 could be seen slowly moving toward the prescribed docking point. The roar of the jet engines began to diminish. In a very short interval Earl Norris would be stepping onto New Zealand "soil." The arrival of the Air New Zealand flight from Christchurch reminded Lynn of the moment when she and John had stepped onto the tarmac here in Invercargill. *When my life was starting over. And such a good life it has been ever since—except for John's death.* A wistful and somber mood replaced Lynn Lindsay's nervousness. She recognized and affirmed herself as a New Zealander, the wife of John Lindsay, and now his widow. That was that.

But then when Earl emerged from the cabin and began descending the steps her heart "missed a beat." He certainly didn't look his years to Lynn. From a distance she could imagine him as he was in his youth. She quickly pointed him out to the Pattersons. "There he is."

"Ah, yiss. Our new pastor, Tricia!" Graham noted to his wife.

Their reunion was awkward for Lynn. She stepped forward as the stream of deplaning passengers came through the doorway into the terminal. Soon Earl appeared. He smiled his greeting from a short distance and then when he came close she noticed that he was about to greet her with a hug. But she did not feel comfortable with such a display of familiarity. She was all too aware that Graham and Patricia knew her as John Lindsay's wife, and that there should be no other man in her life. Somewhat stiffly she held back, discouraging any initiative on Earl's part. Instead she held out her hand for him to shake as she greeted him.

"Earl, it's good to see you again." She added the traditional New Zealand greeting. "Kia Ora!"

Earl responded with his own hand. Bewilderment showed as he heard her words of welcome.

Lynn quickly brought the Pattersons into the exchange. "Earl, meet Graham and Patricia Patterson."

"Well, Mr. Patterson. We meet face to face! And Mrs. Patterson, so good to meet you both."

Graham responded. "It is our pleasure, Mr. Norris."

"So good to meet you," Patricia added as she and Graham greeted Earl with handshakes.

"And, by the way," Patricia added helpfully. "Kia Ora means, 'Welcome!' A Maori expression of welcome to New Zealand, Earl—may we call you, Earl?"

"Of course. I like that, Patricia."

Tricia's soft warmth tended to dispel whatever nervous awkwardness remained among these four who would be destined to work together in the Oreti parish. She had set the tone for the often difficult process of getting acquainted.

"First, you will find your baggage over here," Graham announced as he began leading the little group to the baggage area.

After retrieving his luggage Earl followed the Pattersons out to the car park. While Lynn accompanied him they exchanged small talk until they reached the car. Graham put the bags in the boot and ushered Earl and Lynn into the back seat. He and Patricia took their places in front leaving Lynn to sit in the back with Earl for the relatively short drive to Drummond.

It would be starting over for Earl as he prepared to resume his work as a parish pastor and all that such a position entails. Whether this would also be a starting over with Lynn, remained yet to be seen.

Fortunately for Lynn, Graham and Patricia presided over Earl's first tour by pointing out various sights as they passed through Invercargill and then drove northward to Drummond. She could remain quiet, immersed in her own thoughts as her old acquaintance was taken care of. The familiar travelogue brought back to Lynn her first journey with John and his parents from Invercargill to Drummond. She listened carefully to Earl's responses, trying to determine what he was thinking about as he saw his new surroundings. *I wonder how he likes what he sees. I hope he likes it as much as I did—and do.* She tried to put herself in his shoes. *It's different for him than it was for me. Earl will be here alone and only temporarily, and then he will return to the U.S. When John and I came, I knew down deep that I would be staying as John's wife.* Lynn had to smile to herself when she thought. *But John still wasn't sure.* She pondered the temporary nature of Earl's visit to New Zealand. *He'll not be staying here. After he's goes back to Montana I can get back to where I was before.* She thought about this and then questioned herself. *Or will he go back?* She thought about the implications of this possibility. *Oh my! What am I thinking?*

As they drove into Drummond, Graham broke into Lynn's thoughts when he announced to Earl, "Patricia and I would like to have you in our home for the night, and then in the morning we can get you installed in the manse."

"I'd like that very much, Graham."

"You can drop me off at the Drummond store. I left my car there." Lynn then addressed Earl, "It's good to have you here with us, and I hope that you'll find us a hospitable bunch!"

"Thanks. A good start already. I'm really looking forward to these months with all of you."

Graham pulled up next to Lynn's car. Earl got out to bid Lynn a good bye.

"I'll see you Sunday, Earl."

He returned to Pattersons' car.

"Our farm is just a wee distance from town," Graham said as he drove off onto a gravel road. Soon the road turned gently to the left and ahead Earl could see a farm house. As they got closer Graham announced, "That's our farm on your left."

Earl acknowledged this information and looked even more closely at the house and its surroundings. Between the house and the road he saw a pasture of grass filled with sheep, and another in the distance behind the house.

The house was white stucco. It was a single story much like an American ranch style house in the suburbs, of about that age as well—1950s or 60s he surmised. They reached the entrance gate which was flanked with stone work. On one side the name *Anstruther* done in metal was attached to the masonry. Graham entered the open gate and drove into a circular drive which brought them to the front of the house. Earl noticed that the drive continued, returning to the road at an exit gate similar to the entrance. Graham stopped the car and announced. "Welcome to Anstruther, Mr. Norris." He spoke this in a formal way, which Earl matched with equal formality. "Thank you, Mr. Patterson."

And with that Earl's first "home-stay" in New Zealand began.

In anticipation of his new experiences as a temporary resident in New Zealand and his six months' service to the Oreti Parish, Earl had decided to record his observations and reflections in a personal journal. Had this been earlier in his life when Kaye was alive, such thoughts would have been shared with her. But now, alone, Earl would write to himself as it were. He would not obligate himself to a daily entry, but would write whenever he felt like it. He would begin on the day after his first night in the manse in Drummond.

Day 1

June 1! Here I am at the beginning of winter in the Southern Hemisphere. It is fortunate that Patricia showed me how to fire up the kitchen range. It was cold in the house this morning and the stove feels good. She told me to use pine cones as tinder. I'd never heard of that. Worked great. It was thoughtful of her to stock the cupboards with some groceries to get me started. So my first New Zealand breakfast consisted of guava juice, rolled oats which she called porridge with what I call raisins but they are sultanas, toast and instant coffee. I hope I get used to instant. It's the way they fix it here.

During the afternoon, Graham drove me around the parish for a tour to show me where church families live and a little bit about each one. It reminded me of a similar tour Homer Stein took me on years ago when I first arrived at Saline. Interestingly enough, I found myself thinking of Saline, in that both communities are rural and most of the members of the two parishes are in agriculture of some kind. It was a strange feeling as we went by the Lindsay farm, Glen Mor, it is called. I don't think Graham has any idea how close Lynn and I were long ago. And it doesn't look as if Lynn has any desire for that to be known. I shall honor that.

Well, I'm "back in the saddle again" with a sermon to write for next Sunday, and a bulletin to put together. I'm here to work—not to play.—I keep telling myself.

Day 6

Sunday. I feel good about my first services at both Drummond and Oreti. A good crowd at each church. I suppose curiosity brought some, but the old timers told me that this kind of attendance is what they used to have each week. But lately it had been falling away, probably because of not having a regular minister. So, hopefully I can ride the crest of this resurgence.

This parish could be seen as an outpost of the Church of Scotland. For singing and the reading of the Psalter they use *The Hymnary of the Church of Scotland*. The pages are cut in two across the middle. The upper half pages contain the music of the hymn tunes. The words of the hymns are on the bottom. In this way a selection of a certain hymn tune can be fitted to the words. The book has onion skin paper. Very hard to turn pages with such cold hands as I had. It was cold in the church building. No wonder they have electric heaters down the center aisle at every other pew. However, in the vestry behind the chancel there was no heat. It was cold putting on my pulpit gown back there. Another touch of Scotland was the fact that an elder met me in the vestry to help me with my robe and for prayer. Then when it was time he preceded me into the sanctuary and ushered me into my seat on the platform. Like the beadle in Scotland. At the appropriate time in the service he made the announcements—*intimations*, as they are called.

The elder's name was Mervyn Lindsay. I found that he was a cousin of Lynn's late husband, John. She was in the congregation, of course. I found it a bit distracting for her to be in the third row. We didn't have any chance to talk. She didn't stay long after the service. Most of the folks did. The men gathered in little clusters on one side outside the entrance to the church. The women a few feet away having their conversations. This reminded me of Saline pot lucks where we had gender separated socializing. In fact, despite the interesting differences, the congregation and my part in the service reminded me of back home in rural Montana.

I had a half an hour to drive down the road to Oreti where I had a similar experience. Oreti, however, does not have a town as such surrounding it as Drummond has. Only the Oreti school across the road.

I thoroughly enjoyed the morning, and found that through the afternoon at home in the manse, I basked in the warm glow of this new ministry and the fellowship of this great group of people.

I am enjoying this new start. Like a new life for these old bones! I guess I'd have to give one modifying thought. I am perplexed by Lynn. She seems distant. It feels like she is denying any closeness we might have had in the past. Maybe it is out of a fear of any of her friends here recognizing something in our relationship. There are some Lindsays and in-laws in the congregations. Seems like a lot of people in this parish are interrelated. A word of caution to myself!

CHAPTER 48

On the Shore Again

Lynn slipped out of church during the final hymn. She wanted to be gone before Earl went to the back to greet people as they filed out of worship, the first he would lead during his temporary assignment. She had felt very uncomfortable sitting in the congregation while Earl led the service. She didn't know why, really, but she was sure that she did not want to greet him on the way out. In fact she wanted to get away from everyone for a while in order to sort out her thoughts and feelings. Hurrying home she picked up some clothes and a few necessities and headed south through Isla Bank and Thornbury. She was on her way to Riverton on the coast.

As she drew closer to her destination she thought about the first time John's father had introduced her to Riverton rocks where the Lindsays' summer house, called a crib, is located. It had been the first December after she and John had been married. Trevor and Meg had taken her along while John had some work to do on the farm. Her father-in-law gave her a brief historical lesson about the location of their summer home.

"Riverton is strategically located on what we call Jacob's Estuary. This is formed by the flowing together of the Pourakino River and the Aparima. In fact *Aparima* is the old Maori name for the area which became Riverton after the European settlers arrived. That was back in the 1820's. Before that in the late 1700's some sealers and whalers from New South Wales used this location as a supply depot. It got its original name of Jacob's River from an old whaler named Jacob. This was the oldest European settlement in New Zealand. It's been a fishing port ever since, but more important for us it has become a popular resort area." Trevor concluded his introduction.

In succeeding years, Lynn and John and their children had come to their crib at Riverton rocks every year in the weeks right after Christmas. A favorite haunt for the whole family, it remained close to Lynn's heart because of the precious memories it held for her, especially now after John's death.

On this Sunday afternoon Lynn made the trip alone, driving some twenty or so miles to Riverton and the Taramea Bay end of town where the Lindsay crib was located on Rocks Highway facing the bay. An unpretentious house, its most appealing feature was its closeness to the sea. This, more than anything, brought Lynn back time after time. The soothing effect of looking out onto the ever swelling ocean breakers while sitting on her deck or on the beach had a way of bringing solace to her spirit and order to her mind. She needed this medicine for the soul. Earl's coming into her life was upsetting, and she needed to work through her feelings.

She parked into the short drive next to the house, took out her suitcase and went into the cabin. The sun was out and the air was warm which induced her to put on her swim suit and to head for the little beach across the road. Finding a spot of shade she unfolded her chair and sat down to give herself some pondering time. It was so good to be on the shore again

Earlier, she had thought it would be fun to have Earl in the church at Drummond, but now that he'd come her feelings were at odds. The old pull from Earl was there, but she was repelled by it. Just the mere look from him made her feel disloyal to John. This confusion of feelings made her want to avoid any contact with Earl, but she knew that would be rude. *How would he feel about that? In fact, what must he think of my leaving church this morning as I did? And yet I don't want to be drawn to him. I wish he hadn't come, but then it was my fault that the church found him.*

But then there was John's mother. After his death she had said to Lynn, "Don't let this end your life too, Lynn. After a time you need to live again." Lynn pondered what she meant by *live again*. She felt that this referred to finding another mate, but she couldn't believe that Meg Lindsay would say that to her.

"May I join you?" Lynn's reverie was halted when a woman about her age came up and started to place her chair next to Lynn's.

"Yes, of course." *What else can one say?* Lynn had not met this woman. "I'm Mrs. John Lindsay."

"Hello. I'm Reggie Stewart. Good to meet you. Do you live here?"

"Yes. We have that brown cabin across the road."

"Year around, are you?"

"Oh no, we—I farm up at Drummond. Are you from Riverton?"

"My husband and I just bought a house back on Myrtle Street. Peter's an artist and we have just opened a studio and shop around the corner on Lionel Street."

"That's interesting. Did you have a shop somewhere else before that?"

"Oh no. I worked in a bank in Invercargill and Peter worked at the bank to pay the bills. We met after my first husband walked out on me."

"Oh." Lynn didn't know what to say.

But Reggie had become energized by her own narration. "Yes. I'd thought everything was fine between Donald and me, and then one day he told me he was leaving for a job in Australia and he didn't want me to come along. In fact it became clear that he didn't want me. *Period!*" She paused for this to sink in. "That would make me mad, wouldn't it?" Lynn recognized this as one of those typical New Zealand exclamations worded like a question. She waited for more of her neighbor's story.

"I was so angry I told myself that I never wanted to see him again. I now know that I really did want him back at that point, but I couldn't face it.—at first. There was a young man working around the bank, just on odd jobs. Mostly janitorial. Peter was his name. I must have caught his eye. He became quite friendly—in a decent sort of way. In fact he was a really nice fellow. One day he asked me if I wanted to go with him to a nearby take-away for lunch. He took me by such a surprise that I told him I would. Well I did and afterward I felt terrible. You would have thought I'd been the one to leave my husband, instead of the other way around. So after that I refused his invitations—for a while."

"How soon after your husband left was this lunch?"

"Oh, about a month, I think. Much too soon. I was still mad. I hadn't washed Donald out of my system yet."

"Was that the end of Peter?"

"Oh, no. Peter Stewart and I married about a year after that. In the meantime Donald divorced me and that set off my anger all over again. But I didn't contest it."

"Did you ever get over your anger at Donald?"

"Had to. Or I wouldn't have married again. And any other feeling for Donald had to go. Couldn't have feelings for Donald and married Peter, could I?" This seemed to bring Reggie to the end of what she wanted to say at this point. "So, tell me about yourself. I see by your ring you're married."

"My husband, John, was killed fifteen years ago. I live alone. Our son and his family live nearby. He took over the farm after John was killed."

"You mean you've been a widow fifteen years and you're still wearing the wedding ring?"

"Of course. He's still my husband."

Reggie looked at Lynn and thought for a long time before giving what might be called her testimony. "The day I decided to eliminate Donald from my life I took off my wedding ring. This was also the day I admitted to myself that I was ready for Peter to come into my life . . ." Reggie then uttered a slogan which she made up on the spot. "You can't wear two wedding rings, can you?"

As Lynn thought about this she couldn't help but feel that this was a message meant for her. All this was getting a bit too close for comfort. She changed the subject. "Tell me about your shop."

In the coming weeks Lynn found herself making trips to Riverton much more frequently than she had for years. Most often she came on the week ends. When she was in Riverton on Sundays, she often attended services at the Presbyterian church in Riverton. It was her ambivalence toward Earl which kept her away from church in Drummond on some of those Sundays. Over the course of this time, she and Reggie developed a friendship.

One afternoon when the two women were on the beach Lynn told Reggie about Earl, concluding by telling her about Earl's preaching at Drummond. When Reggie heard this surprising revelation, she chided Lynn. "You mean he's in Drummond and you spend your Sundays here? You're hiding, aren't you?"

"Maybe . . . ."

"And I see you still wear the ring."

Lynn looked at her watch and announced. "I must get back. I'll plan to see you after I get back."

"From where?"

"I'm going to Australia for a bit of a trip. I'll see you after that."

"Without the ring!" Reggie shouted after her as she went up to the cabin to prepare for her return.

CHAPTER 49

On the Rocks

Earl was feeling good about his work in the Oreti Parish as the first few weeks flew by. The only negative was Lynn's disconcerting absences from Sunday worship. *Almost as if she is trying to avoid me.* His constant companion was his journal.

Day 23

My first session meeting went fine. A few differences, but basically the same as at home. Meeting here in the manse made it a bit more informal. When the session clerk asked me to sign his minutes after they had been approved by the session, it took me by surprise—sort of a nice touch!

They want me to be sure and take a day off each week. They seem eager for me to see their country, which I'll be glad to do. But I wish I didn't have to tour by myself. If only Lynn would offer to show me around. But I haven't even seen her the last couple of Sundays. I overheard someone say that she was spending some time at her crib. I learned that a crib is what we call a cabin. But I didn't catch where it is located. On one of the lakes northwest of here, I should think.

So far as session business is concerned, most of it was routine program items like deciding to order Sunday School materials and curriculum for fall. Some financial matters, and then there was the report of the committee to seek a pastor. They think they have a couple of interested names, which they are pursuing. This prompted them to make my time here a three month position. But it could be renewed if no one was coming by then, to be their pastor. On the other hand, if by chance they should get a pastor I could be terminated with a "fortnight notice." I can live with that, I told them.

As Earl's days progressed, he found himself doing pretty much what he'd done in Saline, especially at first. Study in the mornings in his office in the manse, and calling on parishioners in the afternoons. With the exception of a few calls at KEW hospital in Invercargill there wasn't much pastoral work. No impending weddings or funerals that he knew of.

About a month and a half after his arrival Graham Patterson stopped by the manse. Earl saw him drive into the front circular drive, and went to the door to meet him. "Hello, Graham. Come in."

"Yes, thank you, Mr. Norris." Graham was one of a small number in the parish who always addressed Earl as "Mister."

Earl showed him to a seat in the lounge and joined him. "May I fix you some tea?"

"Ah, no thank you. I won't be long but I have an item of importance."

"What is that?" Earl had a premonition which was a bit unsettling.

"The committee . . . ." at this point in the life of the parish everyone knew that the committee" referred to the group interviewing prospective pastors. ". . . has interviewed a young woman pastor from Dunedin who is interested in coming to the Oreti parish."

"How does the committee feel about her?"

"They are impressed. She is presently working as a hospital chaplain there, but would like to come to a parish."

"What is the next step?"

"They have invited her to come here and to preach before the congregation. Someone from Southland Presbytery will come and moderate a congregational meeting to see if she might be the one for us." At this point Graham sounded a bit unsure of himself. "Ah . . . it sounds as though the committee is quite hopeful."

"When is she to come?"

". . . . Ah, by the way . . . ." Graham seemed uneasy. "Have you taken your day off this week?"

"No, why?"

". . . Ah, you might take Saturday and Sunday. She's to preach here on Sunday."

Earl understood why Graham had sounded unsure. "That would be just fine. I'm glad that you are making some progress."

Patterson looked relieved. "Good. Then we will firm things up with the candidate." He looked at Earl. "Thank you for your flexibility."

"Certainly, Graham."

"Ah, well . . . I must be on my way."

The two men rose and went to the door where Earl asked one more question.

"When would the new minister take over? Do you know?"

Graham once again was hesitant. "Ah . . . her contract with the hospital is due for renewal and so it appears that were we to vote for her, she would come in a fortnight."

"I see . . . Quite soon."

"Ah yiss, isn't it?"

Graham took his leave and Earl returned to his office. *Wow! A fortnight. Looks like I may be back in Saline sooner than I thought.* He surveyed the unfinished work on his desk and spotted Sunday's sermon. *Won't need that. I won't even be here.* He then began to wonder where he would go to church. He got out his Southland Presbytery directory to see what churches were nearby. He spotted Riverton and turned to his map and concluded that its location would afford some good coastal views. His New Zealand Accommodation guide book listed a Riverton Beach Motel. He phoned and obtained a reservation for Saturday night. Once again, looking at the map he thought, *I can get an early start and go up to TeAnau and drop down to Manapouri and follow the back roads down to Waewae Bay and over to Riverton, stay the night and go to church Sunday morning. Then after church I can explore the Catlins east of Invercargill.*

Earl was beginning to feel elated over Graham's news.

Later that day Earl wrote in his journal.

Day 46

> Well, my New Zealand odyssey may be coming to an end. If this new preacher is hired, I'll be outta here! My anticipation of renewing some level of relationship with Lynn certainly went down the tube. I have hardly seen her since my first Sunday. Oh well, back to Saline and the family. That's all to the good.

It was 8 PM when Earl found the Riverton Beach Motel on Marne Street and checked in for the night. He'd taken a light supper at a little take-away he'd found in Orepuke. He asked the desk clerk about the location of the Presbyterian church.

"Cross the Jacobs River Estuary. The church is in downtown Riverton on Palmerston Street between Napier and Princess Streets." The clerk gave Earl his key. "Have a fine stay here with us, sir."

After he put his things in his room, he walked down to the beach along the shore which was across the road from the motel. Mesmerized by the endless sea, he had a brief flash of memory. He was on the lake shore with Lynn. The memory faded as he considered the difference between this Pacific view and that of Lake Michigan. As the sky over the water darkened, he returned to his room.

The next morning, after a light breakfast at a local restaurant, Earl parked his car near the church and walked up to the door. Once inside the building he was greeted by an usher, given a bulletin and shown to a seat half way down the center aisle. Those who came down the aisle to find seats near him were quite friendly, greeting him and shaking his hand before they were seated.

There was nothing unusual about the service. A good sermon, he thought, but otherwise not too memorable a service. But as it turned out he would long remember this Sunday in Riverton because of what happened on the way out. As the congregation rose to walk to the back of the sanctuary, he found himself speaking with the woman seated in front of him. She had introduced herself as Meg MacDonald, and had asked him about himself. They were very interested in the fact that he was serving as an interim minister in the Oreti Parish.

"Ah, yiss. We have some friends who have a crib near ours out on the Rocks who are from Drummond."

"Oh, is that right? What are their names?"

"Lindsays. Actually it is a Mrs. Lindsay now and her children. Her husband passed away a some years ago." The woman paused and then asked. "Do you know them?"

The mention of her formal name didn't ring familiar at first. Then he realized it was Lynn, but by that time the woman was continuing.

"In fact, I think she might be here this morning." Meg looked back toward the oncoming worshipers who were leaving. "Ah . . . there is Mrs. Lindsay now." She broke away from Earl momentarily and found Lynn and brought her to Earl. "This is Mrs. Lindsay." Then turning to Lynn, she stopped when she saw that the two knew each other. "Oh, you've met?"

Earl admitted, "We certainly have . . . . Mrs. Lindsay! So good to see you."

"Pastor Norris. You have found me!" She turned to Meg. "I've been remiss in my church attendance at home. I have been here for a number of weeks."

"So that's the reason." Earl looked at Lynn with a sly grin in his eyes.

Just then Meg MacDonald excused herself. "I must get on home. My husband will be waiting for me. We are going into Invercargill. Good to have met you, Mr. Norris." With that she was gone, leaving Lynn and Earl looking at each other with embarrassed faces.

"Earl, you're the last person on earth I thought I'd see here. How come?"

"Your congregation is hearing a candidate this morning, and I am *persona non grata* in that situation." Then he added in a light hearted manner. "And you won't be there to vote on her."

"Her?"

"Yes, a woman minister who is currently a hospital chaplain in Dunedin."

By this time they had walked out of the building and onto the street. It was an awkward moment for each of them. Would they separate and each go about the day's plans, or might they take this as an opportunity to catch up?

Earl was about to let it pass. "Well, I guess I'd better . . . ."

"No. Earl. I need to talk to you."

"Yes?" Earl felt a surge of excitement.

Lynn seemed to ponder the situation further before suggesting. "All I've got is some soup and bread, but there's enough for two. Please come out to my crib—I mean *cabin*, would you?" She seemed to hesitate. "Unless you really have to be on your way."

"No, I'm not in any hurry. I could come out. If you show me the way."

"Good."

With that they made arrangements for Earl to follow Lynn out to The Rocks and to her crib.

Once inside Lynn apologized again. "All I have is soup and bread. I hope that's all right."

"Sure. I'm glad for the chance to visit with you."

"That's why I thought it would be good if you could come here this afternoon. Just make yourself at home while I get things ready."

Earl sat down and leafed through some magazines Lynn had stacked next to an easy chair which he occupied. He didn't have to wait long.

"Soup's on."

They sat down. Lynn offered a blessing and served the soup.

"Good soup. What is it?"

"Pumpkin. A favorite around here."

"I've never had pumpkin soup."

Lynn was eager to get on with a more important subject. "Earl. I owe you an apology . . . ."

"For what?"

"I have practically snubbed you ever since you've come to New Zealand. I've run out on you and hidden here in my crib. And I'm about to go to Australia for a while. If you hadn't come today, I'm sure you would have thought my ignoring you was total rejection."

"Well, I have wondered . . . ."

"It's different here at Riverton. At home everyone knows me as John's wife. And I just have been afraid to start any talk about . . . you know . . . who you are and what's going on between you and me. Drummond's a very small community and if any kind of story started going around I'd have to live with it. So I guess I just decided to avoid it and so I acted as if you weren't around. Now, I'm really sorry and feel really bad . . . ." Lynn paused as if to get some sort of response.

"I think I can understand. Saline's small too." Earl thought about how to put it. "But it has been a lost opportunity. That's what makes me feel badly. At first, I thought it might be our chance to see if we might want to . . . you know . . . get together."

"I know." Tears began to form in Lynn's eyes.

"Are you sure your reluctance is only a matter of what the people will think?"

This took Lynn by surprise. "Oh, Earl, I don't know what to think—or to feel . . . ."

Earl didn't want to push her any further on this. "You're going to Australia?"

Lynn recovered her composure when the subject changed. "Yes, a week from Monday." She saw the question in his expression. "A former Southland neighbor lives on a cattle station there. Her husband sold out here and bought a place in Australia. They invited me for a visit . . . they have been especially solicitous since John's death."

"I see. So we really are about out of time."

"I know."

There was silence between them for an extended moment. Lynn struggled with what she had to say.

"Earl, I need to level with you . . . ."

"How so?"

"The reason I've been here so much of the time since you came to New Zealand . . . is that I'm afraid . . . ."

"Afraid?"

"Yes, I am fearful of re-starting our old relationship. So much has happened in our lives since then. We are different people, Earl." She seemed to be pleading for understanding.

"Well, yes. But we are still Earl and Lynn . . . ."

"That's just t. You may be Earl, but . . . Oh, Earl, I've been Mrs. John Lindsay for so long . . . And now I know I'm no longer Mrs. Lindsay, but I don't know yet how to act without wearing his ring, so to speak."

Earl understood to some extent what Lynn said, but he didn't know how to respond. He thought that it would be fruitless to push Lynn at this point, so once again he changed the subject. "Say, I haven't seen your shoreline yet. May I go outside and look around?"

"Sure, let me clean up our dishes and then I'll show you around." She watched as Earl went outside *He seems so alone*, she thought. *Ever since he came to New Zealand.*

In a few minutes Lynn joined Earl on the porch overlooking the bay. They walked down to the shoreline. Earl was quite taken with the surrounding view.

"You have an enviable spot here. Down here near the water it reminds me a little of Shore Crest."

"I often think that too. In fact in the past when I would miss Shore Crest, I'd come here and imagine being there." She thought some more and tentatively added, "And sometimes I thought I was at the beach with you." Lynn then did something which surprised Earl, in the light of her earlier conversation. She stopped, turned to face him and took his hands in hers. "Every so often I thought of you, and when I did, I felt warm inside . . . ." she confessed. "That was before he died, and I knew it was wrong. Now after he's gone, it still seems wrong."

"Oh Lynn. It's not wrong now." He took her in his arms and they held each other close for a long moment.

The spell was broken when she separated herself. She wanted to say more. "But now . . . I'm reluctant to . . . ."

"To come to me when I'm here and . . . real?"

"Yes. It doesn't seem right for me to become close to you again, Earl." With that she turned toward the house and they began walking back.

Earl got the message. "I guess I'd better let you go. I need to get back to Drummond."

"I'm sorry we don't have more time, but then . . . ."

"I know. Are you returning to Glen Mor any time soon?"

"Actually, I'll be back later on this week. I have to get ready for my trip."

Earl felt a certain amount of desperation. The time was running out for any sort of continuing relationship. "Lynn, can we have dinner next Saturday? Maybe in Invercargill."

"Why, I guess so." She thought some more about this. "In fact I'd like that. I feel better talking with you somewhere besides Drummond. The people see me as John's wife, even though he's gone."

"And do you still regard yourself as John's wife after all these years he's been gone?"

"Not really . . . now that you put it that way . . . it has more to do with my place in the community . . . coming from so far away . . . my acceptance here has always been as Mrs. John Lindsay, never as Lynn Ellerton . . . ." she seemed to be caught up in pondering what she had just thought out loud . . . "and besides, Glen Mor is my home, as nowhere else has ever been."

Earl pushed her further. "Lynn, if I may say it . . . you need to let go, and become your own person again."

"Have you let go of your wife?"

"I believe I have."

"I don't know how, Earl." Her expression was plaintive. "When I was growing up—really until the time I quit working for Daddy, and moved out and found a new job—I wasn't my own person. I was Ellertons' daughter."

"Did John treat you like that . . . as his possession, and not as person in your own right?"

"Oh, no. John was never like Daddy was to me."

"Well then, talk to him, Lynn." He could see her puzzled look. "It's sort of like prayer. Tell him what you're thinking. Ask him . . . ." Earl felt he was on unsteady ground. "Ask him what you think you can ask him. Know what I mean . . . about letting go?" Earl thought he saw a glimmer of understanding. He also thought he'd said enough. "Where shall we meet for dinner Saturday?"

Glad to get off the subject, Lynn was quick to answer. "How about six o'clock at the Kelvin Hotel? On Kelvin Street at Tay street. In the Molly O'Grady Restaurant in the hotel—OK?"

"Great. I'll be there." He refrained from any kind of hug or embrace, feeling that it would be inappropriate . . . at this time. He took his leave. "So long, Lynn. See you Saturday."

"Good bye, Earl . . . Cheerio."

CHAPTER 50

Neither Here nor There

Lynn stood on her porch and watched as Earl's car disappeared on its way back to Drummond. *For a few more days. Then will I ever see him again? Do I want to? On the other hand I know what he wants. He never said it, but I know he wishes we could marry each other and live happily ever after. But where? I want to stay here in Southland. This is my home. And Montana is his home. I'm sure that's where he thinks we'd live. Maybe I want to live neither here nor there. Not anywhere with Earl? I wonder . . . .* The confused widow returned to her crib and began the process of packing her things and closing up the place. Originally she had thought she'd stay four or five more days, but this dinner date with Earl changed her mind. She wanted to get back to Glen Mor . . . and to church during this transitional time.

That night, her last at the Rocks for awhile, she had a dream. She was at the dining room table at Shore Crest. There were others at the table, but she couldn't identify most of them. They were all immersed in conversations. Seated next to her was . . . her mother? No, it was John's mother. And on the other side of her was . . . John? At first, but then it was Earl. John's mother and Earl were engaged in an animated conversation as they spoke back and forth in front of her. Then suddenly she was seated in a chair in her father's office. She was facing the desk behind which was a person whom she thought at first was her father. Then, when she looked more closely it was John's father. And John and his mother were not there. The sound of the waves on the beach seemed to get louder and louder, making it difficult to hear what Mr. Lindsay was saying. But to the best of her ability she thought he said, "Lynn. You must live again. John is alive with his heavenly Father. You must not remain so tied to Glen Mor as if your husband was not dead. Find a bit of heaven for yourself now. Our family and John will give you his permission . . . if you ask him, child."

The dream scene must have changed once more, for when Lynn woke up, the picture in her mind was the local cemetery and John's grave. The dream left her feeling a vague bur eager anticipation. But she had a busy day ahead of her and she went about her final tasks before closing up the crib and packing her car for Glen Mor.

Instead of taking the back road up to Drummond, she headed east to Invercargill and from there up to Winton. The road north out of Winton passes the cemetery where John is buried. When she saw it, the dream flooded back into her consciousness. She stopped and found her way to John's burial plot. She knelt at his grave, bowed her head, and burst into tears. She heard the incoming waves of Lake Michigan again and over the tumult of the raging water a voice, dimly heard and yet clear. John's voice. "Good bye, Lynn Ellerton. Cheerio." Then it was quiet. And Lynn heard the noise of traffic out on Highway #6.

Fortunately there was no one in the cemetery at the time. If there had been, that person would have witnessed something quite strange. After her prayer, Lynn very tenderly removed her wedding ring, held it in her hand for a few moments as she wept. She kissed the ring and then took an empty plastic film canister from her purse and placed the ring in it, securing it with its lid. Next she took a sturdy ball point pen from her purse and began to dig a hole at the head of the grave next to the stone marker. When she had excavated a few inches down the side of the concrete slab, she placed the small container with the ring at the bottom of the hole, which she then carefully filled and compacted. She collected some dead leaves and other plant debris and covered the black soil where she had dug. Satisfied that it would not be noticed, she stood up, and rather quickly walked to her car, and drove off to the west on Highway #96. She drove on to Glen Mor—shaken.

A few days later, when the two had finished tea, Earl lifted his napkin off his lap, lightly crunched it together and placed it next to his empty dessert dish. Lynn did the same and they both took their coffee and rose from the table and walked out to the lobby of the Kelvin. When they were seated Earl announced. "Graham informed me that the new minister will be coming in a couple of weeks. He told me that I'm free to leave for the U.S. at my convenience."

"Oh, so soon?"

"I plan to book a flight out of Christchurch and do some sight-seeing on my way there."

Lynn was quiet, taking this news to heart. They had ended their meal with conversation about Earl's experience at Drummond and in New Zealand. But now in the lounge they turned their attention to the weightier matter which had been on both of their minds.

Lynn was the first to speak seriously. "Earl, on my way back from The Rocks I stopped by John's grave. I had a vague idea that I might 'speak to him.' But before I could compose myself to tell him what was on my mind he spoke to me!"

Earl knew that it was not his place to ask what it was that John had "said" to Lynn.

"I'm glad you stopped at the cemetery. Was it unsettling to you?"

"In a way, and yet there was something freeing about what he said to me."

"Yes . . . . ?"

"He said, *Goodbye, Lynn Ellerton . . . Cheerio.*"

"What did that do to you?"

"It made me do something I never dreamed I'd do."

Earl was startled.

Lynn continued. "I dug a little hole in front of the burial marker and I took my wedding ring and I buried it there with John."

Stunned, Earl responded by taking her hand and offering, "Oh Lynn, that must have been difficult for you."

"Actually not. It gave me a settled feeling . . . . It's a start, I think." Lynn pondered more to herself than to Earl. She turned to Earl. She hesitated before speaking. "Earl, seriously, if after I sort things out and if we should plan to get together, where were you thinking we'd live?"

"Well, back when I thought about that, all I could come up with is six months here and six months there."

"Oh?"

"But then as I realized that your feelings were not as mine, I put the matter out of my head, thinking the question to be merely academic. That you bring it up now is a shocker, Lynn."

Lynn looked at him in a sympathetic way. "Oh, Earl, you seemed so alone. I guess that's what triggered my speculations."

Earl resumed his train of thought. "But when I did think about it, it just seemed to me that neither of us would want to give up our home." Earl thought some more about this and commented. "Yet without Kaye, Montana is not the same, and without John . . . . ?"

"But for me, even without John, it's Glen Mor itself, and New Zealand, that I don't want to leave."

Lynn became stressed over the question and wanted to end it. "Well, it's all theoretical at this point isn't it? Academic, as you say."

"Is it?"

"Yes—until I can sort things out . . . ." She didn't want to say it, "which means letting go . . . . I guess," she said without much conviction. "I mean letting John go fully and finally. I've made a start with burying the ring, but there's still lingering feelings . . . ."

"Yes." Earl could see that there was nothing more to say. "I imagine we'd better be getting back."

A pall of sadness covered them on their way out of the hotel and to their separate cars.

They extended their conversation to other less significant topics as they stood on the sidewalk near Lynn's car. Finally Lynn said, "It's time to head back to Glen Mor. I need to pack for Australia."

"Lynn, I don't want to let you go."

"I know you don't, but I leave for Australia a week from Monday."

An idea was forming in Earl's mind. "What's your flight schedule?"

"I'm on the morning flight to Christchurch on Monday—a week. Then after a bit of a lay-over I fly out of Christchurch." she added. "What about you?"

"I haven't nailed it down yet, but what I'm thinking now is that I could perhaps book the same flight to Christchurch, and forget about sightseeing before I fly home."

"Are sure you want to miss seeing more of New Zealand?"

"Not at the expense of a bit more time with you, Lynn."

"That's sweet of you."

"Do you know your flight number?"

"I think I have it here in my purse." Lynn brought out a slip of paper on which she had put her departure information. "Let's see. I'm on #1301."

Earl jotted the number down on his pocket calendar. "So that's what I'll do," Earl announced.

"That'll be fine." She responded once again without much conviction.

He wished Lynn had shown some interest in his being with her for a longer time.

With that they went to their cars. Earl to finish his duties in the Oreti Parish. Lynn to pack for Australia. As it turned out, Earl would have one more Sunday in the parish, for on the following Sunday the new pastor would be on hand. So it was, that he was ready to leave New Zealand at about the same time that Lynn would be leaving for Australia.

A week later on Sunday after worship in Drummond a farewell reception for Earl was held in the local community hall, only a short walk from the church. When all had arrived in the hall, Graham Patterson made a presentation to Earl. "On behalf of the Oreti Parish it gives me great pleasure to offer you, Mr. Norris, our most sincere appreciation for all you have done for us during this period between pastors. As a token of our appreciation we present you with this farewell gift." Graham brought forth a wrapped gift and formally presented it to Earl.

Earl took the gift, broad and flat, about eighteen inches square, and an inch or so thick. He carefully removed the blue ribbon and white tissue paper.

Just as Earl uncovered a rather large coffee table book, Patterson announced. "This is Jonathan White's NEW ZEALAND. He is one of our famous painters and this is a series of his paintings of New Zealand—something to remember us by."

Earl quickly looked at a few pages and exclaimed. "These are gorgeous. Thank you all so much for this, and for all that you have done for me during my stay here. I will never forget your gracious hospitality."

Everyone applauded and then began to gravitate toward Earl, and finally to the table spread with an assortment of sweets.

He and Lynn had only a passing formal greeting at the reception along with everyone else who thanked Earl for his brief ministry in their church and wished him well.

The next morning he met Lynn at the Invercargill air terminal where they were scheduled on the same flight to Christchurch where there was a connecting flight to Sydney for Lynn with two hours in between, and a flight to Los Angeles for Earl. His delay would be a little over three hours. On the short flight to Christchurch they had little to say. In fact the silence was awkward.

Once on the ground, they found a spot for coffee while waiting for Lynn's flight. When they were seated with their coffee, Earl broached the subject which had been unspoken. "Lynn, our surprise meeting in Michigan and the time we've had together since then will be the high point of my year. In fact—of my life since Kaye died. I just want you to know that, no matter what happens in the future."

"I appreciate that, Earl. The surprise and what has followed have really been something! In fact disturbing would be a better word for it." She looked pensive. "But I'm not at all sure about all this . . . . Whether it's just been a brief re-play of when we were kids . . . or something new . . . and with some sort of future. I just don't know how to think about it."

"As I turn all this over in my mind, I can say, Lynn, that what might have once been called a good case of puppy love, has been transformed into love, as far as I'm concerned . . . ."

Lynn started to interrupt, but Earl continued.

"Which is to say that I love you, Lynn." He thought about what he was saying and added. "I believe I always have."

"Oh, Earl, it's too soon . . . for me to say . . . I don't know my own mind—and heart. One minute I think one way, and then the next minute, it's the other way."

"That's OK. I don't want to push you. I know. There was a time after losing Kaye that I was sure I could never love anyone else . . . And then—Shore Crest!"

Lynn began to cry. Earl reached over and held her hand. She started to say something. Earl kept her from it.

"You don't have to answer. Let's leave things the way they are for right now. And when you get back to Glen Mor, write me."

Just then over the loud speaker: "Quantas flight 571 for Sydney is on the ground. Boarding passengers should be at Gate C."

Lynn gathered her carry-ons and they got up to get in line. "I'll write you when I get back from Australia, Earl . . . Goodbye."

"Goodbye, Lynn. I'll wait for your letter."

They got up and hurried to the gate and found the boarding process had already begun. They embraced, but did not kiss.

"Goodbye, Earl."

"Good bye, Lynn. I'll wait for your letter."

Lynn showed her ticket and entered the walkway, turning around briefly to wave. She was gone.

Earl ambled back along the concourse toward his gate. He had a book to read, but found he couldn't concentrate. Finally his flight was called.

The cabin door closed. The 747 rose into the sky over Canterbury Plain of the South Island, and then veered to the right and was soon ascending over the Pacific and into oblivion for seventeen hours or so. Not wanting to visit with the stranger in the seat next to him Earl put his head back and closed his eyes, feigning sleep. Instead he thought about his time in New Zealand and his living on South Island for a brief stay. *I've been on an island very far away from the world in which I've been living my life. It seemed as if I'd stepped back in time, into a society like Montana was forty years ago. But it's changing they say—getting to be more and more like the U.S.* As Earl thought about all this it came to him *"Being in New Zealand has been like living on a shrinking island, just like my life has been feeling since the class reunion . . . and Lynn is on that Island . . . the same Lynn from forty years ago?* The question startled him. *No, she says that she's not the same Lynn . . . and maybe I'm trying to be the same Earl!* Eventually he fell asleep and remained so, on and off for most of the flight to LAX. Finally as the huge plane began to descend, Earl looked out the window. *Los Angeles—U.S.A. Welcome to the world!* The touch down was a jolt to Earl in more ways than one.

Suddenly he was in the customs hall and then he was soon walking through the exit gate and emerging into the bustling terminal at LAX. Home at last. Soon he perceived that all of the faces around him were those of Americans, and he was no longer surrounded by New Zealanders. He walked out of the International Terminal building and boarded an airport bus, which took him to the Delta terminal, where he located the gate which listed the flight to Salt Lake City as leaving in twenty minutes. Enough time for a quick cup at Starbucks and a phone call.

He set his coffee down on the shelf under the phone. "Hello, Davey, this is Dad. . . . in L.A. How's Barbara? . . . . Great! . . . . I should be in Billings in about four hours. . . . Flight 1715 at 5:50 PM . . . . Thanks . . . I'll be so glad to see you. . . . Goodbye."

He took his coffee to a seat in the gate waiting area. *Saline—here I come.* He took out his journal to make the final entry of his three month odyssey.

Day 101

By tonight I'll be home. But at the moment I'm neither here nor there, no longer New Zealand, and not quite Montana. A good time to make my final entry. It was a good three months assignment. I did some good. The people appreciated my being there in their parish. I fell in love with New Zealand—but not enough to want to live there full time.

Lynn?—I don't know where I'm at. We discussed where we'd live and came to an impasse. Each of us wants to be where we are now.

But I wonder if down deep all this talk of *where* is a cover for her reluctance to marry. I declared my love, but she could not—at this point. So, who knows!

It's back to Saline now. I'm anxious to get home again—but not at all sorry that I got into this venture. Overall I'm the richer for it.

So long 'til next time!

Earl's flight was called. He put away his journal and prepared to board. Finally he passed the flight attendant standing inside the cabin door and found his seat. Soon he was airborne on the next leg of his return to Montana. He had only a few minutes in Salt Lake City. And then a very short hop to Billings for a late afternoon arrival.

CHAPTER 51

Home Alone

Earl walked through the walkway into Logan International Airport in Billings, eager to be home. Davey and Barbara were there to greet him with hugs. He was home in Montana. In a few hours he'd be home in Saline. The three jabbered as they moved with the crowd from the gate to the baggage pickup, and all the way to Saline, each catching up with the other. They stopped in Miles City for a quick supper at the Olive, before going home.

It was dark when they arrived at the ranch and drove up to Earl's house. Before letting him leave to go to bed, Barbara offered, "Dad, we want you to come to the house for breakfast in the morning. The kids want to see you, and we want to visit further."

"That will be fine. What time?"

"How about seven-thirty?"

"Fine with me. I'd like that."

Jet lag caught up with Earl as he opened his bedroom window. He wasted no time climbing into bed. He hit the pillow and was out for the night.

At first light, Earl was awakened by the gentle sound of the fluttering of leaves outside his window. The countryside around Saline is almost completely bereft of trees, characteristic of the northern plains. What trees there are can be found along flowing streams and around farm houses. The W Lazy N had both. Mature cottonwoods lined the river nearby. When the house was built, young seedlings had been planted. These now made up a wind-break of large cottonwoods on the north and west sides of the farm buildings. It was the rustling of these bright yellow-green leaves which welcomed Earl to his home in Montana the morning after his sojourn in a far off country.

Earl splashed some water on his face, and slipped on his sweats for his brisk walk along the river past Davey and Barb's place, a ritual he'd started before going to New Zealand. This time the morning exercise included breakfast. He stepped out onto his tiny back porch and inhaled the pungent smells of new mown hay mixed with cattle. He noted the blue sky, a different hue from what he'd gotten used to in New Zealand—a little darker blue.

He hurried down his steps to begin his morning walk. A gentle breeze accompanied him as he took the familiar trail. Across the river in the distance was the county road. On his side of the river Black Angus grazed. Beyond them, further north stretched the endless prairie, sun dried under an unclouded sky. *So very good to be home—home where I belong.* For all the pleasure and new-found friendships Earl had enjoyed, and for all the new and intriguing geography, he could now admit, *I never felt that I fully belonged—always an outsider. Maybe it was such a feeling which Lynn experienced before she was seen as John's wife.* He pondered this feeling as he walked the river trail to Davey's. *Maybe it was because Lynn never really accepted me. Her intentional distance kept me at arms length not only from her but from everything else. Maybe, because I was a part of her former life, my being there made her feel like she didn't belong there either. A strange twist.*

The trail led Earl beyond the ranch house and then it connected to a ranch road leading back to the barn and house. As he made his way back to the house he met Davey on his John Deere pulling a wagon loaded with hay bales.

Davey shouted, "I'll be in for breakfast in a couple of minutes."

Earl passed over a slight rise in the road bringing the house into view. Josh came bounding off the porch and waved. Earl waved back and Josh came running toward him.

"Grandpa!"

"Well, for goodness sakes, there's Josh!"

Josh giggled and held out his arms to be lifted up. And to be carried back to the house.

"Here, let me hoist you onto my shoulders."

The two reached the house just as Jenny appeared. She gave a shy smile and waited for her Grandpa to come up to her.

"Hi, Jenny. You look so nice this morning!" Earl put Josh down so that he could hug Jenny. She demurely let her Grandpa hug her.

Earl took both children by their hands and the three marched into the house and to the kitchen where Barbara was at the electric range tending the bacon. She smiled. Jenny and Josh ran off to play.

"Good morning, Barb. My such a good aroma!"

"Good morning, Dad. I'm so glad you're home. So are the children."

"I can see that. Thank you, Barbara. I certainly am too."

The door opened and in came Davey. "Dad! You're a sight for sore eyes this morning! Welcome home!"

"Thank you, Davey. I couldn't be happier." A brief doubt seemed to cloud his face—a fleeting thought of Lynn.

Barbara called to the children. "Time to wash hands. Breakfast is ready."

When everyone was seated, Earl took up a canvas bag he'd been carrying and brought out gifts. They weren't wrapped, and he gave an immediate explanation. "Jenny, this is a Kiwi bird from New Zealand." He handed her a little stuffed Kiwi.

She immediately held it to her chest in a loving gesture.

"And, Josh, I brought you a model of an Air New Zealand jet, like the one that brought me home. You can hang it from the ceiling in your room."

Josh was obviously delighted. "Grandpa, this will go nicely with the other planes in my room."

"I know. You've got quite a collection."

Turning to Barb and Davey, he handed each a hand knit woolen sweater, each with a Kiwi bird on the front. "Jerseys, as they say!"

"Thank you, Dad." Barb held her pink sweater against her in an act of appreciation.

Davey slipped his on immediately and displayed it with a smile. "Thanks, Dad."

Breakfast was what franchise restaurants tout as "a hearty farm style breakfast." Bacon, eggs, hash browns, toast and homemade chokecherry jelly. And of course freshly perked coffee.

"This is a treat, Barbara. Haven't had much perked coffee lately. Freeze dried instant is the usual style of coffee in New Zealand. And the bacon and hash browns are uniquely U.S."

"I guess it's one more way of saying, 'Welcome home, Dad.'"

The talk around the table turned to a continuation of the conversation of the previous night when each had been sharing what had gone on for the three months in their lives.

Earl made sure to ask the children what they'd been up to. Jenny was particularly attentive and when there was a lull in the jabber she asked, "Tell more about New Zealand, Grandpa."

Earl tried to think of the various things which were different. "Do you know which way the water swirls down our sinks?"

"No, I never looked," Jenny confessed.

"Well it circles to the left—counter-clockwise—as it goes down."

"It does?"

"Here, but in New Zealand it swirls to the right, clockwise!"

"You're kidding." Barbara had never heard of this.

"No. It's true." Earl turned to Josh. "Josh, where does the sun rise in the morning? Point to the direction."

Josh pointed east.

"O.K. then where does it go as it moves toward night time?"

This time Jenny pointed south.

"Right. But in New Zealand it follows an arc in the North."

"Why?" both kids asked.

Earl tried to explain about the Equator and how New Zealand is south and so the sun is north.

Jenny understood. "Cool!"

Josh looked confused.

"After breakfast I'll draw a picture to show you what I mean."

Davey and Barbara had begun to discuss some of the things which they needed to do.

Earl felt that the time had come to let the family get busy with their day. He'd be glad to return to his house and to be on his own for a while.

However, Davey had a question. "Dad, we have been wondering just how it was that this parish in New Zealand contacted you?"

Earl felt a brief surge of embarrassment, because he had not wanted to mention Lynn. "Well it turned out that there is an American in the parish who had known me back in my school days in Illinois—and thought of me, I guess, when the parish needed a preacher." Earl thought this might suffice.

Barbara, however, wanted to know. "How come an American was way down there?"

"She'd married a New Zealander from that area."

Fortunately for Earl, nothing more was said. But the unspoken thought of Lynn suddenly saddened him. He wanted to be alone. "I must get home now. You all have lots to do."

After thanking Barbara for the farm style breakfast, Earl got up and let himself out of the ranch house. He walked over to his house with his heart heavy with thoughts of Lynn as well as his continuing sorrow over Kaye's untimely death. By this time Earl had come through the valley of depression over his loss, and had come to an acceptance which allowed him to move on, so to speak. But he would always cherish a place of love and of sorrow for Kaye in his heart.

When he returned to his house he sat down to sort his thoughts of Lynn before getting busy with chores around his home. *There's no way we are ever going to get together. I lost that chance years ago.* He had thought that the day would be one of pleasure as he got back into the routine of his life in Saline again. Instead his house felt unbearably lonely and there seemed to be nothing to cheer him.

However, as the days progressed Earl's retirement projects took over and brought him joy. He had lots of time to do the reading he'd always wanted to do. He felt free now to spend time with fiction. His association with his family nearby took on some regular rituals like Sunday dinners together, usually followed by recreational activities outdoors when the weather was good, and indoor games during other months of the year.

A high point in the year following his return from New Zealand was a brief visit from Anne and Bob. This was several years after Bob had retired. He and Ann had bought a house on the outskirts of Spokane not too far away from Whitworth College where they had found a number of events and special interest seminars to keep them "young in mind and heart" as they said. After their return to Spokane they kept up with Earl through a steady stream of e-mails back and forth.

In addition to his regular church attendance in Miles City, Earl volunteered at the food bank in Miles City and did some meals on wheels deliveries as well. Also on a weekly basis he spent an afternoon playing chess with a young man in the Saline community who had lost a leg in an auto accident. With time on his hands, he'd welcomed Earl's tutoring him in chess, and now they played the game regularly. Earl had missed his chess partner, Martin since his death some years previous. In the weeks following his return, Earl kept busy, and keeping busy raised his happiness level. *It's a good life. God is good! But I'm still lonely.*

The letter which would confuse Earl's future arrived a month after Lynn returned from Australia and some weeks after his return to Saline. He picked it up from the rural mail box on the road and hurried to the privacy of his living room, sat down in his chair and opened it.

> Dear Earl,
>
> I've been doing a lot of thinking and at last I think I know my own mind. First, I now know that I've been able to let John go, as they say. That means that I'm free to consider some kind of relationship with you. But I'm still not sure. I can't get over the feeling that you and I are both very different people from what we were when we were "in love" in the old days. I wish we had more time. I still kick myself for missing the opportunity for us to get to know each other while you were here. Now we are worlds apart.
>
> I've come to realize that I really don't have to live here at Glen Mor, or even New Zealand. But I still don't want to return to the U.S. I know that's hard for you to understand. I don't understand it either. There's something about NZ and what you might call "British soil" that appeals to me so much that I don't want to leave it. I sometimes think that I'm drawn to NZ because it seems that the men here are

not at all like my father was. They seem so gentle and gentlemanly here. I know that must be hard to understand, but it is how I feel. When I was in Australia I realized the "British soil" feeling. I found that I could live there, but I know that doesn't solve the problem, does it? You still want to live in Montana—Saline to be exact, don't you? I keep wondering if there is someplace neither here nor there that we'd both like.

Oh, Earl—I'm so confused. I know this is no way to end a letter. But please, let's write some more.

Love from the old days,
Lynn

Earl put the letter down, leaned back in his chair, closed his eyes and pondered what Lynn was saying . . . . *very different from what we were* . . . . *Someplace neither here nor there.* Earl didn't know what to think.

Little changed in the weeks following his return. Apparently his loneliness had become known to Barbara and Davey. So much so that they began to hatch a plan. One Sunday after dinner Barbara brought up the plan.

"Dad, we've been thinking. We think you need a change of scenery . . . ."

Earl began to protest, but Davey cut in. "And we have an idea for you. You've always wanted to see them. Ever since I was a little kid, I've known your desire to go out there."

"Where?"

"Can't you guess?"

"No, but you make me very curious. Where have I always wanted to go?"

"The Butchart Gardens—Vancouver Island—Victoria! You know, Dad."

"Oh that!" At first Earl wanted to downplay this idea, but then as he thought about it. He had to admit, "Yeah, you're right. That is a place I've always wanted to see."

"Well . . ." Barbara beamed as she reached into a buffet drawer. Pulling out an envelope she gave it to Earl. "Here, Dad. This is for you."

Earl took the envelope, opened it and pulled out a round trip Northwest airline ticket to Vancouver, B.C. "What's this! No! You shouldn't . . ."

"Yes, we should," Davey announced.

"What else is in the envelope?" Barbara prodded.

Earl brought out a travel agency itinerary with vouchers for the ferry to Vancouver Island. Two nights at the Red Lion Motel in Victoria, a car rental voucher, and a ticket to Butchart Gardens. He was overwhelmed.

To break the embarrassing spell, Davey quipped. "Two things, Dad. We couldn't get you into the Empress Hotel, and you're on your own for meals."

Earl didn't know what to say and gave a nervous laugh.

"Better start packing. The plane leaves in ten days!" Davey added with a broad smile.

"Thank you both! Such a surprise. And, yes, that is a place I've wanted to go."

That night in bed Earl thought about the gift his kids were giving him. A cloud passed over his countenance in the darkness. *A trip Kaye and I always wanted to take.*

Though not as frequently, Earl maintained his journal entries when something big or significant happened. The gift of a trip to Vancouver Island qualified.

April 12, 2000

Some times well intentioned gifts reflect the tastes and desires of the giver more than they do the wishes of the receiver. I guess I'd have to admit that this trip to Butchart Gardens is like that. I imagine Barbara and Davey would love to take such a tour. But I am less enthused. I know I should be. But to go there alone without Kaye? And now I'll be wishing Lynn were with me the whole time. I remember one time when she and I were with our youth group on a trip to the Garfield Park Conservatory in Chicago. Lynn loved looking at all the flowers and plants. I wonder if she still likes flowers so much. I don't know. Anyway, all this money on myself.

CHAPTER 52

Naomi

The shiny new Toyota Camry was neatly tucked in one of a number of lines of vehicles in the hold of the ferry. Earl got out and locked it and took the stairs to the upper deck. He walked outside the cabin and found a spot on the railing of the forward deck. Soon he felt a slight motion and the dock began to move away. He watched the prow cut its way along the channel. The huge ferry gently plied the gray waters of an overcast day in late October. He always enjoyed boat rides small and large. This one reminded him of a cruise on Lake Michigan he and Lynn had once taken. *Wish she was here* now . . . wish *I had somebody to talk to—to share this experience with.*

Anyone observing Earl Norris as he leaned over the railing on the forward deck would have had to conclude that his countenance was somber. The railing was crowded and most people seemed to enjoy gazing out to sea beyond the ferry's bow.

The person leaning next to him left, and immediately the spot was filled by a woman about his age, wearing what appeared to be a Land's End wind breaker. Her gray streaked hair blew gently around her bronzed face. She looked out onto the water and said to no one in particular. "A gray day—for sure."

Earl thought he should respond. "It is that." He added to himself *grayer than you know.*

She looked at him as if surprised he'd heard her. "Oh—hello. My name's Marie—Marie Butler." There was an easy friendliness about her expression.

"Hello. I'm Earl Norris."

"This your first time on the ferry?" she asked knowingly.

"Yes it is. Not for you, I take it."

"Oh no. I'm a regular. But I never tire of watching the water as we go."

That seemed to be the end of the conversation until a bit later the woman surprised Earl with, "You wouldn't want to go down for a cup of coffee with me, would you?"

"No, I think that would be OK." Earl thought that sounded less than willing. "In fact, that's a good idea. It would put a little warmth to a gray day."

She led the way to the snack bar where they each ordered a Starbucks coffee. She then found a table for two and they seated themselves facing each other. Earl could now see her more fully. Her unforced friendliness showed in the creases around her mouth and eyes, which sparkled behind rimless glasses. He was struck by the tiny earrings she wore. They were the brilliant blue paua shell he'd seen so often in New Zealand, a perfect match to her jacket. She unzipped it to reveal a form fitting white turtle neck He noticed her well manicured fingers as she lifted her cup to sip her first taste of what appeared to be a favorite morning elixir.

"Mmm . . ." she intoned, "No gray morning should be without it!"

"No morning—period!"

"A man after my own heart!"

"There seem to be more and more who don't drink plain coffee." Earl looked at her for a response.

"Oh, I know—the boomers all go for the specialty coffee drinks these days. But that'll pass. So, what brings you to Vancouver Island?"

Earl thought a moment. "The simple answer is, Butchard Gardens. But there is a bit more to it. My son and daughter-in-law gave me the trip." Earl hesitated, but then this woman seemed to be so open and inviting that he shared more. "They thought I needed it. It had been some time since my wife passed away, and I'd just returned from a three month stint in New Zealand where I met an old high school friend . . . ." He stopped.

Marie Butler picked up on his hesitance. "He or she?"

"She, in fact, an old girl friend . . . Lynette Lindsay. She wasn't interested in continuing a relationship, and my visa was running out and I had to come back to the U.S."

"I see, and you wanted to hold on to her!"

"You're on the mark. Anyway, my family thought I needed cheering up. They couldn't come along so I'm on a solo trip."

The woman gave him a quizzical look. "Until you met me!"

Earl thought he'd go along with this little game. "Until I met Marie Butler leaning over the railing on the ferry on the way to Vancouver Island, B.C. in the middle of October—the year of our Lord, 2001!."

"Well, you're religious at that! These days most people's years are not 'of our Lord' anymore. But under all sorts of other gods."

"No, that's seems to be the case. And your years? They are under . . . ?"

"Of our Lord'." She said this reverently, as she crossed herself.

"You are Roman Catholic?"

"No, Anglican. And you?"

"I'm Presbyterian . . . a clergyman, in fact"

She nodded recognition. For a few moments there was silence between them. Earl felt a slight lurch as the boat changed its angle slightly. Marie was looking across the snack bar to the window and apparently watching the water and the weather. Earl found himself looking at her. She turned to look at him and he quickly mentioned her pendant hanging from a delicate gold chain around her neck. Also fashioned in gold, it appeared to be a tiny sheaf of grain.

"That's a unique pendant you are wearing—and most attractive."

"Thank you . . ." She hesitated before saying more.

He observed. "Is that a representation of wheat?"

"Yes it is. A sheaf of grain. Notice the few stalks lying beneath it." She decided to share more. "I'm a member of a very special group in my church, but it includes Christians of many denominations. It's *The Order of Naomi*."

"I've not heard of that."

"You know the story of Ruth in the Old Testament, I'm sure." She was nevertheless eager to tell the pertinent part of the story. "Naomi was a recent widow and she was bitter. She had lost her sons as well. Ruth, also widowed, was Naomi's daughter-in-law. She asked, in effect, to be adopted by Naomi. Naomi accepted her plea for help. It was through Naomi's love and care for Ruth, that Naomi herself found happiness. Naomi then brings Ruth and Boaz together. Ruth becomes his wife and will become the mother of a son. Near the end of the book of Ruth are these words spoken to Naomi: *'Blessed be the Lord today, for he has not left you without a next-of kin . . . . the child will give you new life . . . for Ruth who loves you, has borne him.'*"

"How does the sheaf and stalk of grain fit into the story?"

"We see the stalk of grain as a metaphor. Ruth had been invited to harvest the stalks of grain left behind after the reapers had put most of the grain in sheaves. The grain left behind is a metaphor for Ruth herself whom Naomi saved. And in whose salvation Naomi found new life."

Earl was quite taken with this explanation. "And the Order of Naomi—what does it do?"

"We are widows who find new life as we find the Ruths of this world—the left behind, the lost, the losers, the lonely, and the hurting among us. When we find them we offer the spiritual grain they desperately need."

He noticed that she did not have a wedding ring, but on her right hand was a diamond of some size. "Then you operate homes for women in need?"

"Oh no, we are not institutional at all, and it isn't just women whom we try to help. It's men as well. This is entirely one individual reaching out to another individual. Sometimes this may be confined to praying for someone whom we know is in need. Many other times this involves taking active steps to help another person, or perhaps a kindly word of guidance."

"Does your order have meetings?"

"No, we do not even know each other. If I come across someone else wearing this pendant I'll recognize that person as a sister in faith, but that's all."

"That's interesting. Different. The world is so full of meetings."

Marie continued. "Each of us makes a commitment to serve others in this way. And then it is entirely up to each of us to determine how we fulfill this commitment."

Earl thought about what she had shared. "You know, Marie, what you tell me really is what every Christian is called to be and do."

She smiled graciously. "Yes." Her expression saddened. "But so many do not realize that."

Earl had another question which he hesitated to ask. "But, if I may be personal, you seem to be wearing an engagement ring—on your right hand."

"That's another indication I forgot to tell you. We wear our engagement rings on the right hand to signify that we are engaged in Christ's work."

This was an *Aha!* moment of truth for Earl. The only response to rise to the surface was Jenny and Josh's way of saying, "Cool!" It did not occur to Earl that Marie Butler had already taken up the task of *Naomi* in her conversation with him. And that as a result already some of his sadness had begun to melt away. He could not yet know that before he and Marie parted company in Victoria she would have helped him to perceive a way out of his dilemma, a way to companionship again.

By this time their coffee was long gone, and with it any further reason to stay together, except that Earl found himself wanting to remain longer with Marie Butler. "Shall we go back up to the deck?"

"Looks to me like it's begun to rain." She saw disappointment on his face. "But we could go up to the forward lounge."

When they were seated, Earl asked. "Besides being Naomi, what do you do?"

"I have a little gift shop in Victoria. That's where I'm going. I've been to Vancouver to visit my grandchildren—and their parents."

"How old are they?"

"Lawrence is twelve and Jennifer is nine."

"They are about the same age as my two. An eleven year old girl and an eight year old boy."

Just then the announcement came over the loudspeaker for passengers to go down to their vehicles in preparation for docking at the Port of Victoria.

"Well, Marie, I've enjoyed talking with you. You made this voyage seem shorter."

"Yes, but I was wondering what your plans for the island are."

"I'll drive to my motel now, and then in the morning go out to the Gardens."

"What about dinner, where will that be?"

"Someplace out by my motel, I suppose."

"I think you should come downtown when you get settled. You shouldn't miss old Victoria, and especially the Empress Hotel. That's where my shop is. Why don't you come down? I'll show you my shop and the hotel, and then we could find somewhere to have dinner together."

"I'd like that. Tell me when and where."

After firming up arrangements for dinner, they each went down to the vehicle deck to find their cars.

The street level entrance to the Empress Hotel in downtown Victoria leads into a complex of upscale shops, art galleries and boutiques. Earl discovered that Marie's shop was among the most elegant. He arrived at closing time and Marie met him in the hall after closing the shop.

"There's a nice restaurant a block away. We can walk."

With that she took his hand and they made their way out of the Empress and into the waning sunlight. She led the way to the entrance of a restaurant which was on the second floor over a gift and souvenir shop. They both ordered grilled salmon and spent the hour talking.

When it was time to leave Marie said to Earl, "I've always considered it a shame when people visit the Gardens alone. Such beauty must be shared to be etched into one's memory."

Earl appeared saddened by this remark. "But I shall try to make the most of it."

Marie continued her thoughts. "That's why people feel they must photograph scenery, or better yet to sketch it. Some way to appropriate the scene as one's own. The very least is to remark about it to a companion."

"Or write about it? I will take my journal."

Marie became serious and turned to Earl. "In your speaking of your work in New Zealand, you mentioned Lynette Lindsay, whom I believe you said is an American, whom you knew previously." This was obviously an invitation for Earl to say more.

"Yes, we'd been in a high school church group back when we were in high school in a suburb of Chicago—in fact we were more or less engaged to be married."

"Oh!—'more or less' you say?"

"Well yes, we were engaged, but we broke up. She—mostly her father—couldn't accept my becoming a minister. The tacit understanding had been that I would be joining the old man in his business."

"Hard on you?"

"It was. In some ways, as I think of it now, I never really got over her rejection of me."

"So when you re-met was it 'love at second sight' so to speak?"

"At first, it was for me, but then I began to feel a marked distance between us, which leaves us as we are today."

"How's that?"

"I really don't know. We—mostly I—talked about getting married, but the question always ended up in an impasse over where we'd live. She couldn't bear to leave New Zealand. And I really want to remain in the U.S., if not Montana itself."

Marie Butler asked Earl a great many questions about Lynn's life in New Zealand, most of which he couldn't answer. "Why is New Zealand so important to Lynette? Do you know?"

"No, I can't really say. The U.S. is her home."

"Is it?"

"Well, I should think so."

Marie gave a knowing look and changed her line of questioning. "Does she have children?"

"Two."

"What about them? How old are they? What are they like?"

Earl was hard put to give much of an answer to these questions.

Marie then asked, "How did she adjust to the life of a farm wife after her very urban background?"

"I wondered that too."

"Forgive me. I must sound like an interrogator."

"Oh, that's ok. I'm just sorry I don't have good answers."

Marie smiled, but didn't say anything at that point.

Dessert was served and while the two lingered over their coffee Marie reopened the conversation about Lynette.

"You know, Earl, if I may be bold to make an observation."

"Sure, go ahead," Earl said, but wasn't quite sure what he wanted to hear.

"As you have told me about Lynn, I've been trying to put myself in her shoes, and what I think I'm discovering is that you have been hanging on to the Lynn of your high school and college years, but the present day Lynn is someone you don't really know too well. . . ."

Earl thought about this. It took him aback, but he felt there might be some truth in what she'd said. "You could be onto something."

"And if that is so, Earl, she would realize this and not feel comfortable relating to you in anything but a sort of nostalgic superficial way. Know what I mean?"

"Yeah, I do."

"Good."

"Not a very good basis for marriage is it?"

"Right."

"In fact, the two of you have not gotten acquainted all over again, after all those years, so in a way each of you is bound to be a 'new acquaintance,' so to speak."

"I guess we ought to go on some dates! And that's a bit unhandy just now, considering where we both live." Earl seemed to be saying this to himself.

"You need to court her! I should think." Marie felt that she'd said enough. "Well anyway, I thought I needed to share with you my sense of it all."

"Thank you. You make me think. . . ." But he wanted to do his ruminating alone—now that he had been given something new and somewhat disturbing to think through. "Well, Marie—or should I say *Naomi*—I've enjoyed meeting you and your thoughtful input. But I need to go to my motel, I've got some letters to write." But Earl wondered just to whom these were to be written.

"Yes, I have a big day at the shop tomorrow so I guess I need to retire as well. I has been good to meet you, Earl. And I hope you have a very good day at the Gardens tomorrow. I know you will. I often think the fall flowers there are the best."

They rose from the table and went out onto the street. As Earl turned to go to his rental card they said their "good bye's." It was then that Marie intoned: *'Blessed be the Lord today, for he has not left you without a way to new life.* He turned to acknowledge this benediction, but she had turned a corner to go to the hotel.

Earl's tour of the Butchart Gardens was everything he'd hoped for, but throughout the day he was frequently distracted as he pondered Marie Butler's counsel. By the end of the day he was eager to return to the ferry and to *get on with it* as he said to himself.

Once again, Earl found a place on the railing of the forward deck. As he peered ahead at the breaking water of the Pacific he mused. *Two days ago a stranger stood here next to me. She appeared out of nowhere and now is gone from my life. But while she was with me, she entered into my sadness and left me feeling better.* "The Order of Naomi!" *She tried to do for me what Naomi did for Ruth! The rest is up to me. There's work to do if Lynn and I are ever to get together. That was Marie's counsel.* Earl pondered the matter further and concluded. *But not much chance.*

Earl left the rail and went down for coffee, this time alone. Coincidentally he found the same table he and Marie Butler had occupied two days earlier. As he looked at the empty seat across from him, he thought about her, and how she appeared. He pictured the pendant. Then he heard the announcement coming over the loudspeakers.

"We are due to dock at Vancouver shortly. Passengers with vehicles are to go down to the vehicle deck and go to your vehicle to be ready for disembarking."

Earl joined the line of passengers descending to the lower deck. He found his car and waited for the signal to begin driving out onto the dock.

The ferry docked at Vancouver on time and Earl drove to the Vancouver airport where he returned his car and boarded his flight to Seattle. His return schedule called for an overnight in Seattle before the connecting flight to Billings the next morning. When he checked into the Seattle motel in which he had reserved a room, a phone message was awaiting his arrival. He was to call Davey. After warmly greeting each other Davey hastened to relay a message he'd gotten the day before.

"Dad, there have been a series of phone calls for you. Finally yesterday I was given this message . . . ."

"What's that?"

"For you to call a Mrs. John Lindsay at a number in California as soon as possible."

"What number?" Earl was excited, knowing that this would be from Lynn.

"Here, let me get it." Davey picked up a slip of paper from the kitchen counter. "Here it is—209-638-5682."

"Thanks." Earl jotted down the number.

"When will you be home, Dad?"

"I'm flying out of here tomorrow morning. Should be in Saline by noon."

"Good, we miss you."

CHAPTER 53

The Pendant

"Alaska Airlines flight No. 2469 to Fresno is now in the general boarding process. Please have your tickets ready to present at the gate."

Earl closed his book and got up to walk to the boarding gate. His plans had changed. He'd arrived by motel limousine at SEATAC at 7 A.M., and after coffee and a doughnut had been waiting at an Alaska Airlines gate in order to board an 8:30 flight to Fresno, California. Three hours later he would pick up a rental car he'd reserved. By noon he'd be driving south on Highway 99. *To meet Lynn* he kept thinking. A very helpful ticket agent had given him the option of postponing his SEATAC to Billings flight, and had put him on a flight to Fresno in the meantime.

His return phone call to Lynn the night before had completely changed his plans. She told him that she had been summoned to California to care for a cousin. On the outside chance of seeing Earl she had called Davey in Saline in an attempt to reach Earl to tell him of this development. Earl's response had been immediate. And now he was on his way to be with her.

After arriving in Fresno he drove about twenty miles south to Manning Road which he took east a few miles to the town of Reedley in the heart of orchard country. He turned left onto North Reid Avenue and drove a few miles north to the house of a citrus grower, a well kept low appearing brick house flanked by four large palm trees. He walked up onto the front porch and pushed the door bell.

The door opened and Lynn Lindsay threw her arms around him.

"Earl! You're here! I'm so glad."

The two former friends continued in their embrace, each shedding a tear.

When they let go, Lynn exclaimed. "I haven't even let you come in off the porch." She led him into a sitting room off of the entry hall. "Here. Let's sit for a minute. Howard's asleep right now. We can talk."

Earl was the first to speak after they were seated facing each other. "When you told me over the phone why you had come and said that you hoped to see me, I knew right away that this would be a chance to see one another which we couldn't miss. The truth of the matter is that I couldn't wait to see you."

"Oh, Earl, you're so sweet to come." She smiled at him in a way that left Earl without any sign of her former reticence. "I need to start at the beginning. I know I didn't give you much information on the phone."

"I do want to know more about what you're going through, Lynn."

"A fortnight ago Julio Rodriguez, my cousin's orchard manager, wrote me to tell of Howard's stroke. Julio's wife was taking care of Howard, but that kept her from her responsibilities at home and with her extended family. I could see that they would not be able to take care of my cousin for long. There was nothing for me to do but to come to care for him myself."

"Aren't there other relatives closer than New Zealand?"

"No. He has no one, Earl. He was an only child and he never married. All he has are a few cousins, and I'm the only one who has stayed in touch with him. My brother certainly hasn't kept in touch with Julio . . . or with any other family. So here I am."

"Lynn, you are an angel of mercy!"

"No, I'm just doing what I'm supposed to . . ."

"Which is?"

"To bring a grain of help and hope to the lost, the losers, the left behind, the lonely, and the hurting of this world."

Earl was taken aback. Within the last week he'd heard those very words. But at first couldn't think where.

"And when it's to the next of kin it is all the more profound. In fact in the Book of Ruth 'next of kin' is known as the *redeemer*."

The Book of Ruth—the second time lately that I'm hearing something about Ruth, Earl thought. *It was Marie Butler who spoke about Ruth*. "I guess the term fits what you're doing here, Lynn."

"Just part of my promise and commitment."

Earl didn't yet know what she meant. "How'd your cousin come to be in California?"

"His father, my uncle on my mother's side, moved out here after the war. He'd been stationed at Ft. Ord for part of his service time and liked the area. Both my uncle and aunt passed away and left the farm to their only child, Howard."

Earl remembered Lynn's aversion to living in the U.S. "The last time we talked, when I was in New Zealand, you told me that you had no intention of returning to America, and now you're here, Lynn. For how long, do you think?"

"That's impossible to tell. All I can say is that Howard's condition is deteriorating."

"Forgive me for looking ahead, but when . . . when you are free, do you plan any U.S. travel while you're here?"

"Not really. Why?"

"Oh, I just wondered if you might be able to see Saline, and my set up . . . ." Earl watched her expression to see any hint of her feeling about this suggestion.

She looked at Earl with a friendly smile. "That would depend a lot on how soon . . . ."

"I understand. What is his condition right now?"

"You can see for yourself, Earl. Come with me."

They went to Howard's bed, a rented hospital bed which had been placed in the dining area of the house. "I've put him here so that he's close to me while I'm doing other things."

Lynn's cousin was lying on his back. His eyes were open and he appeared to be staring at the ceiling. He turned his head slightly toward Lynn and grunted an acknowledgment of her presence.

"Do you need anything?"

He grunted again and tried to shift his weight.

"Adjust your sheets?"

Another grunt. Lynn leaned over him and pulled the sheets which had bunched up beneath him. She re-adjusted the blanket. He gave a faint smile. "By the way, this is Earl Norris. I don't believe you remember him. He came to the beach house after you left for the west, I think. Earl, this is my cousin, Howard."

"Hello, Howard," Earl said gently.

Howard uttered a soft prolonged sound, which could have been a "hello."

Lynn, aware of the awkwardness, said, "Earl and I will fix you some supper."

Lynn led Earl to the kitchen and closed the door. "He can't speak, but his mind is good, so all he can do is grunt and a make a few other sounds. He has very limited mobility, so I pretty well have to do everything for him, if I can." She qualified her explanation. "Some times when I need to move him, like to change his bed sheets, I call on a young man next door. He comes over to help me with the heavy work."

"Like I said, you're an angel of mercy, Lynn."

She seemed embarrassed at this approbation and said almost to herself. "Just being Naomi."

Earl could barely make out what she said, but heard what he thought was *Naomi*. It dawned on Earl. *Lynn must be in the Order of Naomi!*

Lynn set about to prepare a simple supper, first for Howard and then for herself and Earl. "If you care to, Earl, you could put together a salad for us while I'm doing the rest of the meal."

"Sure. What do you have in mind for the salad?"

"There's lettuce in the fridge and some other fresh veggies. Just make a simple tossed salad."

"OK." He found a mixing bowl and took the lettuce and vegetables out of the fridge and began work. The two worked quietly until Lynn had a tray ready for Howard. "This will take a while for me to give him his meal. You might want to settle in the living room. There are some magazines to read there."

Earl slipped into the living room while Lynn took the tray in to her cousin and began to feed him. Earl retired to a chair in the living room, but he didn't have much of a mind for paging through magazines. His mind was filled with thoughts about Lynn. There was something new and striking about her "take charge" attitude. But there was also a softness in the way she spoke of Howard, and in some of her responses to Earl. He thought of Marie Butler's comments and he had to admit that she was right. *I don't know this person who used to be Lynette Ellerton. In some ways a stranger to me—Mrs. John Lindsay.*

Lynn appeared in the doorway and announced, "Give me ten minutes and we can eat." She disappeared into the kitchen.

"Can I help?"

"No, you stay there. I'll be a minute."

When she returned she had taken off her apron and had given her hair a brushing and had put on some make up. She stood in front of Earl and smiled as she offered her hand to lead him to the dining room where she had the table set for two. The supper was on the table in warming dishes and she'd lit two candles.

Earl held her chair and then took his seat. Lynn offered a brief word of thanks and they began their supper. He was taken with both the formality and the familiarity of the meal.

"This reminds me of the suppers John and I used to share. He always liked it when I lit candles. We would sit opposite each other like this . . ." She seemed to drift off into memory and then thought of Earl. "Anything like you and Kaye?"

"I guess a little." Earl preferred not to say any more. "Tell me about John."

As Lynn tried to put into words her description of her husband and their relationship, Earl found himself discovering more about Lynn herself. Obviously John and Lynn had loved each other deeply and had had a good marriage. On a rational level Earl was glad to hear this, but emotionally he felt a tinge of jealousy.

When it was his turn to describe Kaye, he found himself doing so by drawing comparisons and contrasts to what he'd heard of Lynn's experience. He found Lynn to be a very sensitive and sympathetic listener. He told of Kaye's sickness and untimely death, and as he came to the end of his sharing he looked across the table and was moved by Lynn's obviously warm and understanding expression. The candlelight reflecting in her eyes had a mesmerizing effect upon him.

"It feels good to share Kaye with you, Lynn."

She smiled but didn't say anything, knowing that he had more to say.

"Not since her death have I had a chance like this to tell anyone about her . . . . and to share my feelings." He noticed a moistening in her eyes.

"I too," was all she could say as she choked up.

He continued so as not to embarrass her. "After the funeral it was like everyone wanted to avoid the subject. No one asked me about Kaye or my feelings. Some avoided me. I found that not only did I miss my wife, but I felt a painful isolation from friends. This made me even more lonely."

"That's it exactly, Earl." She reached across the table to touch his hand. as if to verify the truth of what they had exchanged just then.

When she drew closer to him in this way, he noticed her pendant. A sheaf of wheat with a stray stalk at its base!

"The Order of Naomi," he said.

"You know about it?"

"Yes, I met a member . . ." He hesitated to say more.

"And?"

"She helped me."

"How?"

"I'd rather wait to tell you how after we've had a little more time together, Lynn."

She looked puzzled. "That's fine."

"How have you been helping people?"

"Nothing dramatic so far. I just became a member a fortnight ago. I'd been friends with a nurse in my doctor's office in Invercargill for sometime. Her husband died a year or so before I lost John. She'd found out about *Naomi* soon after she had been widowed and she told me about it. But I can't say much about it yet. I've not helped anyone yet."

"You have, though!"

"What do you mean?"

"You've helped me, Lynn . . ." He became quiet and Lynn did not interrupt, but waited for him to continue. "I think it was the openness with which you told me about John that encouraged me to share Kaye with you, and that made Kaye seem to come alive . . . ." He felt reticent about going on but he felt impelled to. "And in the strangest way . . . it makes no sense, I know, but . . . while I was telling you about Kaye, it seemed for a moment that you were Kaye. And suddenly it was like I heard Kaye say *it's OK.*"

"OK?"

"OK to be visiting with you."

Lynn appeared startled when she heard this. Earl felt as though he should not have said this.

'I'm sorry, Lynn. I shouldn't have told you."

"No, that's OK. It's just that you reminded me of something John's mother told me after he died . . . ."

Earl didn't want to pursue this, unless Lynn wanted to.

"She told me *to live again.*" Lynn was pensive.

They heard Howard struggling to call to Lynn. She excused herself to see what her cousin wanted. She was disturbed by what she found. He was apparently having difficulty breathing and was obviously terrified. She called Earl. "Earl, would come here? I think Howard needs some help."

When Earl came to the bedside he immediately felt that Howard needed more than Lynn could provide. "I think you better call 911."

CHAPTER 54

Turning Point

The ambulance sped away from Howard's house. Lynn sat with her cousin, while Earl followed them to the local hospital. Lynn and Howard were met by a nurse wheeling a gurney out to the emergency vehicle. She immediately wheeled Lynn's cousin into the emergency room. Lynn joined Earl in the waiting room while the E.R. staff worked to stabilize Howard and emergency doctors assessed his condition. The wait for these procedures seemed to be forever. Under the circumstances they had little to say to each other as each pondered what this development might mean. Earl could not help but feel that this might be Howard's final struggle. And that if he were to die, Lynn would have no further reason to be in the U.S. Given her feeling about being here, she would most likely go back to New Zealand as soon as she could tie things up in Reedley. He had a sinking feeling that these days of Lynn's involvement in Howard's affairs would be the last he and Lynn would share. He thought of Marie Butler and her admonishment. He told himself, *In these few remaining days I need to get to know Lynn as she is now.* He realized that already he had learned a great deal. *Her involvement with the Order of Naomi says a lot for who she is at this point in her life.* At the same time he realized that she had been less reticent in his presence and seemed warmer toward him. *I need to court Lynn. That's what Marie Butler said. I need to pray for Howard that he doesn't die. That'll give us more time.* Earl caught himself. *What a selfish reason to pray for Howard.*

At that moment the door into the waiting room opened and a doctor dressed in his white smock came toward Lynn. As he pulled off his surgical gloves, she stood up.

"We have decided to send your cousin to the hospital in Fresno. He's being prepared for an ambulance to transport him. You can ride with him or you can go up on your own, Mrs. Lindsay."

Earl hoped she would opt to drive up on her own—with him. Then he and Lynn could visit on the way up.

"What is his condition, Doctor?" There was anxiety in Lynn's voice.

"His airway is partially blocked and it is necessary to surgically relieve the condition."

"Will he be all right on the trip up to Fresno?"

"Yes, we have adequate breathing support in place in the mobile unit."

Lynn seemed to hesitate as she tried to decide whether to accompany Howard. "I guess I better go along."

"Fine, if you'll come this way then." The doctor turned to Earl. "We are taking him to the Community Medical Center in downtown Fresno, just a block off of freeway 41." He took a notebook out of his shirt pocket. "2823 Fresno St. Come to the main waiting room where Mrs. Lindsay can meet you."

Lynn stood up and turned to Earl. Impulsively they hugged. With tears in her eyes she bid him goodbye.

"I'll meet you up there in the waiting room, Lynn." As he got up and began to leave Earl thought about how devoted she had become to her cousin. Disappointed to be alone for this drive Earl headed west from Reedley on Manning. As he slowed down while the road passed through Parlier he saw the flashing lights come up from behind and pass him. They would have Howard at the hospital long before he could travel the twenty or so miles to Fresno. In a few minutes he turned onto Highway 99 and was immediately swept along in the midst of the never ending stream of cars and trucks, all exceeding the speed limit. Earl kept up with the flow and flipped on the radio. He found a Spanish language station and listened to the featured mariachi band.

He exited into downtown Fresno and found the medical center, parked and hurried into the hospital where he found the main waiting room. Preparing for a long wait he took a stack of magazines from the rack and settled down in an overstuffed chair. Only a few short minutes later he was surprised to see Lynn entering the area and coming toward him. She appeared distraught.

"What is it, Lynn?" Earl stood up.

She stepped into Earl's arms. "He didn't make it."

"I'm so sorry, Lynn."

"We were off the highway and a block or so from the hospital, and he died, Earl." She began to weep. "I came all this way to care for him, and he died." She seemed to be accusing herself.

"You did all you could. You can't blame yourself."

"I know, but I do. I'm all he had."

"Come, Lynn, let's sit on the couch over there for a while."

He led her to the couch and they were seated. He kept his arm around her. She continued a quiet weeping. Earl started to speak.

"I just want to be quiet for a moment."

Earl did not know what needed to be done at the hospital, what sort of arrangements needed to be made. Answers came when a social worker appeared and asked Lynn to come with her to her office.

The social worker turned to Earl as Lynn got up. "I'll have her back to you in a few minutes, sir."

When Lynn returned to the waiting room she seemed to have regained her composure. "I'm all done here, so we can go and get a cup of coffee before going back to Reedley."

"The hospital cafeteria OK?" Earl asked.

"That's fine. It won't take us as long."

They found a table and put their trays down and were seated. "What now, Lynn?"

"That's the big question, isn't it?" She went on. "Neither of us lives here. We're both in a sort of suspended animation, aren't we?"

"Yes, and I do need to get back to Montana, at least briefly. How much do you need to do at Howard's?"

Lynn thought for a moment and then seemed to be listing responsibilities out loud. "There's the funeral, cleaning out the house, some legal stuff with his attorney, selling the house, and disposing of his things. That's all."

"Quite a bit, I'd say. A couple of weeks?"

"A fortnight, except for selling the house."

"That you could leave with an agent, and the attorney, I should think." She second guessed some of Earl's questions. "These are things I must do. You don't have to stay."

This took Earl aback. *There go my chances.*

Lynn read Earl's face. "But, you're welcome to stay."

This was getting confusing, so Earl took the matter in hand and suggested. "Lynn, I need to go back, but I can return in a couple of weeks . . . . In fact I'd like to."

"You're sure? That's a lot of traveling."

"You're worth it, Lynn." He reached over and took her hand. He felt a warm response.

She looked into his eyes. "I feel that too, now. So, if you're willing to come back, I'd like that."

"That's what I'll do . . . ." he hesitated. "And then we can come to some conclusion as to what might be ahead for us, Lynn."

"Yes," she said simply.

Earl had been back in Saline for ten days when Lynn called. "Earl, I've sold the house. The attorney is taking over all the other details and I'm free to leave. In fact there is nothing to keep me or make me want to stay here . . . ." He could not hear her next word, which she said to herself. "Unless . . . ."

"That was quicker than I assumed. What is your plan?" Earl was fearful that she was about to announce her departure for New Zealand.

"Well, I've been thinking. Howard used to spend his vacations on Monterey Bay. In fact he has an old friend who owns a motel on the beach. It's the Borg Motel in Pacific Grove. I've contacted him and he has a room which opens up tomorrow. I'm going to drive over and spend some time there." There was a pause during which Earl didn't know quite what she was asking, if anything. "And I was hoping that you might be able to meet me there, Earl? Instead of here."

"I could do that. Sounds exciting."

"Soon?"

"Two and half days' drive, I'd say."

"That long?" She seemed disappointed that it would be so long.

"Well, I could leave yet today and be there the day after tomorrow."

"Please, Earl. I miss you."

Earl was elated. While he was quickly packing, another phone call surprised him. It was from Phil Otis.

"Earl, this is Phil . . . . No, I moved from Spokane to Alaska . . . I'm retired in Juneau . . . Oh, it's great. The reason I'm calling you is to see if you might be interested in an interim assignment up here."

"It depends upon where it is. I did one in New Zealand, so I have some idea of what is involved."

"The church in Sitka is without a pastor just now. They have just begun their search process, and it is going to take the better part of a year. So they elected to hire an interim for a six month contract, which could be renewed for another six."

Earl thought of Lynn and her experience in Sitka and wondered if she might like to go back up there—this time with him. *She might even do some volunteering at Sheldon Jackson . . . .*

"You still there?" Phil hadn't heard any reply.

"Oh, I'm sorry, Phil. You got me to thinking. As a matter of fact I could be interested, but I'd need a week to settle some things and I could let you know then."

"OK . . ." Phil was a bit reluctant. "I will need to be talking to some other prospects, Earl, but if it is still open in a week, we can talk."

"I'll take the chance. Or I may know sooner. I'll phone as soon as I do."

The two exchanged personal news for a few moments and Earl said he'd get back as soon as he could.

Things were happening fast. Earl couldn't wait to share this with Lynn.

CHAPTER 55

Pacific

Pacific Grove is the first municipality along the shore of the bay just south of Monterey. While gorgeous three story Victorian mansions face the ocean across the road from the Pacific shore, many of the original houses nearest the bay are small and close together. Formerly they were associated with a Methodist church camp. These were early day summer houses built by Methodist lease holders when the property was first purchased as a conference center. The church camp has long since ceased to exist and the houses are now privately owned, each with a brass plate commemorating its unique history of ownership. The southernmost portion of the town's shore line is the location of state owned Asilimar conference center, located where the Methodist camp had been located. Up the hill from the original houses is Pacific Grove's main business street, attractively offering an assortment of upscale shops. A harbinger of what one will find further south at Carmel by the Sea.

South of a public beach, the land protrudes into the sea to form a rocky promontory across from which on the east side of the street are upscale eating establishments. South of these is the Borg Motel, which apparently was built before Pacific Grove had moved up the ladder of social class. While the motel itself is a strip of modest units—vintage 1950s—its setting is timeless and appealing as it faces the rugged coast and the enchanting beauty of the Pacific.

Lynn was sitting on the narrow porch of the Borg Motel when Earl pulled into the driveway beside the office. She stood up when she saw him and met him as he mounted the steps to the office. They hugged.

"They have a room for you on the ocean side—next to mine. Why don't you check in. Then we can go down along the shore and talk."

"Right. I've got some interesting news."

"I'm so glad you could come out here to the coast, Earl."

"So am I!"

"I'll be waiting out here."

Across the street from the Borg is a public shoreline with a well used pathway winding along the ridge overlooking the sea. It stretches along an aisle among tropical cactus-like plants. As one walks south every so often one comes to a path going down the sharp descent leading to the rocky shore. Here the rocks are wet and the air is moist where the waves slosh upwards over the rocks. Sea gulls swirl around looking for morsels of fish while some of the boulders further out are convenient resting places for sea lions sunning themselves.

And so it was that Lynette Ellerton Lindsay, an expatriate Chicago native from Southland, New Zealand, and Earl Norris, a Chicago transplant from Saline, Montana strolled hand in hand along the Pacific coast on Monterey Bay. Now with their hair attractively graying, their demeanor was more that of teenagers. For them it was a nostalgic return to the days of their youth when they had walked the beach on the east shore of Lake Michigan. During the intervening decades each had lived a life time filled with real and personal experiences. Each had married and raised their children to adulthood, each had mourned the death of a beloved spouse, and now each was alone. These two high school kids who had sat in the sand at Shore Crest had long since been transformed into the mature "sixty-something" adults who were now sitting on a park bench overlooking the Pacific. Each knew so little of what had filled the life of the other. And yet each knew that their relationship in their late teens and early twenties had been deep, and in a curious way, lasting—and renewable, Earl hoped. And it was becoming apparent, Earl dared to surmise, that Lynn, too, wanted to renew their former closeness.

Lynn's life with John Lindsay, New Zealand sheep farmer, had been full and complete, but her husband's life had been cut short. Earl and Kaye Norland, daughter of a Montana cattle rancher, had enjoyed a happy marriage until Kaye's early death. While their children remained as lasting legacies of two good marriages, these two old friends were now alone and sitting here together looking out onto the huge and timeless Pacific Ocean. Each knew his or her own past years and would share much of that with the other. Neither knew the future—the future which occupied the unspoken consciousness of each as they talked of things current and casual.

Such thoughts as these kept Earl from saying anything to Lynn about his phone call regarding Sitka until finally she broke the mesmerizing silence. "What's this news you have?"

Without any preliminary explanation, Earl told her. "I've been asked to consider an interim pastorate for six months at the Presbyterian Church in Sitka, Alaska."

In that moment, Earl's offer of a future experience intersected with Lynn's remembrance of an unforgotten past. It left her speechless at that poignant intersection of images.

"You lived in Sitka for a short time didn't you?" Earl said this, not so much as a question as a way of linking Lynn to this news of his.

"Yes, I did. I worked in the library at Sheldon Jackson College." She qualified, "as a volunteer." She seemed distracted.

Her response disappointed Earl. He had thought this would immediately strike a positive chord in Lynn. "I thought you'd be interested in this offer."

"I am, Earl. It's just that . . . ." Lynn interrupted the subject pointing ahead. "Lets go down that path to the water."

Perhaps she suggested this to give herself some time.

They got up and made their way down to the rocks and found a dry place to sit above the water.

Earl began to understand her reaction. He returned to their discussion of Sitka. "Because it has to do with where you met John?" He asked. "Is that troubling to you, Lynn?"

"Yes. And now he's gone. And I don't want to think much about Alaska—at least not right now." She looked forlorn. "Are you going to accept the offer?'

"I don't know." His enthusiasm for accepting the offer was shaken. He put his arm around Lynn and drew her close to comfort her. "Lynn, don't be reluctant to talk about John. You're not who you really are without affirming your lifetime of love for John. Anyone who wants to know you as you are now, needs to know John as much as possible."

"Oh, Earl, do you really feel that way? You're not just trying to find the high school Lynn you knew long ago?"

"No . . . I did at first when we met at Shore Crest, and I guess also when I was in New Zealand . . . but I found out that was impossible. The people you and I were in high school and college have been replaced. I've been helped to see that it would be foolish to think otherwise. Now since being with you in California I've discovered Lynette Lindsay, the person you are now, not Lynn Ellerton, the girl you were." Earl paused. "Now of the Order of Naomi."

Lynn snuggled in closer to him. "What do you mean *you've been helped to see* . . . ."

"You asked me about how I had been helped by the Order of Naomi, how someone was a Naomi to me."

"You were going to tell me about that."

"Well, when I took the ferry to Vancouver Island, I met a woman who lives on the island."

Lynn looked at him with a slightly accusatory glance.

"Nothing romantic. She was doing her work as a member of the order. She discovered that I was saddened by my separation from you. When she probed this further she gave me some advice. Which was to get to know you as you are now, and not to relate to you as if we were still in college. She advised me to spend some time and effort getting to know you—sort of like dating. At the time that sounded like something which I'd never have a chance to do. And then suddenly you and I were together in California!"

Lynn took Earl's hand and squeezed it. "I'm glad she put you onto that pathway, Earl. It makes me feel good to have you accept me as I am, wrinkles and all!"

Then Earl declared, "And so, it's you, Lynn Lindsay, John's widow, whom I love." He added, "With you—as you are—I want to spend my remaining years."

Lynn was very quiet. Her response finally was to turn her face toward Earl's inviting a kiss.

Earl bent down and they kissed long and deep.

When they released each other, Lynn was the first to speak. "Let's walk."

They climbed up to the ridge and walked south along the parkway trail until they came to another steep path descending to the water. When they reached the shore line they followed it toward the south. As they ambled along they were quiet, each deep in thought. They reached a small beach and sat down in the dry sand above the water line.

"I've been thinking of Kaye, Earl."

Earl appeared surprised.

"I want Kaye to be as much a part of our . . . ." She hesitated.

". . . of our marriage?" Earl dared to add.

"Yes—if we should marry. Her memory as much as John's should be part of our life together."

They both looked out on the ocean and watched the incoming waves as they rippled up the sand turning it dark brown and then after each run up the sand, returning.

"Can you accept that, Earl?" She saw a puzzled look. "To keep alive our good memories of John and of Kaye?"

"I have not stopped loving Kaye. And you still love John. We don't have to reject those feelings. There is a enough love in me to love you as well." Earl waited for a reciprocal response.

Instead Lynn questioned having two loves. "But isn't that sort of an unfaithfulness—loving another person while you're still married?"

"Not if you have truly let John go—accepted the fact that he is gone—permanently. And you're not still trying to bring him back somehow."

"What do you mean?"

"I've seen it in people grieving. I call it the *What if?* syndrome. Always wondering what one could have done differently so that he or she wouldn't have died. I know it doesn't sound reasonable, but I have the feeling that when you say those *what ifs*, you are in effect trying to bring your loved one back. Sort of bargaining with God, which is ultimately saying to God, *If you let me go back and be a better person will you bring my loved one back to me?*"

In the unspoken response Earl felt from Lynn, he thought perhaps she knew what he was saying, and could identify with it. Earl continued. "Letting go is giving up that kind of bargaining, and accepting the stark reality that your husband or wife is dead, and that you are thereby released from marriage. But that does not mean you must forsake your love for him."

Lynn's response took Earl by surprise. She turned toward him, reached for his hair and ruffled it saying with a grin and a glint in her eye. "Reverend! You're treating me like one of your parishioners—giving me a sermon! Know what I mean?"

"No, but let's go find us a coke or something." Earl relented, "Yes, I see what you mean."

It was time for Lynn to mend her ways. "You're probably right, and, yes, let's find us a coke, while I think about your sermon."

Much to Earl's chagrin, their conversation over cokes amounted to little more than small talk. When they had finished, Lynn appealed to Earl. "I'd like to go back to the motel. I need to lie down for while. I'm really tired. I guess I'm just now reacting to the weeks I spent caring for Howard."

Earl acceded to her request and they paid their bill and walked back to the Borg. When they arrived at Lynn's room door Earl announced. "I guess I'll look around town. How long will you want?" He was obviously disappointed.

"No, Earl. I want you to come in with me. Why don't you take a nap too? There are two beds."

"O.K. I guess I could."

When they were in the room Lynn closed and locked the door. She turned to Earl holding out her arms to be hugged. "You're so sweet—and patient." After nestling her head between his head and shoulder, she lifted her face and kissed Earl on the lips. Both of these old friends seemed to melt into each other, and remained in an impassioned embrace for a long time. When they let go, Lynn led Earl to the other bed and had him lie down. She knelt over him and kissed his forehead, and then loosened his shoes and slid them off. "Go to sleep, darling, and I'll do the same." With that she went into the bathroom where she slipped off her slacks and top and put on her silk robe.

Earl noticed that she had put a picture of John Lindsay on the little table next to her bed. He watched as she came back into the room. She lay down on her bed still facing him, smiled and said. "Good night, Earl."

"Good night, precious." Earl watched her relax as she induced sleep. The expression he observed was one of ease and happiness. He thought about how they had used the terms *darling* and *precious* when they had "gone together" in their youth. He marveled at the natural unembarrassed way she had allowed him to be with her in this way. The emotional warmth of their kiss remained with him. He thought about the fact that here they were: two people alone in a motel room in the middle of the day, seeming to be an "old married couple." *A delicious feeling,* he thought . . . *though incomplete!*

Earl noticed that Lynn's breathing had slowed down. She was asleep. Soon he was asleep as well. After an hour or so he awakened to see Lynn getting up. He pretended to remain asleep. She stood by her bed table and held up the picture of John and looked at it for a long moment. She took it over to her suitcase and put it inside. Earl questioned this. *Does that mean she is finally letting him go? Or is it merely that she doesn't want his picture out while I'm around?* She went over to the clothes rack on which she had hung the clothes she had brought and appeared to be trying to decide what to wear. She looked over at Earl and when she saw that he was awake she came over to his bed and sat down beside him. She didn't seem to care that her robe gapped open loosely and split to reveal a portion of her thigh.

"Lazy head! Time for dinner!" She nudged him. "Good sleep?"

"I'll say. I guess I needed that."

She leaned over and kissed him on the cheek. "I need your help."

He looked at her with a question.

"What shall I wear?" She went over to her clothes and took down a flowered dress and held it against her. "This?" She replaced it and modeled a pink linen suit. "Or this?"

Earl thought a moment. "The suit."

"What are you going to wear?"

"I guess a polo shirt and blazer. Does that sound O.K.?"

"Yes. I'm hungry." She announced. "So, get up, my friend."

Earl got up and went to his room to dress while Lynn put on her pink suit.

Like an old married couple. He thought as he dressed. When he returned to her room, he didn't knock but walked right in. She stuck her head out of the bathroom and smiled.

"I'll be just a minute, dear."

Earl looked around the room while he waited. He saw John's picture had been put back on the bed table. *Now I really am confused.*

When she emerged she looked ravishing to Earl. "Lynette Ellerton Lindsay! You look beautiful." He held out his arm in a formal way. "May I take you to dinner?"

"Earl Norris, my answer is YES. Not only dinner but . . . ."

"But what?"

"Lynette Ellerton Lindsay Norris, it shall be."

Earl was shocked. "Did you say *Norris?* Does that mean what I think it does?"

"Yes." She stepped forward to embrace Earl and to kiss.

"Watch my make-up. We can mess that up big time after dinner!"

Needless to say, dinner at a seafood restaurant on the wharf at Monterey was very special. It was an engagement banquet. The westbound sun set over the Pacific and rose in the hearts of these two high school sweethearts who'd spent their lives apart, but were now together.

When they had finished their dinner they went out hand in hand onto the wharf and found a spot along the railing where they could look out onto the shimmering reflections skipping along the dark night water. They put their arms around each other like teenagers, silently savoring the moment.

Earl was the first to break the silence. "Lynn, when I was in your room this afternoon the way you were napping and preparing to dress for dinner made me feel as if we were an old married couple."

"I know. And how did that feel to you?"

"It felt good. What about you?"

"Well, I have to confess to you that I set that up."

"What do you mean—set up?"

"I wanted to see how living with you would feel after all these years and after living with John. So I wanted to act in a way as if we were married. That's why I wasn't very modest and why you needed to help me decide on this suit."

"I see what you mean. Did I pass the test?"

"You did. You were neither embarrassed nor did you ogle! And you had an opinion on what I should wear. I guess the fact that you slept also clinched it for you."

"I'm glad. Next time may I ogle?" Earl asked slyly.

"Of course. You men are all the same—at 16 or 66!" she said with an accusing grin.

Lynn suddenly became serious when she shared something else with Earl. "That wasn't all that was going on today. I want to tell you about a dream I had this afternoon."

"Oh? What was that?"

"I was in a house which was familiar to me. But I can't quite remember where, or what house. In some ways it seems like it was the house at Glen Mor. But I thought I was with you at first. Then it seemed like it was John. I was in some sort of office or library. It seemed then to be at Shore Crest—in Father's library. At first I thought I was with Father, then I saw that it was John. It was the strangest thing. It was like he had already died. He was holding a photograph. He said to me. '*I found this in your suitcase . . .*" and then he said in a most kindly way something I'd never thought of: '*This photo is not of me. It is a picture of a memory. So you can put it up again, can't you?*' At that point I began to weep. And then I woke up."

"What do you judge your dream means, Lynn?"

"That now that I've let John go I can have you . . . and his memory as well."

"And do you feel all right about Kaye's memory?"

"Yes, darling. You can have me, and Kaye's memory too."

Earl was overwhelmed with love, and joy. They faced each other and embraced, offering each other an engagement kiss.

When they returned to the railing, Earl brought up the very questions Lynn had on her mind as well. "Let's go back to the Borg. It's getting chilly here."

"So the only two questions remaining are . . ."

"When? And where?"

"That's right. When?"

"As soon as possible."

"Where will we live?" Earl looked westbound into the darkness.

"That's tougher," Lynn offered, as she peered out beyond the bay into the Pacific. Thousands of miles to the south was her home on the South Island of New Zealand. *Some seventeen hundred miles to the north,* she thought, *at this very moment these same waters are lapping against the shore of Baranof Island in Alaska.* Lynn had a quizzical look which Earl could barely make out in the darkness of the evening. "Where?" she asked rhetorically. Then she answered. "Who knows? But I have an idea of where we can start out." She waited for Earl to respond.

"Where?"

"Sitka!"

AUTHOR'S NOTE

With the urbanization of America over the past hundred years an increasing proportion of young clergy have come into regions such as eastern Montana with little experience of rural life. For pastors of small rural congregations the culture gap is often quite wide and there is much to learn of each other for both the pastor and the people of the congregation and community. Add to that the fact that for many of these young ministers, this will be their first assignment after seminary graduation. Some consider their call to a small rural congregation in the West to be an entry level position and yearn to return to an urban environment and to a larger congregation. These social dynamics often lead to short pastorates, making it necessary for congregations frequently to look for another pastor—"to train!"

While Saline, Montana and its Community Church are products of my imagination, their story is much the same as that of many actual towns and churches in eastern Montana. If one were to draw a circle with a hundred and twenty mile radius around Miles City, one would find six towns with Presbyterian churches, where once there were fifteen. When Montana opened to homesteading in 1908 towns sprung up everywhere and churches were not far behind. In the years since, many of those towns have dried up and blown away as drought years, together with an assortment of adverse economic factors, caused a depletion of the farm population in the region. And so church membership in many of these towns declined, closing some churches and bringing about mergers of other congregations in order to survive. Similarly in New Zealand the Oreti Parish—an actual parish, has closed with its congregations in Drummond and Oreti merging into the Central Southland Parish based in Winton, a larger town nearby.

Saline is imagined as a town on the Great Plains, a semi-arid region bounded by the 98th Meridian on the east and the Rocky Mountains on the west. It has been a region inhospitable to immigrants from the more populated and humid areas in the mid western and eastern parts of the United States. The late Annie Moore Knipfer, a friend of our family, was such an immigrant who came to the prairies of eastern Montana from Massachusetts in 1919 as a 26 year old school teacher. In Chapter 17, I have included one of her poems, *HOPE CRUCIFIED*, from her early days in Montana. In this poem she expressed her feelings about the new land to which she had come, feelings of disappointment and hopelessness. These have been feelings which have been shared by many such immigrants over the years. I've taken this poem from her self-published collection, *Songs of the Prairies and Other Poems*. (Miles City, Montana, 1975). Another book has been of help for including some historical facts from Custer County, Montana. It is *The First Century, A History of The First Presbyterian Church of Miles City*. In am also indebted to Andy Pehl who farms in Terry, Montana and Dr. George Haynes, an economist at Montana State University for their help in providing me with recent trends in agriculture in Montana.

My descriptions of official church procedures have been those of the Presbyterian church. This is not to discredit in any way other churches and their procedures, which would be similar in many respects.

Finally my account in Chapter 48 of Riverton and Riverton Rocks on the south shore of New Zealand was greatly aided by friends in New Zealand, Diane and John Macdonald and their family, of Oreti, Southland, who have a second home at Riverton Rocks. Among the materials they sent me, was an especially helpful ten page *RIVERTON HISTORY*, a school report which their eight year old daughter, Jeannie, researched and wrote some years ago!

Finally I want to give my deep appreciation to Jody McDevitt whose editing has been especially helpful, to Dan Krebill for his photo from Red Rock Lakes National Wildlife Refuge in south western Montana, which appears on the cover, and to my wife Doris for her editing as well, and for her support and encouragement.

—Paul Krebill

Comments from readers of Paul Krebill's novels—

HARRY'S LEGACY
—an entertaining mystery set in present-day Montana. Author Krebill sets his protagonists on a quest for the redress of an old injustice in which their greater reward is a growing love for each other. His characters are well-drawn and appealing. I found the book an entertaining read.

—Stan Lynde, Author of
The Bodacious Kid and *Vigilante Moon*

—a wonderful story . . . the weaving together of Montana and New Zealand mining histories, and the ties to the Civil War . . . all these threads held me to this story.

—filled with suspense and had me fooled as we thought we had it all figured out. The ending was a total surprise.

HERITAGE HIDDEN
—really enjoyed it, especially the part about the characters feeling like they have lived before.

—it held my interest all the way as the two mysteries unfolded . . . with a good amount of suspense.

—Thank you for another good "read." I loved it . . . the best yet.

—I was so engrossed in the book that I missed my band rehearsal . . . very mysterious and kept me turning the pages.

A PLACE CALLED FAIRHAVENS

—Definitely a *'don't put me down until you're finished.'* Krebill has created a refreshing plot tying together his knowledge of geography and life in two areas a half a world apart.

—The simple, calm backgrounds of these places were an interesting backdrop for the turmoil and angst of the main characters: Max, Bronwyn and Conrad.

—a magnificent story . . . a masterful job of putting it all together.

—it gave me hours of pleasure.

MORIAH'S VALLEY

—a remarkable job bringing together the story of changes in people's lives over several generations with the historical events that influenced the migrations—World War II, the McCarthy era, the Vietnam War . . . these historical events and sociological changes are constructed in a rich tapestry of characters and their lives . . . the rich and real story of change mending and growth. Krebill does not take the easy way out! Jim and Laurie do not just come together and live happily ever after—they have to work through their losses. The reader is given all the ingredients for a happy ending, but is taken to a richer resolution—change for the area as well as for all the people involved.

—Paul Krebill's book documents many of the changes that are taking place in Montana and surrounding states . . . fascinating to follow the myriad of broader social and economic developments in Montana.

—James Sargent—former County Agent in Montana.

Author of *Too Poor to Move, But Always Rich,*

a study of the lives of people in the Big Timber region of Montana,

and of *One Hundred and Ninety-Nine Years Late,*

a Lewis and Clark Story.

Printed in the United States
60230LVS00003B/34-36

9 781425 716318